BEYOND THE END OF THE WORLD

AMIE KAUFMAN & MEAGAN SPOONER

HARPER TEEN

An Imprint of HarperCollins Publishers

Welcome back, dear reader.

Before we plunge once more into this tale of two worlds, we offer you a short reminder of the story so far—read on to retrace your steps through *The Other Side of the Sky*, and then continue on to *Beyond the End of the World* . . .

Our story takes place in a world divided: above, the technologically advanced sky-city of Alciel, ruled by kings and queens; beneath, the beautiful and chaotic Below, a world of magic, prophecy, and fate, led by a living divine.

Below, the line of divinity has been passed down for a thousand years—when one divine died, another received the gift. A generation ago, the goddess Jezara fell in love. Forbidden by divine law to touch another human being, she was cast out of the temple when she found herself with child.

Her successor was Nimh, now Nimhara. She was a powerful magician, but as the years passed and she failed to fully manifest her divine powers, the faith of her people was shaken.

Splinter groups arose: the Graycloaks, who wished to live

in a world without magic; and the Deathless, who followed a shadowy figure they believed to be the true divine.

Finally, Nimh received a vision—a new part of an old prophecy. It promised the Last Star would fall and the Lightbringer would come.

The Lightbringer, also known as the Destroyer, would bring the end of days. It was easy for Nimh to believe her dark, failing world was close to its finish. It was tempting to believe she had finally found her purpose as a goddess.

She set out in secret to follow the prophecy, and found not a star, but a boy who had fallen from the sky—Prince North, grandson of the king of Alciel. What she called a spell, he called science—though magic ruled her world, technology ruled his.

Meanwhile, Inshara, leader of the Deathless cult, wrested control of the divine temple and murdered the high priest, Daoman. North and Nimh were forced to flee with the aid of her Master of Archives, Matias. Stealing a boat to escape downriver, North and Nimh grew closer, unable to deny their chemistry and attraction—but the divine law held. They were forbidden to touch, and Nimh would not risk damaging the faith of her people as Jezara had done.

Finding themselves in a village filled with mist, the wild and dangerous source of magical power Below, they were rescued by a mysterious woman who turned out to be Jezara herself. From her, North and Nimh learned Inshara's true identity: Jezara's daughter, obsessed with the idea that she herself is destined to become the Lightbringer.

They left Jezara, taking with them an ancient scroll she had stolen from the temple when she was exiled. That night at camp, a drop of North's blood touched the parchment of their prophecy scroll and unlocked centuries of messages from previous divinities. It transformed before their eyes, revealing dozens of messages, all speaking to Nimh, all telling her the same thing.

She was the true Lightbringer.

Her long-overdue manifestation brought with it new magic—she could directly control her world's powerful, magical mist, as no magician had been able to do before her.

She spoke a new, terrifying prophecy that described the sky falling and the blood of the gods raining down. She told North the sky would fall and life would be wiped away, both their worlds ending so they could be reborn together.

Then a message arrived on North's chrono, announcing a rescue party had arrived from Alciel to rendezvous with him. He refused to aid Nimh in fulfilling the destructive prophecy and resolved to leave her. Nimh gave him a protection stone, a ward against hostile magic, and heartbroken, they parted.

North soon discovered the rescue party was a trap laid by Inshara, who promised to send him home if he helped her capture Nimh. She carried a device from his own world, a chronometer, claiming the Lightbringer had spoken to her all her life through it. This mysterious speaker knew many impossible things—including that North was a prince.

North discovered that Elkisa, Nimh's trusted bodyguard, was a traitor. She loved Inshara and believed she was the true goddess.

Nimh, returning to fight for her city, met Jezara, and they

were joined by Elkisa, who was still posing as an ally. She tried to prevent the coming confrontation between the two goddesses by telling Nimh that North was dead—and triggered an explosion of uncontrollable power within the newly manifested Lightbringer.

In the city, North was very much alive and forging an unlikely alliance with Techeki, the Master of Spectacle.

Anticipating Nimh's coming, Inshara and the Graycloaks had readied anchors made of skysteel—a substance that negates magic—to be lowered into the river around the city. Inshara had inherited immunity to skysteel when her mother was forced to drink it while pregnant to destroy her own magic—this would make it impossible for anyone except her to use magic within the ring formed by the water around the city.

A wild mist storm appeared, Nimh riding it in her manifested form of the Lightbringer—the Destroyer—leaving carnage in her wake and vaporizing the river in a terrifying display of power.

Jezara appealed to her daughter. She told Inshara that the voice she heard from her chrono was not a god, but simply a man, her father, a cloudlander like North. Furious, Inshara killed her mother.

Nimh and Inshara did battle. Afraid she would destroy the city, North threw himself into the mist storm after her, surviving thanks to his protection stone but wounded by the debris caught in the storm. As he tried to talk Nimh down from her rage and grief, Inshara managed to grab Nimh's ankle, violating the divine law.

In that moment, Nimh reached for the crown, her fingers stained with North's blood—and just as it had unlocked the prophetic writings in the ancient scroll, North's royal blood unlocked the power within the crown.

A golden light surrounded them, and though North tried to reach them, he was too late—both Nimh and Inshara were transported to Alciel.

The crown was destroyed, and with it, North's way home. He was left with Techeki and Matias the archivist, who revealed himself to be the leader of the riverstriders, the Fisher King, and one of the mythical Sentinels, a guardian of the way between worlds.

Onward, now, to a story worthy of the Fisher King himself . . .

THE MAID

The maid creeps into the chamber, her eyes accustomed to the dark. Her duties this early are few, but she likes the quiet—likes hearing the soft breathing of the queen and her wife as they sleep, the whisper of her footsteps on the lush carpet. She likes the sense of anticipation that hangs in the air.

She quietly, carefully pulls each curtain open, one after the other, so that the room's occupants may wake with the sun. She opens the vents in the floor for the palace's central heating to begin warming the royal suite. She gives the bathroom a quick clean, and then refills the jug of water for the queen's nightstand.

Only as she creeps close to put the jug in its place does she realize: the bed is empty.

She's about to slip back out of the suite again when she hears voices coming from the private sitting room that adjoins the bedroom. A sliver of light illuminates the carpet along the bottom edge of the door.

She knows she ought to creep away, but there's an edge to the tones that makes her hesitate. Heart in her throat, she tip-toes to the door just in time to leap back as footsteps approach.

The door flies open so that Anasta can storm through, too preoccupied to notice the presence of the maid—the queen's wife heads straight for the doors of the suite, slamming them behind her.

"She'll come around." The queen's voice is lowered, but

full of certainty. "Anasta is very fond of tradition—all of this change is difficult for her."

"Most insightful, Your Majesty." That voice, relatively new, has nonetheless become familiar to the maid in the last two weeks. She gathers her wits after the shock of Anasta's exit and creeps close again to listen. "It is difficult to explain the importance of my mission here. We must keep searching, though."

"You think this person could be a danger to my people. I understand, Nimhara. And I am grateful you're working so hard to keep us all safe."

There's a strange quality to the queen's voice that makes the maid lean forward, greatly daring, and ease the edge of her face around the door so that she can peek inside.

With a dull jolt, she realizes that there are tears on the queen's cheeks. It isn't the first time since the girl from another world arrived that the maid has seen the queen cry. Then again, she's in mourning. Of course she cries.

The girl—Nimhara—stands not far from the queen, her red robes seeming to glow in the lamplight. "I am so glad to have found you," she says softly. "And I think your son would have been glad to see us together."

The queen smiles at her a little, her gaze fierce. "Come," she says, not bothering to wipe away her tears. "All of Alciel is about to learn that we have been visited by a goddess. Are you ready?"

Nimhara smiles, reaches out, and squeezes the queen's hand. "I am," she murmurs. "This is fate, a thousand years in the making. This is my destiny."

ONE
JAYN

Sunrise, in the sky, comes from below. The massive buildings take on the color of dawn before anything else, glowing against the darkness of the night sky above. White stone and polished metal catch at the light, a pale canvas for the sunrise. Soaring above the rest of the city is the intricately designed palace, its tallest towers the first to shimmer pink and gold in the morning light, gilded tiles on the roof gleaming like fiery beacons in the night.

Do not fear, they seem to call across the sleeping city. *Morning still comes.*

The balcony of this house is built out over the edge of the island, and I find myself staring at the clouds that separate this world from the one below. Lit by the rising sun beneath them, they make me feel as though I am looking down at a strange ocean where the water is pink and all light emerges from its depths instead of beaming down from the sky.

I shiver, drawing my sweater more tightly about my shoulders. Even the sunrise makes me feel strange, one in a long string of details that create a sense of unease that I've never quite managed to explain to the electrician who's been my host these last two weeks.

"The doctors will know how to help you," she told me in that voice of hers that invites no argument. "My cousin is the best cerebrist in all of Alciel. Don't you worry."

I close my eyes, which burn with the sting of tears. I may not know what's happening to me, but some part of me remembers I am lost, and keeps reminding me with a ruthlessness more befitting an enemy than my own mind. I catch only glimpses of why I have come to find myself here—I am not sure I want to know the truth.

Every night I wake to the feeling of fire like a burning wreath around my ankle; every night I realize, in the dream, that it is not fire at all, but the hot and desperate clamp of fingers around my ankle, grabbing me, *touching me*. When I look down, I see the twisted face of a woman, teeth bared in rage and madness, with eyes that shimmer with a strange, otherworldly light. I wake, smothering my scream, for in the dreams I cannot fight her, and I *know* that all I am is shattered, that I am lost.

But some nights, when I look down, the face I see is not that of the mad-eyed creature. Some nights, I look down and I see soft brown eyes watching me; a strong, aquiline nose; lips that smile and shape a word as if in silent prayer. My name, I think, though I cannot be sure, because I do not know my name. The fire on my skin is still there, but the fingers that touch me are gentle, and heat washes up along the curve of my calf, into the sensitive crook behind my knee, and up the slope of my thigh.

Those nights, I still wake gasping. I only wish, then, that I had never woken at all.

Turning my back on the strangeness of the sunrise, I draw in a long, deep breath, trying to summon calm. This place is the first that has felt like anything other than a half-waking nightmare. Where all else in the world seems full of chaos and noise and harsh, bright lights, this balcony is like an oasis of calm. There are no screens, no broad avenues lined with dizzyingly tall buildings, no crowds of people chattering through their chronos or auto-vendors singing in tinny mechanical voices about food and drink for sale.

Other balconies dot the edge of the island, stretching away into the distance on either side, though I rarely see any of our neighbors on them. The stonework has been left unpainted, and some clever gardener—the electrician's mother, I feel sure—has coaxed vines sprouting sweet-scented blooms to climb the walls and spill out over the balustrade to wave in the stiff morning breeze.

Here, among the greenery, I almost feel . . . at home.

A groan and a creak from inside the house bring me back to myself. Stepping inside, I see Monah, the electrician's mother, in her favorite chair by the hearth, which is still cold and dark. She cradles a wide mug in both hands and lifts it for a sip—I can smell the rich, bitter scent of her caff-ley drink in the air.

"Good morning, my dear," she says, without lifting her head.

I slide the door closed behind me and pad over to another

chair. "You do not wish to attend the coronation today?" I ask in some surprise, for I had thought the electrician's whole family went with her when she tapped on the shed door to bid me farewell on her way to join the crowds.

The old woman smiles. It seems to me her smile should be set in wrinkles, deep and proud, a sign of years and wisdom. She is ancient, both her husband and her wife gone now, which brought her back to her daughter's house. But the only sign of her age is in the nuance of her expression, in the depth of her eyes, and in her hands—though smooth and fair, the bones and joints of the fingers curled and knotted the tiniest bit against the mug. There is a procedure, I have learned, that makes the people all seem young until the very end of life, a seeming of youth that appears to display shame in age, rather than pride. There are such wonders in the world, it's hard not to believe it is a kind of magic.

Not magic, a wry, laughing voice in my mind keeps telling me. *Technology.*

I know that voice, and yet I cannot remember whose it is. That loss feels somehow greater than all the others, that gap in my memory throbbing like a hole in my heart.

"My bones ache today," Monah admits, the smile turning rueful. "I don't feel like fighting the crowds." The old woman's gaze falls to the dark hearth, as if watching the memory of a fire there, and she adds in a low voice, "And I remember another coronation, not so very long ago. I'd like to keep remembering that one, I think."

So much grief—and yet I feel some deeper, greater grief

11

hidden in the things I cannot remember. And my grief, I cannot share.

They loved the old king, these people. He died two weeks and one day ago, having suffered a stroke, as the news stories said. I have never seen a picture of him—or at least, I do not remember him, for my memories do not stretch back that far. The custom here is to put away images of the lost for a year after their deaths so that when they see the faces of their loved ones again, they can feel joy with their sadness too.

The stories that play from chronos and screens are dry and concerned only with the facts, but I could see the truth in the faces of the people: the old king died of a broken heart, grieving the loss of his beloved grandson, the prince who had perished in a glider accident a few days before.

When I first learned of this, the day after the electrician took me in, I half leaped up from the table and blurted, "But the prince is not dead!"

The electrician exchanged glances with the members of her family. "You must not remember the tragedy—it's a lot to take in, especially when you're struggling with your own memories. Take it easy, one step at a time, Jayn."

The prince's face, like the king's, has been hidden from the people of Alciel. I have never seen his likeness. But the sound of his name, nearly as taboo as his image, is still whispered here and there, and only confirms that strange, deep knowledge in my heart that I cannot explain.

The prince lives.

"You've some time before your appointment at the medical

center," Monah says, bringing me back to myself. "Shall we watch a little of the coronation footage together?" Perhaps she wishes to distract me if she is willing to watch the ceremony after all. This family has been so kind to me.

I murmur an assent and rise to my feet. "Can I light the fire for you too, grandmother? It is cold this day, and the warmth from the hearth will ease the ache in your bones."

She laughs, though the sound is kind. "I love the way you talk," she tells me, nodding and gesturing toward the hearth. "Hang in there, little poet—the doctors will know what to do."

It is the electrician's theory that I am a student at the Royal Academy. When the queen shut down the school, an event that coincided with her suspension of the trains that travel between islands, hundreds upon hundreds of students from neighboring islands were stranded with no place to live. The electrician, believing me to be one of these abandoned children who suffered some accident to damage my memory, told me I could stay with them while I await my appointment with the doctor. She thinks I must be studying poetry, and that this is why I speak the way I do, why I seem to them as though I have one foot in some other world than theirs.

I have not the heart to tell her that I feel no spark of recognition from that theory, or any of the others they've suggested in the two weeks I have stayed with them.

I kneel at the hearth and slide my fingers along the underside of the mantel until they find the ignition button. A neat little row of flames springs up from the stones.

The first time I saw this done, I leaped back with a little

cry, prompting the electrician's ten-year-old son to laugh at me, delighted by my ignorance. My first instinct was that it was some kind of awe-inspiring magic, although I have since learned that that is nonsense. The stones have minute holes drilled into them, and pipes lead to the holes, and in the pipes is a fuel that burns hot and clean and flows to every house in the city.

And yet, every time I see the fire lit, my body jumps with the same quaking fear I feel whenever one of those screens comes to life. Though I get better at hiding my reaction, my heart shrivels just a little bit more every time I witness one of these wonders. For my heart knows something my mind and my memories do not—a strange suspicion, an impossible belief.

I do not belong here.

I straighten and turn on the screen over the hearth before going back to my chair.

For all that I know how to dress myself, how to comb my hair or tie a lace, the gaps in my understanding frighten me. To the electrician's family, the use of the screen is as easy and mundane as the use of a comb.

To me, it seems . . . like magic.

On the screen is an aerial image of the crowded streets outside the palace gates. Many of them must have left their homes even earlier than the electrician and her son, because there are hundreds of them—hundreds of hundreds, numbers I've never thought to imagine. The thronging masses of people wash up against the closed gates like wavelets on a riverbank, the sheer volume of bodies making my nerves thrum tight.

The electrician had apologized to me that my appointment

with her cousin the specialist fell on coronation day, as if missing such a spectacle would be to miss the display of a lifetime. It was the reason I could get in with only a two-week wait—nobody else wanted the time. But while the gathered crowds seem stirred by excitement and anticipation, the thought of being among them makes me feel faint, and I close my eyes.

My host and her family accepted very quickly that I did not want to be touched. But out there, among that mass of bodies . . . there would be no escape from them.

A murmur from the other chair brings me back to myself, and I open my eyes to look at Monah. She is gazing steadily at the coverage, solemn, as if she is preparing herself to bear witness to something.

The screen has shifted from the aerial shot of the crowds to a dais in the palace courtyard, surrounded by the machines that capture images and sound to broadcast them across the city. Beyond the machines is a thick crowd of others, clad more richly than those outside the palace gates—counselors and other important statespeople, though I do not know or remember their roles. To judge by the sound of impatience from Monah, she cares as little about them right now as the machines—*cameras*, my mind supplies, one of the new words I've had to learn these past weeks—seem to. Every one of the cameras is pointed at the empty dais, and the curtained pavilion from which the queen will emerge at any moment.

Monah may not have chosen to celebrate the coronation, but I do understand why she wishes to see it.

As much as everyone loved the old king, the new queen's

father, the people of this world seem uncertain about their new ruler. Rumors are everywhere, citing strange decisions and uncharacteristic secrecy from the throne. There are some who say that when she ordered the suspension of the train service that travels between islands, she had no intention of ever starting them again.

They whisper that she gives no thought to what will happen when the stores of food in Alciel run out, for there are no farms on this island—they get everything from the smaller islands farther away.

They ask why the queen does not speak to her people anymore, why her daily audiences have been canceled, why no one has seen her but servants and guards who never leave the palace grounds.

They say the new queen has gone mad.

On the screen, the curtain parts, and Beatrin, Queen of Alciel, steps through onto the dais. The audience of her court bursts into thunderous applause, though the sound is entirely drowned out by the roar of the throngs beyond the gates, watching the same images we are on massive screens throughout the city.

She is tall and beautiful, in a remote way. Her skin is a flawless brown a shade or two darker than mine, and her black hair is plaited into a coronet of braids in imitation of the crown she will wear by the end of this ceremony. She is thin, thinner than the pictures I've seen of her from months and years past, and her eyes seem somehow distant—but then, she is gazing out over an audience of hundreds.

Her lips move for some time before her voice becomes audible over the roaring crowds, and she raises her hands in an appeal for silence.

"Thank you," she says, her voice ringing. "I admit I am heartened, seeing you here before me on this glorious morning. Our people have suffered so much grief, so much loss and uncertainty, in these last dark weeks. But I hear the strength in your voices—I see the devotion in your faces—and I know that Alciel will recover. We have survived this darkest of nights, and together, we will see the rise of hope and prosperity to light this land once more."

Queen Beatrin pauses as the crowd screams its approval. My own heart stirs to the words she speaks, for she is an orator, and she plays her audience well.

"You may ask me how I know this to be true," she goes on when there is space for her to speak above the cheering of her subjects. "I could cite the long history of our people and our ability to adapt. I could cite the strength of this royal blood in my veins, the blood of my father and his father's mother, generations that span a thousand years. But the truth, good people, is this: I have had a visitor."

The roar of the crowd fades, and I have no need to look at Monah's furrowed brow to know that this last announcement strays from what is usual in such a speech.

Beatrin waits a moment longer for quiet, and when she speaks, her voice is grave and certain and brimming with a strange passion. "You came here today to meet your queen after the end of the mourning period and see her wear her crown for the first time. But I intend to introduce you all to another. You may find what she has to say hard to believe—I did myself, at first. But I have spent many long nights speaking with her, and I have come to believe her—to believe *in* her—with all my heart."

The queen, whose eyes are red-rimmed with emotion, takes a step to the side, turning so that she can gesture to the pavilion. The curtain stirs—there's someone else back there. "I know you all will come to rejoice in her as I do: Nimhara, Forty-Second Vessel of the Divine, goddess to her people, and history's first emissary to our lands from the world Below."

The stunned silence that follows is a stark contrast to the roaring of the crowd only moments before. A young woman steps out of the pavilion to stand beside the queen, her face not quite in focus, for the camera operators are as stunned as anyone else. Beside me, Monah is spluttering about impossibilities, protesting that no one lives Below, her voice choked with emotion.

But I scarcely notice. I can no longer hear her—can no longer hear the gathered masses on the screen, though they have exploded back into animation now, so much so that the queen cannot regain control of the crowd.

All I can hear is a dim ringing in my ears.

I know that name.

The woman wears red, a long robe of diaphanous material that catches the morning sun and turns it to fire. Her long dark hair is crowned with gold, and she carries a staff of some kind, tipped with a wicked-looking edge. She has turned to speak to the queen, who has tears running down her face now. The red-robed woman has her own face mostly hidden from

18

the cameras, but the sight of her strikes at me so viscerally that I cry out.

I know her.

Nimhara. Vessel of the Divine. Goddess. The words ring with bell-like clarity, fragments of memory stirring in my mind like ashes on the wind.

I hear the name, over and over, from a hundred different throats. Faces I do not know flash before me, and yet they are somehow more familiar to me than my own. I see another terrace, another balcony, another garden; I see a river, far, far below me, gleaming in the moonlight; I see that cloud-ocean I saw this morning from the balcony, but I see it from *beneath*, lit by the rising sun, suspended over a vast plain of waving grasses and ancient ruins.

I lurch to my feet, lost memories surging against the walls in my mind like waves battering at a breakwater. The heavy barricades tremble—but they do not break. I am left only with a singular flash of understanding.

I do not belong here.

That certainty, which I have been running from ever since I woke beside the train tracks that bitter night two weeks ago, solidifies in my chest with a sickening lurch. That truth, too terrifying to contemplate and too insane to speak of to anyone, courses through me like a poison. Like a sickness, a plague that forever wrenches me away from these people who have been kind to me. I can never be one of them, for this is not my home.

I come from another world.

TWO
NORTH

"North, did you sleep here?"

I swim up out of my dream toward the voice, my brain full of fog, eyes aching. I had my head resting on my folded arms, and I'm stiff and sore as I try to unbend them. I scrub my face to wake myself up, and surreptitiously check for drool. I scrunch my eyes closed and then force them open to find the cat sitting on the table in front of me, giving me a Look.

Techeki stands over both of us, arms folded, expression stern, but not unkind. He looks a little more ragged around the edges these days, but his head is still shaved cleanly, bronze skin gleaming in the torches that line the temple archives, where I apparently spent the night.

"Is it morning?" I ask.

"Yes. What are you doing sleeping here again?"

"I didn't mean to," I say, looking at the cat as if he's going to back me up. He only continues to stare round-eyed at me.

The Master of Spectacle—and now the leader of the temple and Nimh's priests and staff—sighs in a way that reminds me of my mothers. "North, the attendants won't wake you. Nobody's going to tap the Last Star of prophecy on the shoulder and tell him it's bedtime."

"One of your Graycloaks did yesterday, actually," I reply, needled by his tone. He makes it sound as if I'm a troublesome child.

"Please." He's clearly reaching for tolerance now—he's better at schooling his expression than almost anyone I know, and I'm not sure if it's a measure of his own tiredness or of our new familiarity that he lets me see that I'm getting under his skin. "They are not 'my' anything, except perhaps 'my temporary solution to a problem I see no other way to solve.'"

To say the Graycloaks and Nimh's priests make uncomfortable companions would be like saying I was a *little bit* surprised when magic turned out to be an actual thing.

The Graycloaks, led by a hard woman called Elorin, say Nimh's people should abandon magic—should abandon their religion. The Greycloaks filled the river with sky-steel to keep the mist, the source of all magical power, out of the city and make it one of their Havens.

But Nimh is the goddess of her people—and the first in their written history to be able to control the mist directly. She dealt with the Greycloaks by going into terrifying-magical-badass mode, riding in on an out-of-control mist-storm, *possessed* by the mist. With a single wave of her hand she just . . . evaporated the entire river.

Since then the water has crept back in and the river has refilled.

Nimh is gone, the water links the sky-steel anchors once more, and the city is a different place.

The lamps that have nearly extinguished themselves in the early morning light are oil, not spellfire. Even the air inside the temple feels different, giving everything a strange, muffled quality that sets me on edge.

It's strange, missing something I barely knew.

Then again, I miss Nimh so much it's like someone's got their hand around my throat, and they're squeezing all the time.

"Nimh would never accept the Graycloaks here," I say stubbornly. "And you invited them in."

"If Nimh was here, *they* wouldn't be," he snaps. "But unless and until she returns, Elorin and her Graycloaks are the only thing stopping the mist from overtaking every soul in this city. You know that, and I hope that one day I'll have an opportunity to explain it to Nimh. If she cannot forgive me, then so be it."

"There must be——"

"There isn't." His voice is flat as he cuts me off. "North, we've had this argument already. I know you're spoiling for a fight with Elorin, and frankly, I'm tired of running interference. She has no use for instruments of prophecy, and for now, our interests align with those of the Graycloaks. We *must* keep the mist out of the city, and if that is at the cost of magic, so be it. At least then Nimhara will have people to return to, even if she doesn't want to count me among them."

Our eyes meet, and he doesn't look away. We both know I'm silent because he's right—we don't have the luxury of scruples. Not with our goddess gone. Not when the threat is so large.

"Sleep, North," he says eventually, softer. "You're no good to anybody if you read *past* something because your mind is nothing but a tired blur. You need to be slow and deliberate about this and get it right. You are the Star, and if anyone can find a way to bring her back, I believe it's you."

The Star.

Everything I have here, everything I'm worth, comes from being a part of Nimh's prophecy.

I reach for my glass of water to see if I can get my mouth tasting a little less like shoes, and when I find it empty, he softens, filling it for me from the jug as he continues.

"Any progress?"

"No." My reply lands heavy between us.

Two weeks of desperate hunting through the archives, and I'm no closer to a way home than I was before. The first days were a furious, frantic search for something, anything, that would hint at a solution. But Techeki's wisdom sunk in, and I'm trying to be methodical, to make sure that when I'm done with the archives, I know I haven't missed anything.

"We need Matias," Techeki mutters, looking up at the huge shelves that disappear back into the early morning gloom. "But our Master of Archives is too busy playing at being the Fisher King with his riverstriders, and he doesn't want to be found."

I nearly say something—*I can tell you where to find him*—but at least for now, I keep my mouth shut.

Techeki does sound tired—of course he is. He's worked as hard as I have.

He had my glider brought in on a barge, in case it could somehow be repaired, but it was a melted heap of slag. He spared metalsmiths from the effort to salvage the city, but there was nothing we could do for the *Skysinger* or the crown that sent Nimh and Inshara from here to Alciel.

He's tried everything we could think of, anything that might hint at a way home for me. He's barely slept. Half the city saw Inshara touch Nimh, and touch is fatal to a goddess's divinity. The city is in ruins, and he's holding its faithful together with his bare hands.

He wants his goddess back. I want to go home.

At least, I think that's what I want.

I can almost see the faces of my family, imagine the reunions when my mothers learn I'm still alive. My grandfather's face, his worry lines easing in relief at the sight of me. Miri and Saelis, warm and comforting, wrapping me up in their arms. My heart aches with missing them, and yet, when I close my eyes . . . Nimh's face is the one that comes back to me, over and over again.

"Get some sleep," Techeki says again, quietly, gathering himself to depart.

"I will," I murmur, beginning to pack up my papers, piling them into neat stacks. My gaze falls on the one I'd been reading before I fell asleep, and abruptly, memory comes flooding back, and I lurch to my feet. "Wait—I did find something odd."

Techeki pauses, folding his hands into the sleeves of his robe. He thinks it's a way of concealing any body language that might betray his thoughts, but it's a tell on its own: he's trying not to look hopeful. "Yes?"

"The further back I go in the records, the more references I keep seeing to something called the Oracle connected with the Ascenscion. Er, Exodus, I mean."

Techeki's eyebrows rise, and he fixes me with an affect of surprise that he knows grates on my nerves. "Do you not have this story, in your own land? Are you so busy being gods that you have forgotten the way the world began?"

"No. Ours is just . . . different." I have to speak through clenched teeth. He certainly knows how to suck the satisfaction out of learning anything new. "So the Oracle is some kind of god who made the world?"

Techeki sighs, as if annoyed at having to educate me like I'm a child. "The Oracle is the one who gave us the story of the world's beginning. Without them, we wouldn't know where we came from, or why we're here, or even that there have been other cycles of existence before this one."

"So how come nobody mentions this Oracle anymore in modern stories?"

"Theologians started to have issues with their very existence. If they were a god, then that was problematic, because there's only supposed to be one god who stayed behind after the Exodus—the living divine. If they were just a person, then how could they have known how the world began? So, in the manner of religious scholars throughout time, they just sort of edged the whole idea out of canon."

I snort, my annoyance with Techeki overtaken by amusement at the idea of a bunch of grave scholars just tucking away part of their history under beds and behind cupboards so they wouldn't have to figure it out. "So how do I find out more about this Oracle? Or the story it gave you? If it's connected to the Exodus, maybe I can learn something from it."

Techeki's lips twitch a fraction. "Be glad we can't find Matias anywhere. He'd make you sit down and listen to the entire saga."

I keep my own face very still. Techeki doesn't need to know what I know about the former Master of Archives. "The short version will be fine, I think."

Techeki pauses for a moment, tucking his hands behind his back. Despite his mockery of the old man whose domain this was, he still stands like someone about to deliver an epic poem or impart some crucial piece of wisdom.

"We live in an endless cycle. All that has happened will happen again—all that is happening now has already come before. Our world exists in a neverending chain of creation and destruction, joy and suffering, life and death. This incarnation of the world should have been ended a thousand years ago, but the Lightbringer, the god destined to bring about the end, could not bring himself to do it."

"I know this part," I interject, not cowed by the flash of irritation on Techeki's face at my interruption. "Nimh told me the story. He didn't want to end the world, so he ran away to the sky with the other gods." I manage, with an effort, to keep a straight face through the implication that the people of Alciel—myself included—are gods. "And he left behind a prophecy that some day he would be reborn and return to finish what he failed to do a thousand years ago." I stop just short of adding, *And Nimh believes that power—that responsibility—has fallen to her.*

"More or less." Techeki nods. "But what the Oracle tells us—and what most theologians like to forget when writing and rewriting the saga of the Lightbringer—is *why* the Lightbringer left in the first place. In the Oracle's version, he saw the world around him and was conflicted. It was full of violence and suffering and strife, but also beauty and love and forgiveness. He couldn't reconcile the good and the bad, couldn't bring himself to wipe out the darkness if it meant destroying the light too. The Oracle tells us that he left us because we broke his heart."

It's certainly poetic, but it doesn't seem to have much to do with the actual mechanics of how our ancestors managed to lift a city into the sky—and how I might get there myself.

Techeki isn't done, however. "The Oracle's version of the story is that the Lightbringer put half of his heart in the land of the gods and left half of his heart here. In that version, only when the two pieces of his heart are reunited can the world be ended and the cycle resumed."

I wince. "So I suppose the half that's here is meant to be the divine. Does that mean the other half is just floating around somewhere in Alciel? I guess that's why your theologians don't like this story."

Techeki lifts one shoulder. "There's nothing in the Oracle's version that suggests they were referring to the living divine when they spoke of the Lightbringer's heart. Some think they must be referring to twin artifacts of great power, or even the cloudlands themselves. I admit I don't know much more than that—our rituals now rarely invoke the Oracle's version of events. People tend to prefer the Song of the Destroyer—that's the version of the Lightbringer's story that Nimh told you."

"Well, thanks anyway." I don't bother to hide the

disappointment in my voice. Still, something about it nags at me, like a splinter in my foot too small and too deep to pull out. If this Oracle's version of the story is the odd one out, the one that doesn't match all the others . . . surely that means there could be something in it that might help me where all the others have failed.

Techeki stands for a long moment, watching me, then murmurs, "Seriously, North. You look terrible. Get some rest." His footsteps echo as he walks away.

He's right. I'll sleep a few hours, refresh my brain, and then go through what I've gathered. Maybe I missed something. Maybe something in his story will give context to one of the ancient documents I've been reading.

I lean back in my chair, pushing one hand into my pocket to automatically check on the protection stone Nimh made me. I've always got it with me.

It's wrapped up in red thread now, wound around until not even a sliver of it shows through. Just two weeks ago I wore red silk as my riverstrider's sash, making a declaration to Nimh that brought her heart into her eyes. That sash is long gone, but I found the cat playing with a tangle of red threads the other day, and for reasons I haven't examined, I slipped them into my pocket. That night as I tried and failed to sleep, I picked at the knots and smoothed out the thread, then wrapped it around the stone, and so it's been ever since.

Two halves of one heart: above and Below? My world of Alciel, and this land of Nimh's? Or two artifacts, separated in the Ascension. Or . . .

Or two *people*?

I rub my thumb along the grain of the thread wrapping Nimh's protection stone. My mind replays the words she spoke to me the night of the Feast of the Dying, in those few precious moments we stole together before Inshara destroyed it all.

I believe the prophecy brought us together, she told me. *North, this is our destiny.*

I pull my hand from my pocket and rub at the bridge of my nose. Maybe I just want it to be true. Maybe I want our shared destiny to be symbolized by these two pieces of the Lightbringer's heart, because then the prophecy would tell me that we would have to be together again before the end.

If only I could find out more about this ancient Oracle, maybe I'd find some kind of answer.

I groan and drag my attention back to the here and now, deciding I'd better follow Techeki's advice and get some real rest. "Want a nap?" I ask the cat softly.

He steps in closer, carefully licks the skin of my wrist, and then deliberately bites it.

"Ow! What was that for?"

He backs up a couple of steps and gazes past me. There's a hooded figure approaching us—not unusual, all the acolytes have their hoods up to symbolize their separation from Nimh— but the cat's making a clicking noise to greet this one.

Oh, no. This again.

The figure joins us at the table, taking the seat at a right angle to mine, and turns her head so I can see her face. It's a woman—a riverstrider who used to know Nimh, though I've only come to know her myself in the last couple of weeks.

Hiret. Her braids are shorn away to mark her recent widow-hood, the short hair allowing her to pose more easily as an acolyte. She has a gaunt face and medium brown skin, much darker under her eyes.

"Tell Matias no," I say, soft but absolutely firm. "Again." This has been happening almost daily, and I'm wearing thin. Hiret's sister Didyet has left the riverstriders, abandoning their magic and their faith to become a Graycloak. But blood ties aren't severed so quickly, and she's almost certainly the one secretly letting Hiret into the temple.

"I can't tell him no," Hiret replies, just as soft. "You are the Last Star. Nimhara's people need your light in the darkness of her absence."

"What *I* need is your Fisher King to help me search for a way back to the sky," I snap, forcing myself to keep my voice down.

"But the prophecy brought you here," she points out. "This is where you are meant to be."

Usually the conversation ends here. Usually I'd keep my mouth shut, because her husband died the night I met Nimh, one of the riverstriders willing to escort her as she chased the prophecy that brought us together.

He believed in her, and Inshara's Deathless murdered him for it.

But this morning anger swells up in my chest, and my reply bursts out of me in a furious whisper. "Screw the prophecy, Hiret. It yanked me out of my world, away from my life, my family, my friends. It put me in front of Nimh, made me fall in—into the middle of all your in-fighting. It sent her to the sky, and then your prophecy tossed me aside."

She opens her mouth, but I'm not done.

"Your prophecy has done nothing but harm the people I care about, and I'm done looking for some kind of clue about what it wants from me next. All I want is a way home. *That* is the problem I need to solve right now. Given my home's where Nimh is, it should be the problem you want to solve too."

Hiret waits me out, and when my words finally run dry, her reply is simple—she juts her chin out with determination as she delivers it. "The Fisher King of the riverstriders has called for you to come, cloudlander."

"Why should I do as he asks?" I demand. "He lied from the moment we met right here in these archives. He stood here as Nimh's humble librarian and he pretended he was nothing more—not the Fisher King of the riverstriders, not a Sentinel. I was asking for his help to find a way home, and he neglected to mention that he's part of an ancient order literally dedicated to *guarding the way between the worlds.*"

"He had his reasons," she hisses.

"And no doubt he has them now," I snap. "Or he'd be helping me, instead of guarding the way home still, while I tear this place apart to try and find something that will show me the path."

"If he knew how to find her, he would tell you," she insists.

"Then what does he want with me?" I demand. "If he's not going to help me?"

"He will tell you that when he sees you."

"Which he won't be doing."

"You *owe* him," she whispers fiercely. "How dare you not answer his call?"

Her eyes burn into me, and I can feel my cheeks heating. "I can't leave the temple," I point out. "There are Deathless all over the city. I'd have to be an idiot to let them get their hands on me."

"So you hide?" she demands. "The river is empty of fish. Our crops are dying. Before long, people will starve."

"I'm not much of a gardener," I snap.

"More and more people are turning to the Deathless, and their stockpiles of ransacked food. The rest are starting to believe the heretical words of the Graycloaks, who are speaking here from Nimh's very temple. The faith of the people is failing, and if we don't find a way through this together, we'll all die alone."

"I can't save you from that," I tell her, my voice gravelly with exhaustion.

"You're the Last Star! You're the *only* one who can save us."

I grind my teeth until a pain runs through my jaw. I try to steady myself with a slow breath. It doesn't help. "Hiret, I gave up everything to fight for Nimh. I gave up everything to serve your prophecy. And now I'm *done* with it. I'm not anyone's Star. My only work right now is to find a way back to Alciel, where everyone I love is in danger, if it's not too late already. You tell the Fisher King, your Sentinel, that he can get on board that train or he can wave me farewell."

"I—"

But this time I'm the one to cut her off. "You should go now,

Hiret. I've kept my mouth shut out of respect—Matias found me a way out of his temple when Inshara was screaming for my head, and I'm grateful for that. But *enough*. Come here again and I'll call the temple guard. Techeki will be thrilled to meet someone who can lead him to his old rival."

Her mouth drops open. *You wouldn't*, say her eyes.

I narrow mine in response. *Try me.*

Our gazes lock as the moment stretches—as she tests my resolve, and I hold. Then abruptly she looks away.

She pushes to her feet, adjusting her hood. "Someone will be waiting in the usual place this evening," she says, turning her back to walk away.

I wait until she's cleared the main doors before I lever myself to my feet, gathering up my armfuls of papers. "Come on, fluffy butt," I tell the cat. "Let's get some proper sleep for a few hours."

The cat stares at me, and then sinks his claws into a pile of papers.

"What?"

More staring.

"I'm doing the best I can," I say softly. "Going with her doesn't get us closer to Nimh. It means giving up on Nimh. And I'm not ready to do that yet."

I think the cat is half the reason the riverstriders think I'm the one they need. Nimh's the only one who's ever had the beast's loyalty, so they see his attachment to me as some kind of sign.

I told them I don't command him. I'm just the one who feeds him.

The cat and I make our way along the hallways, past the sleepy acolytes and staff on the first shift of the morning.

I have my own quarters, but we're heading to the one place nobody dares interrupt me—a place that's only for the divine. The cat led me to this secluded corridor half a dozen times before I figured it out—as far as I could see he just kept bringing me down a hallway to a dead end, meowing at a blank wall, and then staring at me with judgment in his eyes.

Now I bundle my papers into one arm so I can find the button recessed into the stone scrollwork carved around a seemingly ornamental pillar. The hidden door begins to slide open, and the cat slips through it ahead of me, to Nimh's garden sanctuary.

Skylights and mirrors overhead bring in the morning sun from outside, illuminating a space perhaps twice as large as my bedroom.

Delicate vines cling to stone walls, and water trickles down their cool surface to a pool in the far corner that's edged with moss, overlooked by a stone bench. Flowers reach up to the light, red and orange and yellow, long-stemmed and delicate, bouncing slightly in the faint breeze caused by the closing of the door behind me. There's a whole tree in here, with smooth white bark and branches that rise and then arch gracefully back down again, gray-green leaves, and bunches of vividly pink blossoms.

I've dragged some cushions and blankets in so I can nap beneath it, completely undisturbed—none of the temple's staff would dream of banging on the door to a place reserved for the gods, and as far as I know, nobody's told Elorin and her Graycloaks it exists.

If I'm honest with myself, this beautiful place is beginning to take on hints of my bedroom at home—piles of paper sit in stacks next to my mattress, old plates are stacked by the door where I keep meaning to carry them out. I've tacked up rows of documents along the one free wall, half of them covered in my messy scrawl. I'm the one who put it together, and even *I'm* starting to think it looks like the collection of a conspiracy theorist who has lost half his mind.

It's a sacrilege, my things in this space, turning something beautiful and quiet into a reflection of the chaos of my own world—my own mind.

Here, wedged into a flowering vine is a cluster of pages—diagrams of wings made by some batty old inventor who never got anywhere imitating birds. If he'd ever seen something like my glider, the *Skysinger*, his eyes would've popped out of his head. And yet I cling to his pages, because I don't have the *Skysinger*, and I'm almost desperate enough to try anything else I can find.

I built my glider with tech I salvaged from the engines under my city, and I was sure that, given time, I could improve on my design, create a skyship that would be able to ascend under the power of its own engines. I stood and told the council so the day I fell Below. I still believe I could, but all the tech I'd need to do it is in the sky.

It's torture. Being able to visualize every piece of what I need. It's like standing on one side of a chasm, wanting to cross to the other, and staring at the plank I could use as a bridge . . . on the other side.

Just next to the sketches of the flying machine, there's the stack of scrolls from when I found records mentioning the Second Exodus. They broke my heart, those scrolls—for a moment they offered a glimmer of hope that someone may have found a way into the sky *after* the Ascension, when Alciel rose into the sky. The Exodus, to Nimh's people. The way it was done is lost to history, and for a wild moment, I thought the cracked scrolls might tell me how to do it a second time, how to ascend, but I could barely make out any of the words.

By the edge of the water, weighted down with a stone, I've placed a little nexus of myths I've found about the Sentinels, who have existed as long as this place's records. They're supposed to know the way between this world and mine. But they talk a lot about magic doors and true hearts. Are they the same pieces of a broken heart from the Oracle's version of the story? I wonder. But otherwise they give no hint about what the hearts are or where any of them might be. They don't even allude to the fact that at least one Sentinel *still exists*—Matias's revelation on the steps of the temple after Nimh and Inshara ascended seemed to shock Techeki and the others as much as it did me. But if Matias knows a way to the sky, he's not telling me.

Another dead end.

Because this is hopeless.

Two straight weeks of searching for a way home, and I'm absolutely nowhere.

Trying not to let the stab of disappointment overwhelm me, I add my little stack of notes about this Oracle of theirs to the myths about Sentinels. More stories, more perspectives on the mythology of the Exodus. Nothing that will ever help me do what our ancestors did and reach the other side of the sky myself.

Back when I first found this place, the garden was dying. A few discreet questions made it clear that nobody but the Divine One would ever set foot inside her sanctuary, and she hadn't been here to tend to the growing things inside. When I walked through the stone door and it silently closed behind me, the leaves seemed to shiver in anticipation of . . . something.

And then I saw it, lying by a patch of wilting cream-and-gold flowers: a small trowel. Just set down, as if Nimh expected to return at any moment.

I told Hiret I wasn't much of a gardener, but that wasn't completely true.

I've used Nimh's tools plenty of times since I found them, and now I sink down to sit on the grass, letting my fingers wrap around the carved wooden handle of the trowel that Nimh once held. For a moment, the image of her sitting here is so strong in my mind that I can almost feel her hand under mine. The handle even seems warm in my palm, as if she had just been here and touched it moments ago.

I *thought* I knew nothing about gardening, but it didn't take long for my memories to come back. My grandfather's voice . . .

He loved the palace gardens. I had tools just like these—miniature versions, because I was no more than five or six years old in my memory. The same age Nimh was when they found her and brought her to the temple.

The palace gardens were never my thing. If I ever get home, I'll weed them end to end for my grandfather. For now, I begin

37

my daily work, the way I wind down before I sleep—though usually I'm not dumb enough to attempt to sleep first thing in the morning, after an all-nighter in the library.

Slowly, I start to clear away the grass that's closing in around the flowers, to gently remove the dead blossoms.

The cat takes up position beside me, watching my work, and after a few moments he starts growling softly. No, wait, this isn't growling—Nimh told me the name for this.

Purring.

"I'm trying, Fuzz," I tell him softly. "I swear, I'm trying hard as I know how."

He just twitches his tail at me, and I keep on with my work. The quiet here is different from the quiet of the archives—this place is filled with life, with its own purpose. And though I've always loved learning, loved libraries, the last two weeks in the archives I've felt like a very small light in a big, dark room, the edges so far away I don't even know where to search for them. The archives have been lonely.

Here, even though I know there'll be more flowers to water tomorrow, more branches to trim, there's still something comforting in this kind of work—in knowing I can finish it today, and do it right, and do it well.

Growing things are the place to look for hope, North. I can hear my grandfather's voice, echoing between our worlds. *No matter what else is happening, the garden is always putting forth a new shoot, readying itself in the certainty that tomorrow will come.*

Nimh tended these little signs of hope, even though outside were Inshara's Deathless cultists, who said she'd never manifest her power; the Graycloaks, who wanted to kill all magic to protect themselves; the mist storms threatening her people, who all looked to her as their sole protector.

I miss her so much, the ache of it exhausts me. My anger is my shield—I need it to hold off the constant fear of what Inshara might have done—to Nimh, to my family, my friends, my people. My anger is my fuel too, but it's not propelling me anywhere useful. I'm no closer to an answer than I was when I began searching the archives.

I ease back from my knees to sit cross-legged on the edge of the mattress, and the cat climbs quietly into my lap, claws retracted for once, curling in against me without a hint of a protest as I gather him up in my arms, press my face to his fur.

"How did she do it?" I whisper to him. "How did she find the energy, the hope, to face the world when none of them thought she could do it? When even *she* didn't know if she could do it?"

He's quiet now, warm in my arms. He's always gentle when we're here. I'm gentler too. Perhaps this place can give *me* strength—just enough to try one more time.

Growing things are the place to look for hope, North.

How do I keep searching for a way to reach her? I could spend another ten years in the archives without finding what I need.

I know what I have to do.

I need someone who knows more than me. And I'm going to find a way to make him help me.

THE NETWORK SPECIALIST

The network specialist hovers, his palms sweating, at the edge of the crowd that surrounds the queen.

Every now and then, he catches a glimpse of filmy crimson out at the podium. *She* is there, the girl from Below, speaking to the cameras and the crowds.

When she finishes and steps off the dais, she's surrounded by courtiers and reporters all clamoring for her attention.

This is exactly why the specialist chose to work with tech systems—he's not cut out for politics, not made to jostle for position. Give him a nice, quiet server room any day.

Still, his orders were clear. Gathering his courage, he steps forward, expecting to have to fight to be seen. Instead, a gold-crowned head snaps up, and a pair of penetrating eyes fix on his face.

"You're back!" she exclaims, her eyebrows rising. "Did you learn the nature of the malfunction?"

The specialist shifts his weight from foot to foot. "I—uh—It wasn't a malfunction after all, ma'am." The woman's eyes narrow a touch, and he hurries to correct his address. "I mean, Divine One. It wasn't a mistake, the towers last pinged that particular chronometer in the gardens two weeks ago, around the time you arrived."

The woman waits, sensing that there's more. He swallows, dipping his hand into his pocket and pulling out the dirt-encrusted object there.

"Someone buried it, ma—Divine One."

"Buried it?" She stares at him, her strange, compelling eyes flashing with a momentary anguish. "You mean it was abandoned? He tried to get rid of it?"

The specialist nods, nervous. He knows this is not the reply she wishes to hear.

"Someone of . . . great importance, spoke to me through this chrono," she says. "There must be another explanation."

"It was smashed and buried nearly an arm's length underground, among the red flower display in the south garden," the specialist replies, wincing.

A shiver goes through him as she approaches to take the chronometer. He surrenders the object with relief, hoping against hope that he won't be summoned back to the palace until the next time their chrono network starts acting up.

Nimhara studies the broken chrono in her palm, those alien eyes intent, her lips tight. Then, in a quick gesture, she tosses it aside, and it clatters to the ground. "Never mind," she says, her voice tight and controlled, focusing somewhere past him. "I don't need him. I am my people's *goddess*. And now yours, too."

The specialist takes a few steps backward, listening to the crowds milling around outside the palace gates—there is some cheering, but mostly he can hear raised voices, confusion, uncertainty.

He waits until Nimhara has turned away, striding back to the queen's side before all the cameras and the reporters shouting questions—and then he flees, leaving the broken chronometer abandoned on the floor.

THREE

JAYN

Mumbling an excuse to the old woman by the hearth, I stagger out the door into the cold, crisp morning air of Alciel. For once, the sheer towering height of the sleek white-and-silver buildings rising on either side of the avenue doesn't rob me of breath—for my mind is ringing, screaming, with the truth I suddenly know: that I am not from this world.

The pavement beneath my feet gives a tiny quiver, as if the wide, empty streets are cold and shivering to find warmth. I ought to be used to it, but the movement always leaves me unsettled and unsure. The first time it happened, I am told, was a few days after the old king's death. While no one knows what's making the islands of Alciel quake, I can't help but wonder if the people's grief for the loss of their king has made the very ground unstable.

The streets are mostly deserted here in a way I've never seen before. A few clusters of people gather around the screens that line the exteriors of the buildings to listen to the visitor from another world, but most of the city is at the palace for the coronation. One of the spectators, a boy about my age, turns and spots me standing on the corner. My body wants to freeze, certainty rushing through me that he can somehow tell that I'm like the girl in red on the screen—that I don't belong here. I force my feet to move, picking a direction at random. An older woman standing next to the boy says something to him, and he turns away from me.

They cannot know by looking at me, I tell myself, though I cannot explain why I'm so afraid of anyone knowing. *I lived with the electrician's family for many days, and none of them suspected.*

But that was before the people of this world knew mine existed.

In the distance I can hear the windy roar of thousands of voices—the crowd still gathered outside the palace. My heart pounds along with my footsteps, fear making my limbs heavy and awkward. A shadow swoops along the ground in front of me, making me gasp. Overhead, a glider wheels in a slow, graceful circle, enjoying the freedom of the relatively clear sky.

There must be some reason I am not with the other girl, the one with whom the queen has allied herself. It cannot be coincidence that two visitors from a lost world arrived here within days of each other.

But if we traveled here together . . . why am I not with her still?

Nimhara.

The name strikes in me a chord of unease and dread that I cannot explain any more than my fear. The sight of her in her red robe, standing at the queen's side, is fixed in my mind's eye, but every time I reach for the feelings stirring inside me, to try to understand them, they flee like wild povvy before a bright light.

My steps falter, and I stop by one of the posts that, in evening, light up the streets. There is never darkness here, every corner and alleyway glowing with screens and signs all through the night. No darkness, and no animals—how had I never noticed that before? I know the word *povvy*, can picture the little furry beasts running on their short little legs. I know there *should* be animals. And yet here there is nothing. Only birds, and the wind, and the gliders in the sky.

I pause in the mouth of an alley, checking to be sure that no one is watching, and try to catch my breath. There is a way of reaching for calm and stillness, an exercise of meditation; I don't pause to wonder how I know this when I remember so little, but instead I close my eyes and focus on the rise and fall of my own breath. The feeling is so familiar that my heartbeat settles quickly, and my racing thoughts slow. My mind reaches out for all the things I cannot remember, a tangible presence that I can sense there, as if waiting just behind a ceremonial curtain. All I must do is draw the curtain back—and yet I cannot make myself do so, for I fear the thing that waits there.

The hairs lift along the nape of my neck, and I open my eyes, startled. For a moment, I'm confused, caught between fear of the monster behind the curtain in my mind, and fear of . . . what?

And then I see him.

He stands on the opposite side of the street, fair hair combed immaculately and posture straight. Though he wears ordinary clothes—a black jacket zipped up to his throat and gray trousers—some deep instinct recognizes that he should be in a uniform, for some part of me knows how to recognize a guard in any guise.

Heart sinking, I realize I must have been a thief in my former life.

Or someone worth guarding.

He is watching me. Forcing my gaze to slide past him, as if nothing about him held my interest, I urge myself to turn my back and keep walking. Every instinct tells me to glance over my shoulder and see if he's following, but I manage to wait until I reach the next corner, where a shop window gives me a blurry, distorted reflection of myself.

And there, some distance behind me, a black-and-gray column of a figure, moving quietly and slowly after me.

My throat closes as panic threatens to rob me of sense. I can't think of what to do, so I just keep walking—he doesn't seem inclined to close the distance between us, so I'm safe as long as I keep moving.

Why should a royal guard be following me? My mind races even as my eyes flick to another shop window and another glimpse of the dark figure. *I did not know until today where I was from, so how could the queen?*

But then my mind supplies the answer: the girl in red must know I am here. She must have reason to search for me.

Nimhara.

Except that she isn't Nimhara. That certainty nearly makes me stop, and I keep walking only with a monumental effort.

Somehow, I know this truth the way I knew about povvy, the way I knew the man following me had the bearing of a trained guard.

The emissary from another world is lying to the queen.

My eyes keep darting this way and that, finding reflections of the man on my trail. Then I see something that robs me of breath: there are *two of them.*

A second guard has joined the first, wearing similar clothes, except that his jacket is gray and his hair dark.

Abandoning pretense, I quickly change directions and turn down a narrow side street between two dizzyingly high buildings—and stop dead. A third guard, a woman with short brown hair and a sharp face, waits at the other end of the street. My heart gives a stab of panic, and I whirl around and break into a run.

I have the advantage of surprise, and I can hear one of the men somewhere behind me stifle an oath as they scramble after me while I sprint across to the opposite side of the street and into another alley.

I barely have time to register the wall at the end of the alley before I'm upon it and scrambling to climb. I manage to swing one leg over before the first man is there, and I glance down to see him reaching, hand outstretched, for my foot.

I see her face, the woman in my dream, as she grabs hold of me. . . .

I shriek, and a sickening crack splits the air. The man goes flying back. He hits the pavement and rolls to a stop in front of the other two guards, who skid to a halt, staring first at him and then at me, where I sit straddling the brick wall and panting for breath.

My hands still grip the brickwork. My feet still rest against the wall.

I did not move, did not reach out. We did not touch, and yet . . .

I make myself move, trying not to think about what just happened. I hit the ground on the other side of the wall, stagger two steps, and then break into a run again.

I don't stop until I'm half a dozen streets away.

All of Alciel is celebrating this night. Colorful explosions light up the indigo sky, and music spills out across the streets, different tunes and beats blending together at their edges to form a pulsating web of merriment. The smells of frying foods from vendors' carts cover the acrid smell of smoke from the sky-fire, familiar and alien all at once. Lights projected from the buildings looming overhead cast dizzing patterns against the wide, smoothly paved streets and the people gathering there. This part of the city is even grander than the sector where the electrician lives, with broad avenues and buildings so intricately constructed that they seem more like sculptures carved from ivory and obsidian. Sections of wall that seem like windows by day are now screens, projecting images of the coronation and the celebrations taking place across the city.

Ever since I woke two weeks ago by the train tracks, the city has been somber in a way I didn't fully understand until now. Despite tonight's attempt at joyous, wholehearted celebration, there's still a current of uncertainty beneath the festivities. The city is still grieving the loss of its king and its prince—and still trying to process the appearance of a woman from Below at the queen's side.

The owner of the caff-ley parlor I've been hiding in all afternoon comes by my table again. They ask if I need anything, though I know what they are actually saying: *It was fine for you to sit all day nursing one small drink when the world was at the coronation—but now I have customers and you no more coin.* Still, their face is kind enough, and when I tell them I need nothing and that I'll go soon, they tell me to take my time.

I've kept myself tucked away all day, frozen by indecision and fear. A part of me longs to simply go to the palace and ask the woman who calls herself Nimhara who I might be, but some instinct seated deep within my heart tells me I cannot trust her. If nothing else, she is allied with the queen—and the queen's men are the ones chasing me.

Neither can I go back to the electrician's house, for it would be a poor show of gratitude for her kindness to me if I brought danger to her doorstep. I have no way of knowing how long I've been followed, and whether they know where I've been staying.

And I cannot simply flee, for this place is a floating prison, surrounded on all sides by sky, and my home an entire world away.

The wide window at the far end of the shop flashes blue-green a few seconds before I hear the distant muffled pop of another celebratory explosion in the sky. I don't know where I am—the streets in this district are unfamiliar, for I've never ventured very far from the electrician's house, and I don't have one of the chronos that people here use to find their way.

I cannot help but remember the first night I spent in this place, body aching from injuries I could not remember, and mind empty except for fear, with nowhere to go and no idea who to trust. I wandered, street by street, until I crawled between two bushes to try to sleep with my back against a wall—a wall that turned out to belong to the house of the electrician.

Slowly, telling myself that I am stronger and better armed by knowledge than I was then, I get up from the table. I fish my last coins out of my pocket and leave them on the table; just enough to cover the small caff-ley and a few extra for the shop owner's kindness. Then, carefully making wide detours around the other patrons so that no one jostles me, I weave my way to the door, which hisses open at my approach.

A scrape from behind me makes the hairs on the back of my neck lift. *Coincidence,* I tell myself—with a shop full of patrons, it's not so strange that someone else stood so soon after I did. Turning just a fraction, I watch out of the corner of my eye as a woman approaches the shop counter, waving the proprietor away as she peruses the array of baked goods on offer. I'm about to let my breath out when the woman casts a quick, furtive glance my way.

My heart slams against my ribs, and I hurry out the door as my mind floods with questions. How long had she been sitting there, watching me? She must be one of the queen's guards—but if so, why did she not try to seize me or have me arrested?

My eyes scan the streets even as helplessness threatens to choke me. I already know I have nowhere to go.

I jerk my gaze up as a burst of laughter above me heralds

another of those colorful explosions, one of the smaller ones set off from a balcony that hangs over the street. The burst of red and gold nearly blinds me, and leaves my vision blooming with afterimages against the dark night. I focus on the sparks as they fall like gilded petals from a weeping hirta tree.

Below them stand a boy and a girl, facing each other. She has her head bowed, and he moves closer to her, one hand stroking her lavender curls, which glow pink and peach in the light of the sky-fire. Time itself slows, the sparks dancing around them, and for a moment I forget my fear and distress and just stare at them both.

A shock of recognition runs through me.

I know them.

For a moment I cannot move—my whole body is numb, my staring eyes unable to so much as blink.

An image unfolds in my memory.

I am looking at a picture. They have their arms around each other in the picture, and they are laughing, smiling, pink with pleasure. They are also embracing a third figure, another boy. . . .

My eyes fill and burn, and I stagger back against the wall of the shop, choking on my tears. I stare at the two figures from semi-concealment until the boy lifts his head, eyebrows drawing together, and turns, as if sensing the weight of my gaze. His eyes move past me once, but as his head turns back again, he sees me. He murmurs something, and the girl lifts her head too. Her gaze turns hard as her eyes meet mine, and she tugs on the boy's arm, leading him off into the crowd.

"Wait!" I cry, my paralysis falling away as urgency takes its place. "Wait—please."

But they keep moving, and though I try to follow, they don't mind being jostled—whereas I have to hurry out into the middle of the street, where the crowds are thinner and I can move without being touched. They are the first familiar things I've found in an alien world, and I cannot let them vanish again.

Then, shaken by my need, a tiny dam in my memory breaks. "Miri!" I shout, voice cracking. "Saelis! I need your help!"

In the distance I see a head of lavender curls pause and turn. But then I sense movement behind me, and I turn just in time for a pair of bright white lights to blind me, freezing me in my tracks as the tramcar bears down on me.

FOUR
NORTH

It's dark, and the hour is late when I reach the alleyway outside the temple. Last time I used this passage, Nimh and I were escaping through the archives.

It was the first time I truly saw her power. Saw something my rational mind couldn't explain. Nimh collapsed the stone roof right in front of me, blocking our pursuers.

It was the night I realized both death and magic were real, and they were here, and I couldn't outrun them.

Last time I came out through this door, we were on our way to borrow a boat from the riverstriders. To escape the city, find Jezara, and learn the truth about Inshara, who believed *she* was the true leader of her people—and wanted Nimh dead.

That night aboard the riverstrider's ship, as the moons rose, we told each other our stories.

I thought I could have stayed there with Nimh. Forever.

The idea terrified me.

At first, the alleyway seems deserted. Then the cat trots past me with a meow of greeting, and a shape unfolds from the shadows.

He wears the sash of a riverstrider, a man in his thirties with an open, friendly face, and a build on the heavy side. Light brown skin, a mess of dark curls, and a one-sided smile I'll bet wins him plenty of admirers. Another day maybe I'd be one of them, but tonight I'm a little preoccupied.

"Greetings," he says politely to the cat, bowing slightly. Then he looks up and turns that easy grin directly on me. "My name's Orrun."

For a moment, all I can do is blink at him. I was thinking only a moment ago of that other night we crept out through the tunnel, and here stands the man whose boat we took. Techeki tells me that the ship was found burned out on the riverbank.

Briefly, I wonder if Orrun knows I owe him a boat. But then I remember why I'm here.

"You can take me to Matias?" I ask quietly.

He sketches another little bow, lips quirking. "The Fisher King awaits."

Our journey down to the water is short and silent—fuel is scarce now, and the streets are dark, so it's easy to keep to the shadows. The ruin Nimh wrought on the city is everywhere, great blocks of stone tumbled across the streets, homes and shopfronts broken open and left empty.

Orrun leads me along the riverbank and onto the gently rocking dock. There's a boat moored there, the smallest sliver of light escaping the cabin around the edge of thick, dark curtains.

I follow him down a few worn wooden steps, then he parts the curtain and we're in the cabin itself—it's crowded with bodies and filled with the sound of conversation, lit by the steady glow of lamps dotted around the place. So the riverstriders have fuel, it seems, in a city where almost everyone is scrambling for it.

Matias is at the center of them all, resplendent in his turquoise velvet coat, dozens of strings of beads clicking and shifting across his chest as he moves.

Slowly the noise dies away, as one by one, the two dozen riverstriders crammed into this small space turn to regard me, mouths opening in surprise. A few shift back a step, as if I shouldn't be touched, just like Nimh. More than a few cover their eyes, in the same gesture of piety they offer their goddess.

Their respect hits me like shock of cold water. These people truly *believe* that I'm a part of their prophecy. That the Last Star will have answers.

But I have none.

Before I have time to consider my words, they're tumbling out of me. "Enough, Matias! I'm not your savior, I'm not a god—I'm just a guy trying to get home. Tell them to put their hands down."

The surprise with which the assembled riverstriders greeted me turns to outright shock. Matias, for his part, just blinks at me with slow deliberation, reminding me for one unnerving moment of the cat, who stands quietly at my feet.

Then he nods politely, levering himself to his feet with the aid of a stick. "It's good to see you, North, welcome. Come take a walk with me, my boy."

Hearing my name releases something inside me. I've barely heard it since Nimh disappeared—nobody calls the Last Star by his name. And Matias utters it with such kindness. The cat stalks forward to meow a greeting to the old man, as if to highlight what a jerk I am for snapping.

Already deflating, leaking my fury like a faulty airship, I mumble a response and turn to shuffle after Matias, who lifts a lantern and pushes the curtain aside. The riverstriders let us pass in silence. Even after we've emerged onto the deck, when I expected them to explode into gossip behind us, they're quiet.

"Is it safe to walk out here?" I ask, breaking the silence and casting a nervous glance out at the darkness beyond the lantern's pool of light. I can hear something splashing softly in the water, and none of the possibilities my mind supplies sound fun to me.

Matias makes his way to the ramp leading to the dock. "Here, where the riverstriders gather, it is safe enough for us. I do not think the Deathless will test their luck tonight. And after all, we have a light."

That's when I get a better look at his lantern. It's not flickering in the way the oil lanterns in the library do—it's a clear, steady light like I haven't seen in a couple of weeks now.

It's spellfire. In a city bereft of magic.

"How did you get that?" I demand, jabbing one finger at the lantern. "How is it working?"

He lifts the lantern, setting it swinging, and studies it as if he's as surprised as I am to find it there. Then he tilts his head out toward the river itself, and I follow his gaze. By the light of the lantern, cast wider now, I can see that something *is* moving in the river to cause those splashes. There are people down there, diving below the water, then surfacing for air, before they repeat the exercise.

A hint of ice creeps into the pit of my stomach.

"Matias, are you messing with the sky-steel anchors?" I whisper. "Those are the only things keeping the mist out."

"They're keeping the magic out too," he observes.

"Have you *seen* what the mist does to people?" I hiss. "What use will magic be if everyone's lost their minds? If Techeki finds out you're doing this—"

"He'll tell his Graycloaks?" he asks, lofting one brow.

"They're not *his* . . ." But my words die out. This is the exact argument I had with Techeki this morning, except now I'm somehow on the other side of it. Skyfall, can *anything* be simple in this forsaken place?

"Come," says Matias simply, handing me the lantern and setting off along the bank, leaning on his stick.

Left with no other choice, I fall into step beside him, forcing myself to take small, slow steps to match his. The cat has stayed behind, to be spoiled and swap stories with the riverstriders, no doubt. I might not want their adulation, but I'm pretty sure he won't object.

"You've got to stop sending Hiret to the temple to hassle me," I mutter, leaving the question of the sky-steel for now. "I'm doing exactly what I need to be doing: trying to find a way home. I could use *your* help, by the way—that's what I came to say. I'm searching through the archives without a map, without the man who knows where everything is."

Matias doesn't reply, tipping his head back to shift his attention from the docks to the star-studded expanse above, and the dark place where the underside of Alciel blocks the sky beyond it.

"I did everything your prophecy asked of me," I point out, my steps quickening for a moment with restlessness before I slow again. "You know I'm not a god, Matias. I'm just a guy from somewhere else. I'm no use to you."

This, too, fails to earn me a response from the old man. Impatience leaping in my chest, I draw breath to demand he answer me or else let me go—but just as I'm about to speak, Matias lets out a little chuckle, as if thinking of something else entirely.

His tone still amused, he asks in his resonant baritone, "How much do you know about the Fisher King of the river-striders, North?"

I stop walking for a few seconds in surprise and have to quicken my pace again to catch up. "You're . . . their leader. You keep their stories and oral traditions from generation to generation."

"Leader?" Matias lets out another laugh, this one a quick, sharp shot of surprise. "What made you think I was their leader? Nowhere in any of our traditions does it say that the Fisher King is anything other than a storyteller."

I resist the urge to grind the heels of my hands against my eyes in frustration. "Well, I mean, obviously there's no official leader, but you're sort of . . . the closest thing they have, I suppose."

Matias gives a little shake of his head, lowering his eyes back to his feet, and giving me the undeniable impression that he's still laughing.

Annoyance surges in me, but I get it under control—my bloodmother would be appalled at the way I've been losing my temper. I gather myself, applying one of her earliest lessons and focusing on my senses, rather than my thoughts.

I hear the *shhh-clomp*, *shhh-clomp* of Matias's shuffling footsteps and the thunk of his walking stick against the wooden dock, the soft splash of the riverstriders dismantling the sky-steel anchor out in the dark. The night air smells like campfire smoke and the dampness of the river, and something else I can't quite identify, something that disturbs the serenity of the evening.

It isn't until the dock gives way to the spongy terrain of the riverbank that Matias speaks again.

"When I was chosen to be the next Fisher King," he says, "I was already a Sentinel. My father was a Sentinel, and his mother before him, you see—it was always my destiny to be one of the secret guardians of the way between worlds. But none of the other riverstriders knew that I had already answered destiny's call."

"So . . . what, being the Fisher King is some sort of cover for your real identity?"

Matias glances in my direction, the darkness too thick to make out anything other than his eyes, gleaming. "It does make a rather splendid cover, don't you think?" He strokes a free hand down the rows and rows of beads he wears around his neck. "At that time, I wanted nothing to do with storytelling—after all, I had just learned that the story of the Sentinels was true. My life had changed utterly, and not in a way I had chosen."

"I can relate," I murmur.

His smile is wry. "I had been told to pledge myself to secretly protecting the way between the worlds. My life had been signed away from me in servitude to a cause no one would ever know about. But the old Fisher King bade me come to him, and in those days, when the Fisher King called, you went."

Another little gleam of his eyes, and I find myself a little relieved that he can't see the rush of heat to my cheeks. The Fisher King has been calling *me* for two weeks.

"So I went to the Fisher King's barge, and I sat before him. The heir to the Fisher King is a secret, you know—they reveal themselves only when their predecessor dies, so he was asking me to take on a second secret identity. To wrap myself in more lies to those I loved. He listened to me tell him why I didn't want to follow in his footsteps—though of course I could not tell him my real reasons—and did not attempt to argue with me. Instead, he opened a little jeweled box and drew out a round gray stone, perfectly polished by the river. It is common for young riverstriders to fill their pockets with such stones and practice swimming, for it makes them stronger, but this one was different. He explained that it was a powerful and secret relic of our people and that I must keep the stone with me at all times for a month and a day, and never lose it. This stone, he said, would reveal to me in that time whether I was destined to become the Fisher King or not."

Slowly, Matias's hand dips into a pouch dangling from his belt. There's just enough light cast from the slivers of the moons to see the little round stone resting in his palm. A shiver runs through me, and I have to fight the urge to step away.

Oh, for the love of . . . do not *give me your precious artifact, Matias!* My mind races, trying to come up with the words I'll need to convince him that a magic rock wasn't going to change my mind about being their divine savior in Nimh's absence. Still, I can't help but think of the stone I already have—to anyone else, a smooth stone wrapped in red thread. To me . . . all I have left of Nimh.

But the old man just looks at the stone in his palm, a faint smile on his face. "I did as he instructed, certain that I was right, and that the stone would not choose me. I wanted to just throw it in a drawer until the month had passed, but I was afraid someone would take it and I would be the one who had disrupted this long chain of tradition. I began to feel as though it were watching me, though—I would notice its weight in my pocket as I went about my day, and sometimes I would wake in the night, straining my ears, convinced I had heard some distant whisper from deep inside it. I was a fair magician back then, and I could sense the power within the stone; latent, hard to reach, but a power nonetheless. Something waiting. Something searching."

I feel my pulse quicken, and in spite of myself I murmur, "What happened when it called you?"

Matias curls his fingers around the stone so that he can stroke it with his thumb and cast me a sideways glance. "Such impatience, my young prince. Don't you know you cannot rush a good story?"

My breath huffs out of me in a laugh, a little of the tension in my chest easing. "Fine, sorry, I'm listening."

Matias takes a deep breath and comes to a halt, turning to gaze out over the river. In the darkness it looks like it always has, glittering with the reflection of the moons, the surface gently rippling with the movements of those farther upstream.

It's as if the river is alive, but I can still hear Hiret in my mind. *The river is empty of fish.*

I had never seen a fish before I came here—their darting quicksilver beauty reminds me of the birds swooping near the palace at dusk.

After Nimh vaporized the river, the waters came back, seeping in from the rest of the forest-sea, in a day. But the *river,* the whole ecosystem of it, is changed forever.

In the dark you can't tell that it's full of debris and dirt—that it is a dead thing, now.

"I held the stone for a month and a day, as the old Fisher King had instructed me." Matias's voice is quieter now, thick and grave. "I went back to him at sunset on the final day, and I told him that the stone had never called me. That he had been wrong to choose me to succeed him, and that he must give this stone to some other young riverstrider. That he must let them carry it, not me."

Matias stops speaking, breath hitching as if he's forgotten the next words, or like some other thought came in to distract him. He stands there, rubbing his thumb over the stone, staring out over the river.

I'm still half-afraid he's going to try to give this magic artifact to me, to make it "call" me like it must have eventually done for him. But despite that worry, I can't let the story go unfinished, and after a moment I whisper, "And what did he do?"

Matias glances my way, a tiny smile on his lips. He holds up the stone between thumb and forefinger. "This," he replies—and then, drawing his arm back, he heaves the stone out over the river.

A strangled cry bursts from my lips, and I take half a step forward, as if I could somehow catch the thing. My eyes lose it in the dark as it arcs away, but I hear it strike the water with a tiny, neat splash.

Matias is already laughing by the time I whirl around to face him, spluttering questions. "It was just a stone," he explains, grinning, resting one hand on his belly as if to contain his mirth. "I had already stripped half my clothes off, preparing to dive into the water after it, when the Fisher King told me: it was just a stone. He said, 'All I did was tell you a story. It is your belief that gives the stone its power.'"

I lift the lantern to stare at him, and I know he can see my chagrined expression, because the Fisher King keeps chuckling away, shaking his head.

But as I gather myself to retort, the laughter flees from his face, and he turns to face me directly, meeting my eyes.

"Hear me, North." He raises his walking stick and then slams the butt of it down on the damp earth. As if jostled loose by the impact, half a dozen stones fly up—no, hundreds of them, maybe thousands. All along the riverbank, the stones rise up, hovering in midair, damp and gleaming in the faint moonlight like tiny black gemstones—like distant stars lining the ancient waterway.

"There will always be another stone," he says, watching my face intently. "I know Nimh's was not the first call to destiny that you have answered in your life. Nor will it be the last. You must choose which stones to carry, for if you try to carry them all, you will be dragged down by their weight and drown in the depths. But you may find that as you swim, you grow stronger for the stones in your pockets. You may find you can carry more than you knew."

I swallow hard, shaken by the careless ease of Matias's magic. I try to meet his gaze without flinching. "I can't do this, Matias," I whisper. "I'm not divine. I'm not chosen. I already *have* a people who need me, and they're up there. So is she and . . . and I can't leave her there alone." Memories of Nimh flood my mind's eye—those large eyes, the gold-dusted lips, the quiet mirth in her voice whenever she teased me about magic. I slip my hand into my pocket and curl my fingers around her protection stone. "I can't give up on her."

"I would never ask you to," Matias replies. His voice is grave, and he doesn't shift his eyes, giving me no room to escape. "But I do know that without a road to another world, we find ourselves *here*, and this is where we must choose our actions. You can do more than hold our people together, North. You can unify them, and you *must*.

"The Graycloaks wish to trap us within their sky-steel ring, to drain the life out of our faith. Then there are the Deathless. They have perverted everything we know about our world, twisted it into pain and terror in their worship of Inshara. They will fight the Graycloaks and the temple, seek to conquer them both in her name. Techeki is clinging to the middle like a man stranded on a rock in a raging river. The people are afraid. The city is in ruins."

"Your prophecy said Nimh was meant to destroy the world," I remind him, though I think I find that idea more disturbing than he does. "Perhaps this is just the start of it."

"No, my boy," he replies. "Destruction is not what comes next. As the keeper of my people's stories I am calling on you, as we were called on by Nimhara. And we gave her everything. We riverstriders will be the last of the loyal, cloudlander. And you? Your part of the story is not finished yet. There are still far more of the faithful than you think, but someone must unite them—someone who has seen. Someone who *believes*."

I squeeze my eyes shut but I can't block out the truth.

I *have* seen. I *do* believe.

"If the faithful go to the Graycloaks, or fall to the Deathless, that will be the end of this place, the end of its people. It is your choice, Last Star of prophecy. No one can force you to carry a stone you didn't choose. But I do not think anyone else can do it."

A strangled sound escapes my throat. I open my eyes once more, looking back across at him. All around us, the floating stones are gone, scattered once again across the muddy riverbank.

"You know," I manage hoarsely, "there aren't any rivers in the sky. I never actually learned to swim. I would drown without any stones in my pockets at all."

Matias sighs, sounding so like my grandfather in that moment that for a heartbeat I feel the old man standing right beside me. He wouldn't like hearing me shy away from a call to duty, I know that.

Then I hear the squelch of Matias's stick against the mud

before he reaches out to take my shoulder. I can sense his surrender in his slow breath out.

"I understand, lad. This world has survived for a thousand years without your people—we will find a way through. But there is something you can help me with, which requires no stone-carrying at all."

I breathe a sigh of relief. "Whatever it is, I'll do my best."

"There's an artifact of great power in the temple. We riverstriders could use it to help restore balance here and in the city." Matias's gaze is serious, but no longer penetrating. "I had one of my people hide it after Nimh vanished, for there was no safe way to remove it from the temple unobserved, and I didn't want it to fall into Techeki's hands—he'd only use it to solidify his own power."

"Matias," I protest. "Techeki is doing his best to hold the temple together. He's done nothing but help me while I try to find a way to get to her."

Matias raises an eyebrow. "Indeed. Did you never wonder *why* he's being so helpful?" When I stare at him blankly, he gives a little shake of his head. "There's really only one person who could be a threat to Techeki's current power and position, North. One person to whom Nimh's people might turn, one symbol of her divinity that still offers hope. It seems to me that Techeki would be very happy to let Nimh's Last Star of prophecy stay hidden in the temple, his nose buried in books, desperate to find a way back to the other side of the sky. I do not suggest he is glad Nimh is gone—but I think that while she *is* gone, he would like to be in charge."

The back of my neck's prickling. There's no evidence he's right . . . and yet his words are sinking into me slowly, like the cat's claws—with a sting. The first moment I met Techeki, my instincts told me he was a slippery sort of person. It sounds like the sort of thing a clever politician—and he *is* a politician, even if in service to a religion—would do.

"I should tell him what you're doing to the sky-steel," I say, unwilling to accept his point, but not completely sure I can dismiss it either. "The mist-storms out there are wilder than ever now, since . . ."

Since Nimh's fury. Neither of us say it out loud.

"We will speak of it when you return," he replies.

"And in the meantime you want me to get this thing without Techeki finding out. What is it?"

"You'll know it when you see it," he says, with an infuriating air of calm. "You're the only one who can retrieve it—you can move freely around the temple, after all. I will tell you where you must go."

"This is unnecessarily mysterious," I protest.

He laughs softly. "Young man, I was being mysterious when your mother was just a gleam in *her* mother's eye. I am unlikely to stop at this late stage. Now, will you do as I ask?"

I'm itching to know what it is—what it can do. Maybe some sort of magical relic to help the crops, or bring back the fish, or rebuild the city in the blink of an eye. When I reply, it's with a mix of curiosity, duty, and resignation.

"I'm not going to be anyone's god, Matias. But I'll be your errand boy. Just this once."

THE CAPTAIN OF THE GUARD

The captain of the guard stands stiffly to attention, trying not to let his face reveal his thoughts.

"What do you mean, you've *lost* her?" The emissary from Below's expression is stricken, her fingers clutched tightly around the staff she carries.

The captain glances from her to the queen, who stands listening, her own expression stern as she regards the man who served her father loyally and faithfully for over two decades. Finding no hint of sympathy there, the captain turns back to Nimhara.

"Begging your pardon, Divine One, but my men aren't trained for reconnaissance. Our job is to protect our people, not follow them—"

"Your job is to do as your queen commands!" the woman in red snaps, causing the queen to blink and look over at her.

"Nimhara," she says gently. "Don't fret. I have faith in you."

"She could ruin everything," Nimhara murmurs, her hand white-knuckled in its grip on the staff. "I am finally where I was meant to be, *finally*—" She whirls, fixing the queen with an intent, almost hungry look that makes the guard captain half reach for his weapon. "I have *your* heart, do I not?"

"Mine," agrees the queen, her eyes glimmering with tears, "and thus the hearts of every loyal citizen of Alciel. We'll find her, this girl you're looking for. Just as we'll find that other one—what was his name?"

"The Lightbringer," whispers the goddess from another world, her voice hollow. "But I do not think he wishes me to find him."

"It doesn't matter," declares the queen, gazing at Nimhara with such fondness and devotion in her eyes that the guard captain shivers. "You don't need him. You're exactly where you need to be, doing exactly what you need to do. I'm—I'm proud of you, Nimh."

The goddess blinks, glancing at the queen, her expression unreadable.

Slowly, the guard captain takes a step backward, hoping to ease out of the room undetected. Before he can make it more than a few paces, however, the goddess turns, lifting a hand to summon him back.

"You," she says shortly. "If she is beginning to remember, then it won't be long until she comes here. We must be prepared. Bring me . . ." She pauses a moment, then lifts her chin, a bit of her calm returning. "Bring me a locksmith."

FIVE
NIMH

The face from my nightmares looms over me, long-fingered hand reaching out to grab me. I try to scream and pull away, but all I can do is scramble feebly and croak, "Don't touch me!"

"Whoa," says a low voice. "It's okay. I won't, I promise." The face leans back, and when I blink, the nightmare is gone, replaced by something strangely familiar. A fair, round face, soft green eyes, a look of grave concern on his features. The name comes to me after a moment. *Saelis.* He's crouched at my side.

I try to sit up, and he makes a quelling gesture, though he keeps both hands in view, held up before him. "You should stay still," he says, voice soothing. "You're hurt."

"I don't think she is." The other voice belongs to a girl— *Miri*—standing in a flood of bright lights, her curly purple hair in disarray. She's inspecting the front of a tramcar that's been mangled, a large dent in its grille. "Look at this. I don't think she was hit. I think . . . she stopped the tram."

Saelis lifts his head, then gets slowly to his feet, staring. I follow his gaze back to the dent in the tram, not understanding at first what has him so transfixed. Then I watch him run his hand across the dent, which is a smooth arc of compressed metal, without any of the divots or angles that would be left by collision. "That's . . . not possible," he murmurs, frowning.

Miri's watching me, face unreadable. Beyond her, the passengers from the tram gather in loose clumps, talking to each other, inspecting themselves for injuries.

Blinking, I realize that others on the street are acting the same way—gazing at each other, stunned. I must have missed another of those island-quakes. Miri leans in close, pulling my attention back to her. "What did you mean, when you were coming around? That thing you said."

"What?" My dazed mind is starting to pull itself together. Somewhere beyond the ring of onlookers is the woman who was watching me in the caff-ley parlor. I have to get out of here.

"You said 'He's alive.'" Miri drops to a crouch in front of me. "When Sae and I first ran up, you looked at us and said 'He's alive.' Who were you talking about?"

I don't remember saying it, but I don't remember stopping the tram either. I know what I must have meant, though. It's what I kept saying my first few days here. *The prince is alive.* But everyone around me kept telling me I was confused and just didn't remember anything of the last few weeks, so clearly didn't remember the prince's death. I swallow and shake my head. "I—I'm not sure."

Miri's eyes narrow. Her sharp face is appealing, attractive with its dusting of dark freckles, but there's no warmth in it. Still, I can see the image of her that came swimming out of my memory: the picture of her smiling, laughing, her whole being showing her affection for Saelis and for . . .

"North," I blurt, giving in to the instinct that I can trust her and the boy who stands over us. "The prince. He's alive. And I know you were his friends. More than his friends. I remember . . . I remember a picture of you."

Her face is still hard. "Half the city saw him fall," she says in a taut voice.

I glance from her to Saelis, whose gaze has dropped to the ground at his feet, and then back again.

A swell of desperation makes my voice rise. I must make them understand—I have to believe that they will help me. "Have you not just had it proven to you that there is life Below? That the sea of clouds that surround this island conceals the truth beneath your city of wonders?"

The two exchange a look; when Miri meets my gaze again, I can see the emotions warring in her face. She wants to believe me, to see a glimmer of hope—but then she might have to lose him all over again.

From somewhere beyond the pool of light cast by the stopped tram, I can hear a commotion—someone asking questions, trying to push through the onlookers.

I lower my voice, not bothering to hide my urgency. "Please. Yours are the first faces I recognize—I do not know who I am or how I came to be here, but I *know the prince is alive.* Someone is following me. I called out to you because something told me you would help me. Like a voice in my heart. His voice."

Miri's watching me, suspicion still battling hope in her eyes, but after a moment she looks up at Saelis, and some silent communication seems to pass between them.

"When are your first memories from?" he asks.

"The first thing I can recall is from a fortnight ago. Perhaps fifteen days."

"That's how long *she's* been here," he murmurs, eyes widening a little as he looks me over again. "They speak the same way too."

Miri pushes up to her feet. "Then we should bring her to Nimhara."

"No!" My voice is loud enough to interrupt the whispered conversations of those nearby, and I have to concentrate to speak quietly. "I do not trust her. I know she lies. The people following me—I think they are the queen's guards, and Nimhara stands at the queen's side."

"Right." Saelis's voice is quiet, but firm. "Okay. We'll take you someplace safe, and we'll figure out our next move."

"What?" Miri casts him an incredulous look. "You believe her?"

"I don't know. But I do know that if she's actually from Below, and she did somehow know North, he'd never forgive us if we didn't help her. Especially when she had no one else to turn to."

Miri glances back at me, her cheeks flushing. But she doesn't waste another moment. "Come on," she says, glancing around at the onlookers and then choosing a path away from the well-lit street with its ivory towers and gleaming screens. "This way."

✦ ✦ ✦

It doesn't take very long to tell Miri and Saelis what I know, for I know very little. My memories stretch back only a fortnight, and I've spent most of that time in the electrician's home, doing what I can around her house to repay her for her kindness. I tell them what I can: they call me Jayn; something terrible happened to me; and I am not from this world.

Miri continues to pepper me with questions, though, as we wind our way through the back streets of Alciel. How did North survive his fall? When did I meet him? Did I help him? Did he ever speak of her and Saelis?

I can sense her frustration, though she tries to conceal it, each time I tell her that I do not know, that I cannot remember. It's Saelis, though, who treats me to silence and thoughtful glances. For all his reserve compared to his partner, I get the feeling he can tell from my voice, or my face, or the lengths of the pauses between question and answer, that I know more than I am saying.

But I don't—not really. My mind remembers very little. But my heart . . . my heart, with every repetition of the lost prince's name, beats a little faster.

This part of the city is farther away from the palace, and the buildings are closer together, less polished, less soaring. More stalls crowd the streets, with human salespeople rather than auto-vendors, and bright, hand-painted banners proclaiming what goods they have on offer. We pass a cart behind which an old man is ladling fragrant noodles into a dish, and I nearly stop walking, my empty stomach momentarily seizing control of my body. Suddenly it feels like the single caff-ley I had to drink today was many, many hours ago.

Miri leads us to what seems to be a blind alley—but then she touches her chrono a few times and waves it just above a round disc sunk into the street, which slides open with a faint hiss. Saelis eyes me askance as I jump back, catching my breath, but says nothing. For all Miri seems to dominate, I have the feeling that very little escapes her partner's gaze.

The hole in the street leads down into a tunnel by way of a ladder. My heart balks at the idea of voluntarily lowering myself into such darkness, but the relief at finally having someone else to help me, to tell me where to go and what to do next, is stronger than my fear.

So I descend, concentrating on the feel of the metal beneath the balls of my feet, until I nearly choke on my own heart when my foot hits stone instead of another rung. When I look up, only a tiny circle of light above marks the entrance to this place, whatever it is. I know I must turn away from it and move on through the darkness, but I find I cannot move forward, or retreat, or do anything but stand there with my face tipped upward like a dying flower seeking light from the cracks in the canopy.

Canopy. The word conjures a flash of a wondrous image. Trees many times larger than any that grow here, so many that they grow together in arches and vaulted ceilings like the architecture of a great temple. Sunlight filtering through, warm on my skin as I walk. Damp soil underfoot. Distant cries of animals and birds, the whisper of leaves disturbed by a troop of lying monkeys swinging through, the rat-a-tat-a-tat of a wood-bore marset tapping to find insects hidden beneath the bark of her tree.

I blink and blink, but the image doesn't fade—until a loud hiss and clunk tears me away from the memory. The cover slides back into place high above, and I see that last circle of light vanish like the instantaneous waning of a moon, leaving me in utter blackness. There's a strangeness to the atmosphere here—strange in its familiarity. I hadn't realized how alien the very air felt to me in this world. Now I take a deep breath, and a little ripple shivers its way down my spine. Something about these tunnels feels like . . . home.

"What is this place?" I ask, as much to hear the voices of my new companions as to actually get an answer.

"Maintenance tunnels," Miri replies. A moment later, a light shimmers into existence, revealing a long, rounded corridor vanishing into the darkness ahead. My eyes fix on the light, which comes from the chrono she wears at her wrist. Familiarity, as tangible as a shiver, seizes me. Misinterpreting my blank stare, Miri adds, "They stretch all across the underside of Alciel. North used to use them to get around the city unseen, and that's how he found the place he turned into his hangar."

"What is a hangar?" I ask politely, still distracted by the strange, distant memory of a light on someone's wrist. Unlike all the other flashes, this one lingers, as though it's truly a memory and not a clip of a story from someone else's life.

"It's where he kept his glider. The one he crashed in. No one else knows about it, so it's a safe place to lie low while we figure out what's going on. If North is really alive—"

"He is." My voice is sharp, and with an effort, I soften it and add, "I swear it. That much I know to be true."

"Even if he was alive when you came here," Miri points out bitterly, "it's been weeks, and he's all alone."

"I would know if something had happened to him."

Silence stretches for a moment, and though I keep my eyes on the light from the chrono, I can tell Miri and Saelis are exchanging glances over my shoulder.

It's Saelis's soft voice that breaks the quiet. "How can you be so sure, when you have no way of contacting anyone Below?"

Even expecting the question as I was, I'm left shaking my head helplessly. "I cannot explain how I know, any more than I can explain how I know I am not from this world. I just *know*."

Miri makes a frustrated sound in her throat. "No one wants North to be alive more than us, it's just—I can't let myself think he's okay just to lose him again. You don't know what it's like to watch someone you love die while you're helpless to stop it."

I do know.

I don't speak the words aloud, but they fill my head and my heart. I'm left speechless with the effort of not adding one more certainty to the list of things I know but can't explain.

"Miri," says Saelis, "maybe this can wait until we're at the hangar? She's been on the run all day. She must be hungry too." I glance at him, meeting his keen, soft eyes. He must have seen the way I half stopped when I smelled those noodles.

Miri shakes her head, stubborn. "No, Sae. She expects us to just take her word for what she says, when she doesn't even remember her own name. Claiming North isn't—" She stops short, clearing her throat. "I want an explanation."

I place one hand on the cool, steadying surface of the stone beside me. "When I woke, I thought I knew nothing—but there were small things. I could tie the laces on my clothing. I could brush my hair. I knew my own face in the mirror. I cannot tell you how I know these things when I have forgotten so much else, but they were all I had in those first few days. You say I do not know what it is to lose a loved one—I say *you* do not know what it is to lose yourself. To you, tying a lace or holding a brush is nothing. To me, it was all I had."

Miri's eyes shift toward Saelis's, then fall. Her arms stay crossed, though, the light from her wrist quivering with each breath.

"The only other thing I *knew* was that the prince was alive. The first time I heard his name, I knew." My eyes are burning, but I hold my tears back with a ruthless control I didn't know I had until this moment. "I do not even know my own name, but I know North's. I cannot force you to believe me. But I will not let you take this certainty from me, because it's still all that I have."

Into the silence that follows my voice, Saelis exhales a quiet breath. "You care about him." His eyes search mine in the darkness, and he turns on the light on his own chrono, softening the harshness of the shadows from the other.

"I do not know." I swallow down the reply I want to make: *Yes, gods help me, I cannot remember him and yet I think my heart is his.* "I think we are bound together, he and I."

"And you would know if something had happened to him." Saelis echoes my pronouncement solemnly, without the disdain of his partner, who eyes him quickly. He glances her way, lets his eyes linger on her a moment, and then looks back at me as I nod confirmation. "I believe you."

"What?" Miri's voice is taut and sharp.

Saelis lifts his chin. His eyes are wet, his face weary but touched here and there with a new lightness I didn't see before. "I believe her. Maybe it's because I want her to be right. But I believe her when she says North is alive."

Miri's hands tighten into fists around the fabric of her sleeves, and her expression twists, betraying how badly she wants to believe as well. "I can't," she says finally, turning away. "Not until I see him. Not until I *know* he's okay."

I draw a breath, my heart warring between impatience and sympathy. "I understand," I murmur gently. "You're allowed to protect your heart. You are aiding me—that is more than I could have hoped for."

Miri gives a loud sniff, and Saelis reaches out to take her hand. "Let's go," she suggests. "Before whoever was following you thinks of checking down here."

I trail along after them, for they are less suspicious of me now and don't bother to keep me in between the two of them as we move. The tunnels below Alciel twist and turn in no pattern that I recognize, corridors branching at seeming random, and none of them ever running in a straight line. Some disappear into the inky darkness, and others are lit by whole walls of tiny red and green lights that flash in ever-changing, unpredictable patterns.

We pass through a long section of corridor where the walls are lined on either side with pistons madly thrashing up and down, puffs of steam snaking out across the curved ceiling above our heads, drifting down to paint us with false perspiration. As we reach a crossroads, down a path we do not take, I can see a tangle of vines with faintly glowing leaves.

Miri and Saelis do not hesitate, their path well-known to them, but a hint of uneasiness tickles at me when I realize that were we to be separated, I would have no idea where I was or how to find my way to the world above. Without a chrono, I wouldn't be able to operate the trapdoors in the streets. I would be stuck here until someone else—quite possibly someone far less friendly than these two—found me.

Despite the darkness and the closeness of the air, despite that strange, almost familiar greasiness to it, I find myself breathing more easily, letting go of the knot of tension and anxiety in my chest. Perhaps it's because I am with allies, with friends of the boy that haunts my memory. But some instinct tells me there's more to it than that.

In Alciel, very little attention is paid to feelings and instincts—the dismissal of my insistence on the prince's survival when I first arrived was proof enough of that. I think, though, that my world must value these things more highly, for I feel compelled to listen to those inner voices. And just now, they're telling me that there's something here—something important.

Something alive.

Between one step and the next, my feet freeze. To my left stretches a long, straight corridor, unlike the curving, twisting tunnels we've been traveling. Something about it is different—something more than its one arrow-straight line amid a web of tangled, curving pathways.

The darkness gathers as Miri and Saelis continue, unaware that I've stopped, and my eyes strain as the tunnel seems to close in on itself. It ought to be forbidding, that thick, dark emptiness—but I find I can't look away, can't hurry my steps to catch back up with my companions. I stare so long that my eyes begin to play tricks on me: a tiny light flickers, far down the corridor, bobbing as if beckoning to me.

"Wait," I rasp, my voice barely a whisper as the footsteps of Miri and Saelis begin to fade away. "Wait!"

My second call echoes around the stone walls, and the others come hurrying back. As the light from their chronos washes over the mouth of the tunnel, the light I thought I saw vanishes.

"Are you okay?" Saelis's voice is a little breathless—they hadn't noticed I wasn't behind them anymore.

"What lies down this corridor?" I ask, finally tearing my eyes away from the place.

Miri and Saelis wear twin looks of wary concern, and they exchange a glance before Miri answers me. "That's one of the access tunnels to the engine mainframe."

"Engine," I echo, glancing back into the darkness again. That was a word I didn't know when I woke but have learned in the last few weeks. "That way leads to the device that keeps Alciel in the sky?"

"Well, there are six engines, spread out along the rim of this island, Freysna," says Saelis, "but that's the control room the connects them, and the engines for the other islands. Not that anyone really knows how to control them anymore, but . . . Wait, where are you going?"

My feet have started moving as if by themselves, halting at first, but gathering certainty as I make my way down the access tunnel. "I must see it."

"What the . . ." Miri sounds baffled as she trails off. I hear her steps quicken, and her voice is close when she hisses, "No one's allowed in there except on official maintenance duty. We're not supposed to be down here at all! We're certainly not bringing a crazy girl who claims to be from Below into the place that keeps us from falling out of the sky!"

"I *must* see it," I repeat, aware in the back of my mind that I *do* sound mad, even mist-touched, as I continue down the corridor. "There are answers here—I can feel them."

An argument breaks out behind me as Miri and Saelis debate what to do—I let them fight it out and continue walking. Somehow, it doesn't feel strange to listen to other people arguing about what I ought to do—equally, it doesn't feel strange to ignore them both and do as my instincts tell me.

"Miri, wait—don't—!" Saelis's voice rising is the only warning I get before footsteps race up behind me.

"Jayn, stop! I can't let you—" Miri reaches out for my arm.

I sense her approach more than anything else, and I'm ready as she makes a grab for me. I whirl, my own hand whipping up—and in that moment, I see the flash of the lights from the tramcar that nearly hit me, and I hear the sickening crack of the guard's body as he went flying.

No.

Miri freezes, one foot lifted mid-step, her fingers reaching, halted a breath away from my shoulder. Her eyes are wide with sudden fear, but she doesn't speak—can't speak. She doesn't move, even her hair frozen in mid-bounce while she ran. Curling all around her, like half-invisible flames licking at a log, are flickers of light. Colors like vivid green and dark purple swirl through her invisible bonds.

I know what this is.

The same way I knew the word *povvy*, knew the image of a forest canopy, *knew* the connection between myself and this world's lost prince, I know the name for what I am seeing, what I have tasted down here on the air: *mist.*

Saelis, running after Miri, skids to a stop, staring in confusion between her frozen form and my outstretched hand.

I take a deep breath, surprised to discover that there is no panic there this time at the threat of Miri touching me—only certainty that I could stop her before she did. Tearing my eyes from the deadly beauty of the swirling mist, I see Miri's face. My heart cracks—she's terrified. Quickly, I release my grip on the mist and let it dissipate, and she collapses to the floor of the tunnel, gasping.

"I mean you no harm," I tell her, trying to put my whole heart into my voice, as Saelis hurries up and drops to his knees, his arms going around his partner as she clings to him. "Not you, nor Saelis, nor anyone in your world. But you must not touch me. It is forbidden."

Miri swallows, her very breathing strained. "What did you do to me?" she rasps, the sound tearing at my conscience, for she sounds like someone who's just been throttled.

I take a step back, wrapping my arms around my midsection, and shake my head. "I—I am not sure. I have no wish to hurt you, you must believe me."

Saelis, silent until now, lifts his head—for the first time his eyes are hard and cold. "This is what you did to the tramcar, isn't it? Somehow you can move things with your mind—what if you'd hit her as hard as you hit it? You left a huge dent in the metal, you could've killed her!"

"No, I—I would never. And I'm not moving things, I am merely controlling the mist—it exists even here, in Alciel. There is less of it, and it feels strange, but I recognize it nonetheless." My mouth is running away with me, babbling in the aftermath of what I have just witnessed—what I've just done. Miri and Saelis have little reaction to my explanation, for they do not know what mist is.

But I . . . I *do* know. And I know it ought to be impossible to control it. Channel it, yes. Use it to cast spells, yes. But control it, as if it were an extension of my own body? I could never do that before . . . before . . . But my memory refuses to complete that sentence.

Starting to shiver, I take another step back. "Forgive me," I whisper, still looking from Miri's prone form to that of Saelis, who holds her close, his body between her and me.

"I'm calling the guards," Saelis announces, hurt in his voice and in his eyes as he looks over his shoulder at me. "Like we should've done back there on the street."

I'm not prepared for the wash of despair that hits me at

those words. Even Saelis, now, the one who seemed willing to believe me, to trust me enough to learn what I knew of North, has turned on me. And for good reason.

"Wait." The voice is still raspy, but Miri lifts her hand and places it over Saelis's chrono, preventing him from initiating the call to the guards.

He gives her an incredulous look, but while her eyes are still wide with fear as she regards me, something has shifted there in her gaze. A new spark flickers to life, deep in her eyes.

My heart knows what it is, though my mind refuses to name it for fear I'm wrong.

"You're right, Sae—she could've killed me. She didn't, though." The display of undeniable magic has left her shaken, but certain.

"I saw something," she murmurs, pulling herself up into a sitting position, though her arms are still tight around Saelis. "When that stuff grabbed me, it was like . . . I dunno, like bits of a movie playing in my head. I think I saw a memory—I think I saw the place she says she's from. I saw *him*."

Saelis finally tears his accusatory gaze from my face to stare at Miri, eyes widening. "You mean . . . ?"

Miri's eyes are wet, but she keeps meeting mine, not blinking even when a tear slips free of her lashes and falls onto her cheek. "She was with North."

My heart squeezes. All I want to do is ask her to tell me what she saw, where we were, what was happening. How she could see a memory of mine that I cannot see myself, I don't know—but the mist has granted stranger powers than visions.

Miri fumbles around, and after a moment Saelis seems to come out of his daze enough to help her get to her feet. For a moment they stand there, their arms around each other while they watch me, fearful still, though I'm seeing more and more of that other thing I was afraid to name: *hope*.

Then Miri swallows. "The engine mainframe is just a little bit farther down this corridor. Right at the heart of Alciel."

The door at the end of the corridor is locked, but I can feel the mist permeating the air inside the mechanism, and it's the work of a moment to twist its tendrils around the tumblers and slide them free. From behind me I can hear Miri making a strangled sort of noise, and the whisper of Saelis's lowered voice, but I haven't any attention to spare for them, because the door swings open.

The large, cavernous room is round, with metal walkways around the edge and crisscrossing to the center. A metal column stretches from floor to ceiling, windows at irregular intervals that would reveal what's housed inside the column, if they weren't ancient and covered in dust and mineral deposits. A number of panels stand at different points around the room, with lights that flicker here and there, glass dials, handles, and other things I can't make sense of.

None of this is what seizes my attention, however.

Flickering with power like a thunderstorm on the horizon, the mist curls thickly around the metal column. Like metal shavings attracted to a lodestone, the stuff clings to the metal, stirring wildly.

Unable to tear my eyes away, I take a step into the room,

my mouth falling open. "This place," I hear myself whisper. "It's magical."

Saelis clears his throat from somewhere behind me. "I mean, it's significant, sure. This is how all the engines stay in sync. This is what keeps us in the sky."

Miri adds, "But it's not magic, it's science."

My eyes sting a moment, for I know those words—someone has spoken them to me before, and my heart aches at the lost memory. I swallow that grief and turn to look at the others. "Do you not see the way the mist is drawn here?"

Miri glances at Saelis, who frowns, puzzled. "There's a lot of dehumidifier equipment down here to make sure the tunnels don't take in water from the clouds. There's no fog or mist of any kind."

An impatient noise works its way out of my throat. "Not that kind of mist. This, here, the power that is being pulled in. You may think these engines are made from science, but I *know* magic when I see it—I have lived with it all my life." I step closer, gesturing to the roiling column of mist.

Miri's eyes travel toward where I'm pointing and then back, her gaze wary. She doesn't see what I see. "There's no such thing as magic."

"Except . . ." Saelis casts a sidelong glance at his partner, who looks incredulously back again. "I mean, she did just freeze you mid-step with a wave of her hand."

"Well, yes, but . . ." Miri's eyebrows draw together into a scowl. "But that was something else. Like . . . magnets or something."

"Magnets." Saelis's face is suddenly unreadable, his tone careful. "Uh-huh."

Despite the pull of the mist, I almost can't tear my eyes away from them. I feel a foolish smile tugging at my lips, and when Miri glances my way, I can't help but say, "You are both so like him."

Miri's scowl vanishes as quickly as it came, and her face softens. "Well, we grew up with him."

"He and I would argue this way—he for science, I for magic. He told me that magic is simply science you cannot explain. But I think he was beginning to believe when . . ."

They're both watching me intently, and when I trail to a halt, Miri takes a step forward, her eyes pleading. "You're starting to remember, aren't you?"

The tugging sensation of the mist is growing, from a faint itch at the edge of my consciousness to something far less difficult to ignore. "I think it is this place," I tell her, shifting my gaze back to the mist-shrouded column.

At home, such a concentration of mist would only occur during a storm, and the very sight of it makes my pulse race. But as I take a step closer, and another, the mist shifts in response to my movements, as if welcoming me. My hip connects with the guardrail of the walkway, impeding my progress—without thinking, I grasp the railing and swing one leg over.

I hear a burst of protest from behind me, but I can no longer ignore that pull. I'm reaching, stretching my fingertips out toward the self-contained mist-storm—and then it snaps to me, engulfing my arm.

For a moment I am frozen there, perched atop the guard-rail, held as surely by the mist as I used it to hold Miri. And then the mist sweeps up my arm in a hot, white rush that sears along my body and across my vision, and the world around me is gone.

I know this place.

The sensation of familiarity is almost as frightening as the experience itself—blind and deaf but for a roaring in my ears and a searing white light surrounding me. I can't feel my arms or legs, can't tell if any sound emerges when I try to open my mouth.

But just as a bolt of panic rushes through me—*no, not again, not this*—my vision flashes with something other than white. I see a face: long, well-shaped features, a distinctive, familiar nose, warm brown eyes, lips that curve easily to a smile, hair cropped short on the sides and left to curl over the brow on top. . . .

I try to say his name, but I still can't move, and in an instant, he's gone, replaced by other flashes. Fragments of memory slide past, moving quickly.

Alciel's lost prince standing at my side on a clifftop, wearing my colors, begging me to do . . . something.

High Priest Daoman confronting a woman in indigo robes, a warning caught in my unresponsive throat.

The vibrating warmth of the bindle cat's fur under my fingers, the bump of his spine as he arches his back into my hand.

North's face again, near mine, his eyes sweeping across my features, a look of such wonder and tenderness combined that I cannot breathe.

And then I see memories that I know are not mine, cannot be mine, and yet are mine as surely as my divinity.

A great, writhing ball of red-and-gold light, teeming with life, suspended in the air just beyond my fingertips.

A long line of people climbing a set of stairs—somewhere above, Alciel looms, but the city is not in the sky.

The flashes move more and more quickly, so that I can barely register what I am seeing, but I know these memories—they are a part of the life *I* have lived, not those who went before me.

The lost copy of the Song of the Destroyer, covered in messages from divines before me.

Elkisa, my dearest and only friend, eyes stricken and heartsick.

A boy with lifeless eyes lying on a riverbank with a stream of blood across his throat.

A white-hot flash of rage and anguish so deep it will tear me apart . . .

My body hits metal with a clang that reverberates through my skull. Gasping, blinking away the light and shaking with reaction, I press a hand against the walkway beneath me and lift myself up. Miri is already there at my side, and Saelis is leaping the railing I had been perched on—the mist must have pulled me over it.

"Jayn!" Miri's calling; dizzily, as if swimming out of a dream, I realize she's been calling it again and again.

I try to speak, but my voice emerges only as a ragged whisper. Glancing up, I see the mist—calm now, stirring gently, gathered around that central column at the heart of Alciel.

Beneath me the floor is trembling again, quaking more violently this time, almost as in sympathy to the shivering of my own body.

Miri's hands hover nearby, but she resists her obvious desire to take my arm and help me as I struggle to sit up. "Are you okay? Skyfall, you flew off the railing like something had grabbed you—don't try to get up yet, the ground's still shaking!" A thought seems to strike her then, and she glances at Saelis, her eyes wide and serious. "Did she . . . ?"

Saelis just shakes his head, his own expression rather unsettled. "Coincidence," he mutters, though the uncertainty in his eyes says otherwise.

It's one thing to realize I can stop someone in their tracks with the mist—another thing entirely for them to think my power is causing Alciel's tremors.

I ignore Miri's warning about moving too soon and push myself the rest of the way into a seated position. "We have to get to the queen," I gasp, blinking away tears—my eyes were watering in the blinding light. "We must warn her."

The quake subsiding, Saelis drops to a crouch by Miri's side, his expression grave as he studies me. "We might be able to get you in, but . . . warn her about what?"

"Nimhara." The name feels so strange on my own lips—but then, I rarely say it myself. "The woman at the queen's side—she is not who she says she is. All of Alciel is in great danger."

Saelis's face darkens, but there's little of the shock I would've expected to see there. "Miri and I have been trying to figure out what she's up to ever since the queen introduced her to her inner circle two weeks ago. But I don't know how we can get in to see the queen without *her* being there."

"I do." Miri glances between us. "I know who we can call to get us into the palace. Especially if we can tell him that North's alive."

Saelis's eyebrows lift, and he nods. "But what do we say?" He turns those raised eyebrows on me. "That Nimhara isn't . . . what? Not an emissary?"

"She's not *Nimhara*," I correct him through gritted teeth, reaching out to grasp the guardrail and summon the strength to get to my feet.

"Did you remember something when you fell?"

"I remember everything. Everything up to . . ." I hesitate, the flashes of memory still jumbled in my mind, unsure of anything that happened after standing on that clifftop with North. None of them tell me how I ended up here.

"Jayn?" Miri prompts, concern in her voice.

"No. Not Jayn." That much I know—that much I can put right. "Nimh. Nimhara is *my* name. The woman with the queen is an impostor."

SIX

NORTH

I just walk on in through the front doors of the temple—let Techeki wonder where I've been or try and take me to task if he wants. If Matias is right about the Master of Spectacle trying to keep me distracted, perhaps it's time I pushed a little at the boundaries he's set up for me, if only to see what he does.

There are still a few acolytes around in the silent corridors in these hours before dawn, but nobody stops me, and nobody questions me.

I'm the Last Star, after all.

Once I reach the lower levels of the temple, I take a little more care—Mathias doesn't want Techeki to have the thing I'm here for, so it would be best if nobody saw me looking for it.

I find a heavy door at the end of a disused hallway, just where Mathias said I would. It's the second entrance to a secret place I've seen today, and I can't help but wonder how many other secrets the temple holds, even from its inhabitants.

I don't try the standard lock, to which Matias says the key was lost generations ago. Nobody's bothered replacing it—we're too far below the everyday levels of the temple already, and nobody needs this space.

My fingers search up high instead, on top of the doorframe, for the hidden catch he promised me. It clicks, and I ease the door open silently—someone's kept it in good condition. The cat goes ahead of me, slipping through the crack, compressing himself to half his size—easy to do when you're mostly fluff, I guess. I follow him, unshuttering my lantern once I'm inside.

We find the staircase Matias said would be here, and down we go. Down and down, switching to the next set of stairs, and the next. At first, they're in decent shape and we make good time. The cat flows down them like water, and I hold my lantern aloft, shadows dancing ahead of us.

It's good thinking time, and of course I have Matias's voice in my head, as he must have known I would. I can't forget his call to take up Nimh's mantle and become some sort of leader, to use the way these people see the Last Star to unite them, or at least hold them together.

But that's not who I am, and this isn't my world. I'm not one of their gods. I'm a guy who misses the people he loves—and every single one of them is in Alciel. If I can find a way home, I can solve everyone's problems—deal with whatever havoc Inshara's wreaking up there, see my family again, my friends . . . Nimh.

We reach the oldest passages and doors that only open with showers of dust, and still we descend. I try not to think about how far below ground level we are, all that earth above us pressing down. It seems impossible that it won't just collapse, even though I know, intellectually, that it's held up for at least a thousand years.

There's a tightness in my chest that calls out for the open sky. That quietly, miserably says *I want to go home* more insistently than ever.

I wonder if Nimh's feeling the opposite, somewhere far above me. If she finds all the space beneath Alciel unsettling and yearns to be exactly where I am now.

I press my fingertips to the cool stone wall beside me, grounding myself. *Stay focused, North.*

The stairs grow squarer eventually, which is interesting. They remind me of home, of machine-made blocks and corners. Perhaps whoever built this lower part of the temple also created Alciel, and the ruined city out in the ghostlands, with the shopping arcade buried beneath a grassy hill. My people came from here once, and I know we left traces behind.

There's a kind of symmetry to it. At home, when you descend below the city and into the engines, you find the mist—the part of our world that's closest to this one. Here, when you descend, you come as close as you can to Alciel.

The air turns stale, and my lungs start to tighten, though I think it's nerves, not air quality. I feel like a kid who's listened to one too many ghost stories, but the deeper I go into this abandoned place, the more . . . watched I feel.

I set down the lantern on one of the steps and switch on my chrono instead so I can keep both my hands free. *Hey,* I tell myself. *If you're alone, then there's nobody to see you jump at shadows except the cat, and he's already judging you.*

The cat's tail waves dismissively as he leads the way down, though he keeps within my beam of light.

And then, when I'm so used to going down that it's become an automatic movement, my foot suddenly lands heavily on stone where a step should be. The ground has finally leveled off, as Matias said it would. I stop in place, and the cat looks back over his shoulder at me with a soft sound of query.

I linger so long at the bottom of the stairs that he mews at me, impatient.

"I know, Fuzz," I tell him in a whisper. "Give me a sec. Having kind of a moment here, what with being in a dark, probably haunted place way underneath the temple. I mean, if we were in a vidshow, this is *exactly* where I'd be screaming at us not to go."

But it's more than that. I'm strangely nervous, for a guy who's only meant to be picking up and delivering something. My breath is shallower, harder to catch, and I try to focus on filling my lungs, expanding them.

I walk forward carefully, stepping through an archway into a huge chamber. I can't see much, but I can tell how big it must be from the way my scuffing footsteps echo back at me. I angle my chrono upward, and when I catch sight of the ceiling, my jaw drops.

The dome above me is a gloriously jeweled rainbow, jagged crystals in every color imaginable clinging to it, sparkling back at me as the uneven surface catches the light. It responds to even the tiniest of movements, like a many-hued galaxy of twinkling stars. I've never seen anything like it, never *dreamed* anything like it.

Slowly I let the beam of light play downward, and I find the place where the domed roof ends and the walls begin. They're covered in painted murals, a procession of figures all in a row, all facing in the same direction, like they're walking somewhere together. What was this place, once upon a time? And why was it sealed up and abandoned?

The thing I'm looking for should be in the middle of the room, according to Matias, so I carefully work the light across, and . . . oh.

You'll know it when you see it.

That wily, relentless, shameless old . . .

How did I not see this coming?

Nimh's spearstaff lies before me, resting on a rectangular block of stone, the tip gleaming in the light.

I'm moving before I know what I'm doing, running toward it, reaching for it—but my hand stops short of curving around the worn wood of the handle.

The cat is right beside me, leaping up onto the plinth. He studies the udjet charms at the end of the staff for a moment: the tiny golden version of himself, the stone wrapped in polished wire, the miniature ship in its glass bottle. Then he turns his gaze on me, and the noise he makes is so plaintive it nearly cracks my bruised heart in two.

"She's not here," I whisper. "I'm sorry. I'd do anything to change that, if I could."

I reach out once again, willing myself to pick up her spearstaff, just as I did her tools in the garden. But this isn't for digging out weeds, and my fingers curl involuntarily to make a fist—the air around the staff feels charged, as if it might shock me if I try to take what's not mine.

"It's just a stick," I murmur, the dark around us swallowing up my voice.

And the Fisher King's rock was just a rock.

The light on the spearstaff moves as I shift restlessly, making its shadow writhe as if it were a living thing, and making the crystal beyond it glint and glimmer.

I never saw her without it, and it's as if Nimh's standing silently beside me now, Matias behind us, whispering in my ear.

The mist runs wild, our crops are failing, our city is dying, and some-one must unite us. You are the Last Star. . . . No one can force you to carry a stone you didn't choose. But I do not think anyone else can carry it.

Then the Nimh in my mind isn't beside me at all—she's five years old, picking up this staff for the first time. She's taking on a weight she never asked to carry, but one she's fought ever since to carry well.

She was only five. At least I'm grown.

And I'm the one standing in front of the spearstaff now.

"She's not here," I murmur to the cat again. "But I am."

I let out a slow breath and run my gaze along the spearstaff one more time. The wood is worn smooth where her hand rested most often, the grain dulled.

And slowly, so slowly that I'm not even sure of the moment

when contact is made, I rest my fingertips on it.

The cat purrs, startling me so completely that I jump back, snatching my hand up before I catch myself.

And like that, the spell is broken. I almost laugh at myself for a moment, but the cat's stare instructs me to take this moment seriously.

"I do," I murmur to him. "I promise."

Then I reach for the spearstaff again and curl my fingers around it properly.

It's surprisingly easy to lift. It's perfectly balanced and sits comfortably in my hand.

It doesn't feel wrong.

I heft it again, and something settles inside me. I won't stop searching for a way home. But it's time to be a part of this world, as well. To be able to look Nimh in the eye if I ever see her again and tell her I did what I could.

"I get it," I tell the cat, who butts his head against me in reply. "You've made your point, you and Matias. I'm holding the staff. Time to climb the stairs and figure out what's next."

And then a voice sounds in the darkness behind me.

"Don't go yet, Prince North."

I swing around, spearstaff in hand, the light of my chrono slicing wildly across the chamber—it flies past crystals like jewels, past the silent figures in the murals, to illuminate a single figure.

A woman, not painted but real, standing on the far side of the huge room.

Her hair is still pulled back in two black braids. Cheekbones sharp. Bare arms showing muscle. The light brown skin I remember is washed out by the glow of my chrono, her freckles hidden completely. She's dressed in a plain brown tunic and trousers now, no more black and gold. No more temple guard's uniform.

Elkisa.

I swing the spearstaff up in one movement, all my anger surging up to take control. She's no more than ten paces away, and I take them at a run, lunging for her without a single thought in my head except the one word I hurl at her: "Traitor!"

She ducks in one fluid movement, knocking aside my arm and sending the staff flying to the ground, and then there's a blinding pain in my knee as she kicks at the side of it, sending me sprawling.

I roll and scramble to my hands and knees, grabbing at the staff as I look up, ready to throw myself to the side to avoid her next blow.

But she lifts her hands, palms out, and stands still. The movement shifts her belt and brings her knife into view, but she doesn't reach for it.

"I am here to talk," she says quietly. "Hear me out, before you take up her weapon again."

The cat growls low in his throat. "You're a traitor," I manage, no louder than a whisper. "You were her best friend. Her only friend. I swear, I will . . ."

Last time I saw Elkisa, she was leaving Inshara's side to betray Nimh.

The next time I saw Nimh after that, she was a wild goddess

riding a mist-storm into the city, destroying everything in her path, everything between her and me. Or between me and my killer, as she believed then. Her pain turned her into the Destroyer, and I thought Elkisa was dead, perhaps the first casualty of that terrifying onslaught.

Her voice is quiet when she speaks. "I didn't come here for revenge—yours or mine. I came here because I need your help, and because we each have something the other wants. We should talk."

"I have nothing to say to you," I say through gritted teeth, tightening my fist around the spearstaff.

"Then I will say something to you," she replies as she offers me her hand to help me rise to my feet. "You are seeking a way back into the sky, are you not? I have found one. And I'm going to show you where it is."

THE COUNCILOR

The councilor stares at the queen, his mouth hanging open for a moment. He's never heard her speak that way to *anyone*, much less a member of her government. But Anasta, standing beside him, simply squares her jaw.

"Tell the queen what you told me, after the coronation," she urges him, her eyes never leaving her wife's face.

The councilor swallows, glancing between the two women. The three of them stand together, as they have many times before, in quiet conversation.

"We must start the trains again," he says, struggling to keep his voice even. "Even if they aren't open to the general population, we must be able to send supplies between the islands. If nothing else we will begin to run out of food here on Freysna in another week."

The queen, still looking at her wife with hard eyes after snapping at her, merely shakes her head. "Nimhara says we must not—to allow passage between the islands might allow someone she's looking for to escape Freysna. I trust her."

"More than you trust your own councilors?" he blurts in reply, starting forward and halting only when the queen turns that hard stare on him. "Your Majesty—please, *please* listen to me. Some of us have been talking, and we . . ."

Anasta, at his side, makes a quelling gesture, hand slicing through the air.

But too late. The queen's eyes narrow. "Talking?" she echoes slowly. "About Nimhara, I presume?"

The councilor clenches his hands into fists at his side. "You've changed since she arrived, Your Majesty. Something is wrong—you must see it. You must come to your senses and—"

A quick, hot line of pain; a numbing blow knocks the councilor's face aside. The councilor claps a hand to his cheek as he focuses, finding the queen before him, hand still raised.

"Beatrin!" Anasta gasps, putting herself between the councilor and her wife. "What are you doing? For the love of your people—what is *happening* to you?"

The queen has begun to cry, but there's little in her face to tell of any grief or sadness. If anything, she seems more resolute than ever, more remote. "You will not bring this sort of nonsense before me again," she tells her wife, her eyes cold and furious. "In fact—you will not come before me again at all."

Anasta stands there for a long moment, as the councilor holds his breath, one hand still cradling his stinging cheek.

Then the queen's wife turns, her face unreadable, and walks out of the throne room.

SEVEN

NIMH

"You should try to get some sleep." Saelis's voice is quiet, just audible over the sound of Miri's soft breathing from a pile of blankets on the other side of him. "Our ticket into the palace won't get here until morning, and you've had a rough day."

I huff a soft laugh at the understatement, brushing away the crumbs from the bar of pressed grains and honey he gave me after my stomach began rumbling loudly enough to make Miri stir. "So have you. Miri's not having any trouble—perhaps if you just lie down?"

Saelis smiles at me, but shakes his head. "I'm a night owl," he says, despite the signs of weariness on his face that tell me otherwise.

My heart gives a painful squeeze as I realize: he's keeping an eye on me. They'll sleep in shifts so that one of them is always wakeful and watching. They don't trust me.

I cannot blame them for that—I do not think I would trust me either.

The hangar where North kept his glider is smaller than I expected and littered with pieces of machines and boxes.

Though the glider itself is long gone, the clutter has kept to the edges of the room, leaving an empty place at its heart. As if the glider—and North—might reappear and need that space back.

The overhead lights are off, though a small glowing orb at the end of a dangling wire illuminates the space, for which I am grateful—that space in the middle of the hangar would feel all the more empty in the dark.

Saelis is right—I ought to sleep. I can't go back to the electrician's house, not if I'm being followed by the queen's guards, so there's no telling when I'll next have the chance to rest. But my mind is too wakeful to sleep, buzzing with the torrent of confused memories brought on by that mist-touched machinery at the heart of Alciel. Sorting through them has brought a little clarity.

I can pick out memories up to a fragmented vision of a boat on fire—the boat North and I used to flee the city the night Inshara murdered High Priest Daoman. I remember Jezara, my disgraced and exiled predecessor, finding me by the body of a cultist boy, a boy who killed himself while I stood by helpless. I remember Elkisa. I remember her speaking to me, though I can't understand the words she says in my memory.

And then I remember red.

I shift my weight, causing the boxes at my back to creak a little. My whole body shies away from the memory, muscles seizing with some nameless pain: fear, anger . . . shame? Guilt? I pull my thoughts away as ruthlessly as I can.

"What is all this?" I ask to distract myself, bringing Saelis out of his own reverie. I gesture to the piles of boxes, the papers tacked up on the wall, the lists of names and words written in chalk on the floor nearby.

Saelis hesitates, glancing over at Miri's recumbent form. I wait, though, and after a moment he sighs. "Don't tell anyone. But we're trying to figure out why North fell."

I sit up a little straighter. North never said anything about what caused his crash, except to insist that it wasn't fate or prophecy. I wondered how he could *know* it wasn't destiny, but if he had had suspicions that it wasn't an accident, it would explain his certainty.

Of course, North was certain about a lot of things that he'd probably admit now were wrong. I take a long, slow breath against the ache in my heart. *Gods, I miss him.*

It was almost better when I didn't remember how much.

"No one knew where the glider was kept except us," Saelis is saying, still keeping his voice soft to avoid waking Miri at his side. "Another pilot might have been able to triangulate the hangar's location by seeing the *Skysinger* coming back in to land, if they were in the air at the same time, but no one but us knew that North was the *Skysinger*'s pilot. We can't figure out any motive to sabotage the *Skysinger* unless they knew who the pilot was."

A tiny trickle of suspicion works its way into my thoughts, and I can't stop myself from glancing past him at Miri. If only two people had access to the hangar and knew who was flying the glider, then the number of people who could have committed the sabotaged dwindles down . . . to two.

But somehow, I cannot bear to think of Miri or Saelis doing

such a thing. North trusted his friends—*loved* his friends. Loved them as more than friends. To not trust them myself feels like a betrayal of my own faith in him.

"Who would want to hurt North?" I ask. "Setting aside the question of how they would know to hurt him through his glider, what reason would someone in Alciel have to want him dead?"

Saelis shakes his head, gazing at me helplessly. "That's just it—we can't think of any reason. North is the best—some people think of him as a bit of a party boy, or that he should maybe take his responsibilities more seriously, but the truth is, he's kind to everyone, thoughtful, funny. He doesn't have any enemies, and I can't imagine him making one."

I watch Saelis for a moment, absorbing the hurt in his features, feeling that increasingly familiar ache in my chest as it hits me all over again just how much his friends care for him. I have to swallow and give myself a mental kick before I point out gently, "But North isn't just North. He is also the prince, the heir to Alciel's throne. He may not have enemies—but surely the throne might."

Saelis blinks at me, and then gazes down at the floor, thoughtful and quiet.

What must it have been like to grow up in a world where enemies were so few? One more in a long list of reasons North must have found my world so utterly terrifying. At least, when I found my guards murdered by cultists, I knew what was happening.

"Politics has never really been my thing," Saelis says finally, glancing over at Miri's sleeping form, eyebrows drawn together.

"But while there are definitely debates about things like representation for the smaller islands, allocation of resources, that sort of thing, I don't think any of it is worth murdering a prince. What point would that even make? Better to, you know, kidnap him or something, if they wanted leverage to use against the queen."

"That is true." Politics may not be Saelis's thing, but he's certainly not foolish. Then I sit up straighter, seized by a new thought. "Unless it was not about leverage. In my world, the divinity is an unbroken line from the Exodus—what your people call the Ascension—to now. To me. This is true of your royal family as well, is it not?"

Saelis nods, gravity shifting a little to something a bit more wary. He and Miri didn't ask me too many questions about my assertion that *I* was Nimhara, that it was I, and not the woman at the queen's side, who claimed divinity. But then, North thought divinity was little more than a lie, so his friends probably think it's akin to a ceremonial title.

"Yes," he replies. "The royal family dates back to the Ascension. Why?"

"Where I come from, many people have very little. It makes them angry and afraid, and when they feel that way for long enough, they begin to hate the ones who keep promising to help them." My throat tightens a little, but I manage to keep speaking. "Alciel is a land of plenty, and no one goes hungry—but if there are those who are scared or angry for other reasons, they might blame the royal family. They may wish to change things even if they do not quite know *how* they wish things to change. If you wished to end the royal family's hold on Alciel, how would you do it?"

Saelis's mouth falls open a fraction, gaze tinged with a hint of horror, but he answers me readily: "By *ending* the royal line once and for all."

We stare at each other for a long moment, and then Saelis doubles over to put the heels of his palms to his eyes, weariness in his movements.

I wish I could reach out and lay a hand on his shoulder—anything to remind him that he isn't alone. Instead, I whisper, "I will help you. I only wish for North to be safe when he comes home."

Saelis smiles at me a little, and I shift our conversation, wishing to ease the tension in his body. I tell him stories of his North in my world, stories to make him smile again: North meeting the bindle cat; North tasting meat for the first time; North dodging all the people who tried to invite the handsome stranger to dance at the Feast of the Dying.

I stop there, for the next story on my lips was not one of *his* North, but one of *my* North, and the strangeness of feeling his fingertips so near my skin as he helped me dress, or the addictive warmth of his palm near my cheek on the riverstrider's barge. A part of me longs to speak of these things to someone who might know how compelling such experiences would be, someone who would desire them as much as I do. But the rest of me remembers that these two loved North first, and he them, and I . . .

I am just his destiny. Not his heart.

Saelis doesn't seem to notice the abrupt halt in my voice. His eyes are closed, and his lips curved in a little smile, and as he heaves a little sigh, I realize that the lateness of the hour and the events of the day are overtaking him. Despite his intention of keeping watch, he's falling asleep. I glance between him and Miri, who's still slumbering soundly beside him, and hold my tongue.

My own words come back to me, echoing as if trapped by the vastness of the empty hangar. *I only wish for North to be safe . . . when he comes home.*

In my world, I never thought much about North going home, for the idea seemed impossible. It was one thing to fall from above to below, but to rise from the ground, fly into the air, and reach the other side of the sky? No one had passed between our worlds, from our land to that of the gods, for a thousand years, or so I had believed. But then I learned that Jezara, the goddess who abandoned her divinity to take a lover, whose banishment led to my own calling, had done it all for a cloudlander who had arrived a generation before North fell. Perhaps people had been passing between the worlds in secret for a thousand years.

I know that I may never see North again. But my heart tells me I will—my faith tells me I will. The prophecy did not bring us together only to rip us apart so abruptly—there is more to our story, I believe it. But if I do see North again, it will be because one of us has found a way to travel between our worlds. And that means that North will be able to come home—to his world, his family.

To Miri and Saelis.

Throat tightening, eyes burning, I huddle more tightly against the boxes at my back and wrap the tattered dropcloth around me. But the chill that makes me shiver isn't coming from the hangar, and wrapping myself up only traps the cold inside my heart.

I wish North to be safe. And more than that, I wish him to be happy. Having met his friends, his loves, I can see why he cared so much for them. I can see why they made him happy.

After all, what future could he have with me, when he cannot so much as touch my cheek, much less kiss me or hold me close?

I am my people's goddess—there is no room, in a life like mine, for wanting.

"Nimh—wake up. He's here."

Miri's voice slips into my dream, one of endless, twisting corridors in the temple, of being lost and helpless in the place that is meant to be my home. In my dream I am certain I know who she means, and I turn, drawn by a soft glow behind me, like starlight, chasing away the darkness.

But when I open my eyes, there's only the daylight streaming into the hangar from the windows at the far end, and Miri's face not far from mine. I prop myself up on an elbow, my body protesting the night on the hard hangar floor, and rub at my eyes. They are sore and crusted with salt at the corners—I was crying last night.

Miri's eyes are on the far end of the hangar, where Saelis

stands talking to a man whose back is to us, so I have time to wipe the evidence of my weeping from my face.

"Who is here?" I ask, the confusion of sleep still fogging my mind.

"The guy who's going to get us in to see Beatrin." Miri gets to her feet and offers me a hand, absently; then, when I do not take it, she jerks it back. "Sorry, I forgot."

I smile at her. "I still appreciate the gesture."

She offers a tentative smile in return. She is not so quick to trust as Saelis, but it seems she'll follow where he leads. Miri *wants* to trust me, just as she wanted to believe North lived, before the mist granted her a vision confirming it. "Come on. I told him as little as possible. In theory, chrono comms can be hacked."

I blink at her. "I do not—"

She thunks herself on the side of the temple, a playful gesture. "I keep forgetting you don't know what any of this stuff means. I didn't tell him much because if the woman who showed up at the queen's side two weeks ago can't be trusted, it means someone could've overheard my call."

I get wearily to my feet, glancing at the chrono on her wrist and back up to her face. "Magic seems much more reliable."

To my surprise, Miri lets out a laugh; the quaking of her body makes her curls dance. "No wonder North hung around with you down there."

Before I can ask her to elaborate, she leads the way across the hangar. The man speaking with Saelis wears simple enough clothes, by Alciel standards, though I can see that the cloth and the fit of his jacket are of high quality. He wears his brown hair short, and his skin is lighter than that of most people I have met here. Saelis glances over his shoulder at us, and, following his gaze, the man turns.

I stop where I am, a few paces away, staring, my heart caught in my throat.

North?

An instant later, I am reminded of all the differences—his light skin to North's darker, the hair brown where North's is black, the nose and chin unobtrusive where North's are his strongest features. But the eyes . . . the *eyes* are North's, gazing back at me with a hint of surprise in his own features.

"Are you all right, miss?" he asks, in North's very tones.

Then I understand. This man is like an answer to a puzzle that I had been trying to solve with only half the pieces. I've seen so many images of North's mother, the queen, who has his nose and hair, but skin so much darker than his, and shorter stature, and a voice that struck no recognition in me. I kept trying to see Alciel's lost prince in her, to understand my certainty that I knew him, even before I regained part of my memory, but I could not form his image from her alone. But combine her with this man, and you get . . . *North.*

"You are North's father!" I gasp, still staring at him, unable to take my eyes away. "He spoke of you—he said you were his . . . his . . . bi-logic father?" I feel my face warming, remembering the rest of that particular conversation.

The shock and surprise deepens in the man's features, and he glances between Miri and Saelis. "This is who you brought me to meet." The words are not a question. "Skyfall, she speaks just like . . . just like . . ."

Miri nods, her expression grave—she had flashed a rather delighted smile when I first identified the man as North's father. Now she's solemn. "Yes. This is the *real* Nimhara. She got here at the same time as the false one who's with the queen. You can see why we called you first instead of going straight to the palace. Nimh, this is Talamar. North's biological father."

Talamar, trying to recover from his shock, is still staring at me. "Then *you* are the true divine?"

He speaks the words with more respect than North did at first, and more weight than Miri or Saelis. This man is a politician—I recognize the care in his tone and the deliberation in his choice of words, even as a sliver of relief trickles through me like cool water. I had not expected him to believe me so quickly.

Misinterpreting my silence, he smiles a little, takes a step back, and then—to my utter surprise—he bows his head and puts his palms to his eyes in the ancient gesture of respect and loyalty to the divine. When he straightens, and sees my face, he says quickly, "She may be a false divinity, but she has taught us a lot about the customs of your people in the brief time she's been at the queen's side. Tell me, Divine One—how did you know I was North's father?"

"You look just like him," I murmur, dazed by the man's North-like gaze and the strange experience of being bowed to in that familiar way. "Around the eyes, you do. I would know him anywhere, even in his father."

Talamar's brow furrows. "Know him . . . how? How can you have known him?" There's pain now, in those familiar eyes, and with a jolt I realize he changed the word to past tense. *Known.*

I glance at Miri, who just raises her eyebrows at me. She really didn't tell him anything over the chrono. Taking a deep breath, I turn back to North's father. "The prince survived his fall. He lives. I knew him well in the time before I came here."

Talamar's face drains of its color. His eyes go to Miri's face, then Saelis's. When they do not contradict me, Talamar looks at me again, face taut with intensity. "North—lives? He survived?" He swallows, throat bobbing visibly as he lifts a trembling hand to clutch at his collar. "My son is alive?"

I nod at him, but before I can say more, he coughs and gasps as if the news caused his very lungs to seize—he reaches automatically into the pocket of his coat and draws out a small device, which he puts to his lips. The thing makes a hissing noise, and he breathes in sharply through it, waiting a few moments to lower it, breathing still labored, but better.

"North," he murmurs, closing his eyes. When he opens them, his look is so gentle and warm that I have to resist the urge to weep again, for he looks so like his son that my heart threatens to crack. "Thank you, Nimh. You can't know what this means to me. To all of us."

Miri clears her throat, though the briskness of the sound can't hide how her face is glowing with pleasure at sharing the news of North's survival. Saelis, on her other side, is grinning so widely I fear his face will cramp.

Talamar flinches and lets out a shaking breath. "You're right. There's no time to waste. I believe you, Divine One. Nimhara—the false Nimhara—just appeared at the queen's side one morning. She showed up in the night, I guess. By the time the rest of us even knew of her existence, the queen already trusted her, and trusted her deeply. Far too deeply, if you ask me. But the rest of us . . ." He shakes his head, gaze troubled. "I didn't want to make clouds in a clear sky, because the last thing I wanted was to create ill will between Alciel and the world Below, when we'd been ignoring you all for generations, certain no one lived down there anymore. But I didn't trust her, not least because the quakes we've been having started happening right after she got here."

"We have to warn the queen," Miri says, lifting her chin. I could almost imagine her in one of the riverstriders' boxing matches, fists balled up, eyes blazing. "Nimh says this woman is dangerous, and who knows what she's been telling Beatrin."

Talamar is nodding. "You're absolutely right. And you were right to call me here." His eyes scan the hangar, momentarily distant. I know he must be thinking about his son—to know that he had spent so much time here in secret, this place he never knew about until Miri summoned him. "It's nearly impossible to get the queen alone, but Nimhara—drat, what am I to call her, the false one?—does spend an hour or so by herself in the late morning, doing the sun knows what in her room."

"Her name," I whisper, "is Inshara."

Talamar glances at me and then reaches for his breathing device again. The hiss it makes reminds me of a river-snake defending its nest, and I shiver. He notices, lowering the device. "An old illness," he says gently. "My lungs are fragile and often need medication or else they try to close up on me."

I shake my head, aware that I should not stare at the man for his infirmity. "I am not afraid of you—she is the one I fear. It is the first time I have spoken her name since remembering she was my enemy."

Saelis turns his head, his eyes sympathetic when they fall on my face, but Talamar is already speaking again.

"I should be able to get the queen out into the audience chamber by herself for a few minutes. Can you be at the palace at exactly eleven hundred hours? That will give me enough time to make sure the guards on duty will let you in. Enough time to think of a reason to bring Beatrin out alone."

Miri nods. "We'll be there." She steps up beside Talamar to walk him out, the two of them discussing what entrance to use, which guards to alert.

Saelis is still watching me, though, and after a moment he steps closer. "*We* will be there," he says gently. "All of us. Whatever happened down there between you, you won't have to face her alone."

I answer him with a smile and a shake of my head. I cannot explain the dread in my heart, the nameless quality to the fear at the idea of being face-to-face with Inshara again. It is the same fear, or shame, or regret that I feel when I try to remember past that moment on the riverbank when I saw the cultist boy die, when Jezara found me, when Elkisa found us both. It isn't fear of death, or pain, or even of what may happen to my new friends, or me, or North.

Saelis ducks his head to catch my eye in a way that stops the dread spiraling around in my heart, for it reminds me so of North, and I wonder who learned it from whom. "For what it's worth," he says with a smile, "when it comes to a showdown between you and her? My money's on you."

I smile at him, because his faith helps, and I can push that dread to the back of my consciousness, back where it has lived since I first woke in this place and could remember nothing. But I can only keep the smile in place until he turns away to meet Miri returning from seeing Talamar off.

I know what the fear is, now.

I am afraid to remember.

EIGHT

NORTH

I'm trying not to ask myself if I've lost my mind, because the answer is definitely *yes*.

There *has* to be another way, anything that means I don't have to ally myself with this woman who looked Nimh in the eye for years, heard her secrets, saw her rare, precious smiles, and then stabbed her in the back.

But if there is, I can't find it, so I've gathered up everything on Elkisa's list, and I'm preparing to leave the temple once again, this time in broad daylight. Getting across the city is going to take a series of disguises, but this one might be the riskiest—because if I'm recognized, then Techeki will probably chain me to a shelf in the library or something.

I'm bundled up in acolyte's robes I've just lifted from the laundry, with the hood up like everyone else's. The real issue is the spearstaff, which I'm sure as sky not leaving behind, but which isn't the most unobtrusive thing to smuggle out. I've wrapped the spear and udjet charms in rough brown cloth, and I'm holding it along with an armful of brooms I found in a supply room.

I have to take the risk. Nimh's people need her back. If I can give her to them . . .

My thoughts want to linger on the fact that if I can get her back down here, that means I can get myself back home. What my mind refuses to do is acknowledge that this means we'd still be apart. So I pack that away for later and decide to limit myself to dealing with sixteen or seventeen problems, worries, or panics at a time. I'm not a god, after all. They only think I'm one.

I muffle a pretend yawn as I walk out the front door of the temple, ducking my head and using one hand to hide my face, and the guards at the top of the great stone steps leading down to the city clearly think that I've drawn the short straw among the acolytes—that I've been sent out on some early moring task. They don't pay me much attention or volunteer to join me on cleaning duty. All the way down the steps I'm waiting for someone to call out after me, ask where exactly I'm going to sweep, and it's only when I reach the dusty street that I let a slow breath out.

I follow Elkisa's instructions, turning right and ducking into an alleyway, making my way to a small, abandoned house a few blocks away. The door's hanging off its hinges, rubble spilling out through it from the inside. I step over it carefully to find one of the internal walls has collapsed. Elkisa is sitting on the only unbroken chair, waiting for me.

Neither of us speaks as I pull the robes off over my head, revealing the simple tunic and trousers I'm wearing underneath. She doesn't break the silence until I'm bundling the acolyte's robe into my bag.

"You're too clean," she says, looking me over.

She's not wrong—nobody in the ruined city is doing laundry the way they are inside the temple. I drop to one knee and scoop up a handful of dirt from the rubble, starting to work it into the fabric.

"I was beginning to think you weren't going to come for it, last night," she says, nodding at the spearstaff. "I wondered if I'd overestimated the Fisher King."

I know what she's doing—I've been trained to do it myself, and no doubt all of Nimh's guards were. Small talk, de-escalation. People are much less likely to attack you in the middle of a harmless conversation.

"How did you know I was going to come for it at all?" I ask, keeping my tone even.

She lifts one shoulder in an idle shrug. "I know lots of things."

Someone must have told her, if she was down there ahead of me. But who? Who in Matias's camp even knew what he planned to say to me? There's been a messenger waiting in that alleyway every night for more than a week, since he first started sending Hiret to me. How did any of them know that last night was the night I'd say yes?

If you don't know what's happening, my bloodmother often says, *then your best move is to shut up until someone tells you, rather than revealing your ignorance.*

So I don't reply. Instead I unwrap the cloth I was using to hide the head of the spearstaff. I rewrap it with several layers this time, and tie it all up with a knot at the top, so when I rest it on my shoulder it just looks like a stick with my belongings tied into a bundle at the end.

I test the point of the spearstaff through the layers—I could still use it to stab at someone, though the idea of bloodying it makes my skin crawl. I glance up to see Elkisa watching me and smooth over my expression.

"Are you armed?" I ask, looking her over.

In response she nods toward the broken table, and I see her knife resting on it. She stands up and pulls her clothes taut against her body to show she has nothing concealed, turning in a slow circle. We both know she could probably take me—again—without a weapon, but I see no need to make it easy. And if it brings her even a hint of discomfort, I'll take that too.

I buckle the knife onto my belt and heft the spearstaff and its wrappings onto my shoulder.

"It's a bindle," she says, nodding toward it. "That's fitting."

"A what?"

"The way it's all wrapped up, to carry things," she says, pointing at the staff. "That's called a bindle. It's how the cat got his name."

"Nimh told me you never name a cat," I reply, frowning.

"Well, it's what she calls it," she replies, waving away the objection. "The bindle cat. Because he was found in a bindle, in the river."

"What was he doing in . . . ?" My voice trails off. *Oh.* Someone threw him in there. No wonder he has trust issues.

I didn't know Nimh called him that—I've never heard her say it. Time for my own moment of discomfort, as I'm reminded for the thousandth time how little we know of each other. Compared with how well I know Miri and Saelis, Nimh and I are practically strangers. And yet, she's the one I think about when I wake in the morning, when I sleep at night, when I try to get through each day here without her. I miss the two of them—but I *need* her.

As if our talk has summoned him, the cat comes stalking in through the door, tail high and swishing back and forth in displeasure.

"You can't walk with us," I tell him. "Not unless you're willing to reopen the discussion about dyeing you a different color. You're too famous. Can you keep to the shadows?"

He just stares at me like I'm beyond help, which in my experience means *yes*.

"It is time we moved," Elkisa says, rising slowly to her feet.

"You can get us past everyone out there?" I ask again, my gut clenching at the idea of just strolling onto the streets of the broken city.

"I know where the Deathless will patrol," she replies. "I know how the guards were trained. The daylight hours are when the highest number of people are moving. This is our best chance of passing unnoticed. But we must begin."

We head out together, making our way down the main street that leads away from the temple. When I glance back over my shoulder, the temple towers above the city, the tallest structure in the valley—it rises even above the hills to either side. Its spires reach straight for the cloudlands above, for Alciel, its wide base larger by far than anything else in the city. To the right, I can see a work crew, and after a moment I realize they're repairing the hole Nimh blew in the wall the night we escaped. I haven't thought of it since, but now I can see a few of them carefully climbing down toward it from above, strapped to towers with rope harnesses, and I know there must be more down on the ground.

"Careful," Elkisa snaps, and I look up just in time to dodge a man carrying an armful of wooden planks, so large he can't see around them. I turn my attention to the city around me, and there's plenty to see. I haven't walked through this place during the day since the first time Nimh and I limped in after my crash. It's like someone's turned down the color contrast—everything is duller than it was before.

The place is coming to life now the sun's cleared the horizon, though people move slowly, and pick their way across the broken city carefully. Some wear gray strips of cloth tied around their upper arms, declaring their loyalty to the Graycloaks who've shielded the city from magic—and from the mist Nimh called in. Others keep their opinions to themselves.

Neither of us speaks as we move to the left-hand side of the road—a building has collapsed, its timbers and bricks strewn out across the road, leaving only a small gap through which we can pass. Nimh did this.

The cleanup is beyond everyone. Survival is the only game in town right now. Most of this place lies in ruins.

"Star!"

I just about leap out of my skin as a voice screeches up ahead of us, and Elkisa's hand flies to her waist, grabbing at the place where her knife should be.

"A star, a bright star!" It's a mist-bent old woman, her eyes huge in her face as she stares at me. Filthy clothes hang loosely around her thin frame, layer upon layer of ratty shawls clutched in gnarled hands. Techeki told me there were plenty of the mist-bent out in the city now—Nimh's storm turned them as she swept into the city. My heart hurts when I imagine how she'll feel when she realizes the carnage she left behind.

A man, obviously the woman's son by their shared chins and eyes, hurries to try and gently herd her away, and Elkisa and I edge past her, but I can't help but wonder. If I'm Nimh's star, from the prophecy, did the old woman somehow sense that about me?

We pick our way past stalls that smell of rotting produce— perhaps their owners never returned to claim them. Up ahead is a checkpoint, the broken beam of a house stretched across the road, manned by temple guards in black and gold. They're accompanied by several Graycloaks, but they're facing away from us—more interested in keeping others out than us in. Beyond them lies the bridge across the river.

"This feels like a really bad idea," I murmur as we casually turn left, working our way through the side streets, to find a crossing point where we won't be inspected.

"Have you a better one?" Elkisa asks, checking around a corner.

I don't answer, but I do catch sight of the cat slinking along ahead of us, and I hope that means he's on board with this terrible plan. "Tell me more about where we're going," I say. "About the way to the sky you've found."

She pauses as we reach the edge of the river, casting about for a moment, then commandeering an unattended boat. I don't bother arguing—I climb on carefully, the cat a moment later, and Elkisa pushes off with a pole.

The river runs in from the north of the city, splits around the temple to leave it on its own island, then rejoins on the other side. The whole temple island, the highest point in the city, is set in a valley, hemmed in to the east and west by hills.

We're leaving that island now, crossing to the west, where the ground begins to rise almost immediately. As it grows higher the houses become bigger, and it's clearly a wealthier area, though that didn't save it from the fury of Nimh's mist-storm. The streets are steep, often turning to staircases set into the hill. The large windows look down on the rest of the city.

"You see the building in the middle of the largest hill?" Elkisa asks, not looking up from her work. "Bigger than all the others?"

"I see it."

"That's where the Congress of Elders meets," she says quietly. "The place is inside the hill, beneath it. That's where the secret is."

"And what's the secret?"

She shakes her head. "A way up to the sky, cloudlander."

I stare up at the Congress hall, trying to ignite some spark of hope inside my chest. "Have you been inside it?" I ask. "I don't see how the way home could be so close and Matias not know about it."

She snorts. "You speak of a man who concealed from you that he was the Fisher King, concealed from you that he was a Sentinel. Interesting, that you are so sure he has no more lies to tell."

I buy myself a minute to choose my reply as we climb up onto the bank and set off through the streets. "I'm not so sure," I say in the end. "But I believe he has Nimh's best interests at heart, and I believe he knows that leaving her up there with Inshara a moment longer than necessary is unthinkable."

"Perhaps," she agrees. "But in this case, he did not lie. He doesn't know the vault is there. The Sentinels lost the knowledge of it a long time ago. There are too few of them. The high priests still knew, though. Daoman taught Jezara, and Jezara taught Inshara."

"And Inshara told you," I conclude.

"She knew you could unlock the crown with your touch and send her to the sky," Elkisa replies. "And she was right. She also told me about this vault, and that she believed your touch would gain her entry. She was right the first time, and I am hoping she will be right the second. I am the only person in the city or outside it who now knows where the vault lies. You are the only one who can gain entry. Thus, we find ourselves allies."

I square my jaw and adjust the spearstaff-bindle over my shoulder.

She believed. I am hoping. It's a tenuous offering, and from someone I have no reason to trust. But then again, Matias tells me half the truth, and Techeki kept me hidden away inside the temple while following his own agenda. There's nobody in this world, except the cat, I can trust completely.

I've spent weeks searching for any other way home and come up short. I have no other choice but to take a risk.

And perhaps she's right. My royal blood *was* the key to activating the magic in Nimh's crown and sending her and Inshara to Alciel. Scientifically, there had to be tech embedded in it that was DNA-based. Perhaps this other way to the sky has the same safeguard.

I'm beginning to understand why my family's so obsessive about continuing our bloodline.

Probably best not to mention to Elkisa that all she needs is my blood, and not my touch, or she might decide to take some of my blood with her and leave the rest behind.

We follow a street that zigzags up a hill, half the windows to either side boarded up. It doesn't take long for my legs to start aching, sweat slowly trickling down my back.

"If Jezara knew," I say after a while, "then how come Nimh didn't?"

"She had not been taught yet," Elkisa replies. "Daoman would have told her, after she manifested and came fully into the knowledge of the divine."

"Was that why Inshara wanted him dead?" The words are out before I have time to consider them, puncturing the fragile civility between us. I can't make myself sorry, though—I watched Nimh's light go out as the man who raised her died to protect her. And it was Elkisa who stabbed him, pretending that she was under Inshara's control. That Inshara was using impossible magic.

She glances back at me, then looks straight ahead once more, her mouth a thin line.

"Nimh trusted you," I say quietly. I should keep the peace, but I just can't bring myself to bite my tongue. I want her to see it. To understand what she's done.

"And Jezara trusted Daoman," she snaps. "Until he threw her out of the temple, leaving her to raise Insha all alone in a world that hated them both."

My own temper breaks, and I only just manage to keep my voice down, moving faster so I can come up alongside her. "You don't get to judge anyone. You took Nimh's trust, and you tried to kill her with it."

I see the moment that lands—I see the cracks in the composure she's so carefully cultivated. Her gaze is hard, but there's a desperation hiding in her dark eyes. There's a tension to her jaw, to the way she holds her shoulders—there's a storm in her, hiding behind the clear blue skies she's trying to show me.

"I would never have let Nimh die," she says quietly, and there's a hollowness to her voice she can't hide, though she's still trying.

Suddenly I wonder—where has she been? With the Deathless, trying to convince them to wait for Inshara? Or all alone?

"Did Inshara know you wanted to keep Nimh alive?" I'm already wrestling my anger under control, but I keep my tone barbed. If I can think more clearly than her, perhaps she'll tell me something she didn't mean to. After all, the moment we know how to get to Alciel, our interests diverge. "Because I'm pretty sure Nimh understood you were prepared to let her die."

"Neither of them are here right now," she replies through gritted teeth.

"And yet you still fight to get back to Inshara," I point out. "She stabbed her mother right in front of my eyes. Don't tell me you care about Nimh, when you did everything you could to throw her in Inshara's path. She's a killer!"

She stops in her tracks, wheeling around to face me, throwing up one hand to take in the broken city with a wild sweep. "Look around you! So is Nimh!"

And I stop, staring at her.

After a long moment her face closes over, and she turns on her heel, resuming her walk up the hill in silence.

Neither of us speaks for the next hour or so—it takes time to cover the ground that would be so quick if we could move directly. But instead we take backstreets, make sure none of the growing morning crowd get much of a look at us, walk slowly, as if we're as tired as everyone else. Eventually she slows, glancing up a quiet alleyway.

"We should stop and eat," she says. 'The guards will be changing shifts, and there is no need for us to put ourselves in their way as they go back to the temple."

She inspects a house through its window and assures herself it's empty, then neatly breaks the lock on the door. We sit by someone else's cold hearth, eating bread from my satchel along with a nut-based spread I've come to love from the temple kitchens.

"How do you become a guard?" I ask, around a mouthful. "Born into it, or recruited?"

"Most are chosen," she says quietly. "Invited. I sought the honor."

"For Inshara?" I ask, keeping my tone neutral. "Or did you switch allegiances later?"

"I entered my training when I was eight years old. It was the day after I first saw Nimh."

I'm interested in spite of myself, taking a sip from my water bottle, then passing it across to her. When I was eight, my whole focus was on finding ways to evade my tutors. "What made you choose to become a guard so young?"

"She did," she replies. "They took her through the city on a platform so people could see their new goddess. She was five. I thought she looked frightened." She takes a swig from the bottle and passes it back. "She wasn't, but I thought she was. And I didn't want her to be afraid."

I let out a slow breath, studying her profile. This woman is a mass of contradictions, and I'm only just beginning to realize how barely I understand her. "What changed?"

"Nothing," she replies, almost emotionless, though she glances across at me in response to the way my voice grows quieter. "I have never wished for Nimh to be afraid."

"Maybe not," I allow. "But you speak about her like you think you're doing the right thing for her, and I'm trying to understand, Elkisa. Because it doesn't look that way from here."

"You have known her less than a month," she points out,

sounding uncomfortably like the voice in my head. "I have given my life to her."

I lean toward her. "So help me understand how what you did was best for her. Because she's seen people she loves die, seen her city fall, and now, if we're lucky, she's alone in a foreign land. This can't be what you meant to happen."

She pushes to her feet, crossing over to check outside the window. "The first day I saw her, when I thought she looked frightened?" she says, her voice quickening a touch. "She wasn't frightened. She was *lonely*. She had thought, when they brought her out of the temple, that they were going to let her see her mother." She shakes her head, lips pressing together for a moment. "She never wanted any of this."

I close my eyes, like I'm trying to deny myself the sight of that five-year-old version of Nimh, looking out into the crowds, hoping for a familiar face.

The sight of eight-year-old Elkisa, wishing to give her one.

"You thought you could free her from her divinity," I say slowly. "Pass it on to Inshara, who *did* want it."

Her voice has gentled when she replies. "The first time Insha spoke of who her mother was, of what she believed to be her place in the prophecy . . . I wanted it to be true. I wanted Nimh to be free."

"I—" I cut myself off as she raises her hand sharply, her gaze suddenly fixed on something at the mouth of the alleyway. Her whole body's on alert, and slowly I reach down to where the spearstaff lies on the floor beside me.

A few moments after that I hear voices—they're unintelligible, but getting closer. She looks across at me, dropping to a whisper. "Deathless. They're searching each house."

"You're one of them," I whisper in reply, coming to my feet. "Tell them—tell them something to send them away."

She shakes her head, glancing around the room and concluding about the same time I do that it's not rich on hiding places. "I'm alone," she murmurs. "I'm not on patrol. And you—"

My heart sinks. "Half the city knows my face, and I'll bet the Deathless do too." That's exactly why Techeki's had me hiding in the temple. Nimh's Star would be the ultimate prize for them, while they await Inshara's return.

In two quick paces she's at the rich curtains that border the window, pulling free the cords that hold them back when they're drawn. "Hide the staff," she hisses. "Put on your river-strider's scarf and sash!"

I don't need telling twice, dropping the spearstaff down behind an upholstered chair and crouching beside my bag to dig through its contents. It only takes me a few moments to knot a black sash around my waist, then pull a scarf on over my hair, at least hiding my curls. But when she gestures for me to join her, I hesitate.

"I must bind your hands," she whispers, glancing out the window again. "You must be my prisoner. North, *now.*"

"What will you—"

"*Now!*"

I hold perfectly still for two heartbeats, the possibilities stretching out in front of me, running calculations. It's a gamble no matter what I do. Then I hurry across to her, holding out my wrists.

She knots the cord around them in seconds, yanking it tight so quickly I yelp, and for a moment we're so close I can feel her breath on my cheek. Then she pulls the knife's sheath from my belt and ties it to hers.

"We're going to walk out of here, as if we've come across the alley," she murmurs. "If they find us in here, they'll want to know what we were doing. Keep your head down, say nothing."

I simply nod, my heart pounding in my chest. We're in this now, and we'll come through it together, or not at all.

She peers out the door and waits until they're in the house a couple up from ours, then drags me into the alleyway, giving me a push to get me moving ahead of her. We're nearly at their door—I'm beginning to wonder if we could possibly just get past them, wondering how to double back for the spearstaff—when they emerge as a group.

The quickest of peeks tells me there are five of them, in varying degrees of pseudo-ceremonial garb, weapons drawn as if they're hoping for trouble. The leader—or at least I assume he is, because he has slightly better clothes and thicker black paint around his eyes—spots us and stops short.

"It is the divine's consort!" he proclaims, and for a hideous moment I think he's talking about me, and I nearly lift my head—and then Elkisa speaks behind me.

"What are you doing, dawdling in this district? What do you plan to find in such rich houses? The cloudlander, or

133

perhaps something you fancy to line your pockets?"

I force myself to stand perfectly still, to keep my head down, to let her handle this. She wanted me badly enough to find me in the first place, and I have to believe she still wants me badly enough to bluff her way through this, instead of taking advantage of the fact that I'm tied up and she's got the knife.

"No, we were—" He's flustered enough that she's clearly got it right, but he recovers as well as a politician. "Do you require our assistance in any way? Can we perhaps escort your prisoner somewhere?" There's a hint of curiosity in his voice, and I wind my fingers together, squeezing hard. *Would a riverstrider be silent now? Or defiant?*

"I require no assistance," Elkisa says calmly. "They are up to something, down in the river, and I mean to find out from this one just what the Fisher King has planned. I will escort him myself, but I thank you for your willingness to help. When the Divine One returns, she will know which of us served her best."

Somewhere beyond my fear, I'm genuinely impressed—she's just managed to shut down the conversation, subtly threaten them with the consequences of noncompliance by reminding them of her connection to Inshara, and done it all while sounding like she's discussing the weather.

"May she rise," the man murmurs, half inclining in a bow, and the others echo the words and the movement, only just visible out the edge of my vision.

"May she bless us all," Elkisa agrees. "I think you will have better luck rooting out enemies closer to the river."

The two of us stand in silence as they turn to go, and it

takes everything I've got to keep my gaze on the cobblestones beneath my feet. Elkisa rests one hand on my shoulder to keep me in place, and for now I let her. It takes approximately forever for their footsteps to round the corner.

"A moment more," she murmurs, and then she's walking past me. Finally I risk looking up, and I see her check around the corner and satisfy herself they're making their way down the hill. With a nod, she turns back to me.

She doesn't move right away, but instead stands where she is, face impassive as she studies me. One moment becomes two, and my skin begins to prickle.

Is she going to untie me at all?

Her lips press together, and she tilts her head, then begins to walk toward me. There's no doubt in my mind that she's asking herself the same question as I am, but the moment I speak—the moment I name the possibility—it feels like I'll make it reality.

So I wait, hoping, holding my breath, trying to keep my own expression blank.

Her footsteps slow, and she comes to a halt in front of me. Meets my eyes.

Then she reaches for her belt with one hand, and with the other, grabs the thick curtain cord wound around my wrists, using her grip to yank them up.

She doesn't break eye contact as she saws through it, nor as she tugs it away and throws it through the open door, into the room where we were hiding.

"Get the spearstaff," she says quietly. "We should go."

THE ELECTRICIAN

The electrician hurries along the corridor, her pulse racing with nerves. Another day she'd be admiring the palace architecture, marveling at the fact that *she*, of all people—or rather, her mother—had been summoned to the palace. As it is, something isn't sitting right with her. The message her mother left for her was brief to the point of being worrisome.

Summoned to the palace. Back later.

A pair of guards at the next set of doors tries to stop her, one of them stepping forward to stand in her way.

"My mother is in there," she protests, half-fearful, half-confused. She can't explain the urgency she's feeling, but she knows something is wrong.

"Let her come in," calls a voice from inside the room. The guards exchange glances that only make the electrician more anxious—she's never seen the royal guard look *afraid*. It wasn't the queen's voice, and yet the guards stand down, backing away from her and leaving the door clear.

She bursts into the room to find her mother sitting on a divan before a fire, her back to the doorway. Across from her, face lifted in anticipation of the electrician's arrival, is the woman she saw on the screens that morning—the visitor from below.

"Uh," she says, trying out a clumsy curtsy, uncertain how

to address the woman her queen called a goddess. "That's my mother—is she—"

At the sound of her daughter's voice, the woman on the divan turns—and the electrician's heart skips a beat. Her mother's face is streaming with tears.

"Oh, Sofee—I'm so glad you're here. Come, meet Nimhara."

The visitor from Below is younger than the electrician would have guessed, with dark makeup lining her eyes and a gold crown on her head. Her eyes, though—the electrician can't get past her eyes. There's something strange about them. Something unnatural. "Welcome, Sofee," she says in a low voice. "Join us here by the fire."

The electrician, too unsettled to reply to Nimhara, hurries to her mother's side. "Mama?" She reaches for the older woman's hand, only to discover that her skin is cold—far too cold for someone sitting by a roaring hearth. "Why are you crying? Are you all right?"

Her mother shakes her head. "I'm just so overwhelmed. This woman . . . she is a *goddess*, love. You cannot imagine—she has come to save us all." She turns her glistening, shining eyes on the woman across from her.

The electrician, her skin crawling and her every nerve singing alarm, keeps hold of her mother's hand. "What's going on?" she manages, raising her voice. She keeps her eyes on the woman in the gold crown, but she can hear the guards shuffling uncertainly by the door.

The visitor from Below—the goddess—smiles at her. "Your mother has been telling me all about the girl who has been staying with you these past weeks. Perhaps you would like to tell me what you know."

The electrician, caught by those strange eyes—beautiful eyes, really, unlike anything she's ever seen—hesitates. Her pulse quickens, and she swallows to clear her dry throat. "Y-yes," she murmurs, feeling tears sting her eyes. "Actually, I would."

NINE
NIMH

We enter the palace grounds by the eastern gate. Miri nods conspiratorially to the guard in a way that makes Saelis smile, though he's quick to hide it before she can see. The guard pays us little attention, for which I'm grateful—Miri and Saelis might be enjoying themselves, but my nerves have been screaming at me ever since we spoke to Talamar and he promised a way into the palace to see the queen.

The path leads through a small but meticulously landscaped garden, with sweeps of grass cut to a precise length, small trees trimmed to be symmetrical, and, at its center, a lovely fountain that gives a musical tinkle as we walk by. I find myself longing for my own garden, for all its differences from this structured place; but I like its wildness. With a pang, I realize that the new flowers that had begun to bud must be wilting, even dying, by now—new things need water, and nourishment, and tending. And I have been here, hiding in the electrician's house, too afraid to remember what I need to know.

I pull my thoughts away. *I'm doing something now,* I tell myself. The palace, at this close distance, looms in an unsettling way—though perhaps it's just because I know who waits somewhere inside it. If Talamar failed in his mission to get the queen away from Inshara long enough for us to make our case, then the enemy who has haunted my nightmares could right now be just on the other side of the broad double doors at the end of the path.

But the guards there, as well, simply nod at us, and one moves to open the door before us. North's father got us this far—we have to trust him.

Miri and Saelis navigate the palace with obvious familiarity. As North's closest friends, they must have spent quite a bit of time here. Still, the grandness of the architecture inside rivals that of the temple itself, and I find myself casting about nervously as I trail after my companions. I don't remember a time when the temple felt this imposing, though I suppose it must have when I was young and newly called to divinity.

We head down a long corridor that intersects with a broad gallery, windows all along one side. Thick gold curtains line the windows, tied back so that the morning light streams through the thin, perfectly manufactured glass. On the far wall of the gallery hang a series of portraits. The faces are stern and forbidding, and unlike the lively, brightly painted depictions of former divines in our manuscripts, but I recognize them for what they are: the previous kings and queens and rulers of Alciel.

I search for signs of North in their faces as we walk, but I don't see much of him until the very end of the gallery, where an older woman with a long, sharp nose and bright black eyes stares down at me. The next portrait is covered—the most recent king, whose picture will stay covered until a year after his death.

His body will be held in stasis for that year as well, in a manner I do not understand. It will be covered too, but at intervals the vault will be opened and different parts of society will be invited in to pay their respects—from councilors to tradespeople to farmers, all will be represented.

Then, at the end of that mourning period, his portrait will be uncovered, and his remains will be taken from the vault where they have waited for that year. His body will be burned and scattered to the clouds, and this world will turn its face forward. They will look to the next in the row of portraits—but when I do the same, I find only an empty frame. Beatrin's picture has yet to be painted.

I can't help but pause before the covered portrait of North's grandfather, wishing I could tug the black silk away and see the man he admired so much. I didn't remember enough to understand the ache in my heart when I first heard of the old king's passing, but now I do. North was filled with so much admiration for his grandfather—it will hurt him so badly to have been so far away from him when he died. It will be break his heart that he could not say goodbye.

"Nimh," whispers Miri, appearing at my elbow, "come on. We might not have a lot of time to talk to the queen before Inshara shows up." Saelis is at the end of the gallery, gesturing at us to follow.

With one last, lingering look on the featureless sweep of black fabric, I hurry after them.

I recognize the next room immediately. One audience chamber is much like another, I suppose—I can see the architecture, designed to focus the eye on the raised dais at one end. Back home, there would be clusters of finely dressed dignitaries scattered here and there, waiting to speak to me. This room is disturbingly empty, but for a few servants and guards. The dais holds two chairs—*thrones*, I correct myself—though one is unoccupied. The other . . .

My steps slow, as I break my eyes away from the dais, scanning the room for any signs of a familiar, malevolent face. Saelis catches my eye and raises his eyebrows in question. I shake my head.

Inshara's not here.

There's also no sign of Talamar—I hope he is watching Inshara, wherever she is, and that he can make certain she doesn't interfere while we speak to the queen. I lift my chin, imagining myself in my divine robes instead of fresh clothes borrowed from Miri—at least the jacket she loaned me is red, the color of divinity in my world—and turn to approach the queen.

"Your Majesty," I say, upon reaching the dais, as I incline my torso in a bow. I stay there, falling back on the quick and dirty lesson in palace etiquette I received from Saelis this morning, until the queen's voice releases me, and the others at my side.

"Miri, Saelis," she says, her voice liquid and affectionate. "It has been so long since we've seen you here. I hope you know that even though North is no longer with us, you are always welcome."

Straightening out of my bow, I take the opportunity to scan the queen's features. The news feeds on the electrician's screen often use the same picture of her, from some long-ago event where she is smiling and waving to the crowd. This woman is changed from that other—her cheeks are thin, her hair more frizzy than curly, her eyes sunken. *Grief,* I think, my throat tightening. Though there is no flicker of her expression when she speaks the name of the son she believes dead; but then, she is a politician and practiced at controlling her features.

"Thank you, ma'am," says Miri. "But it's not the same being here." She doesn't add the rest, but the words linger in the air anyway, unspoken: *Without him.*

"Who is your lovely friend?" asks the queen, those dark, dull eyes sweeping across until they fall on me. In spite of myself, I shiver—that emptiness in her face isn't grief. I know grief, have walked beside it all my life. This is something else.

"She's why we came, ma'am," says Saelis, glancing between me and the queen. "We came to warn you—this is Nimh. She's from Below."

The queen's eyebrows lift a little, the first sign of interest or curiosity. "From Below? Like my good friend Nimhara?" Her lips curve then in a faint smile. "Nimh, Nimhara . . . Are the two of you related? Sisters?"

The muscles in my jaw clench, and I have to take a deep breath before I can unclench them. "No, Your Majesty. *I* am Nimhara. I am the divine vessel; I am my people's goddess. She is an impostor."

The eyebrows draw together, the tiniest of wrinkles

appearing between them; the queen looks merely puzzled, more like she would if someone had rescheduled an appointment with her, as opposed to informing her of an impostor inside her palace. "That can't be right," she mumbles. "You must be mistaken."

Miri stiffens at my side. "About her own name? Ma'am, we wouldn't have come to warn you if we didn't think she was worth listening to. Ma'am, she knows *North*. She says that North survived the glider crash—North is *alive*."

But Beatrin just continues to watch Miri, puzzled, the dull eyes registering no sign of shock. "No, that's not right. My son is dead. I'll ask Nimhara—Rojer, would you . . . ?" She raises a hand toward a harried-looking man in white-and-gold livery, who steps forward and bows.

"Wait!" "No!" Saelis and Miri speak at once, and Rojer pauses in confusion.

"Don't send for her," Saelis continues, glancing from the steward to the queen. "Ma'am, you have to listen to us." He pauses, eyes flicking toward the empty chair beside the queen's. "Ma'am . . . where is Anasta?"

Beatrin lifts one shoulder, waving her hand vaguely. "I don't know. She's no longer welcome in the throne room."

Miri and Saelis exchange a look that makes my heart sink further. Something is very, very wrong. Even I know from the newsfeeds how closely the queen's wife works with her—co-ruler of Alciel in truth, if not in name.

"Your Majesty," I say, taking a step forward. The movement makes Miri stiffen, for it is a breach of etiquette to cross the invisible line separating the queen from her petitioners. I ignore her, though—I am a goddess. I am not afraid of queens. "The woman you call Nimhara is a murderer and a traitor, responsible for countless deaths Below, and guilty of usurping my own seat of divine power in my temple. You must take her into custody before she does any such harm here. North would never forgive me if I let anything happen to his mother."

I will her to listen to me, keeping my eyes on hers, letting my earnestness show in my face, leaving it open to scrutiny. I want her to see that I am a leader of people who depend on me too—that Inshara could destroy this world, if she wanted, if she isn't stopped. But Beatrin only blinks at me, that faint frown appearing, as if she's staring at some mathematical calculation that doesn't add up.

"North is gone," she says slowly, as if repeating something that's been told to her over and over. "Isn't he?" Her eyes meet mine, and in their dull depths, something flickers.

My heart leaps. Whatever's wrong with her, she's reachable.

"Oh, yes," comes a voice—smooth and hard, like obsidian—from behind and to the right of the queen's throne. The edge of a tapestry lifts aside as someone enters through the door it had been concealing. "He's quite dead."

Memory flashes, and for a moment, all I can see is the twisted face in my dream, wreathed in mist, the clawlike hand grabbing my ankle. My breath seizes, and I stay where I am only because shock overwhelms my need to flee.

She wears red—my red, robes of Alciel soy silk that she must have had made for her—and gold bands circle her arms. Her eyes are painted not with the solid band of black she affected when she invaded the temple, but more gently, rimmed in dark like mine used to be. A band of gold rests on her head, and she even carries a spearstaff, which clicks against the marble floor as she crosses behind the queen's throne to stand by Anasta's empty chair.

And her eyes . . . Now she's close enough, I can see flickers and glimmers of mist in her eyes. My dream, the one where she grabs me—her eyes looked like that in my dream.

The queen has straightened in her throne, her head turning toward Inshara, her eyes lighting.

"Inshara." My voice is sharp and taut—I scarcely recognize it as my own. "You lie—North survived the crash."

Inshara smiles—her lips are dusted with gold, like mine would be for a religious ceremony—and gives a minute shake of her head. "Of course he did. But not for very long."

"What are you talking about?" Miri's voice is high with tension, and after a moment she shifts her stare from the woman in red robes back to me. "What is she talking about, Nimh?"

I open my mouth, but Inshara beats me to it. "I see you have remembered some of who you are," she says, with a look so like concern that I'm momentarily thrown. "Tell me—how *much* do you remember?"

"How do you know I was—?"

"I asked my friend Beatrin to have you watched as soon as they could locate you." Inshara gets a sickeningly devoted look from the queen as she continues. "You've been living these past weeks with an electrician in the Leeward District. Her mother is quite the talker."

Ice trickles its way through my limbs, making me once again fight the urge to simply flee. "You have known where I was this whole time?"

"Nearly. But why bother with you, when you didn't even know your own name? I am encouraged to know that Beatrin's people can be discreet." She gives the queen a nod.

"You told me it was important," the queen replies, her voice brimming with a strange sort of urgency now, a stark contrast to the way she was before Inshara entered the room.

"She's lying to you," Miri breaks in, her brow furrowed as she watches the queen. "Whatever she told you, it was all lies."

The queen's eyes slide away from Inshara's face to fix on Miri. Any warmth those eyes had held when we first arrived, however dilute, has gone. "I will not hear you say such things about this woman," she says in a low, intent voice. "She has my utter confidence. She is a *goddess* in her world."

"But, Your Majesty, Nimh—the *real* Nimh—knows North! He's alive, he survived the fall, he—"

"Enough!" The queen's voice cracks like a whip. There's no hint of grief or doubt in her voice, though her eyes are wet with tears now. Instead of seizing on Miri's words, she turns back toward Inshara, like a flower seeking the sun, to gaze at her with disturbing reverence.

I look from Inshara to the queen and back again. "What did you do to her?" I demand, my suspicions confirmed when the queen barely reacts to the question, too busy gazing raptly at the woman in red.

Inshara opens her eyes wide in a look of exaggerated surprise and innocence. "Do to her? Gods, Nimh, you have a suspicious and evil little mind. Why would I do anything to her?"

"This isn't the Beatrin I know." Saelis, all but quivering with outrage, starts to move toward the queen, but Inshara lifts her arm and snaps her fingers.

The queen stiffens and levels a glare at Saelis. "You will not approach the throne," she says, in a low voice, making Saelis freeze. The tears have spilled out of her eyes, carving wet tracks down her cheeks, though there's little in her expression to tell of sadness—she might almost be crying with the depth of her devotion to Inshara, quivering with misplaced belief.

Inshara turns her attention back to me. "Now, answer my original question, please. How much do you remember?"

My heart thuds a little more quickly, and I draw upon my training, keeping myself still and straight. "I remember you invading the Feast of the Dying and murdering Daoman," I hiss at her. "I remember being forced to flee my own home. I remember North and I learning who you were from your mother. I remember watching a boy scarcely old enough to shave cut his own throat in your name."

Gods, I wish I didn't remember that part.

Inshara's eyes sweep across my face, cool and thoughtful, but for the flickering, lightning-like heat of the mist in her irises. She takes her time before speaking, and when she does, her voice is almost sympathetic—almost *kind*—in a way that makes my skin crawl . . . until her words sink in.

"So you do not remember murdering Prince North?"

Dimly, I hear Miri cry out; Saelis whirls to face me, his form blurring where he stands. The blood rushes in my ears, horror choking me and making my eyes burn.

"No," I croak. "No, I would never—I could *never*—I loved him!"

"I know you did." Inshara moves around Anasta's chair and steps down a little onto the steps of the dais so that she's only a few feet from me, looking down on me. "I can only assume that is why you did it. When you learned that he had betrayed you to help me travel here, you were so enraged that you snapped his neck. Or the mist did, under your control."

Miri lets out a choked little sob. When my eyes find her, she's watching me in utter horror, not even seeming to notice when Saelis wraps his arms around her. What I did to North— what Inshara *claims* I did to North—I very nearly did to her in the tunnels below Alciel.

Shock makes the very ground seem to tremble beneath my feet, and I put out a hand, wishing I had my own spearstaff. "No," I repeat, my voice sounding thin and tiny now, and nothing like that of a goddess. "I would never hurt North. No matter what he chose. I would *never* hurt him."

Inshara takes another step, stopping on the last riser of the dais, so that she's looking down at me from a breath away. "It's not as though you didn't regret it. You did—instantly. But you let the mist take you, I think—you summoned the greatest storm I had ever seen and brought it down upon the city. You killed countless people and left your own temple in ruins."

"No, I—" But that fearful barrier, the bonds holding back the memories, tremble at the words. I see that flash of Inshara's mist-touched eyes again, her hand grabbing me, and beyond it . . . *a mist-storm.* "Gods, no. I would not . . ."

Grief hits me as powerfully as if I'd summoned another storm. Dropping to my knees, I double over, palms on the cold stone, bracing against the memory. *I remember . . . I remember . . .*

I remember North being dead.

Miri gives a strangled, gut-wrenching moan; but no, her face is turned into Saelis's shoulder. She wasn't the one who made that sound. The world seems to tremble again—and this time, Saelis gives a strangled oath, as if he felt it too, his eyes wet with tears.

I manage to lift my head and find that Inshara has knelt down before me, echoing my movements like some twisted reflection, wearing the crimson and gold that used to be mine.

"You took the crown, and you used the prince's blood to activate it. I had only enough time to grab hold of you before it sent you here." The mist in her eyes is swirling more quickly now. "Yes, I lied to the queen about who I was. I took on your name and title and tried to be what you weren't. A true leader. Someone who could ask these people to aid the world you left behind . . . in pieces."

She straightens back to her full height again, towering over me, a vision of red robes and the glint of gold. "Perhaps you never meant to hurt anyone. But hurt you did. And now the rest of us must try to mend the pieces of all you have broken."

Another sob tears its way free of my lips, and the floor vibrates beneath me. Inshara looks down with a faint frown on her face, and behind her, the queen lets out of quick breath of surprise.

"More quakes," she announces, turning her gaze toward Inshara again. "What must we do to stop them?" The tears are running freely down her face, though she scarcely seems to notice. It's as though Inshara has, somehow, reached directly into her heart and is squeezing.

I had thought the ground had only seemed to shake, in my grief—but one look at Saelis's ashen face as he cradles Miri against him tells me it's true.

Inshara ignores the queen, instead flashing me an incredulous look, surprise penetrating her aura of sympathy. Then an idea strikes her, writ as plainly across her features as if she had struck her forehead and exclaimed. Her eyes refocus on me, glowing with realization. "The engines," she murmurs. "No one could give me an answer as to why the engines were failing—but all this time, it was *you*."

I wrap my arms around myself, trying to brace against the onslaught of grief and confusion. "Wh-what was me?"

Inshara's smile shifts, and she leans back a little. "The villain," she says softly. "All along, you thought I was the one—the obstacle to overcome, to save your people and be with the person you loved. And in the end, it was *you*. You are the one they should have spat on in the streets as a child—*you* are the one who brought them all to their dooms." Her voice, quickening, halts abruptly as she swallows, checking herself—there's a fury behind her words, a pain that lances me straight through the heart.

"You couldn't just stay gone," Inshara adds, her expression rippling. "I would have let you be if you would just—now you've come to ruin everything *again*."

The ground gives such a shake that the marble floor splits with a violent crack, and I cry out in shock, scrambling back from the split in the floor that travels right below my feet.

Saelis gives a sudden gasp. "Skyfall, it's the engine mainframe. I noticed the tremor when you fell into it, but I thought it was just coincidence."

Miri turns, pulling away from Saelis's arms to drop to the floor by me. Her face is close to mine, her eyes red and skin streaked with tears, but her voice is sharp with urgency. "Nimh, you're affecting it somehow—you've got to calm down!"

"North," I manage, tears falling from my chin to patter into the dust of the shattered floor. "I cannot—"

"Forget about North." Miri's voice is ruthless, and somehow, the words penetrate the fog of grief. "This is about every human being in Alciel. You *have to calm down*."

Inshara is laughing, somewhere above us, delight in her tone. "Oh, girl, it is far too late for that. You came here to take everything from me again—but you'll end up with nothing. Your grief will destroy it all." Her eyes narrow on me, the swirling irises moving so quickly that I find myself dizzy, nearly falling back onto my palms again. "There is grief enough in you to bring down a host of cities. Gods, Nimh—how could you have forgotten the sound it made when you broke North's neck? What kind of monster could ever forget that sound, just to spare herself the guilt?"

"Don't listen to her." Miri's face is drawn, her own eyes full of grief, but she doesn't let me look away. "I don't believe her, and you shouldn't either. Shut her out. *Don't listen.* Sae, we need—"

"On it," he replies, turning to hurry toward the throne and speak to the queen. "Wake *up*—can't you hear this woman? Please, listen to us!"

But Inshara just glances over her shoulder. "Don't bother. The queen is mine. Beatrin—don't you think you've heard enough from these two?"

Beatrin's eyes sweep from Inshara to Saelis, her son's best friend, the boy who must have practically grown up in the castle with him. Her red-rimmed eyes streaming those strange, telltale tears, she nods. "Yes. You have both always been a threat to the royal line—North never could resist you." Her eyes flick back toward Inshara. "You can dispose of them."

"Wh-what?" Saelis reels back, grabbing for the arm of Anasta's throne when the palace quakes again, harder this time.

Inshara makes a tsking sound. "Killing them seems a little harsh. Perhaps just lock them up somewhere out of the way, in case you need them later?"

The queen nods slowly. "You are wise. I trust you to do what must be done."

Inshara gestures, summoning the guards by the nearest

entrance, both of whom look nearly as shaken and confused as Miri and Saelis. "Arrest these two."

I focus on the pattern of the marble, trying to shut out the sounds of Miri's curses and Saelis's protests, and the clank of manacles locking into place around their wrists. My mind is spinning, thoughts scrambling to catch up. The quakes in Alciel began shortly after the king died—but that was also when *I* got here. I try to think of the moments I remember them happening: when I realized I could not remember who I was; when I realized I came from another world and did not belong here; when I touched the mist enveloping the engine mainframes below Alciel.

Gods help me . . . it was me all along.

The ground gives another shudder, and I close my eyes, focusing my mind, drawing on every lesson in mental discipline that Daoman ever gave me. I let the grief and shock go somewhere else and find a tiny grain of calm inside the storm in my heart. The lives of everyone in Alciel depend upon that minute space.

I focus on it, let it grow, let the other thoughts slide away. Dimly, I hear Beatrin asking what to do about me, and when footsteps approach, I open my eyes.

Inshara is there, and as she meets my gaze, she halts, surprised by whatever she reads there in my face. But then the ground heaves so violently I nearly go sprawling, and she gives a strange laugh that crackles like a snap of pent-up mist, holding onto her staff for support.

Calm isn't helping.

I scan the room, meeting Miri's terrified gaze, seeing my own confusion mirrored there and in Saelis's face too, where they stand bound at the queen's side, held by the wide-eyed guards.

"I remember those same lessons in mental discipline from my mother," says Inshara, not bothering now with her facade of kind sympathy; her lip curls with anger and triumph. "She must have learned them from that old priest too. They don't seem to be doing much for you, do they?"

"How are you controlling the queen?" I gasp. "It cannot be possible—there is no magic that can seize control of someone's mind."

Inshara's eyes bore into mine, so intently that I can almost feel the mist in their depths pushing against me, trying to reach past my own mental defenses. "I have you to thank for it," she whispers. "That mist-storm you summoned on the temple steps granted me this. You may be able to control the mist, Nimh— but it's just a cold, dead thing. *I* have their hearts. I can make them love me."

I glance at the queen, her tear-streaked face transformed by devotion, the depth of her passion for her people and her duty to the throne perverted to something twisted. So much so that she barely noticed us talking about the son she thought she'd lost.

The floor bucks beneath my feet and begins to tilt just enough to send a few crumbling pieces of marble skittering toward the far wall with each tremor. I crane my neck back around, wishing I had something to hold on to—but there's only Inshara there.

"How are you doing this?"

"Me?" Inshara straightens, looming over me. "This is your doing, Divine One. Your instability—and the arrogance of our so-called gods. The royal family has known the engines were failing for years. They debated the sinking of the cities in their council meetings and did nothing but wait for their fate to overtake them. And here you are—someone powerful enough to give the last dregs of mist in those failing engines that final push."

I stare at her, my grip on my calm faltering.

"You want to be the goddess—the Lightbringer—to these people and those Below?" Inshara adds, those mad eyes fixed on my face, hungry for whatever scraps of fear and despair they can find. "If you cannot stand to let me be these people's savior—then you shall be their Destroyer."

TEN
NORTH

I haven't gotten much exercise over the last couple of weeks, and by the time we approach the top of the hill, my legs are killing me and my back's starting to ache. Elkisa, of course, is still striding along without a sign of flagging.

The hall of the Congress of Elders sits at the crest of the hill, looking down into the valley below, the sweeping view taking in the river, the temple on its high peak in the middle, and everything around and beyond. The building itself must be the largest in the city except for the temple itself, and it's built to impress. It's two stories high, with a pitched roof, all carved from white stone. The entire front of it is covered in carvings of the twisting trees of the forest sea, and, I assume, a selection of the fearsome animals found therein. The whole thing involves a disturbing number of open, snarling mouths and plenty of teeth.

We stand in the shelter of a large tree, and I adjust my grip on the spearstaff-bindle as we take in the view. Then, without a word, Elkisa leads me down the laneway to one side of it, the cat trotting ahead of us along the compacted dirt track.

"You know a way in?" I ask quietly, hefting the spearstaff over one shoulder.

"Nimh came here to meet with the Congress of Elders," she replies, just as soft. "I made it my business to know every inch of this place. Then, it was the gathering place for the most senior priests, guild leaders, others of that kind."

"And now?"

"Now it has been taken by the Graycloaks," she says. "But there is a back entrance near the kitchens, where deliveries are brought. I am hoping none of the staff has told Elorin about the less obvious entrances where she might post guards."

"That's the price you pay for a hostile takeover," I muse. "Nobody's in the mood to make your life easier."

With a confidence I can't help but be impressed by, she leads me in through the delivery door while the guard is at the far end of his beat.

I can hear someone moving in the next room—a woman humming to herself as bowls clatter on a tabletop. But in the middle of the afternoon there's nobody in this part of the kitchen, and the two of us move through it as silently as the cat.

Elkisa considers a row of gray jackets and cloaks hanging along a wall, then dismisses them in favor of my disguise from this morning—what worked to get me out of the temple will hopefully work to bring us right through the congress building, as well. Nobody pays attention to the cleaners. She takes a couple of mops and brooms from where they lean in a corner and hands them to me, then chooses two for herself. With a silent apology to the spearstaff, I flip it upside down so its interesting end is hidden down by the head of the mop.

The whole building is almost eerily quiet—we walk at an easy pace, heads down, both straining our ears for any sign of danger. We see only a few people, and those at the other ends of the corridors we traverse. Which is just as well, because the cat's insisted on following us.

Finally we emerge into a central courtyard on the ground floor. It's open to the sky, balconies from the upper floor looking down onto it. The floor is paved with stones worn perfectly smooth by the trampling of feet over the centuries, and the centerpiece is a huge fountain.

"It's here," Elkisa says quietly, glancing up at the balconies.

"Where?" I murmur, studying the doors that lead off the courtyard.

"In the fountain."

"In the . . . How?"

She's quiet a long moment before she replies. "I thought that would be more obvious," she admits.

"What?" I whisper-yelp. "You got us all this way, and you don't know how to get inside?"

"If it was obvious," she points out, "it would not have remained concealed for many centuries."

"That doesn't mean—" I don't bother continuing, because she's walking away from me, craning her neck to examine the statue in the middle of the giant water feature.

I walk a slow lap around it myself, taking it in from every

angle. But it looks nothing like an entrance to anything, or like anything that might transport me anywhere. It looks like a huge water fountain.

It's made of white stone, the base a huge bowl. In the center rises a statue of two people caught mid-stride, each spilling water from an urn they're upending. The motif of the walking people is repeated all around the rim of the bowl, though the pattern is wearing away under the accumulated weight of centuries of water and weather. It's beautiful work, but I'm just not in an art appreciation mood.

"Are they anyone?" I ask quietly, gesturing up to the pair walking through the water. "They look a little familiar, maybe? Or like I've seen them before?"

"I do not believe so," Elkisa says, pausing her own investigations to study them.

A door opens on the far side of the courtyard, and we both fall silent, bending down and pretending to clean away a little of the black muck that always gathers around carvings near water. Two men in gray jackets emerge, totally ignoring us as they make their way across the courtyard, disappearing through another door.

And that moment spent nose-to-nose with the stone carvings has done its work. I know where I've seen this before. The people marching around the rim of the fountain are the same as the ones I saw in the murals far beneath the temple, where I met Elkisa about twelve hours and half a lifetime ago.

They're not all marching in the same direction—rather, they're in two columns, marching toward each other. I shuffle around on my knees to the place where the two groups meet, the leaders reaching out to take each other's hands. I feel underneath the rim of the stone bowl, just beneath that handshake . . . and there it is.

There's a catch there, just as there was above the door when Matias sent me for the staff, and when I press it—oh *skyfall*—the huge statue in the middle of the fountain starts to break in half.

It swings open like it's hinged on the far side, a low divide keeping the water from flowing into the new space it's created. Inside the open statue is a set of stone spiral stairs leading down.

Elkisa and I both twist around, she rising to her feet, as we try to check the courtyard from every angle. But we're unobserved, which means there's no time to waste.

I set down my mop and broom, but keep the spearstaff, scooping up the cat in my other hand, and wading out across the fountain. The water spills in over the top of my boots, stingingly cold, and my feet are wet in seconds.

I step carefully down into the spiral staircase, then take another step, making room for Elkisa to follow me. She presses a switch beside her, and the statue silently closes once more, leaving us in total darkness until I switch on my chrono. It's a slow, cautious journey down a very steep, very tight spiral staircase with a low roof that keeps us constantly stooping. I can't bend down to let go of the cat, so I jam my elbows against the center pillar and the wall to my right, trying to make sure I don't take a tumble.

I lose count at fifty steps, and I think it's closer to one hundred when I finally see the floor leveling out in front of me.

The dust there has dried to show someone's footprints—the last person who waded through the fountain, I suppose.

How many centuries ago was that? Who were they, the person who came down here and left a footstep behind? One of my ancestors, perhaps, if my blood is needed to open this place. It's strange—but perhaps a little comforting—to think of someone from my line standing here so long ago. Did they ever imagine I'd be here?

I step into their footsteps and find myself face-to-face with a pair of metal doors. Elkisa reaches the bottom of the stairs, looking past me at them, waiting for me to push them aside.

But I'm not quite ready yet.

"I want you to promise me you're going to try and keep Nimh alive," I say softly. "Before we go in there. Whatever we find, promise me that."

"I want her safe too," she replies, meeting my eyes. "That is no lie. I only wish—I only wish I could speak to her and try to explain."

I find myself searching her face for signs of dishonesty even as a tiny part of me hopes not to find any. "I will promise you this: if we can figure this out, and if you come back to the temple afterward to face the consequences of what you've done, I'll make sure Nimh knows the part you've played in getting her back."

Her lips tremble a moment, and she blinks twice in rapid succession. The silence stretches out, my own heart thumping in my ears. I can't blame her for whatever internal struggle is taking place in her head—I'm essentially asking her to turn herself over to imprisonment, or whatever worse punishment they might have here for betraying the divine.

But if she really loves Nimh as she says . . . I *have* to believe any shot of redemption is worth what I'm proposing. She has to be able to come back from this.

Elkisa draws a slow breath, then inclines her head in a slow, graceful gesture. "I swear it will be so. I will return with you when we have finished here."

I let out my own breath, trying not to show the wash of relief that sings through me. I know I can't trust her—but I find myself *believing* her.

I nod back at her and then turn to push at the doors. They swing open silently, and Elkisa steps up to hold them in place while I go through.

My first step inside, something crunches under my foot.

I swing the light of the chrono down, and shattered glass glitters back up at me, broken into sparkling grains no larger than my fingernails.

Heart sinking, I lift my wrist and take in the rest of the space. We're in a large, round room with a domed ceiling. Murals of marching people make their way around where the ceiling meets the walls in a painted frieze, culminating in a painting that reaches all the way down to the floor on the far side of the room. There's a chest-high stone counter in the middle, facing us like someone's about to arrive for a shift at customer service.

Beneath the murals, there are sleek, elegant *electronic* display screens lining the walls. They stretch from either side of the doorway where we stand, sweeping around seamlessly to that big painting opposite us. They're like nothing I've ever seen down here—I'm not even sure I've seen something this advanced up above. With touchpads set below them, they look whisper-light, almost translucent. The design is so beautiful, so out of place hidden deep below part of Nimh's world, that it takes me a moment to understand the rest of what I'm seeing.

Every single one has been smashed to pieces.

"No. NO!" I think that roar is me as I stride into the room. "Not again, not—" Not another dead end. Not another. *Please.*

Elkisa stands in the doorway, face grim, as I kick the nearest console, then kick it again, focusing on the pain instead of my frustration.

A hand closes over my shoulder and jerks me back away, and I blink into Elkisa's face as she scowls at me. "You think more destruction is going to help us? Focus! Which part requires your touch to unlock?"

"How should I know?" I snap, trying to catch my breath.

"Then perhaps we should look," she says crisply, sounding way too much like an annoyed tutor. "Whoever did this may not have shared your ancestry. You may be able to do something they cannot."

I want to snap at her again, but I know she's right, so I grind my teeth and get to work examining every inch of the place for any sign that something of value escaped the destruction. The cat picks his way daintily through the carnage, fetching up under the large painting on the far side of the room.

And that's where I find it. Nestled in among the brushstrokes of some long-forgotten artist, a simple copper plate with a small indentation in the middle.

It looks exactly like the finger-pads at home. The ones I use to get into areas restricted to my family. Can the micro-needles possibly have survived all this?

"Elkisa," I say, taking a breath and pressing my index finger to it before I have time to wonder about all the ways this might go wrong.

Silently the mural slides aside, revealing a dark space beyond.

Then, slowly, the lights start to come on.

They begin in the ceiling closest to us, large circles of light illuminating with a soft *whoof.*

Then the next two turn on, and the next two, like a runway lighting up in the evening, ready for my glider to come in to land. The pattern's interrupted when a few of them remain dark, though, and a couple more flicker intermittently, blinking on and off in an uneven rhythm.

The room they illuminate is huge—it must take up the whole of the inside of the hill, longer than it is wide. The floor looks like polished concrete, and the walls are lined with what looks like opaque white plastic, which is gradually beginning to glow.

It looks far more like home than any place I've seen Below, but nothing about it sets me at ease. There's a layer of dust on the floor, and some of it has floated up into the air as the doors opened—it dances in the stuttering light, giving this place an unnervingly abandoned feel.

"W-w-w-ELLLLLCOME, PERMITTED USER." says a glitchy electronic voice, and I startle back, colliding with Elkisa. It's coming from somewhere up in the ceiling, though I can't see speakers. "P-P-LLLLEASE INPUT PREFERRED FORM OF ADDRESSSSSS." It drags out on the last word, the tone deepening and its voice flattening.

"Uh, me?" I ask, my voice sounding small in the huge space ahead of us. Beside me, Elkisa peers into the room for the source of the voice.

"PLEASE INPUT PREFERRED FORM OF ADDRESS," the voice says again, the words dragging out slowly.

"I'm North," I say, tentative. "Who are you?"

"WELCOME, NORTH. I AM THE OPERATIONAL REVIEW, ADVICE, AND COMPUTATIONAL LOGISTICS ENGINE. YOU MAY PREFER TO CALL ME ORACLE."

"What?" I breathe, going perfectly still.

"It cannot be," Elkisa murmurs, instantly alert, her gaze darting around the room. "Is the speaker here or is it a far-speech spell?"

I'm reaching back for Techeki's words, trying to recall what he told me about the Oracle of this world's stories. "The Oracle's story is about the Lightbringer," I say slowly. "The Oracle's version of the Lightbringer's tale was that the Lightbringer refused to end the world as he was supposed to and broke his heart in two—he left one part here and took the other to the sky."

"North, this is no time for old tales," she murmurs. "We do not know what dangers lie here."

My own heart is quickening, though, my skin prickling. I think Matias might say that this is *exactly* the time for old tales.

If the Oracle of their stories is some sort of computer—and if Inshara was right that this place offers a way up to the sky—then perhaps I've found the answer I've been so desperately searching for.

"Let's find out what it is," I murmur, trying to stuff my giddy hope back down inside myself, to be as wary as Elkisa warns me to be. I'm torn between wonder and utter disbelief. This thing is *ancient*. "I'll be careful. Let me speak to it a minute."

Elkisa makes a distrustful noise, but she doesn't stop me. Together we walk warily forward into the derelict room. Our footsteps echo back at us.

"It's good to meet you, ORACLE," I venture. "What's your function?"

"EDUCATION, INFORMATION, AND ADVICE," replies the glitchy voice. "MY MEMORY IS INCOMPLETE. INCOMPLETE. MY MEMORY IS INCOMPLETE. I WILL REQUIRE ATTENTION FROM YOUR ENGINEERING CREW AND MANUAL SYNC TO CORE MAINFRAME."

"I *told* my mothers I should have been an engineer," I mutter, but the joke sounds as nervous as I am. The cat walks in to join us, pushing against my legs in that way that means he wants to be picked up. I lean down and gather him up in my arms, trying to focus on his solid warmth instead of the rising excitement in my chest. I've been burned too many times by seeming leads in the old texts of the archives not to be cautious now, but even I can't deny this time is different.

"What do they mean?" Elkisa demands quietly, tension in every line of her body.

"It, not they. It's not a person. It's . . ." I search for an explanation that will work. Everybody Below is as intelligent as the people of Alciel—there are just things they've never learned about. Nimh never spoke down to me when she found me dumped in the middle of the forest-sea, though I must have seemed like a complete idiot. "It's like a scroll from the archives" is what I settle on. "Or like a whole bunch of scrolls. But you don't read it, it can speak out loud."

"A spell," she concludes.

"Technology I can't explain," I agree, thinking back to my first argument with Nimh about science and magic. "Elkisa . . . I think this could be the Oracle from the old stories."

"Impossible," she whispers. "It cannot have been here since the making of the world."

"But if it *was*," I breathe, "then perhaps Inshara was right. Perhaps there *is* a way home in here."

"Navigational systems offline," ORACLE reports. "No definition available for term: home. My memory is incomplete. Incomplete. . . ." Its voice slowly fades out as the last word trails away.

I wince, glancing around at the abandoned facility. There's nothing here to tell me how to proceed—just blank walls staring back at me, failing lights, and unexplored shadows. "ORACLE, do you have any diagnostics available for your system damage?"

"My memory is incomplete," it repeats. "My systems are functioning at seventy-eight percent below acceptable levels. Please initiate manual sync with mainframe."

"Mainframe?" There's no reply except that two of the overhead lights go out, and the room grows a little dimmer. My hands curl into fists and I force them to relax. I'm *not* letting go of this chance. "We'll try another way, then," I say. "Do you know the *cause* of your system damage?"

"THREE CAUSES. I HAVE. I HAVE BEEN. MEMORY INCOMPLETE. CAUSE ONE: I HAVE BEEN IN LOW-POWER MODE FOR AN EXTENDED PERIOD. MY RECORDS INDICATE THAT IT HAS BEEN ONE THOUSAND AND SIX YEARS SINCE MY LAST MAINTENANCE, THE PROGRAM HAVING CEASED FORTY-EIGHT YEARS AFTER THE SECOND EXODUS."

For a long moment I simply stare at the abandoned room around me, my mouth open—but I have no words. *One thousand and six years.*

This room has been sitting here—this computer has been sitting here—for over a *thousand years*, waiting for someone to come along and talk to it?

How is it still functioning at all? What kind of world does it remember?

And how do we even begin to explain what it's missed?

"One thousand and six years," Elkisa whispers, sinking slowly to her knees. She covers her eyes with her hands, as I've seen Nimh's people do before her, and her breath catches and shudders. I think she's crying.

"I . . ." I stall out on the first attempt and have to try again. I can't let myself think too hard about the span of time ORACLE's been waiting here, or what it means. I have to keep moving forward. "Okay, I, uh. That's a lot longer than I expected. I guess I—Well, first things first. You said there were three causes for your system damage. One was waiting a millennium for someone to perform maintenance. What are the other two?"

"THERE MAY BE MORE," it replies, the words stuttering, the lights above me flickering. "MY MEMORY IS INCOMPLETE. I AM FUNCTIONING BELOW CAPACITY. CAUSE TWO: SENSORS REPORT A FUEL SHORTAGE OCCURRED FOURTEEN DAYS, SEVENTEEN HOURS, AND TWENTY-FIVE MINUTES AGO. THERE WAS. THERE WAS A SURGE AND ABRUPT REDUCTION IN PARTICULATE MATTER."

"Particulate matter?"

"DESIGNATION: MATTER INDIGENOUS TO THE SETTLEMENT TERRAIN, OR M.I.S.T."

"The—wait. *Mist?*" A part of me wants to laugh. I guess the scientists who designed this computer—the ones who discovered the mist—weren't so different from the ones I knew at home. They do love a clever acronym. In a strange way, it makes them seem more human. More real.

"AFFIRMATIVE, IT IS COMMONLY REFERRED TO AS MIST."

I'm intrigued by the words—*settlement* and *indigenous* make me wonder if ORACLE's teams came here as explorers. From a place *without* mist. It certainly lends credence to the idea that it might know how I could travel elsewhere—that it might have a connection to the Ascension.

My skin's prickling, though, at the strangeness of the idea. How far would we have to go to find a place free of mist? Could the great mountains to the east provide some kind of barrier? Or the ocean beyond that?

"What is it saying?" Elkisa says softly, climbing to her feet, still shaky.

I turn to her, leaving my questions aside for now—I have no idea where to begin. With its thousand-year wait? With the revelation that there may a land without mist, one that might be safe for Nimh's people without her here to protect them? The cat shifts in my arms, gazing up at me as though he's waiting for an explanation as well, and he thinks I'm taking too long.

"It needs mist to run, and it can't get any," I tell them.

Elkisa breathes out slowly. "The Graycloaks have surrounded the city with sky-steel to keep the mist out. The mist fuels its magic?"

"I'm guessing so. The mist runs the engines—the machines—that keep my home in the sky. What's the third cause of your system damage, ORACLE?"

"CAUSE THREE: DAMAGE BY AN UNAUTHORIZED USER," it replies.

Elkisa and I look at each other. Then she glances over her shoulder, and I can't help but do the same, taking in the shadows with a new wariness. I fight the urge to take a step back toward the door. "Can you elaborate on that, ORACLE?"

The nearest of the glowing white walls is suddenly brightly illuminated, and we both startle. The surface of it—it looks like plastic—is covered in a web of cracks. Perhaps the material shifted and contracted over the centuries it waited here.

All the other screens dim as that one bright section of the wall turns into a screen, displaying footage of the anteroom we just came through. There must be a hidden camera somewhere within the frieze of marching figures that links the door to the mural.

We watch in silence as the footage blinks and shakes, turns to static for a moment, then flickers back to life again. Now the anteroom is half-destroyed, and there's a figure swinging a stick at one of the display monitors, which shatters, glass cascading to the ground.

The figure turns toward the camera, mouth moving as though she's shouting, and there the footage freezes, her face screwed up in fury. Then it cuts out, and the wall is simply white once more. The light fades to nothing, and the room seems dimmer, closer than it was before. Low in his throat, the cat makes a growling noise that makes the hair on the back of my neck stand up.

"Inshara," Elkisa breathes. "Before she went to the sky. I did not know she had come here."

"Do you know why she was here?" I ask ORACLE.

Two more lights at the far end of the room go out, and there's a long pause before it replies.

"She requested access to the Exodus colony," it replies. "She was not an authorized user."

"You mean she wanted to go to the islands in the sky?"

"Correct."

"And do you—" I can barely get the words out. I close my eyes against the hope that tries to catch alight inside my chest. "*Do* you have a way? To the Exodus colony?"

"No," ORACLE says simply, and the breath goes out of me as if I've been punched.

"No?"

"Memory incomplete. I am. I am. I am operating seventy-eight percent below acceptable capacity. Travel may be possible, given the proper resources."

Beside me, Elkisa makes a soft sound. I can't help taking a step forward, though of course it doesn't get me any closer to the voice issuing from the ceiling. "What resources?" I demand. "ORACLE, this is . . . If I'm your authorized user, then this is my top priority. What do we need to do to get to the sky?"

All around us the room suddenly shifts—the white, glowing walls down either side begin to slide, retract, and fold in on themselves—one catches, dragging across the floor with a screech, and then stops short. Clouds of dust rise all around us, dancing in the light like a mist-storm, and Elkisa and I both cough as it catches in our throats.

As the dust begins to drift toward the floor once more, I see the room is larger than it was before. Almost all the walls have retracted, except for the one that broke halfway across, and those at the far end of the room, where the outside of the hill must be.

To our left and right are what I can only describe as . . . offices? There's a divide between the bays laid out along the sides of the room, and each forms a U-shape, monitors and panels of instruments laid out so that the operator at its center could access them all simply by turning around. There are even uncomfortable-looking but no doubt ergonomic chairs sitting in the center of each one. They remind me of the control station for Alciel's train network, which I visited once with Saelis and one of our tutors. But nowhere can I see the rooms that would hold the computer's hardware—memory banks and servers and cooling rods, all the bells and whistles I'd expect to see in a computer station back home.

173

The workstations are empty and clean, and the silence is eerie—suddenly I can see how busy this place once was, and it only makes the quiet all the more pronounced. It's as if the ghosts of those who used to work here a thousand years ago were around us all along, and suddenly they've stepped forward into the light. I feel . . . watched. I wonder what they'd make of me, a thousand years into their future.

"What was this place?" I murmur, and Elkisa echoes the query beside me.

"THIS FACILITY WAS USED MOST RECENTLY FOR THE PLANNING OF THE SECOND EXODUS," ORACLE says. "MY MEMORY OF THIS PROCESS IS INCOMPLETE. MY MEMORY IS INCOMPLETE. THE RESOURCES YOU HAVE REQUESTED ARE LOCATED IN THIS BAY."

A green light appears on the ceiling most of the way up the room, shining down to form a spotlight on the floor outside a bay that's blocked from view by its dividing wall.

I take a few steps, then break into a jog, tired muscles protesting. Elkisa's right beside me. Our footsteps echo around the room once more, dust kicking up, and then we slow to a stop as we approach the green light.

This bay isn't occupied by a workstation.

There's a machine inside it, about twice as long as my glider, much bulkier, but unmistakably related. Elegant wings sweep back from a snub nose, and I see the windows that mark a cockpit. It's covered in dust, the silver surfaces tarnished and blackened, but I know what I'm seeing.

This is an aircraft.

Suddenly I'm moving, running forward to stretch up and press a hand to its nose, like I need to check it's real, my breath coming quick and uneven, my heart trying to beat its way out of my chest.

"ORACLE, is this craft capable of travel from the surface to Alciel?"

"THEORETICALLY, YES."

I'm dizzy with relief. My glider had no way to rise from Below, but if this craft has propulsion . . .

This thing can *fly*.

It can take me home.

"What resources do you need?" I demand, whirling back to face the rest of the room. "How do we get it in the air?"

"FUEL IS REQUIRED," ORACLE replies.

"You mean like your fuel? It needs mist?"

"AFFIRMATIVE."

"Okay, how much?"

"I AM UNABLE TO ADVISE," it says, continuing before I can shout a protest. "MY MEMORY—"

"Is incomplete, yes, I know! ORACLE, this is life and death. Tell me what you *do* know."

"I CANNOT OFFER A VIABLE SOLUTION. MANY OF MY FILES ARE INACCESSIBLE DUE TO DAMAGE AND LOW POWER. I AM OPERATING SIGNIFICANTLY BELOW ACCEPTABLE CAPACITY. I REQUIRE REPAIR BEFORE I CAN ADVISE FURTHER."

"Can you instruct me on repairing your systems, then, so you can advise me on how to make fuel for the aircraft?"

"Negative."

"Dammit!" I barely restrain myself from thumping my fist against the aircraft.

"North," says Elkisa. "Explain the words I did not understand." It's more a request than an order, but barely.

"This craft can take us to Alciel," I begin.

"That much I understood."

"But—you know the keystones that the riverstriders use to power their boats? It needs fuel, like that. Like wood for a fire. Only there is none, and ORACLE can't tell me how to get it, because . . . the ink on its scrolls has faded. We have to restore them, first, so it can remember. But it doesn't know how to restore itself either. And nor do I."

"Then we must find another craft," she says simply. "One that will operate. Your people cannot all have sailed to the sky in such small boats. There must be other ways."

"Do you wish to authorize this user to submit queries?" ORACLE asks.

Elkisa meets my eyes. This alliance between us is new and delicate, and whatever promises she's made, her loyalty is to Inshara, not me. The best way to stay safe around her is to be the only one who can communicate with this machine she needs.

So after a long moment, I shake my head. "No," I say slowly.

Something flashes in her eyes, and I can't quite read it, but I stow it away for later.

"But please answer that query," I continue. "What information can you provide on how and why the Exodus, uh, members, went up to the sky?"

"Initiating educational program," ORACLE replies.

And suddenly a man stands directly in front of us, and my heart skips a beat. He's dressed in black and teal, his hands folded behind his back. He has the pallid white skin of someone who rarely ventures outside, dark hair with a bald spot on top, and a superior expression.

"Where did—" I begin, and then he flickers and wavers, before regaining his solid appearance. He's a hologram.

"What spell is this?" Elkisa demands, body tense and ready for action.

"It's a kind of storytelling program—er, spell," I say, my eyes on the man. His resolution isn't *quite* right—there's something eerie about his stare, and he doesn't blink often enough. "We have something like him at the Academy."

"Welcome to History Lesson 9F," he says, in a slightly nasal voice, using the clipped tones of a man who's very proud of his elocution. His image flickers again, and he repeats that same phrase. "Welcome to History Lesson 9F. Today we will learn about the Second Exodus."

"There was more than one Exodus?" Elkisa asks, her eyes wide.

"I—I don't know," I tell her.

"Do you wish to suspend the program and undertake History Lesson 9B?"

"No," she says, waving a hand in a way that momentarily reminds me of Nimh. "Continue."

The tutor pauses, gazing into space vacantly, until I remember she's not an authorized user. "Continue," I repeat, and he turns toward us with a too-bright smile. His face wasn't built for smiling.

"In order to understand History Lesson 9F, we must first refresh ourselves on the content of last week's History Lesson 9E," he says, adopting a cheery tone that doesn't sit well over his austere mannerisms—almost like an Academy professor being forced to teach tiny children. It's jarring, too full of energy for his disapproving face, and unsettling against the backdrop of the dark, ancient facility. "Let us commence. Lesson 9E: All About Mist! The mist is all around us all the time, like the air we breathe. And all of us are interacting with it all the time! But a few of you may have discovered by now that you have special ways of interacting the mist: you can use it to do *magic*."

He waits, as if expecting a chorus of "ooooohs" to arise. I glance at Elkisa, who looks back, her eyebrows raised—so I say, somewhat belatedly, "Uh. Yes. Yay, magic?"

The virtual teacher's brow furrows, making no effort to hide his disapproval. He starts to speak, but glitches halfway through, his uniform flashing briefly from teal to crimson, and then back again. "Hmm. Well, what you may *not* know is that even those of you who can't perform magic are still able to use the mist. You're all channeling it, right now. Do you know what *channeling* is?"

"Oh. Uh . . ." I blink at him. "Pouring it into something?"

The teacher sniffs, flashing me a look that tells me he's just mentally lowered my final grade.

"Just tell us what you mean to tell us!" Elkisa demands, her hands balling into fists, her stance ready, as if she might try fighting the hologram in a moment.

He flickers in and out of existence, blinks twice, and begins to speak with a kind of manic energy. "Information! Yes! While a few people can use the mist on purpose to perform magic, the rest are all channeling it subconsciously—that is, without realizing it—into whatever they believe in."

"Can you give me an example of that?" I ask.

"You will see two in today's lesson," he replies, before glitching again. "Now we must hurry, or we will be late for the announcement of the treaty resolution! The moment the Second Exodus was birthed!"

"How can we be late for something that's already hap—"

With a grand gesture, like a showman unveiling a masterpiece, he throws up his hand. All around us the abandoned **ORACLE** facility starts to vanish, overlaid by holographic scenery. Giant chunks of the image are missing, though, and I can still see the dilapidated walls through the holes.

The parts of the projection that are working make it look like we're outside, even though the air still has that stale, indoor quality of a space long sealed off. We're standing on a dais in front of a huge empty square, and when I swing around, I see we're on a hill that rises from the center of a long, narrow valley, steep slopes climbing to either side of us.

Beside me, Elkisa turns in a slow circle. "It's the temple. This is where the temple should be," she says slowly, softly, and I realize she's right. For now, there's just a large, low building behind us.

Nobody on the dais seems to notice we're there, and a woman dressed in red steps forward. Camera drones are hovering around her in a slow, bobbing orbit, capturing her from every angle. Lights click on, artfully illuminating her, their tint subtly changing as she moves. Even knowing my ancestors came from this place and this time—that there must have been tech here for them to bring with them—it's jarring to see it in a place I've only ever seen lit by torches and spellfires.

The woman in red raises her arms to signal to a crowd she wants their attention—but there's nobody in the square below. I stare at her, and for an instant I see Nimh in her place, the setting sun turning her robes to fire.

When the woman speaks, her voice is amplified, and as she speaks, the crowd begins to appear—it's patchy at first, square sections popping into existence, the algorithm beneath all this glitching and jerking as it tries to render all the individual figures. It's uncomfortable—hard to watch for any length of time.

"I have come to announce that there has been an accord," she announces. "There has been too much bloodshed, too much pain, too much uncertainty in this place—we can no longer pretend to live together in peace.

"And so we will part ways. There will be no further violence. We will put an end to the growing war between our factions by forming two worlds.

"One will be here, below, wreathed in mist and magic. The other will be above, leaving magic behind, turning instead toward that which we create with our hands and our minds.

"At the heart of each society will be our proudest, boldest

tech—two creations that could only have come from the unique beauty of our world and the ingenuity of all its citizens. We have worked with ORACLE to create this tech—these two hearts."

"The two hearts from the story," I whisper.

"One to the sky and one below," Elkisa murmurs. "To create the world as it is now."

The red-robed woman is still speaking, her voice ringing out. "One heart will allow those of us above to channel the mist into our engines, keeping our new home aloft by our very belief that it will be so.

"Those below will channel their belief through their own heart and into the creation of one magician beyond any we have seen before. One who will protect and guide them, who will meet the needs of their time, whatever they may be, strengthened by their people's faith."

"The divine," breathes Elkisa, her eyes wide. I wasn't sure she'd been following, but this much she unquestionably understands. "The divine manifests the aspect of the harvest when times are lean. Music, when all is well." Her voice catches, and she closes her eyes. "Healing—Jezara—when the world is dangerous. And nothing at all when faith wanes."

"They chose," I murmur. "Some chose science, some chose magic. They created a world for each. They created their worlds, just like the Oracle said. The old story must have been some sort of record from this place."

"We will never truly be parted," continues the woman in red, raising her voice once more. "In each society will be a failsafe against times of need—a pair of keys that will unlock the way between worlds. Those above will encode it in the DNA of their elected leader. Those below, in their chosen magician, as they—"

Abruptly the vision is gone, and Elkisa and I are left blinking at the white light of ORACLE's chamber. All the lights are stuttering now, failing one by one.

"ORACLE, what did—"

"You cannot—"

The cat's yowling—I don't even know what just happened from his point of view, whether his eyes could see the simulation at all.

ORACLE speaks over our protests, its voice rising and falling without warning, words dragging like music on a player with a dying battery. "LOW POWER WARNING. LOW POWER WARNING. NOW OPERATING AT EIGHTY-NINE PERCENT BELOW ACCEPTABLE MINIMUM CAPACITY."

"What just happened? It was at seventy-eight before!"

"EDUCATIONAL PROJECTIONS DRAIN POWER AT AN UNACCEPTABLE RATE."

"We just cost eleven percent of your power? Why did you play it if it was going to drain your reserves?"

"MY MEMORY IS INCOMPLETE."

I groan. "Of course it is. Forget the tutor. If we can't use that aircraft to get to Alciel, then our question is just this: Is there any other craft available we could use?"

"MY MEMORY IS INCOMPLETE. POWER WILL CONTINUE TO DRAIN WITH EXPONENTIAL SPEED. I HAVE BEEN UNABLE TO PERFORM A REMOTE BACKUP. MY CALCULATIONS ARE INCOMPLETE. I

PROJECT THAT EVEN AT THE LOWEST POWER USAGE LEVELS, I HAVE NO MORE THAN THREE DAYS REMAINING."

My heart stutters. "Three *days*?"

There's a soft hum, and just behind us a white pedestal rises from the floor, though I didn't see any seams when I walked past that place a moment ago. Slowly it pushes up from the ground, then with a grinding noise, it stops.

There's a small half circle on top of the low column, and as Elkisa and I swing around to watch, the little dome retracts to reveal a thin . . . bracelet, maybe?

"MY DATA STORE IS AVAILABLE TO AUTHORIZED USERS," ORACLE says. "PLEASE WEAR THE BAND AROUND YOUR WRIST."

I reach for it, sliding it on over my wrist. It's made of a cool black metal I don't recognize, with a green crystal set into it, traveling about a quarter of the way around the circle. My skin tingles as it tightens to fit me, and the crystal momentarily glows.

"AUTHORIZED USER RECOGNIZED," says a tiny voice from the bracelet.

"THE BAND CAN ANSWER LIMITED QUERIES," ORACLE says. "LIMITED. LIMITED. MY MEMORY IS INCOMPLETE. YOU CAN COMMUNICATE WITH ME THROUGH IT UNTIL MY POWER STORES ARE DEPLETED."

"But if we can power you," I protest. "If we can get you some fuel, some mist, can we—"

I'm cut off when an alarm abruptly sounds with a low blare, like a foghorn, and all around us the lights turn red, then break into fractal patterns, wheeling over the room and casting ghastly bloodred shadows.

"ORACLE? What's happening?"

It responds with a burst of static, and then it speaks. "Cat-astrophic mainframe failure underway."

"What?" I cry. "But you just said we still had time——"

"Calculations underway," it replies, and it's only when my shoulder bumps against Elkisa's that I realize both of us have instinctively drawn closer to each other. Then a series of needles sink into my leg, lightning fast, and a second later the cat's in my arms, his fur standing on end.

The three of us stay perfectly still as the lights wheel around us, and the alarm blares so loud I can't imagine how the whole city isn't hearing it.

Then, suddenly, everything is utterly still, utterly silent.

No lights, no alarms.

"Catastrophic mainframe failure underway," repeats ORACLE, calm as ever. "Stabilization is not possible."

"ORACLE, please elaborate," I say, fighting to keep my own voice anywhere near calm.

"Visual confirmation is available," it says, and at the very far end of the room, up past the aircraft, there's a soft hiss. White light outlines a rectangle the size of a doorway. Wait—it *is* a doorway. And that's daylight beyond it.

As one, Elkisa and I start to run.

ELEVEN

NIMH

I stumble along the corridor, mind reeling. My skin aches where the cuffs rest, my thoughts sluggish, my body seeming not to respond to my orders to keep walking. My memory keeps replaying it over and over, the moment when Inshara tossed a pair of gleaming manacles at my feet, linked by a short chain.

"Put them on," she demanded, eyes never leaving my face. When I failed to move, she smiled, and gestured over her shoulder.

The queen, getting to her feet more quickly than I would've thought possible in her sluggish state, seized Saelis by the arm and drew the ceremonial dagger at her waist.

Ceremonial, perhaps. But also sharp and gleaming.

"Put them on," Inshara said again, smile still in place as she gestured to the manacles.

And then, the blinding shock as the metal closed around my wrist, and the realization hit me: *sky-steel.*

Only now, as I try desperately to regain my equilibrium while the guards escort us to whatever prison awaits us, do I wonder: *Why didn't she just touch me and put the chains on me herself?*

A sharp shudder of the ground sends all of us—me, Miri, Saelis, and the guard escorting us—reeling into the wall. My head strikes stone, cushioned slightly by my hair, and I stay there, leaning against the cool rock for support.

"Yorsa, you *know* us." Miri gasps, her voice penetrating the fog in my mind. "We're not traitors!"

The guard—whose name must be Yorsa?—is just behind us, fear writ plainly across her features. Still, she shakes her head, wild-eyed. "I can't betray the queen," she protests, swallowing hard. "I don't know what's going on, but—"

Another quake interrupts, her words ending in a cry of alarm as Saelis goes crashing to the floor. Miri drops to her knees next to him, and then looks up at the guard, her eyes flashing. "That wasn't the queen!" she hisses. "I know you know that. Skyfall, any cloud-brain would know it. Something's very wrong. That woman is controlling her somehow."

Yorsa closes her eyes, removing her uniform hat and running a hand over her close-cropped hair. "I—I swore an oath . . ."

"You can drop your oath over the rim for all I care!" Miri bursts out, her frustration flaring.

"Miri," groans Saelis, accepting her help to sit up. "It's not her fault." He looks up at the guard, bracing himself as another tremor ripples through the corridor. A fine rain of dust and chips of stone patters down on my head, but Saelis just regards the woman calmly. "You swore an oath to serve the throne, right? If you accept that Beatrin isn't herself—that Inshara is affecting her somehow—then the Dawes Proclamation holds. If the monarch is unable to carry out their duties, their heir may temporarily step into power as necessary."

"But the prince—"

"Is alive." Saelis's voice is firm and calm. "North would want you to help us. She"—and Saelis tips his chin in my direction—"is the only one who can stop whatever's happening to the engines."

As if on cue, the ground quivers again. Yorsa groans and looks over at me, eyes pleading. "You can stop this? Really?"

I open my mouth, but before I can speak I can see both Miri and Saelis, behind the guard, nodding frantically at me. I swallow and amend what I'd been about to say. "I can. But not while I am chained by sky-steel."

I can see the word means nothing to the others. Yorsa, still hesitating, closes her fingers around the hilt of the ceremonial sword at her side, her knuckles white.

"I will take responsibility for them."

The voice comes out of a dark doorway several yards down the corridor. For a moment my heart seizes, but then its owner steps out.

"Talamar!" gasps Miri with relief.

"We have to get Nimh away from here," he says, striding up to us and stooping to help pull Saelis to his feet. "If we can get her far enough away, maybe she'll stop affecting the engines."

"How do you—" Saelis begins.

"I was listening," Talamar interrupts. "Hidden, in case you

couldn't get Beatrin to see reason." He takes a breath, his face grim. "It seems I was right to do so. Come, guardsman, the key."

Yorsa stiffens, though I can see the relief in her gaze at the thought of us not being her responsibility anymore. "I have to see them to the prison—my orders were to escort them personally away from the palace. And I'm not allowed to unlock them, especially her." Her eyes swing toward me, nervous.

Talamar's face darkens, and for a moment I feel a strange shiver, seeing North's eyes so chilly. "Fine, then," he says finally, his frustration evident, though he manages not to shout at the guard trying to do her sworn duty. He pauses just long enough to lift his breather, inhaling the medicine for his weakened lungs. "Come with us. We'll put them on the royal train, instead of locking them up somewhere here—they'll stay chained, but they'll be moving as far away from the mainframe as possible. You can message the guards stationed at the other end to be ready for them."

Yorsa hesitates, but when another shake of the island sends another round of detritus raining down from the ceiling, she nods and straightens. "Let's go."

Talamar leads us to the end of the corridor and up an ancient set of stairs, though a series of adjoining storerooms, and then out onto a gravel-lined path. The train station adjoins the palace grounds, a convenience for the royal family and their staff—and, just now, for us. The place is abandoned except for a few guards, who are milling about in confusion until we approach. One of them snaps to attention—the others seem to be too preoccupied with the intermittent shaking of the ground beneath their feet—and Yorsa hurries over to converse with them.

Talamar signals us closer with his chin. "I'm putting you on a train for my own island, which is about as far as you can get from the engine mainframe while still staying in the sky."

"You're not coming with us?" Miri's voice is higher than normal, fear and nerves jumping as the ground shivers.

"I have to stay and try to talk sense into Beatrin. If you can stop the engines from falling apart, then someone's got to stop what's happening here." His face is grim, eyes distant and tinged with fear even his skill at diplomacy can't hide. "This has to stop."

"Nothing I do affects the tremors," I say, now that Yorsa is out of earshot. "Calming down does nothing. And I cannot try anything magical with these on me." I lift my hands a little behind my back with a clink of steel chains. "They . . . they stop my magic, make me helpless."

"I'm hoping that just getting you far away will stop whatever's happening." Talamar reaches out, resting one hand on Saelis's shoulder and the other on Miri's. "Take care of her," he says seriously. "She may be our only hope against Inshara."

They nod, just in time for Yorsa to come hurrying back over, while the guard she was speaking to begins opening the gates to the platform, where a gleaming train waits at the monarch's disposal.

"Tell me you're not betraying the throne," says Yorsa, looking from Talamar to us. "Tell me I'm doing the right thing letting you on board."

"You are." Talamar straightens, and then moves as if to help escort us up to the trains, taking Miri's arm as Yorsa leads the way. "If we can release Inshara's hold over the queen, she herself will thank you for this, I swear it."

As Yorsa turns to key a code into the door on the train, Talamar makes a furtive gesture, pulling Saelis closer for a moment and then releasing him. The guard hurries us all on board, flashing one last, agonized look between us before the doors hiss closed, and the train's engines kick into gear, rising to life with a soft whine, though the carriage does not move.

Wasting no time, Miri hurries over to Saelis. "What did he give you?" she asks. She saw the same thing I did—Talamar pulling Saelis close enough to slip something into his hand, concealed behind his back.

Saelis turns, working the thing around in his palm until we can see it: Talamar's breather. For a moment, no one speaks—I glance between the others, baffled as to why he would have bothered to give us his medicine. Then I notice Saelis grinning.

"Skyfall," exclaims Miri. "Clever, clever man." Seeing my confusion, she explains, as Saelis starts turning the little machine over in his hands, prying a long metal pin from its casing to remove a panel and access its insides. "Our manacles are electronic—we can short-circuit them with the right tool, which we can make out of Talamar's breather."

"Get over here," Saelis calls, pulling out a bundle of multi-colored threads. "I need your nails to strip these wires."

Together, their bodies half concealing what they're doing,

they pull apart the breathing device, dropping its metal casing onto the floor and focusing on the machinery within.

I could cry with relief, and with a tiny flicker of something that would have been delight, if I wasn't so afraid. Of course North would be friends with a boy who can pick a lock.

They sit back-to-back so he can work—I have picked a lock or two myself, in my quest to chase down pieces of prophecy denied to me, but to do it without the ability to see? All I can do is wait, silently, and hope.

"Hold still," says Saelis, his face a study in concentration as he gets to work on Miri's manacles. I can tell she is barely breathing.

Then, with a sudden jerk, the train is underway—and in the same moment, Saelis is crying out, and the makeshift lock-pick is clattering to the floor.

"Sae, are you all right?" Miri demands, twisting around as he drops to his knees, trying to pick up the device from the floor, angling his body awkwardly. But I can see the same thing as her—it must have driven into his finger, for blood is pouring freely from a wound.

"Skyfall, it's too slippery," he mutters, trying and trying again. "I can't get hold of it." He pushes to his feet, backing up to one of the curtains, and pressing his hands into the rich fabric with a grimace, letting the blood soak in.

"It's still bleeding," Miri reports, looking over his shoulder.

"Then you'll need to try," he says, teeth gritted against his obvious pain.

"You gave me three lessons!" she protests. "And I wasn't even listening in one."

"Mir, life or death," he points out.

Without another word she drops to her knees, leaning back to grab the bundle of wires. He gives up on stopping the bleeding and turns back-to-back with her once more. His eyes closed, he describes each step to her, his voice low and steady.

My breath catches as she inserts one of the wires into the lock on his chains, the tip of her tongue protruding from one corner of her mouth.

If she can get him free, and he can help her, then maybe together they can get the sky-steel off me, and I can . . .

What? Stop the engine mainframe from melting down? Inshara implied that I'd set into motion something that could not be stopped. That Alciel was doomed, no matter what anyone did.

I can't feel anything with the sky-steel circling my wrists, as if its presence has robbed me of sight and hearing and touch— only I can still see and hear and feel. Some other sense, though, is missing, a sense I never quite knew I had.

The train is gathering speed, turning the landscape beyond its windows into a blur of green and milky-gray stone. The train shudders beneath us—I cannot tell if it's another quake, or just some side effect of the magic that keeps it levitating over the tracks—and then, abruptly, the landscape is gone and we're in the sky.

Miri is still concentrating on her task, her eyes on the ceiling as she navigates the lock by feel, while Saelis cranes his neck to try to look over his shoulder at what she's doing. Neither of them seem to notice the heartstopping shift from speeding across the land to being suddenly, impossibly, suspended in the clouds.

Unable to resist, I hurry to the window and lean close. Far ahead of us, I can see the tracks executing a gentle curve through the sky, vanishing into a bank of cloud. In the distance, a smear of gray green tells me of the existence of an island ahead, connected to the one we just left by a tenuous, tiny stretch of track.

The train gives another quick lurch, sending me into the glass of the window with a bone-jarring thud. Before I can pick myself up, my eyes detect movement out the window that makes me blink and try to refocus my eyes, certain I must be imagining what I saw.

The long sweep of track spread out before us is *moving*. Rippling, like a rope bridge suspended over a canyon.

Like a long bridge . . . just before it falls.

Miri lets out a laugh of triumph, and Saelis's manacles fall to the carpeted floor with a clank. He turns with a whoop of approval to throw the uninjured arm around her, making her squeak a protest, though she's laughing too.

For a moment, I cannot speak—I cannot bring myself to tell them what I've seen.

"Tell me," I croak finally, "wh-what keeps this track in the sky?"

Saelis lifts his head and looks over at me, blinking. "It's anchored at either end on the islands and held up with miniature engines at intervals along the track. The islands are kept at exact matching altitudes because their engines are synced up at the . . ." He trails off, the color draining from his face.

"At the mainframe." I finish for him, my heart and stomach sinking. "And what would happen if the mainframe stopped controlling their altitudes?" The unfamiliar words make sense to me in this moment, the urgency of the situation transcending my lack of knowledge.

For a moment, nobody moves. Saelis and Miri look from each other, to me, and back again, our eyes all meeting, the fear rising, no one willing to break the tableau. Then the train gives a sickening lurch, throwing us all to the floor, and everyone scrambles into motion.

Miri inches her way toward me, still shackled, one hand gripping their makeshift electronic lockpick. Saelis kicks his manacles aside and breaks into a run, grabbing a bar that runs along the ceiling and using it to help vault over Miri to my other side, where he starts working at the door to the train. His injured hand leaves great smears of blood on whatever he touches.

"There's a safety mechanism that means you can't open the doors while the train's moving." He kicks at the door at knee height until the outline of a panel appears, denting under the onslaught, and he drops to his hands and knees to start prying at it. "If we can get out of the train, maybe we can get back along the track before . . ." He doesn't finish the sentence, focusing on his task.

Miri grabs the chains linking my hands and pulls herself the rest of the way to me. The train shudders again, and I feel her curls brush my arm. Everything I am tells me to jerk away, but I hold myself still with ruthless willpower.

I remember Inshara grabbing my ankle.

Either she touched me, and I somehow retained my divinity, or she touched me and I am nothing. In this moment, I can't tell which—but divine or not, we *will* die unless Miri can get me free so I can work some kind of magic to save us before the train falls.

Saelis rips the door panel free, tossing it away before starting to pull out bundles of brightly colored threads. "How's it coming over there, Miri?" he asks, voice taut and anxious, as he starts tracing the threads with his fingertips.

"It's a different lock than ours, differently made!" she cries from just behind my shoulder, the manacles quivering—from her trembling or mine, I do not know. "It's not electronic. I think Inshara must've had these cuffs specially made."

My heart sinks, tears pricking my eyes. "She did. She made them from sky-steel. To stop me using magic if I ever tried to confront her."

"We need something stiffer—something metal, but small enough to fit in here." Miri turns, casting her eyes about.

Then something slams into me, knocking the wind out of my lungs.

Dazed, I lift my head—Miri has gone flying, hitting the far windows hard enough to crack them, tiny glinting lines spiderwebbing out from under her body. Saelis is nearby, clinging to one of the seats. For a moment, I can't identify the strange *wrongness* of it, until suddenly—horribly—I realize that Miri *lying* on the window, and I'm dangling from the leg curled around the bar, my head ringing from where it struck the seat back.

The train is tipped up on its side, only connected to one of the two tracks, careening around the corner.

Gasping, eyes streaming tears, Saelis inches toward Miri while I'm forced to watch, helpless. Holding on to a safety bar, he stretches out until his fingertips brush her manacled hands. She stirs, lifting her head, and then freezing when the movement causes the cracks in the glass to spread a fraction more.

"Grab my hand," Saelis gasps, his whole body one long line of tension.

"Wait—" Miri shifts her head again, carefully this time, to look up. Just beyond her head, lying on the glass, is the casing from the breather—and the pin Saelis pulled from it to open it.

"Forget it!" Saelis cries, following her gaze. "You're going to fall!"

"We're *all* going to fall if we don't get her free!" Miri retorts, her eyes wet with terror, but fixed on the narrow bit of metal—narrow enough, maybe, to fit inside the lock on my cuffs.

"Yes, I saw what she did in the tunnels, to the tramcar, but magic . . . magic doesn't exist! You can't just believe in someone you barely know, when what they're telling you is impossible!"

Miri's moving slowly, a fraction of an inch here, a tiny shift there, testing the way the broken glass creaks beneath her. She's bracing a foot against the window frame, trying to use it to stretch just the tiniest bit farther.

She pauses, her eyes finding those of Saelis, her tears spilling down across her temples. "You didn't see what I saw. Feel what I felt, when she grabbed me with that stuff. I saw North. I *felt* North."

"So?" demands Saelis, his voice pleading with her to stop, to reach for him instead of for the tool.

"Sae—*he* believes in her."

Miri's eyes move to meet mine, and for a moment, I see that look of North's there—that same aura of decision he had when he tied the red sash around his waist and chose my colors for his.

And then I also see her decision.

I have only time to shout a warning before she's moving, shoving off with the foot braced against the window frame, lunging for the little pin. Saelis moves at the same time, but his hand closes around metal and not Miri—the sound of shattering glass rends the air, which begins to roar, sending everything not bolted down screaming out of the broken window and into the empty blue below it—

A sob drags my eyes back from that gaping blue emptiness to find Saelis there, dangling from the manacles he'd kicked away—one side is locked around the safety bar, and he's clinging to the dangling end with one hand. The other hand is hooked around Miri's waist.

I let out a cry of relief as he gives a horrible groan, pulling himself—and Miri—back to relative safety inch by tortured inch, the muscles standing out along his arm, his face reddening with the effort. She goes limp in his grasp until he's got her close enough to grab the edge of the window—and then she's scrambling over onto the wall next to it as Saelis rolls back from the edge.

For a moment they lie there, tangled together, chests heaving, murmuring to each other frantic endearments and reassurances. I hear Saelis's voice rise briefly to say, "I could bloody well *kill* you!" before he kisses her soundly. He helps her up to her knees, and Miri looks up at me.

"I've got it," she says, turning so I can see her hands behind her back and the pin clutched between her fingers. "Can you get down here? We've got to—"

The sudden screech of tearing metal interrupts her, a stomach-lurching shift in momentum nearly dragging me from where I'm wedged against the seat. More shattering glass—the high-pitched whine of some kind machinery suddenly whirring out of control—a shudder that makes my bones ache—

And then nothing but the whistle of wind past the broken windows, and the twisting, shifting pull this way and that as the train car begins to spin in midair.

The train is falling from the sky.

TWELVE

NORTH

I clutch the cat against my chest as we sprint for the newly appeared door in the wall of ORACLE's chamber. Elkisa reaches it a moment ahead of me, shoving at it and sending it flying open. It must be set into the front of the hillside, because when we burst out, the valley and the city spread out below us.

Everything looks perfectly normal.

I run my gaze from one end of the valley to the other, along the length of the river, past the place where it divides to run to either side of the great rise the temple sits atop, all the way to the place it disappears from view between the hills.

Nothing. My heartbeat begins to slow.

"North," Elkisa whispers, her voice hoarse.

"Do you see something?"

She doesn't reply, and after a second I glance across at her. She's staring up, her mouth open, her face frozen.

For a long moment, I can't make myself follow her gaze. I just stand there, watching her, noting the smear of dirt at her brow, a tangle in her hair.

Then the cat shifts in my arms, and it's like he wakes me up. I wrench myself into action, tipping my head back, and . . .

. . . Alciel is falling from the sky.

Freysna, the largest island—my home—is in freefall. The smaller islands are following, the train tracks between them torn free of their moorings and trailing behind. I see a carriage plummeting toward the ground. How can this be? How can the engines I've known all my life—the engines that held us aloft a thousand years—have failed?

I hear a sound that I think is me, the sound of pain dragged from deep inside my lungs, as I stare helplessly at my home. Everyone I love is there—my mothers, my friends, my people . . . and Nimh.

And all I can do is watch as they fall.

THIRTEEN

NIMH

The train carriage gives a massive lurch as it tears away from the rest of the train, then starts to spin all the more violently, wind screaming past the broken window. Eyes streaming tears, I try to look for Miri and Saelis, and it takes me a moment before I spot them, wedged into the space between two seats opposite me.

Miri had been trying to get my attention, her voice carried away by the wind as we fall—*oh gods, we're falling*—and now that I'm looking at her, she makes a hurried, indecipherable gesture. Before I can think how to tell her I don't know what she's trying to say, she kicks off the back of the seat, and with Saelis's help, launches herself to my side of the train, hitting a safety bar with a thud that carries vibrations through to my own body, making me wince.

For a moment, I can't tell what she's doing—and then something grabs the chain linking my manacles behind my back, jerking at my shoulders painfully, and my breath catches.

She's still trying to unlock me.

Her knees hooked around the seat back, the pull of the train car shifting this way and that as it tumbles through the air, she's barely able to get the pin salvaged from Talamar's breather near the lock—because she's trying to pick a lock in a falling train while *still* trying not to touch me.

A memory flashes into my mind—I see North's face, stricken, staring at me with his heart in his eyes. We are on the cliffs near the back exit of Jezara's house, and in my despair over his failure to read the lost stanza of the prophecy, I have lost faith in my own divinity—in my own worth, without it.

Which is worth more, I asked him, *my divinity or my life?*

That look on his face—that horror that I could ever not know that the answer to that question was *me,* my life, that anyone had ever made me believe different—flashes before me now.

Enough.

"You cannot do it without holding on to me," I shout over the wind, straining to be heard.

Over my shoulder, I see Miri's head crane around, her eyes wide with desperation. "Are you sure?" she yells back.

"Yes!"

Inshara touched me once, and I am still here. Her touch won't rob me of magic, only my divinity, and perhaps that is gone already.

But there is a chance that, at least, I will be able to save their lives.

Her body bumps up against mine and I close my eyes, trying to take myself somewhere else, trying to hold still. A moment later Saelis joins us, helping to hold Miri close to me, his other arm wrapped around my shoulders.

My instincts scream at me to squirm away, the feel of

someone else's body in contact with mine triggering a panic that transcends that of falling toward almost certain death.

I wanted it to be different. Somewhere else, some*one* else. Not Inshara, grabbing me in her last effort to destroy me, and not these two near strangers clutching at me in a desperate bid to save all our lives. I wanted that first touch to be something beautiful, something I could savor and replay, something that would last me the rest of my life.

I could not help but imagine it—some loophole that would allow me to be touched even just once without sacrificing my purpose and meaning to my people. Some ritual that required it, perhaps—a long-forgotten rite that would suspend that most sacred law of divinity for one hour, one night.

And then I imagined the Lightbringer, when I discovered the lost stanza of the prophecy; imagined he would come into our world, and he and I would help my people side by side, two divines.

And then . . . then I just imagined North.

North. His voice, warm in my ear; his fingers in my hair; his lips on my skin. The sensation of his fingers tying my robe at the Feast of the Dying, the warmth of his hand a breath away from my cheek on the riverstriders' boat, only magnified tenfold when the touch was *real.*

Behind my closed eyes I can almost see his face, almost remember him as if I had never lost those memories.

There is no fate, no prophecy, no pantheon of gods that could ever demand such a thing of anyone: to submit to death rather than be touched. To meet the other half of one's heart and never feel his kiss. To be promised divinity that transcends humanity, but only for one who lives her life as something less than human.

Enough.

Behind me, Miri gives a voice-cracking cry of triumph as something clicks, barely audible over the sound of rushing wind. My eyes snap open in time to see a horrifying jumble of green forest-sea close, *too* close, *oh gods*—

The manacles fall away—the touch of sky-steel vanishes, and I am blinded by mist—

I throw up my arms—

And the world goes white.

FOURTEEN
NORTH

Alciel is falling, the islands careening away from each other.

Freysna overhead is leaning at an angle, the palace like little more than a toy clinging to one end of the island. The engines are still firing, barely preventing the massive floating lands from simply dropping down, but they're gathering speed.

My feet are moving already, speeding down the hillside, my lungs burning.

The islands are on a trajectory to miss most of the city below, but the impact alone will be enough to destroy them—to snuff out every life up there, to scatter the remains of the city across the world Below.

I leap over the prone form of a man on his knees, praying, hands over his eyes. Elkisa's footsteps pound just behind me.

A piece of the underside of the main island breaks away, torn loose by the shifting, inconsistent forces of the misfiring engines. It drops, a boulder the size of a skyscraper, straight down onto the cliffs on the other side of the river. Debris and dust billow up in vast, silent clouds—until, a few seconds later, the roaring crash sweeps through the market streets.

I round a corner, straining for breath but refusing to slow, not sure where I'm going, except that I need to get to the place where my home is falling—I need to find survivors, get help, do something, anything.

Overhead, the massive land mass gives a groaning shudder. Time slows, gravity itself distorting. Everything seems to pause, as if the whole world is holding its breath.

Then, impossibly, the island *changes* direction. For a moment it seems like a trick of the distance, of the way it's moving.

A subtle shift and the palace is no longer tipped to one side, the pace of its fall no longer increasing. Still it drops, but it's as if some giant, invisible hand has reached down to save the city from destruction.

I careen to a stop, gasping, eyes blurring with tears as I stare upward, scarcely daring to believe what I'm seeing.

Slowly, with strangely conscious-seeming deliberation, the trajectory of the biggest island alters. Instead of moving away from the city, now it's coming straight for us—straight for the temple, moving not like a falling land mass, but almost like an impossibly huge glider or an aircraft out of fiction.

My hope tangles in my throat—I change direction too, sprinting now for the temple. Elkisa gives a shout of surprise, her footsteps scraping as she follows after me.

The island's fall slows, and slows again, until it's barely moving at all, time slowing to a crawl. The underside of Alciel is directly overhead now, one edge of it hovering above the temple, the rest of it spanning the river, the far end resting just above the hills and cliffs down the east side of the valley. For a single instant, all is still except for a resonant, ancient groaning

206

sound from deep within the stone.

And then—the temple *answers*.

The ground beneath my feet trembles as a higher keening sound emerges from the temple. I raise my eyes to see something happening at its peak, the top tier of its many layers moving as if in response to the arrival of my homeland. Long, massive steel spires unfurl from the temple's peak like spider's legs, spreading and reaching upward.

And then, with a sound that makes the cobblestones vibrate, Alciel *lands*.

Elkisa and I stand frozen, watching, trying to understand and absorb what we've seen: the cloudlands, her city of the gods, my *home* . . . landing atop the temple as neatly as if someone had parked it there like a tramcar.

The palace is still intact, resting almost directly on top of and alongside the top floors of the temple, the slope of the landmass mirroring exactly the slope of the temple's terraces. Though my mind can hardly process the sight of Alciel perched on the ground like some sort of massive glider in its hangar, a part of me can't help but think that it all looks *designed* to have worked this way.

The islands may have been falling at first, but something— or someone?—intervened. And my people are safe.

For now.

With a groan of effort, I break into a run again, gesturing to Elkisa. If there's a way into Alciel, it'll be through the temple that now adjoins the rim of the palace grounds. I have to get there before anyone else tries to get through—there's no telling what reception will be waiting for my people. It's one thing to believe your gods live on the floating island above you—another to stand peacefully by as they invade your temple. I *have* to be there first.

I have to see if Nimh is . . .

I round another corner—and crash, full-speed, into a merchant's cart laden with vegetables. My momentum knocks it over, and I go sprawling, and the weight of the wooden frame falls fully on my leg—only the strength of the sole of my boot keeps me from a crushed foot. I try to lever myself free and shout out for the merchant—but, faced with this last straw on top of the terror of what he's just seen coming out of the sky, he lets out a scream and bolts, joining the crowds of others running this way and that.

Elkisa comes skidding to a halt beside the cart, her eyes moving quickly, taking in the situation. She crouches, hands hovering over the frame. "Are you injured?" she asks, intent, her voice dry and hoarse with shock even as she readies herself to deal with the problem.

"No," I manage, wriggling my toes a little just to make certain I didn't miss the pain of broken bones in my own shock. "No, but I'm pinned. I can lift this side if you can get the other—on my count?"

Elkisa is still staring at the cart, her hands still hovering above the wood. Then her gaze shifts, her eyes meeting mine.

She doesn't speak—she doesn't need to. Understanding dawns in me like a bucket of ice water thrown over my head.

"Don't do this—" My voice is as cracked as hers now.

"Elkisa, don't—you promised you'd come back to the temple *with* me."

Elkisa doesn't bother to hide the struggle taking place behind her usually restrained features; or else she simply can't, the enormity of the choice taking her somewhere beyond her ability to hide what she's feeling. Her eyes shift again, going from me, to the temple steps, and back again.

"You told me you loved Nimh," I say, trying to hold her eyes, every fiber of my body concentrating on her, trying to summon every bit of persuasive power I've ever had. "That all this started because you wanted her to be free. This is how you get back to her. Don't choose this. Help me—come back with me."

Elkisa closes her eyes for one brief moment.

When she opens them, the flash of guilt and despair I glimpse there tells me her choice.

"Wait—" I cry. "Don't—wait!"

And then she's gone, sprinting away from the cart and vanishing into the crowd.

A shout bursts out of me, a scream of frustration to vent the anger not just at Elkisa's betrayal—but at myself, for ever being stupid enough to believe she meant a word of what she'd told me. My hands, balled into fists, pound at the cart for a few seconds—and then I rein myself in, trying to gather some semblance of calm to keep the panic of being trapped at bay.

I can still wiggle my foot a little, and after some painful attempts at contortion, I manage to slip one of my hands in under the cart frame to reach my boot laces and loosen them, my heart chanting at me every second to *hurry up, hurry up, hurry up.* I have to keep rocking my foot back and forth, the edge of the frame starting to bruise me painfully—but then, with a groan, I'm sliding free of the boot and scrambling away.

I circle the cart until I can see the boot on the other side—without the rest of me attached, I can pull it free and put it back on.

I give myself a second to breathe, telling myself to put aside the sickening tangle of emotions in my chest—I need to act now, not give in to anguish—and then set out for the temple steps again.

The city outside is in chaos—Nimh's people are running, hiding, some simply standing in the middle of the street and staring—and I weave my way through the streets at a dead run, all pretense at disguise forgotten.

After all, the sky has fallen.

One end of the island rests atop the peak of the temple in the middle of the valley. The other lies southeast, resting atop the hills there, so that its shadow draws a diagonal line across half the valley. The other islands, I think, are farther east, beyond the hills at the valley's edge.

When I reach the temple doors, I skid to a brief halt—for there, his tail curled neatly around his hindquarters, sits the cat. Only the urgently twitching tip of his tail betrays his distress, but still, he waits, staring at me, and at the empty door.

Too shaken to feel foolish about it, I tell him, "She's not coming. She chose Inshara."

The cat sneezes, rises to all fours, and breaks into a trot. I fall in after him, and when I quicken my steps to a run, he does the same, leading the way. We head for the stairs that will lead us higher, up toward where the edge of the palace grounds rests.

Up and up we climb, swinging around corners and racing down hallways—I know every stone of this temple by now, save the ones inside Nimh's hidden passageways, and guards, acolytes, and staff flatten themselves against walls to make room as I rush past.

Up and up, and then the hallway is narrowing further, and I'm climbing the final staircase, my breath rasping in my throat as I push aching legs up the stone spiral staircase, as high as the temple will take me—to the peak where I know the edge of my homeland rests.

I burst out into the room at the top and stop short.

Techeki is there already, along with half a dozen temple guards clad in black and gold. They're all staring at a huge, arched doorway that until a few minutes ago, looked out onto the empty sky. Now it leads to a swirling, seething mass of green-and-purple-laced quicksilver, like a mist-storm locked behind clear glass.

"I have to get through," I say, eyes still on the doorway, breathless.

"You must return to the gods," Techeki says, more solemn than I've ever heard him. When I look across, it's there on his face—the faith I've always known he had. The faith that's driven him to hold this place for Nimh, cutting deals with Elorin and her people, letting them into the temple, clinging to power in the raging river of the Graycloaks and the Deathless. "You must go through, North, and bring her home."

"Yes," I murmur, my throat closing around the word. "I'll tell them there's friendship here."

"Wait—Your Highness." A fraction of Techeki's formality falls away. "I don't know how you can get through safely. The mist is trapped here, compressed, suspended somehow. Pushed away by the sky-steel in the rivers but pressed down by the cloudlands. You must be careful."

I take a step forward, and as if it senses my presence, the mist slows and thins for an instant, giving me a glimpse of what's beyond.

I see two palace guards, ceremonial weapons in hands, standing and peering at the mist warily, like they're looking at a mirror they don't realize is actually two-way glass. They spot us at the same moment and jump back—I can't hear them, but I can see that they're shouting something. Then I see one of them mouth what's unmistakably my name.

She charges forward without hesitation, even as Techeki and I throw up our hands, crying out our own warnings. She makes contact with the mist, then goes flying back like she's touched a live power outlet, landing a body-length back from the portal and rolling. My heart nearly stops with relief when she sits up, bruised and shaking, but alive.

The other drops to one knee to check on her, and they exchange a few words, then he takes off at a run, disappearing out of sight.

I slip my fingers into my pocket, taking hold of my protection stone and drawing it out. It's seen me through other dangers—perhaps it can do this, as well. I keep it firm in my fist and move forward tentatively, my skin prickling with anticipation. The closer I get to the wall of mist, the harder it becomes to push forward, until I'm straining to move at all. It's like trying to sink my hand into solid rock. Then a sharp pain runs through my forearm, hitting the nerve in my elbow and sending pins and needles all the way up to my shoulder.

I yank my fist back with a yelp, running the other hand over it. My stomach drops as I realize it was the wrist with ORACLE's bracelet on it, but as if to reassure me, a small green light flashes on the display, then vanishes.

"Okay, not that way," I mutter, watching as the guard on the other side climbs slowly to her feet and makes vigorous signals that I interpret as warning me against touching the wall.

I nod, but I'm thinking about doing it again anyway, when suddenly there's a flurry of movement on the other side.

"Who comes?" asks Techeki, stepping up to my side, peering through the mist.

There are more guards, but then . . . *Oh.*

Then they part, and there stands my heartmother, Anasta. Her black hair is drawn back into a braided coil around her head, her creamy skin flushed with the exertion of her run here, brown eyes wide. Her eyes meet mine, and I see the moment she recognizes me, the moment she realizes I'm not some vision distorted through this barrier of mist. I see her mouth my name, her eyes fill with tears, relief making her legs buckle for just a moment.

Then she starts forward, and Techeki, the guards, and I all

shout a warning, the guard behind her limping forward to try and grab her arm before she can connect with the mist.

But before anyone can do anything to stop her, she simply plunges both hands into the mist and seems to almost grab hold of it, parting it like a pair of curtains. It shimmers around her hands, coiling through and around her fingers, which I can now see are decorated with a series of rings I've never seen her wear before, ornately cut red stones set in intricately wrought gold.

"Quickly, North," she says urgently, holding the mist at bay—I duck under her arm, and in an instant I'm through, and she's releasing it, swinging around to throw her arms around me.

My bloodmother, Beatrin, taught me to lead. She taught me to play politics, she taught me the determination that has kept me going down here. She taught me a thousand things that made me who I am, and she loves me fiercely.

But when I was small, I ran to my heartmother when I scraped my knee.

There's not some simple divide between them—hard and practical on one hand, sweet and soft on the other. They're both formidable. But there's not much in either world that I need more than one of Anasta's hugs right now.

She wraps her arms around my waist, and I bow my head to rest my forehead against her shoulder, and she's soft, and she smells like the berries that scent her shampoo, and all I want and all I need is for her to hold me.

But nothing lasts forever, and as is always the way with the two of us, I'm the one to break the silence, my voice muffled. "How did you *do* that?"

She lifts her head from where she has her face buried in my hair, and when I lift my head too, she smiles, keeping her arms around me and tipping back her head to speak to me. "The door is made up of mist from the engines, and something else as well, something I wasn't expecting. A different kind of barrier."

"There's a sky-steel barrier all around the city," I begin. "The Graycloaks—Wait, how do you know what mist is?"

"Our family knows many things, and I will tell you all of them," she promises. "But we have no time, North. Skyfall, I never thought I'd see you again." Her eyes are brimming, and she pulls me close again, her body quaking as she makes no effort to hide her feelings.

"Ma'am," says one of the guards, clearly nervous about interrupting a personal moment—he's edging forward in a way that suggests one of the others is pushing him from behind. Then his gaze swivels to my face, and his mouth falls open as he finally realizes who I am.

The relief and joy in his face robs me of breath for a moment—I'd been so focused on the feelings of my friends and family that I hadn't really stopped to imagine the fear and uncertainty my people must have been suffering, having lost their only heir to the throne, and my bloodmother well past childbearing age.

Anasta and I break apart, looking over toward the guards— and then for a moment I glance back the way I came. The mist is a slow-moving whirlpool now, and I can't see anything of the other side.

The cat must have come through with me, though, because he sits with his tail neatly curled around himself, waiting to see how all this unfolds, looking like exploring a new world—one in which he's the first cat in a thousand years—was already on his to-do list for today.

My heartmother takes a step back when her eyes fall on the creature—I wish I could pause to take in her wide eyes and shocked face, because in another moment it might be funny to see my own surprise at encountering the cat for the first time echoed in her face. But I just reach out and squeeze her arm. "He's a friend," I tell her.

We're in the palace grounds, I see now, near the outer wall. I can see my grandfather's flowers stretching away from us toward the palace itself, and behind me is an archway that usually has a metal grate across it, looking out into nothing. I used to stand here as a child, staring at the sky and dreaming of flying.

"Ma'am," says the guard again, tentative once more, his eyes still glued to my face. "Should we send word to the queen that Prince North has returned?"

Anasta silences him with a gesture, but the word has already gone through me like a knife.

Queen.

I stare at the guard, taking in the small details of his uniform. The gold braid at his shoulders. The tiny thread coming loose from the embroidery on his crest. Anything I can find to notice, as if a torrent of tiny details will somehow slow down the world enough to stop what's coming next.

"North," says Anasta, a world of sadness in her gentle voice.

And so slowly, so reluctantly, tears already starting to spill down my cheeks, I turn my head to look at her.

"Grandfather?" I whisper, knowing the answer.

"I'm so, so sorry, my love," she whispers in reply. "It was sudden. And we will grieve together, I promise—he is lying in the vault, and he will be there when it comes time to make your farewells. But now, we have no time. There are things we must do first, and they cannot wait."

It takes everything I have to force myself to nod my head.

I understand the sky cities have fallen. *Landed,* as if they were designed to, as if someone steered them somehow. I understand the world beyond the gate is in chaos. I know that I am the one who stands between the two, and I know that I have to—

But my grandfather is dead.

And I wanted to tell him that I tended to Nimh's garden.

I wanted to tell him about *Nimh.* And about Techeki, and Matias, about the cat, about the feasts and the rituals, about my journey along the river, about Jezara and about—

"North," says Anasta, with infinite patience.

"Nimh?" I croak. "Is Nimhara here?"

"Nimhara is here," Anasta replies quietly, though the guards are clearly straining to hear. "She has Beatrin, North. Tell me you know how to fight it, *please.*"

"What do you mean, she *has* her?" I ask, my heart surging. "Take me to her, please. I have to see her."

Anasta reaches out to lay a hand on my arm, drawing me

in close. "No, North," she says, so softly I have to bow my head to hear. "She has Beatrin under her control."

"What?" I just blink down at her. "That can't be right."

"Nimhara is dangerous," she replies.

"Take me to her," I say again. "Whatever's happening, I can fix it, I promise."

"I'm not permitted to enter the throne room," she says, glancing across at the guards.

For a long moment I simply gape at her, and then in an instant, I suddenly pass saturation point. The sky has fallen. My grandfather is dead. My bloodmother is being controlled by *Nimh*? Sure, okay. None of this seems like it can be anything other than a mist-vision, some kind of nightmare, so I might as well keep going at this point.

"I'm the crown prince," I say, raising my voice for the guards to hear. "And I'm going to see my mother. Let's go."

I grab hold of Anasta's hand, leaving the guards to protect the portal to the temple, except for the one who'd been so happy to see me—he strides out ahead of us, leading the way toward the entrance to the palace.

Beyond us, behind us, there are people thronging at the gates to the palace, which hang at odd angles from their hinges, shifted during the fall. Most of the crowd wear expressions of terror, gathering at the palace threshold in search of answers and comfort after Alciel's fall—but a few of the faces there are streaming tears, strangely fixated on us. I shiver and hurry on.

There are two more guards stationed at the side door we're heading for, both wild around the eyes, barely clinging to enough discipline to hold their posts, and I can't blame them for that. I remember how strange it was for me to look up and see the clouds so far away after I first came here. And I only fell in a glider—their whole world has crashed. They barely pay any attention to the cat, registering him as only one more impossible thing in a string of world-shaking uncertainties. Most of their attention is on me—their prince, risen from the dead.

"Y-Y-Your Highness?" one of them asks as the other yanks him out of the way.

"The prince lives," Anasta declares as I march past them, and then I'm inside my home, a place I thought I'd never see again.

I'm overcome by a rush of familiarity as we walk down the hallway together—the colors, the subtle scent of the place, the thick red curtains and the richly embroidered rug running along the floor ahead of us. So many small details that were invisible to me when I saw them every day, and that now suddenly add up to an overwhelming sense of *home*.

There are signs everywhere of the city's fall—a tapestry sprawled across the floor where it fell from the wall, shards of broken ornaments, a jagged crack across the ceiling. But the place has held together incredibly well, and when I turn the corner into the hallway lined with the portraits of my ancestors, I'm relieved to see they're all still in place, if somewhat askew.

I used to run along here as a small boy, playing with Miri and Saelis, debating which of the people in the portraits looked the most fun, which one was the most bored, which ones were keeping secrets, and what they were. Now I turn my face away from them, because I know the very last will be covered in black silk, and I can't let myself be weakened by that until I've found Nimh, until I've understood what's happening and made it right.

There are more guards at the door to the throne room, and they gape as Anasta and I approach, one slowly shaking her head, the other blinking furiously, as if his vision might suddenly clear.

"Ma'am, you can't—" the first begins, with obvious discomfort, holding up a hand to Anasta.

"Stand down!" snaps the guard who's escorting us. "Don't you see the prince has returned? Let him through at once!"

They hesitate a moment longer, exchanging glances, and eyeing my heartmother.

What has happened? How can Anasta not be allowed into the throne room?

"Hello, Prince North," I say loudly, forcing good cheer into my tone and ignoring my misgivings. "Glad to see you're alive, bet you've got a story to tell. We can't wait to hear it, but you'd better go see your mother first."

"Your Hi—"

I brush past, bringing Anasta with me, and make it several steps into the throne room on momentum alone before I begin to slow.

The room is as it's ever been, my grandfather's throne at the far end, with the always-empty one beside it that had belonged to my grandmother before she died. The walls are lined with murals and gilded scrollwork that make newcomers gape, though they've always been part of the scenery to me. I'm not looking at any of the decorations now, though, or taking in the guards who line the walls or the signs of Alciel's fall in the cracked floors and piles of plaster.

There's a cluster of advisors standing in front of the throne, blocking my view of my bloodmother and Nimh. I break into a run as my urgency overtakes me, shouldering my way through the crowd, ignoring their cries of alarm and surprise as I force my way to the front.

My mother is on the throne where my grandfather should be, staring at me with a furrowed brow. She doesn't rise to her feet or give any sign of surprise—or any sign she's noticed I'm here beyond the focus of her eyes on my face.

And then my words die in my throat, and the breath goes out of me like I've been punched in the gut, because on my heartmother's throne sits not Nimh, but Inshara.

For a long moment I simply stare, shaking my head, trying to deny what I'm seeing. Then the words burst out of me in an urgent demand. "What have you done with her?"

"Your Highness," says one of the courtiers, tentative, eyeing the cat and then edging backward even as he speaks. "The queen—"

"No," I say, my gaze still riveted to Inshara, who's enjoying my shock, her lips curving to a slow smile. "What have you done with Nimh, Inshara?"

She tilts her head, adding a note of curiosity to her smile. "I *am* Nimhara, Prince North. First of her name, Forty-Second Vessel of the Divine. I have guided your home safely to ground and reunited you with your people."

"No," I snap, wheeling around to Beatrin. "Mother, this woman isn't our ally, she's dangerous. You need to have the guards take her into custody *right now*."

"North?" My mother is still staring at me, as if my very existence seems impossible to her. Something about her eyes makes a chill run through me, making me take a step back. "No—this cannot be North. My son is dead. Only his grandfather's body lies in state in the vault—North was not here when he died." Her confusion clears—and, to my astonishment, her eyes fill with tears that gather and spill out onto her cheeks. I've never seen my bloodmother cry—and even now, there's something *off* about her tears. Her face doesn't reflect any emotion that could prompt them—if anything, she seems more remote and resolute than ever.

"Yes," Inshara confirms, though her eyes are on me and not on Beatrin. "I am sorry you have to go through this, Your Majesty."

The queen's gaze shifts to fix on Inshara, her eyes softening, her lips curving a little. "I'm not. I may have lost my son—but I have gained a daughter. It is no stretch to see that she makes a better heir than he ever did—she is devoted to my people, not to the pursuit of her own enjoyment."

My mother's words hit me like a blow, and I stagger back a pace, heart reeling. My mind is racing, trying to understand—and then I see Inshara watching us, her eyes aglow with that strange, eerie mist in their depths. It can't be possible—Nimh told me that magic couldn't be used to control people. Even when we thought we'd witnessed such a thing, when Elkisa killed Daoman the night of the Feast of the Dying, it turned out that Elkisa had been play-acting all along.

And yet . . . somehow, now, her power is *real*.

I start forward toward her, then . . . and then I stop.

And I stand there, staring up at the two women on the thrones. Leaders of two worlds.

I think.

Wait, is that right?

My mind's fuzzy, as if I'm trying to see through a swirl of mist, trying to think through a dream, and I can't quite remember what I was about to say, though I know it'll come back to me in a moment. My eyes are burning, as if with unshed tears, and I blink, distantly surprised to find my vision blurring.

I'll just stand here for a moment, though, while I wait to figure out what it was I forgot.

Then there's a sharp yowl beside me, cutting through the mental fuzz. It's the cat. Nimh's cat.

He is his own cat. I can almost hear her voice in my head, correcting me with a smile, and in that instant I remember that Nimh isn't sitting in front of me, she's somewhere else—and I need to find her. I remember something else too, and I slide my hand into my pocket, finding the protection stone wrapped up in red thread.

It's hot to the touch, and I curl my hand around it to make a fist.

Inshara's mist-touched eyes widen, then narrow, her expression twitching with badly concealed fury or frustration.

Whatever she just tried to do to me, it failed.

Thank you, Nimh.

"North?" murmurs Anasta behind me, and something in her voice makes me turn. The courtiers are backing away nervously, leaving the two of us alone as the guards along the walls start to move. Most move with reluctance, exchanging glances, torn between their sworn duty to Beatrin and their consciences and good sense. They *know* something is wrong, and they're not leaping at the thought of arresting their prince.

Then the guard who escorted us here, the one who'd been so ecstatic to see me, whirls around, gripping his weapon and looking between me and my heartmother.

"You had better come with me," he says, his voice halting, some kind of war going on behind his gaze. That passion is still there—but suddenly I've become its target. A threat, where just a few minutes ago I was the savior of the royal line, miraculously alive. "We must protect you, Prince North—we must lock you away, so nothing can ever happen to you again."

As I watch, tears begin to trickle down his face.

I take a step back, looking from him to Beatrin, who sits perched on the edge of her throne, intent on what's happening, urging the guard to carry on.

Only Inshara's eyes carry a spark of alertness as she watches, the corners of her mouth moving to suppress a smile.

She has the guard's mind now, as surely as she has Beatrin's.

"You can't let her do this," I say, swinging around to latch onto the courtiers and advisors who are still edging away from us. "The queen isn't in her right mind, this woman has . . ." But there I grind to a halt, because I have no idea what she's done to my mother.

Inshara heaves a sigh, her eyebrows rising. "Why do people keep flinging that same accusation at me?" she asks, of no one in particular. Then she snaps her fingers at the guards. "Do as your queen commands and seize him!"

Except for the guard with the tear-streaked face, the others all hesitate. Then one breaks, stepping forward with a gasp, her head dropping as she raises a hand to her eyes.

She might not have been able to take me, thanks to the protection stone—and the cat—but Inshara's control is growing.

"Anasta, run!"

My heartmother whirls about to break for the door, the cat a ginger streak ahead of her, and I'm close on their heels.

Chaos breaks out behind us, courtiers shouting, the guards pushing them aside. Anasta and I bolt past the portraits, and I follow her as she swings around a corner toward my quarters.

The door to my suite is ajar, and I follow her through it, slamming the door behind me and pressing my thumb to the copper pad. "Activate door lock," I snap. "No override."

"Quick," she gasps. "She's only ever been able to hold one person at a time before. We must find a safe place to figure out what to do next."

"Nimh's temple," I gasp, trying to catch my breath. When I turn toward Anasta, I realize my receiving room is a disaster— the furniture overturned during the city's fall, a screen hanging from the wall and spitting sparks.

"Please tell me you have a way out of here," Anasta says, eyeing the door. "I always assumed you snuck out somehow to see Miri and Saelis."

"Do you know if—if they're safe?" I ask, gesturing for her to follow as I hurry through to my bedroom.

"I don't—I lost track of them when the city began to fall."

I add their safety to the list of things I'm desperately trying not to think about. I pull open the concealed panel that Miri and I installed underneath the windowsill, keying in the code and holding my thumb over the sensor. "This only turns security off for fifteen seconds—sixteen, and the central unit is alerted, so we had to keep it brief. Be ready to climb."

I press my thumb to the pad, and the window pane retracts inside the one above it with a soft hum. Anasta scrambles through, the cat and I a beat behind her, and we land in a tangle of limbs on the ground just as it whooshes closed once more.

"North!" My heart nearly stops as someone shouts my name, and I scramble to all fours in time to see Talamar running toward us. "North, I—" He stops as he reaches us, doubling over and gasping for breath, bracing his hands against his knees.

Anasta and I scramble to our feet, and she reaches inside his jacket for his breather—but it must not be there, for her hand emerges empty. Instead she takes hold of his arm, supporting him until he can take a deep enough breath to allow him to speak.

"They said you had come—I couldn't—we have to go,

she'll kill you. North, I'm so glad—" He pushes upright, and an instant later, my father's wrapping his arms around me for the first time in our lives. He squeezes me tight, and then releases me, keeping hold of my shoulders.

"We have to go," Anasta warns.

"We have to find Nimh," I protest. "She's the leader Below, not Inshara. If we find Nimh, we can . . ."

But my voice dies away, because there's something in Talamar's face that I can't interpret, but that makes me feel cold all over.

"North," Talamar murmurs, shaking his head slowly. "North, I'm so sorry. I put her on a train with Miri and Saelis—I was trying to get them to safety, you have to know that—and the train . . . the train fell, and . . ."

I don't hear anything else he says.

I barely register it when he takes one of my arms, Anasta the other, and they start toward the portal to the temple. Somehow, my feet move.

Nimh, and Miri, and Saelis . . .

Miri's bright laughter, her dry wit, and her secret softness.

Saelis's gentle hands, his earnest gaze, his steady calm.

Nimh's secret smiles, her huge heart, her sense of duty that was really an expression of her love, over and over again.

All gone.

As if I'm watching from somewhere else, I see Anasta pull the portal open once more with her be-ringed hands—*how does she do that?*—and through we go, the three of us and the cat.

Techeki is gone, but Matias is there with the guards, still

dressed as a riverstrider, looking nothing like he did as the Master of Archives.

Matias is perfectly still for a long moment, only his eyes going from me, to Anasta, and back again.

"North," he says, his voice calm, as if he was expecting us and we're merely a little late. And then he turns to Anasta and sinks into a deep bow. "Sister. I never dreamed we might meet in our lifetime. It gladdens my heart to see that your line has has carried your burden through the centuries, as we have carried ours."

"We have remained true," says Anasta solemnly, and finally I lift my head properly, looking back and forth between them.

"Sister?"

"In a manner of speaking," Matias replies. "We guard the way between worlds, North, so we must be both above and below."

"We?" I ask, my voice going higher, sharp with confusion.

My heartmother inclines her head, meeting the Fisher King's gaze. "The Sentinels," she says.

THE CHAMBERLAIN

"Are you all right, Nimhara?" The queen's voice is quick and anxious—but her attention is all on the girl from another world. Her brow furrows. "Or is it Inshara?"

The chamberlain forces his shoulders away from the wall, his body shaking. The fall of Alciel should have been the worst thing he'd ever witnessed—and yet he'd just had to watch the queen ignore her own son in favor of a woman she'd only known a few weeks.

This is all wrong. Something must be done.

He catches the eye of the captain of the guard, who looks back at him with a slight nod. They've been friends since childhood and have little need for speech in moments like these.

The chamberlain crosses over toward the throne, clearing his throat in a way that makes both the queen and the so-called goddess look his way. "We ought to prepare our defenses," he says, inventing tasks on the fly, only half his attention on what he's saying. "We don't know what kind of reception we'll get among those living here Below. If they breach the barrier before we do, we may have to prepare for war."

Behind the throne, the guard captain is moving. He draws his sword carefully, without any telltale scrape of steel, approaching on silent footsteps.

The queen is nodding thoughtfully. "I certainly couldn't

stand it if anything happened to Nimhara. Inshara. Which do you prefer, my dear?"

"Inshara will do," replies the woman from Below. "I suppose it doesn't matter much now."

"Not to me," agrees the queen with a fond smile.

The captain of the guard creeps closer . . . closer. . . . He raises his blade, braces himself to swing—

And then stops, sword in midair.

The chamberlain can't help but look, though the glance will certainly warn the two women. His old friend's face is transformed, tears beginning to form in his eyes and spill down his bearded cheeks.

"Skyfall," he murmurs, gazing at Inshara with wide eyes. "I—I—I had no idea."

Inshara doesn't even bother to look. Her eyes, instead, swing over to land on the chamberlain. Slowly, the corner of her mouth lifts.

The captain of the guard shifts his grip on his sword and follows the woman's gaze.

He doesn't hesitate before advancing on his childhood friend.

The chamberlain tries to scramble to his feet, to turn, to run—

Behind him, he hears the woman's voice say thoughtfully, "Preparing for war isn't a bad idea, though. Shall we, Beatrin?"

FIFTEEN

NIMH

"Skyfall, is she dead?"

"I mean, she's sitting up, so probably not?" A pause. "We're going to need a new favorite curse word, you know."

"Come on, focus! Should we do something?"

"Like what? What do you *do* when someone's eyes start glowing right before she stops an entire train car in midair with the power of her mind?"

"I don't know. Maybe, like, slap her or something?"

Two silhouettes swim up out of the white fog obscuring my vision, one of them answering the other with just a thin, frightened laugh. Trying to lift my head triggers a massive spike of pain right between my eyes, and I groan in spite of myself.

"Nimh?" Miri leans over me, her eyes wide and anxious. "Are you . . . done?"

"Done?" I croak, squinting against the daylight behind her. "What happened?" But before Miri can answer, memories of the falling train car come screaming back, and I sit bolt upright—and then double over, clutching my head. "Are we alive?"

Saelis laughs again, though, like Miri, I can tell he's not entirely all right, the sound verging on hysterical. "Alive, yes. Okay? That remains to be seen. You don't remember catching the train?"

When I just blink at him, confused, he shifts his weight and tips his head to one side. I follow his gaze over his shoulder and see the train car, its broken window glinting in the sun, the doors half-open. We're on a grassy slope leading down to a creek with the forest-sea on our other side. For a moment, I can't tell what I'm meant to see. Then I realize: *the whole thing is hovering knee-height above the ground.*

I gasp, and as if the sound were some kind of cue, the entire train car goes crashing to the ground, sending leaves and blades of grass shooting out in a cloud around it. Miri gives a little shriek, scrambling back and then eyeing me sidelong. One hand still clutching at my head, I give my neck an experimental twist—the pain is better, now that the train is down.

"You are saying . . . *I* did that?" I ask, bewildered—the last thing I remember is the rush of sensation following the release of my shackles.

"And *that*, I think." Saelis has recovered some of his gravity and lifts a hand to point in the opposite direction of the train.

I turn to look where he's pointing, and then my body stops responding as shock courses through me. In the distance is the city—*both cities.* Alciel sits atop my home, the palace almost exactly centered over the temple, and the other end of the island resting on the hills on the other side of the river. A dim line of color flashes between them, some barrier of mist trapped between the two worlds, but where I would've expected to see destruction—fires burning, buildings crumbling—all seems calm from this distance.

"Gods," I whisper, my staring eyes watering with the strain.

"You turned toward it after you caught the train," Miri says from behind me. "It had been just sort of tilting down toward the ground, but you did something, and it turned and . . . *landed*, I guess, for lack of a better word."

I swallow, thrown more by the gap in my memory than by the apparent display of power I shouldn't be able to command. "Then Alciel—its people—?"

"You know what we know," Saelis says with an eloquent shrug. "But it looked like people could've survived it, for sure."

"You saved them," Miri exclaims. "And us too! And we're Below! And *alive*!" She gives a delighted little whoop, a release of tension that makes Saelis join in with a laugh of his own.

As if in answer, the call of a lying monkey echoes out from somewhere in the trees to the south. Miri's whoop turns to a startled shriek, and she scrambles back, scanning the edge of the forest-sea. "Oh, *what* the hell is that?"

I cannot help but remember North's first few hours in this world, his fear of something so harmless as the bindle cat, his helplessness in the forest-sea. "Nothing to fear," I tell her, searching for a calm tone despite how unsettled I still am over the gap in my memory. "Only an animal back there in the trees."

Miri flashes me a look as though I'd said "bloodthirsty murderer" instead of "animal," and then keeps her eyes on the trees.

Cautiously, I get to my feet, half expecting to be too drained to stand—but instead I feel strangely alive and alert in a way that I haven't since I first traveled to Alciel. Closing my eyes, I take a long, slow breath, reveling in the familiarity of the smells that surround me. Damp earth, crushed grass, the distant, wild tang of the forest-sea.

I'm home.

"You're sure we're safe here?" Miri's asking, still eyeing the edge of the forest-sea nervously.

"The sound was only a lying monkey." But even as I speak the words, I know they aren't truly an answer. Remembering North's first hours here, I can't help but recall what we found when we reached my camp: all my guards and riverstriders dead at the hands of Inshara's cultists.

I shift my weight uneasily, testing my legs once more, and then add, "But we should make our way to the temple. That is my home—they will offer safety and welcome. To both of you, as well."

They turn together to eye the temple, now in shadow, holding up one end of their city. "I'm not so sure *that* seems any safer than out here," Saelis points out, his own eyes wide and scanning the landscape with a mix of fear and wonder.

My own heart quails at the sight of the massive sky-city resting atop my home, but I push my fears aside. "We must go," I tell them softly. "For that is where North will be."

I can feel Miri's eyes on me as I strike out toward the cities. They haven't forgotten Inshara's words in the throne room any more than I have.

So you don't remember murdering Prince North?

I had told her it was impossible, as impossible as the accusation that I had somehow destroyed my own city, killing hundreds of my own people, in my grief. I would remember it, had I done something so unthinkable.

But I have no memory of stopping the train either, or of directing Alciel's engines to land atop the temple.

Eyes burning, I keep my gaze on my path as the others fall into step behind me.

I know something is wrong before we reach the city outskirts. There are no barges tied up at the market, and we pass no one walking in either direction. The river has a strange smell, like decay, beneath its more familiar odors of mud and damp. My nerves are on edge, but nothing prepares me for the moment when we round the rocky outcropping by the bend in the river and the lower city is spread out before me.

Or rather . . . what's *left* of the lower city.

It's as if a massive, violent storm swept through, leveling everything in a direct path leading from the river straight up to the temple steps. Buildings that had stood long before I was born are little more than rubble, ancient stone shattered as if it were pottery. The streets and harbors are deserted, though I can see movement in the windows of a few of the buildings farther away that are more intact.

"Nimh . . ." Saelis stands at my elbow, his voice soft and fearful. "What Inshara said in the throne room, about the destruction of the city—"

"No." My voice is shaking, and I push down my own horror

ruthlessly. "I would never do this. I do not know what happened here, but I could never harm my people this way—I have devoted myself to them since I was five years old."

"But if *this* is true," Miri counters, taking a few steps forward and then looking back at me, "then what if North—"

"North is in the temple," I snap, too shaken to moderate my tone. "He must be. Come."

I lead the others toward the rocky rise at the far end of the city, trying not to weep as we walk through my ruined home. I cannot help but search my memory, trying to push past the gaps—everything between meeting Jezara and Elkisa on the bank of the river and waking up in Alciel.

If I did this . . . this terrible, unthinkable thing, destroying what I've devoted my life to, could I not have also hurt someone I loved?

"It is the Divine One!" a voice cries some distance ahead and to the right, and a sob tears its way from my throat in surprise as I lift my head. We've reached the upper city, where the terraced streets eventually give way to the temple outskirts. A group of dusty, worn-looking people are gathered, kneeling and praying in the direction of the temple—and the city of the gods that now rests on its peak. One of them is staring at me, arm outstretched to point, and the others soon see me as well.

I'm not wearing my divine robes, though the jacket I borrowed from Miri is crimson. A murmur runs through the crowd, and a number of them get to their feet. "The Destroyer has returned!" one of them gasps.

"I don't like this," murmurs Miri, warily drawing closer. When I glance her way, I see there are others gathering, drawn by the commotion, picking their way through the rubble to form a loose circle behind us.

"I am used to it," I tell her, though I'm not sure I am—I *am* used to drawing attention, prayers, crowds. But something here is different. "I am making my way to the temple," I call out, lifting my chin, falling into the role of divinity as easily as if I'd never left it. "I will return and do what I can for all of you once I have learned what has happened here."

"Hah!" The man who originally spotted me barks a harsh, bitter laugh. "You pretend not to know what you've done?"

The words hit me like a blow—and then something else hits me, a wet glob that sticks to my neck. I stagger back, automatically clapping a hand to my throat, wiping away the spittle even as my mind tries to comprehend what's happening.

"Hey!" Saelis's face, normally so sweet and calm, is twisted in an angry grimace. "Leave her alone! Whatever happened here, she doesn't deserve—"

But before he can finish, something else flies out of the crowd, and my head snaps back, a fiery lash of pain across my brow making my vision dim for a moment. A stone clatters to the ground. When I raise a hand to my forehead, my fingertips come away crimson.

As if the sight of blood was a signal, the crowd erupts, pressing in all around us, shouting fury and grief. I feel hands tear at my garments; someone yanks at the edge of my jacket, throwing me down to the ground. Miri and Saelis are still on their feet, but barely, fighting to hold back the rioting people.

I cast a desperate glance up toward the temple to which

they all prayed just a minute ago—am I too far away for them to see my red coat? Where are my guards? My acolytes? It would be impossible to miss the crowd gathering around us—surely someone, *anyone*, would see?

"Nimh, use your magic!" Miri cries out, before yelping in pain as someone lands a blow on her arm.

But I cannot move—my mind refuses to work, refuses to accept the reality crushing in around me. The devotion my people once held for me, turned so hostile and hateful . . . *because I did this to them?*

Another blow strikes me, and another—I hear Miri scream, then I hear someone else shriek as she retaliates. Time blurs as I try to protect my head with my hands, falling to my knees.

Then another shout rises above the crowd, different somehow—familiar?—and more footsteps rush up to join those attacking us. No, not to join them—to *fight* them. I lift my head, blinking blood out of one eye, trying to focus. I see black and gold, the colors of my guards, relief searing through me. They're fighting to get to me, pushing back even Miri and Saelis in their single-minded goal.

They're led by someone wearing the clothes of a temple acolyte, though his hair is not cropped short—someone who must have noticed the growing crowd, heard the shouts from the temple terrace—he knocks aside a ragged-looking woman with another rock in her hand—

A cry tears its way out of my throat, my whole body singing with relief and shock.

North throws himself down into the dust before me, his eyes

searching my face, his hands hovering an inch away, shaking with urgency and with the desire to grab hold of me. His gaze goes to the gash on my head, fingers twitching at the sight of the blood flowing there. Beyond him the guards are continuing to push the angry mob back, forming a perimeter around us, but I can't tear my eyes from his face.

"I thought you were—" My lips won't form the word, but in this moment he understands me anyway, and he shakes his head.

"I'm okay. I thought *you*—" His eyes are wet, his voice hoarse. "Nimh . . ."

We stare at each other, the shouts and sounds of struggles between guards and rioters fading away, time itself seeming to pause. A trickle of perspiration makes its way down one of his temples; his lungs are heaving as if he sprinted here from the temple itself. His face is just as it was in my memory, save for the thin pink line of a wound on one cheek, a week or two old.

For a moment, I forget it all—the violence of my people, the fall of his, Inshara whispering in his mother's ear, the haunting gaps in my memory that suggest something monstrous in me that I can't remember. His lips, forming the shape of my name, are all I can see.

Just let this moment last forever.

"Sae! It's *North!*"

Before either of us can react, Miri barrels her way past a pair of temple guards, throwing herself at North. They tumble to the ground together, North swallowing an oath of surprise— and then Saelis is on them both with a shout of relief. They sprawl there in the street, a tangle of limbs, all three of them in tears.

A guard kneels before me, her face blocking the sight of North's reunion with the people he loves most. "Divine One," the guard addresses me, breathless with exertion. "Can you walk? We must get to the temple, where you will be safe."

I know I must rise, but I cannot seem to make my legs work. *You must move,* I tell myself. *People are watching.*

And I must stand on my own. Nobody can reach for me, can help me. Nobody can hold me, as Miri and Saelis hold North.

Then, just as the guard is drawing breath once more, the bindle cat is there. An orange streak barrels into my chest and topples me backward so he can stand atop me and yowl his defiance at the world. I reach up, as I have a thousand times, and gather him in against me, muffling his opinions only slightly. He speaks so loudly, writhing in my arms, humming with the power of his purr, latching onto me with his claws as he juts his furry face into my chin.

He is so warm, so familiar, so much my *home,* that I am almost undone—my eyes are hot, my throat closing tight, and I cannot make myself release him.

"Easy, Fuzz," comes North's voice from beside the guard, thick with an emotion I cannot name. "You'll smother her."

The moment passes, and I recall myself. The cat climbs onto his place across my shoulders as if he never means to leave it again, and I find that I can push myself to my knees, then rise to my feet, wishing I could better hide the trembling of my body, the way my legs buckle, the white-knuckled grip of my hands.

The mob has subsided, most of them having vanished into the ruined city, with a few of them restrained by guards. The rest of the guard detachment form up around me, including North and his friends in the ring of protection. The three of them are speaking so quickly, talking over one another and interrupting, that it's like they're using some private language of their own; they have North sandwiched between them, their arms around one another.

"Divine One?" The guard is watching me, her face concerned. "Shall I send for a litter?"

"No." I clear my throat and try again, and this time my voice sounds a little more like my own. "No, I can walk. Take us home."

SIXTEEN
NORTH

Miri's still holding one of my hands in a death grip, and Saelis, Anasta, and Talamar are all talking at once. It's chaotic, and joyful, and my heart is full.

We're in my quarters in the temple—they're neat enough, because I barely ever slept here, preferring my mattress in Nimh's garden instead. I'm surrounded by people I never thought I'd see again, and it's incredible . . . but I'm already sort of missing the cat.

He went with Nimh, of course, who was whisked away by Techeki. The Master of Spectacle skillfully separated us, letting her guards bear her away to get cleaned up, and shoving me in the opposite direction with my family, insisting we'd all need a minute to talk. I let him, because I had about a thousand questions. But the moment I turned to my heartmother, the question of how she could be a Sentinel on my lips—Anasta gave the smallest shake of her head and a soft "Later, North."

Techeki was right. We do need a minute. But I'm still living in that moment when Nimh and I knelt together amid the riot, each drinking in the fact that the other was still alive.

"North?"

I look up to see Saelis watching me with a faint smile, as if aware of my daydream. A flash of guilt cuts through me immediately. My heart breaks when I imagine how he and Miri must have mourned me. They've always been a part of my life. I thought they were my future, until I met Nimh. How can I tell them what she means to me, after they lost me and found me again?

And even now, with a strange tangle of prophecy and life-threatening traumas tying Nimh and I together, it feels impossible to tell what's real, and what's just the result of that bond.

How do I reconcile these two worlds, and my heart torn between them?

"North?" Saelis says again, and I blink, snapping out of my tangled thoughts.

"Sorry, I wasn't listening," I admit, and Miri snickers, squeezing my hand.

"Can you tell us who's who?" he asks, and everyone turns their attention to me. Of course they do—they're seasoned palace operators.

I take them through the world I've come to know as simply as I can—Nimh at the center, as its divine.

Techeki, loyal but complicated.

Matias and the riverstriders, traditionalists who follow a path of faith and magic.

Elorin and her Graycloaks, who want to use sky-steel to shut out all magic, and who have risen to power while Nimh was gone.

The Deathless, who believe Inshara is the true divine, and even now will await her return. I leave Elkisa out of it, at least for the moment—I don't quite know how to detangle my thoughts toward her. I also don't quite manage to mention that I'm supposedly the Last Star, a figure of prophecy, and that we're all considered gods in our own right.

I'll have to get to it soon, but there's not a segue in either world that makes that one easy.

"So this world is ready to split apart at the seams," Talamar says, as I conclude.

"It was *before* our city landed on top of the temple," I reply. "Now we also have to deal with Inshara somehow. Not just for the sake of Beatrin, and our people, but because she'll have both worlds up in flames if we don't."

My words fall into a grim silence, and nobody speaks for a few moments.

"You should go and find Nimh," Miri says eventually, and I have to force myself not to bolt to my feet in order to do exactly that.

"Miri is right," Anasta agrees. "From what you've told us about what happened in the city, her grip on power is tenuous. If she's our strongest ally, you should see how you can help her. We may need this place, to evacuate our people away from Inshara's control."

"And if she really did destroy this city," Talamar says quietly, "then make sure you maintain your alliance with her."

I don't have an answer to that, because "she's not dangerous" isn't true, and it's also only one part of a tapestry so complex that I don't know where to start unpicking it for them. So instead I nod and rise to my feet.

"I'll find out what's happening," I promise. "At least nobody can get to or from Alciel for now without those rings Anasta has—that buys us a little time."

But does it buy us enough?

After a little mild intimidation of the temple staff, I find Nimh in what used to be her high priest Daoman's rooms, with Techeki and Matias.

She hasn't cleaned up, and she hasn't changed—it's jarring to see her in what I recognize as one of Miri's jackets, looking like a girl from Alciel, albeit one who's had an extraordinarily bad day. Her hair is still pulled askew, and there's a smear of blood at her temple, though the wound itself has been cleaned.

She's sitting with the cat in her lap, stroking him slowly, and listening intently as Techeki takes her through the current situation, counting out points on his fingers. All his attention is fixed on her as he speaks quickly and quietly. I keep tracing out her features with my gaze, trying to make myself believe she's really here, really alive. Only now can I let myself feel how truly terrified I was that Inshara had simply killed her, and everything I was doing to try and reach her was already too late.

Now I know what ORACLE taught me—that the divine is created by the power of belief, sustained by those who subconsciously channel the mist and magic into empowering her—I'm seeing Techeki in a whole new light. In a strange sort of way, *he's* her high priest, with his shows and spectacles, his ceremonies designed to boost the faith of her people. I touch the bracelet at my wrist, then tug my sleeve down over it. ORACLE and I have a *lot* to discuss, if I make it through the next few hours.

Matias is in the room too, but he only listens and doesn't speak, instead making up some sort of drink from the bottles stored in one of the cabinets. Apart from Nimh's jacket, the tableau of the three of them might be from some time before my fall, from a time when my world was just a distant place, home to the gods.

"The Last Star," Matias says, by way of announcing my presence, and Nimh and Techeki both look across to find me hovering in the doorway.

"And we will have more company in a moment," Techeki says, somehow making me "company," rather than one of their allies without even seeming to shift his tone. "There will—ah, thank you."

An acolyte pushes past me to present Nimh with a robe, and she rises to her feet. "I will ready myself for company," she says, so calm that I know she's reaching for it, and for just a moment she meets my eyes.

There's so much I want to communicate to her, and so much I'm trying to understand myself, but there's no time for any of it. So instead, I twitch my lips to just a fraction of a smile, and I wink.

It's still the two of us, I say silently, and I have to hope she understands.

"Now, North," says Techeki, all business, as Nimh disappears to change into her robes. "Can we count on you?"

My head hurts just considering the question—who's *we*?

Count on me for *what*? I don't know what anyone from Below wants—to make peace with my people, to make war, to send them back the way they came? I'm not sure they know either.

"North will not forget the story he has written thus far," says Matias, with that sort of placid assurance that makes me want to roll my eyes. Techeki's jaw twitches just a fraction, and I'm pretty sure he's grinding his teeth.

Neither of us has the chance to reply before the door swings open to reveal Elorin, the leader of the Graycloaks. I've barely had a chance to meet her—Techeki kept us apart, for fear one or the other of us would start a verbal brawl, but there's no stopping her now. She's a severe woman with her black hair pulled back into a bun so tight it just about raises her eyebrows and pallid skin that clearly hasn't seen the sun in a very long time.

"Well?" she snaps. "What have you discovered so far?"

"We have—" begins Techeki, but he falls silent as the door opposite the one they came in through opens and Nimh appears. Or Nimhara, really.

My breath catches in my throat when I see her. She's once more in her red robe, eyes lined black, gold wrapped around her upper arms. She even moves differently now, more formal, as if Miri's jacket changed more about her than just the way she looks.

Techeki and Matias bow, but Elorin simply glares at her, then swings around to face me, smoothing down her gray clothes with one hand. "Cloudlander," she says, crisp. "Why have you done this, brought your land down upon us?"

"I did nothing," I reply as her eyes bore into me, and I automatically fall back on a lifetime of training to straighten my spine and meet her gaze, keeping my tone firm but courteous. "My people did nothing. The city has been taken over by Inshara, the false goddess. She controls my mother, the queen and ruler of my world, and her intentions are hostile—I assure you, Elorin, we seek the same thing, which is safety for our people. Yours and mine."

The room is silent for a long moment, and though I already saw it in action—saw my bloodmother's tear-streaked face as she watched me without recognition—now the knowledge settles in my bones. I can't banish that image, or the image of those guards succumbing to Inshara's horrifying new power.

Alciel is entirely at Inshara's mercy—nobody above believes in magic, and my family has ruled for a thousand years. Beatrin's power is absolute.

I am gone, and Anasta is gone. In the time it might take the rest of them to raise their voices—to even *dream* of suggesting the queen should not be obeyed, let alone to speak the idea out loud . . . Inshara's influence will silence them.

"Her mind is not her own," I continue quietly. I know what I have to do, and I focus on keeping my voice even, letting that task anchor me in place, when I want to float away and dissolve into the air as I speak the words. I'm doing what Beatrin has taught me, but I can only do it by detaching from my own words. By pretending it's someone else's mother under Inshara's spell. Someone else's city that's crashed to the ground.

It's just one of the Fisher King's stories being told around a campfire—it isn't real. I just have to play my role.

I draw a breath and pull my shoulders back.

"I am Queen Beatrin's heir, and I am therefore declaring myself ruler of Alciel while she is incapacitated. I speak for my people."

Matias inclines his head, solemn, and Techeki as well— even Elorin the Graycloak is silent a moment. Silently I push away my mother's words during our last conversation—that I am no worthy heir, but devoted instead to my own enjoyment. She knows there's more to me than that. Though she's not herself, I have to believe this is what she'd want.

Nimh's dark eyes are grave, there's a softness beneath her resolve. I know that she understands what it costs me to speak those words, and to claim a responsibility that shouldn't have been mine until I was an old man, a whole lifetime from now.

It's Elorin who breaks the silence, of course, swinging around to face Nimh, her tone sharpening. "Why did you stay so long in the cloudlands? And if she is hostile to us, why did you not prevent Inshara from taking their leader's mind?"

"It was no simple task," replies Nimh. "She—"

"You do not lack the power," Elorin snaps. "We need only look outside the temple to see what you have done to the city. It must be that you lack the will to protect your people, which is why—"

"I serve my people, as I have done all my life." Nimh's voice rings with authority, and it's enough to silence Elorin for a moment. "I will do whatever I have to to protect them from her."

Elorin snorts. "We have seen what have done for your people, and what Jezara did before you. The time of the divine is over, and if you think that we plan to rely upon the girl who destroyed our home, and a boy who claims to rule a city that is beyond his reach, then you only prove your foolishness. The Graycloaks have protected this city since you vanished, Nimhara, and we will do so now."

Everyone starts speaking at once—Techeki and Matias both begin to protest, and Nimh makes her own reply as Elorin tries to force her way through by raising her voice, and acting on instinct, I step into the middle of the circle, putting myself between them.

It buys me a moment's silence, and I take advantage of it to speak quickly. "We all have our differences. But we're united in our wish to protect the innocent. Perhaps instead of debating who's in charge, we should discuss how we can work together to protect those who are relying on us."

"The Last Star is right," says Matias. "As soon as the Deathless know Inshara's in the city of the gods, and alive, there's no way of knowing what they'll do. What she'll *have* them do."

I ease my way back out of the circle, choosing a place beside Nimh, facing Elorin.

"You are right," Nimh says to Matias. "We must stop Inshara communicating with her people or there is no saying what harm she might bring. There are only a few ways in and out of the islands. We should post guards to detain anyone who comes through."

I start, my gaze snapping across to her as the others begin to nod. "Hold on a second," I protest, still seeing in my mind's eye the blank faces outside the palace gates. "My people are trapped up there with her, and her power's growing."

"It grows?" asks Matias, his brows lifting.

"My heartmother—the queen's wife—is here in the temple," I say. "She tells me that for a time, Inshara could only control one person at a time—the queen. But when I saw her less than an hour ago, she controlled a number of the queen's guards, as well. We have no way of knowing how well or how long she can do that, but it seems to suggest she's getting stronger."

"And you think this means we should let people through?" Nimh raises her hands, as though I'm just proving her point. "We cannot let anyone else into our world, because any one of them could be an agent of Inshara's."

"Nimh," I protest, starting to step forward. "Everyone else up there is innocent, you know that. We should be helping them get out, not trapping them in there with her. What if we can't reverse what she's doing?" My throat tightens at that thought, the one I haven't been able to voice aloud—because it isn't just about the people of Alciel. It's my mother, too. "What if the minds she takes are permanently controlled? You're talking about condemning thousands to the fate of losing their minds, their lives, to her!"

Techeki intervenes, pulling out a let's-all-be-reasonable tone. "We cannot doom two worlds," he says. "We must at least protect one, if we can."

"This one?" I try to keep my voice level, and I know it's not working. "A little too early, Techeki, to doom anyone, don't you think? We can't simply leave my people where they are."

"North, you know I have seen the people of Alciel, that I care for them too," Nimh replies, her voice shaking. Her gaze darts between me and Elorin, who watches with clenched jaw and fists. Nimh's eyes plead with me to understand—and the worst thing is that part of me *does*. We're both in impossible situations. "We *must* safeguard those we can, and we do not know what Inshara can do."

"So we leave them up there and, what, wait to see what she does?" I snap, something breaking within me. "Setting aside the threat Inshara poses, Freysna—the main island—is cut off from the other islands now. They have to get food and supplies from elsewhere—there are no farms or factories in the city. My people are going to starve if we leave them cut off for too long."

"But we have some time before food becomes an issue," Nimh replies, her voice rising, starting to match my intensity. "There is enough in the auto-vendors alone for at least a few days, leaving aside that which your people have stored in their homes."

It's a jolt to hear her talking about Alciel's food-dispensing machines, and nobody else can possibly know what she means, but Elorin's already talking, elbowing her way back into the conversation.

"I am not interested in what they will eat," the Graycloak snaps. "I am interested in what we will do about them. They abandoned us once, and now they have returned, it is under the hand of a woman you say is hostile to us. For once, I find myself aligned with the *Divine One*"—and there's not an ounce of respect in that title, which she speaks as though it tastes bad—"and I say that we should protect ourselves from these intruders at any cost."

"I did not say—" Nimh begins.

"Your own people attacked you," Elorin snaps. "After you abandoned them for weeks. You speak for nobody, and I am not asking for your approval. I am posting guards to the portal between the temple and the cloudlands."

I lock eyes with Techeki, every conversation and debate we ever had about allowing the Graycloaks into the temple is replaying in my head. "I will have the temple guards join them," he says, crisp. "With orders to turn back—not to harm—anyone who might try to come through."

Elorin turns on her heel, marching for the door, and Techeki takes off after her.

I'm two steps in that direction myself when Matias's hand lands on my shoulder, stopping me in my tracks. I turn back toward him just in time to see the door on the other side of the room closing.

Nimh is gone—it probably leads to one of her private passages.

"North," says Matias, his hand squeezing my shoulder. Just that small bit of comfort is enough to make me swallow, my eyes itching, and I keep my jaw squared with an effort as I turn to him. He meets my gaze, his own carrying an unexpected sympathy. "I think you should take the Divine One her spearstaff, don't you?"

THE TRAINEE

The guard trainee shifts her weight from foot to foot, wishing she knew how to hide the terror coursing through her heart. Fortunately, she's not the only one—her fear doesn't exactly stand out in the sea of similarly fearful guards and recruits.

She never even got to the combat part of training—she was still taking courses at the Academy on mediation, crowd control, and government. She's no better equipped to hold the sword in her hand than her roommate, who's studying to be a sculptor. Even the seasoned guards who've been serving the throne for decades have probably not seen much more action than breaking up the occasional drunken party downtown.

And now—now there is to be a war?

"Divine One," the captain is saying, gazing at her with his wet, red-rimmed eyes in a way that makes the trainee's stomach churn, "I have absolute faith in you. But you say that there are an equal number of trained guards awaiting us in the temple. Even if our technicians can find a way through this magical barrier, I do fear our forces won't have the experience to overwhelm them."

Inshara, the goddess of the people below—though the trainee heard a rumor that she isn't that, either, that the prince himself came back from the dead and denounced her—is standing by the barrier, the entire contingent of the royal guard arrayed behind her. The temple guards on the other side are only dimly visible in uniforms of black and gold. Squinting, the trainee can only make out vague shapes.

And yet Inshara suddenly leans forward, as if she's seen something important, her breath catching. For a moment, she says nothing, her hands clutched tightly around her staff.

One of the guards on the other side lifts her hand in a slow movement—perhaps she's simply brushing her hair back from her face. Or perhaps it's a salute.

Inshara lets her breath out slowly.

"We have nothing to fear on that front," she says, finally glancing over at the captain of the guard, whose eyes begin weeping again under the weight of her gaze. "The temple will be ours before the barrier even falls."

SEVENTEEN

NIMH

The air in the garden is soft and cool, drawn in from the night outside through the gaps high in the walls. Moonlight gleams down from the skylights, gilding every leaf and petal with rose gold. Only Miella shines tonight—her lover, Danna, is at her furthest ebb, and won't rise until near dawn. The quality of the light is different without both moons together. Hollower, somehow.

I'm already inside before I remember that the garden will be dying. I am the only one allowed within its walls, and I was not here to tend to it. It will be one more thing I have destroyed.

For a moment, as I look around, I think I am seeing a memory: the garden as I wish it to be. But I blink twice and still the flowers bob gently on their long stems, the tree's leaves shiver in the breeze from outside, and the smells of damp earth and greenery are thick on the night air. My garden is alive.

The bindle cat runs in ahead of me, going straight to a pallet on the floor, where he begins to turn in a slow circle, flexing his claws into the fabric. A fine layer of hairs tells me he's been sleeping here.

Beside the pallet are stacks of papers, scrolls from the archives, sketches of gliders and more fantastical flying machines. More pages are tacked up on the wall, notes scrawled beside them in chalk. I move toward them, scanning their contents, though I scarcely read the words written there, for my mind is spinning.

North. He is the only one who would have moved a bed into this place, the only one who would've dared to enter a goddess's sanctuary and make it his own. But I would have known he had spent time here even if there were no traces of his presence—I can feel him here, somehow. I can sense him in the garden itself, the delicate flowers, the trembling leaves, the rich earth.

He's the one who kept it alive.

The cat has settled down into what must have become his habitual place at the foot of the pallet and is gazing steadily toward the door behind me. I turn, already knowing what I will see—and still my heart gives a painful, thudding lurch when I see him there by the door, clutching at its frame with one hand, and holding my spearstaff in the other.

I've never seen it in someone else's hands before.

North starts when my eyes fall on him, blinking as if jarred from some daydream of his own. He swallows, meeting my eyes for only a moment before letting go of the doorframe and moving past me so he can start tearing down the notes on the wall one-handed, then balancing the staff in the crook of his arm so he can use both hands at once.

"Skyfall," he mutters. "This place is a mess. I would've

cleaned it if I'd known . . ." He doesn't finish, his voice a little hoarse as he reaches for the higher pages, standing on his toes.

I want to tell him that I don't care, that his minding the garden for me means more than he could know, that the thought of him here while I was so far away makes my heart feel a little less empty. But the words stick in my throat, and instead I have to clear it several times, and the only words I can manage are "May I see?"

North hesitates, but then holds out the stack of papers in his hand. He shifts his weight once I take them, and then turns away again to start neatening the other piles of books and scrolls, as if he can't bear to be still.

The pages are bits and pieces copied painstakingly from archive sources—some are poems, others fragments of prophecy, and still others sections from histories. Tales of old flying machines, songs about the land of the gods, descriptions of artifacts dating back to the Exodus . . . a seemingly random collection, except for the single thread that ties them all together.

"You were trying to get home," I murmur, eyes still scanning the pages.

Silence answers me for a moment, and then North's feet come to a halt not far away. "I was trying to get to *you*," he replies, voice soft.

I raise my eyes to find him there, watching me, having abandoned his attempt to tidy the garden. His hand is still curled around the spearstaff, and his gaze doesn't waver as he holds it out to me, the movement slow, almost ceremonial.

I take it from him, my hand curling around the smooth,

familiar wood, still warm from the touch of his palm. But though it fits into my grip like a piece of me returning home, I find I cannot look away from the boy who kept it safe for me.

He looks just the same—the familiar features, the distinctive nose and cheekbones, the hair curling softly over his brow, just tousled enough that my fingers itch to smooth it—and yet entirely different. He seems older, not in any definable way, but in the set of his shoulders, the firm jaw, the pain in his eyes.

Before I can stop myself, my own pain and regret come surging up as if in answer, and I find myself blurting, "North—I'm sorry. I do not know how you could ever forgive me. . . . I will never forgive myself—"

"Hey, hey . . ." North moves closer, ducking his head to catch my eyes, his own tinged with sudden alarm. He lifts both hands, not to touch me but to show me that he wishes he could. "Back there, with Techeki and Matias and Elorin? Everyone's trying to find a way through this, I know that. Everyone's scared."

I shake my head, the dappled moonlight blurring around his face as I blink away tears. "I did this," I whisper, realizing my hands are aching from gripping the spearstaff so hard—I set it aside, flexing my fingers. "I brought Alciel down. I put your people and mine in danger."

North's expression tightens a fraction, but he doesn't move—doesn't pull away or drop his gaze. "It wasn't your fault. Miri and Saelis told me what happened. Inshara did this, Nimh—she used you, your power. It wasn't you."

"And this place?" The emptiness in my chest yawns larger, trying to swallow me. "The destruction out there? Who did that?"

North swallows, shifting his weight closer, his own eyes damp. "You weren't yourself. *You* would never have hurt anyone. I know that. Everyone who really knows you knows that."

"But I did do it." The words ring hollow, the confirmation of what Inshara told me in Alciel's throne room, of what I myself began to know as I picked my way through the rubble of my own city. "I only remember pain, fury . . ."

"You believed I was dead." He speaks quietly, his face grave. "If I thought someone had murdered you, I . . . I don't know what I'd be capable of."

A breath escapes, some distant relative of a laugh, for the thought of North hurting anyone seems more impossible than anything that's happened in the past few weeks since he first fell to this world. But even as my lips twist to a smile, I stop, for North isn't smiling—he's deadly serious, almost shaken, his eyes on mine lit with a ferocity I've never seen there before.

Before I can stop to think about it, I lift a hand, stretching it out toward his face.

He jerks back, as if he were the one not allowed to touch, ferocity giving way to bewilderment. "What're you doing?" he manages.

"It doesn't matter." I catch the sob in my voice, but I don't bother to hide it. "Inshara touched me. Miri and Saelis touched me when we were falling in that train car. My own people—" Here, I'm forced to stop and struggle for breath before I can continue. "My own people touched me, today in the temple outskirts, trying to make me pay for what I did to them. Whatever I once was, I am not anymore."

North shoves his hands into his pockets, as if forbidding himself from using them in any other way, and shakes his head. "When Miri described how you stopped the car before it hit the ground, she said you started to glow—just as you did when you came through the city as the Lightbringer. Whoever touched you, you *are* still divine, Nimh. Don't give up on your destiny."

I try to take a deep breath, but my head is still spinning—and North's closeness isn't helping. I never knew that I missed the way he smelled until this moment; never realized how much the sound of his voice comforted me.

And never quite knew how all that paled in comparison with how badly I want to feel his touch.

"I wanted it to be you," I find myself saying, that ache in my heart making my eyes start to burn again. "If I was going to break that most sacred law for anyone in this world or the other . . . I wanted it to be you."

North exhales slowly, and I realize with a start that he's shaking, the air trembling over his lips. My hand is still half outstretched, and after a moment he pulls his own hands from his pockets and reaches out toward mine.

His gaze searches my face for a few seconds, waiting for me to pull back or to wave him away. When I don't, he leans forward and lets his fingers slide beneath the back of my hand.

I'm braced for some shock at the moment of contact, some blistering signal of wrongness, for this touch is my own choice—not stolen from me, like with Inshara, or a matter of life and death, as with Miri and Saelis.

This touch is my own, driven by nothing other than my need of him.

But the moments stretch, and I do not burst into flames—there's only the gentle warmth of his skin on mine.

He's waiting too, for me to lift my eyes from our hands, to start breathing again, to show him I am all right. When I meet his gaze, he steps closer, fingers sliding up to circle my wrist until his thumb rests against my quickened pulse. He breathes again, the air gentle as it puffs on my upturned wrist.

"Oh, Nimh." His voice is a bewildering, tantalizing mix of sadness and longing, as his eyes fall to the place where he's holding me. "I wanted it to be me too."

My own breath catches, and for a few heartbeats we stand there, frozen together. His hand tightens around my wrist, just briefly, like a fleeting concession to the desire to hold all of me with such fierceness—and in that moment I find I would quite like to be seized that way.

But then he's shifting again, his thumb moving across the heel of my hand and then sweeping across my palm, gently uncurling my fingers so that he can place something there with his other hand.

With a flash of recognition, I see that it's the protection stone I made for him that morning we parted ways atop the cliff near the western mountains, when he believed I meant to destroy the world and I believed he meant to leave it for his own. He's wrapped it in thread the color of my robes, the color of the sash he wore in my name.

Now, he presses it into my palm and uses both his hands to

curl my fingers around it.

"Don't give up," he murmurs, drawing me closer so gently I scarcely notice the step I take that erases that last little distance between us. "I know you think they've all abandoned you—that no one believes in you anymore."

Slowly, almost absently, he rubs his thumb across my knuckles, as if savoring the texture of my skin beneath his. I cannot speak a reply, for he's stolen my voice—I can only nod, my own heart a confusing tangle of grief and desire.

"*I* believe in you," he whispers, raising his eyes from our hands. His mouth curves a little when his eyes meet mine, the half-hidden smile rueful and fond. "I always believed in you. Before I believed in any of the rest of it, I believed in *you*."

Then he bows his head and presses his lips to my curled fingers. His mouth is soft on my skin, though his lips are firm as they form the shape of a kiss, draw back, and kiss again, as though he cannot quite help himself.

My head is ringing with the rush of blood in my ears, to my face, to the place where his lips press against my fingers. It would take only the tiniest of movements to lean forward, slide that heated wrist against his cheek, curl my arm around his neck to draw him to me. But his touch has paralyzed me, hypnotized me like one of the colorful forest-sea birds in the market. I am caught—I have burst into flames after all, and I cannot move for fear of being consumed.

I pull away with a gasp, stumbling back from him, my heart pounding in my chest.

Eyes wide with alarm, hand still half-outstretched, North is saying my name—I can see his lips moving, though the roaring in my ears is too loud for me to hear his voice. I close my eyes, trying to gather my control around myself with an effort.

"Did I hurt you?" North is asking, his voice rising with agitation. "Are you—did I—"

"I'm fine," I manage, my breathing quickened, the blood still rushing to my face. "I only—When you touch me . . . I fear I will lose myself. Lose control."

His agitation easing away with my reassurances, North's eyebrows rise a hair. One corner of his mouth lifts tentatively, and he says softly, "Maybe that could be a good thing."

My own mouth twitches in response, longing to give in to that smile. My skin tingles where he touched me, and I keep my fingers curled around the stone he placed in my palm. But I shake my head, taking a step back. "Not when I have inside me the power to destroy a city." My breath catches. "To destroy *two* cities. All it took for Inshara to use me was for her to tap into my grief. And this—this feels even more consuming."

For a long moment, neither of us speaks, though I can feel him gathering his breath and his wits, and suddenly, I know I must speak first. I must convince him before he makes me change my mind—and I cannot let him know how easily he could change it.

"Nimh, I—" he manages, before the words tumble out of my mouth over his.

"You know that we cannot, regardless." I swallow, biting my lip at the flash of confusion, and then dismay, over his features. "Back there, debating with the others . . . that is only the start of how things must be between us. It was different when you were here alone, maybe never to return home, but now . . . now you are all but king."

North's eyes fall, and he slips his hands back into his pockets. "And you are your people's goddess."

"We are the leaders of opposing worlds. I must protect my people and you yours, and above all, we must have our peoples' trust. I may already have lost mine. . . . I do not know yet whether I can reclaim their faith. But if they knew how I—" My voice cuts out, in spite of my best efforts to keep it even. "If they knew how I felt about Alciel's ruler, they would never trust me again. They would be right not to."

North is silent, eyes still down, but I can see tension gathering in his shoulders and along his forearms as he balls his hands into fists in his pockets. He turns his back, striding a few steps away. I long to speak, or worse, go to him and run my fingers along that line of tension in his back. Having touched him once has released some terrible longing in me—but I hold myself still with an effort. I know him well enough to see that he's thinking, in that quiet way of his, and I want to let him.

Tell me I'm wrong, I beg him silently. *If anyone can see a way forward for us, it's you.*

When he turns back around, his jaw is firm, lips set in a determined line. "We have to break Inshara's hold over my mother."

I try to hide my confusion at this shift in topic, reminding myself that I can't be hurt by his failure to answer a plea that was only in my own mind.

He sees my distress, though, too well-trained in reading body language to miss it, and his eyebrows lift a little as he steps back toward me. "If we can stop Inshara from controlling her, then my mother can speak for Alciel again, and we won't have to worry about Inshara's agents coming across the borders between our worlds."

My heart thuds in my chest. He *did* understand. "Our two worlds could talk. Peacefully."

He nods, eyes on my face. "Maybe even become allies."

I try to meet his gaze, but mine keeps falling to rest on his lips as they move. I keep myself still with an effort and order my mind to focus. "Then we will stop Inshara. Whatever it takes."

EIGHTEEN

NORTH

I want to close the small distance between us again, to take just one more step and reach for her hands and pull her in against me.

I shove my hands deeper into my pockets, forcing up my shoulders, stretching out the tension singing through my body.

My hands on Nimh.

I thought I'd never feel her skin under my fingertips, and now all I want is to feel it again.

"How is Inshara doing what she's doing?" I ask, forcing my mind to the problem at hand. "Can magic control someone's mind like that?"

"It is impossible," Nimh murmurs.

"Controlling the mist was meant to be impossible too," I counter. "But you do that."

"This is true," she allows. "But only because my divine power manifested that way when I read that ancient scroll of the Song of the Destroyer. Just as Jezara was a healer, as those before her manifested aspects of war or music, my aspect is that of destruction. Only the Lightbringer, foretold in prophecy, could control the mist as I do." She falls quiet a moment, and I see the dread creep into her expression as she follows that thought to its logical conclusion. "Do you think there is possibility she could somehow actually *be* . . . divine, as she claims?"

I lift my hands in a helpless shrug. "Nimh, a few weeks ago I knew magic didn't exist. Given that, anything is possible. When it comes to Inshara, though, I have an idea about who might know what she is. Or rather, *what* might know."

"What are you talking about?"

I puff out my cheeks, considering how best to come at the task of explaining ORACLE. "Let's sit down," I say, admitting to myself that I'm stalling. We both take places on the stone bench beneath the tree, and I find myself automatically leaving a gap between us. I nearly reach out to take her hand then and there, but instead I rest my hand palm down on the cool stone of the bench, and she sets hers just beside it.

"North, tell me what you have learned."

"Well, I found something," I begin. "When I was searching for a way to get you back. It's a computer, which means—"

"I know what a computer is, North," she replies, with a twitch of a smile.

"I . . ." For a moment, I just blink at her. Then it clicks. She's been in my world.

"How can you have found a computer *here*?" she interrupts, as the meaning of my words catch up with her.

"It's ancient. It dates back to before the Ascension—uh, the Exodus. It's badly damaged, and it's running out of power—it's fueled by mist, and now there's none in the city."

"Inshara's ring of sky-steel in the river," she says, brow furrowing. "Not only does it prevent us working magic in the city, it's also preventing this computer from working properly?"

"So it says. It also told me . . ." I trail off, because I have no idea how she's going to take what I say next. "It told me where your divinity first came from."

She simply stares at me, her mouth opening slowly, then closing again. It's a long moment before she finds any words at all. "Where it *came* from?" she manages. "Divinity didn't *come* from anywhere—the power of the divine has been passed down, generation by generation, from the one god who remained behind when the rest . . ."

"When the rest Ascended?" I finish for her when she trails to a halt, confounded. "Nimh, you've been to my world—do you really think we're all gods? Or even all descended from gods?"

Her gaze breaks from mine, and she looks away to study her moonlit garden. I don't know what happened to her in Alciel, but I know that she must have known ordinary people there, met Miri and Saelis: wonderful and fallible and completely human.

"But if there were never any gods," she whispers, hands tightening together in a knot in her lap, "then what am I?"

My own hands twitch with the urge to reach for hers, and I echo her pose, lacing my fingers together. Now isn't the time to drag her even further from what she knows. "You're divine," I reply firmly. "It's as good a word as any, and it *is* real, Nimh. It's just different from what you've learned—the truth of it must have just gotten lost through the centuries, the same way my people forgot how our engines work."

She nods slowly, her eyes closing, her face perfectly composed. "Tell me how it does work, then."

I take the simplest line through the story that I can find. I leave out Elkisa—I'm not sure Nimh even remembers her betrayal, and there will be time enough for that hurt later.

I just tell her that my research turned up a hint about a Sentinel vault somewhere beneath the Congress of Elders, and that I found my way inside.

"You already know that only a handful of people can use the mist to perform magic," I say. "Not control it, like you do, but draw power from it. Apparently, the rest of us are still interacting with it too, we're just doing it subconsciously, without realizing it. In my world, those people were channeling the mist into the engines that kept Alciel in the sky. We all *believed* the city would stay afloat—and it did."

"And here," she breathes, "the people believed in me."

I nod. "A thousand years ago, your people and mine split because not everyone wanted to live in a world where a few people could perform miracles with magic—they thought it was too much power for any one person to have."

Her mouth tightens, but her lashes lift so she can stare at the flowers, their petals closed for the night. "Maybe they were right."

I exhale slowly. "I don't know if they were or not—but while my people's solution was to leave and make their own society in the sky, yours decided to address the problem by having the mist

270

channel into a divinity. Their belief chooses what that divinity's aspect will be—say, healing, like Jezara."

Nimh's eyes widen. "And when Jezara was banished and people's faith fractured—I never manifested as a child because my people's faith was scattered."

I nod, unable to look away from her face. For years, she believed she had done something wrong, or not been *enough* for her people—that her failure to manifest was somehow her fault. "I suppose your ancestors figured that letting the mist choose one magician, one divinity, would keep the rise of any others in check.

"But choose *how*?" she presses, clearly still struggling to understand, and I can hardly blame her. "Mist cannot think for itself, it just *is*."

"There's a . . . machine, I guess, somewhere here Below. It interacts with the mist. There's one in the sky too—ORACLE called them 'hearts.'"

Nimh's face has gone very still. "ORACLE?" she echoes in a faint voice.

Belatedly I remember the stories mentioning this ancient being, and the place it held in the mythology of Nimh's people. "The name of the computer. It's an acronym."

She leans forward, curling her hands around the edge of the bench. "This is—You speak of something sacred. Something so ancient it predates the divine line. You say it spoke of hearts? As in the story?"

I nod. "Each world had one. In Alciel, my people sub-consciously channeled their faith through the heart to keep the cities' engines working. The purpose of the one in your world was to focus the belief of the people into the power of the divine."

"The two halves of the Lightbringer's broken heart," Nimh murmurs weakly. "You mean to tell me they exist? They are *real*? And they—are machines?"

"I can't be sure," I admit. "But ORACLE seemed to suggest that the people of each world built them. And they've got some kind of connection to each other, and to your divinity and Inshara's power. Do you remember encountering something like that when you were chosen? Did they bring you somewhere important or secret?"

"I was only five years old," she reminds me weakly, but I can see her mind is elsewhere. "Up in Alciel, though, I think I saw its heart. *Met* it, almost. The place that keeps all the engines communicating with each other, not far from the hangar where you kept the *Skysinger*."

"The engine mainframe," I reply, my eyes widening. "I thought it . . . well, nobody really remembers, but I thought it ran diagnostics, made altitude adjustments. You think it's the heart? That the mainframe is what Alciel's people are using to channel the mist?"

She nods slowly. "It . . . *recognized* me, somehow, like we were linked. I think that's how Inshara used me to bring Alciel down—because of my connection with it."

I push to my feet, a shiver running through me that feels dangerously like hope. "If she could use your connection with the hearts to hijack the power keeping Alciel in the sky . . . then could you do what she's done, use that connection to hijack *her* power over my mother?"

"I have no idea," she replies. "None of this—the mist powering my divinity, the heart guiding it to me—none of it explains how Inshara is doing what she's doing. These are things no magician has ever done, but I don't understand how she could be connected to the heart, as I am."

I shiver again, though this time I find myself remembering those mad, mist-touched eyes of Inshara's. "She didn't have that power before the mist-storm. Only after she touched you, while you were manifesting as the Lightbringer."

"Gods." Nimh meets my gaze, her own haunted—I can see her withdrawing, remembering the mist-storm in question, when she destroyed a chunk of the city she'd sworn to serve. "When I confronted her in the throne room of the palace, she told me she had me to thank for her powers."

"Her touching you in the middle of a mist-storm, while you were connected so deeply to the temple's heart—it must have been like a lightning strike. A million-to-one chance to form a second bond with the heart."

"The sacred law," Nimh murmurs, her eyes down, resting on her hands in her lap, "that the divine must never touch anyone—that law had to come from somewhere. The ancients must have known it was possible, and they could not risk the creation of another divinity. And so it became forbidden to touch the divine at all."

My own fingertips tingle with the memory of her hand in mine, and I shiver. "You were trying to stop her."

"Instead, I created a monster," Nimh says in a low, remote voice. My heart aches, feeling her pull away. She blames herself for so much. And it's clear she's not ready to be forgiven—by me, by herself, by anyone.

"We'll stop her. If we know how her bond with the heart was created, we can figure out how to sever it again." I wheel around, dropping to a crouch in front of her. "Maybe ORACLE can help us."

"You said you found the vault containing it under the Congress of Elders," she says, and when she turns her head, I know she's not seeing the garden wall but the fear and hatred in the eyes of the people who once worshipped her. "I—I do not think I could disguise myself well enough to be safe crossing the city. The Deathless are out there still, and they would leap at the chance to capture or kill me."

"No need," I say gently, lifting my wrist, and pushing back my sleeve. Beside my chrono sits the bracelet I got from ORACLE, its dark, matte metal seeming to absorb the light. "I haven't had time to figure out how it works."

"This is familiar to me," she says, leaning in to inspect the bracelet. "The metal reminds me of a few of our most ancient relics." Slowly, carefully, she extends one finger, brushing it cautiously over the metal.

An instant after she makes contact with the green crystal set into the band, it bursts into brilliant light, both of us jerking back from each other.

I hit the ground with a thump, and then lift my wrist—the crystal is still lit from within, but the brilliance has been channeled into a series of lines projected in a circle above my arm. The cat gives an inquisitive warble, leaping up onto Nimh's thighs and sniffing at the band on my wrist.

"HELLO," says a calm, somewhat tinny voice, the projected lines flickering up and back in a visual echo of the tone of the speaker. "I AM THE OPERATIONAL REVIEW, ADVICE, AND COMPU-TATIONAL LOGISTICS ENGINE."

The voice pauses, and then adds, "GREETINGS, DIVINE ONE."

"How do you know who I am?" Nimh gasps, scrambling to her feet and clutching the cat to her chest.

"I HAVE BEEN LISTENING," ORACLE admits.

"Were you going to help us at any point?" I ask, caught between indignation and slightly hysterical laughter.

"I HAD NOT BEEN ACTIVATED." I didn't know a computer could sound prim, but this tiny version of ORACLE's voice definitely does.

"ORACLE," Nimh says, standing a little straighter now, "the question I wish to answer is this: Having granted Inshara divinity, is there any way revoke it?"

"YES," replies ORACLE without hesitation. "WITHOUT THE HEARTS, SHE WOULD HAVE NO POWER BEYOND THAT OF ANY ORDINARY MAGICIAN."

Nimh glances at me, her brow furrowed. I blink back at her, then look back down at the bracelet, as if its smooth, featureless surface might have answers. "Without the hearts?" I echo in confusion.

"YES. DESTROY THE HEARTS AND YOU DESTROY HER POWER."

Nimh lets out a gasp and drops the cat, who gives a startled yelp. "Would that not destroy divinity itself? Not just mine, but the entire divine line that has continued for the last thousand years?"

"YES."

"And Alciel could never get back up into the sky," I point out, nearly as horrified as Nimh.

"ALSO CORRECT."

Nimh begins to pace, her steps quick and urgent. "We would never be able to re-create them if we destroyed them now—whatever understanding of that power our ancestors had, it was lost centuries ago. Whatever plan prophecy had for me, for the Lightbringer, would be lost forever. To destroy the hearts and end the divine line before the prophecy is complete . . . We would destroy fate itself." She meets my gaze, my own helplessness reflected in her own. She moves back toward me, speaking into the bracelet. "Destroying the hearts is not an option. There must be some other way."

ORACLE is quiet for several seconds, its conversational light frozen in place. Just as I'm about to say something—to check whether Nimh's broken its brain—it blinks into life once more. "IT MAY BE POSSIBLE TO REPLICATE THE PROCEDURE BY WHICH YOU WERE ORIGINALLY CONNECTED TO THE HEART."

I nearly laugh, memories flashing through my mind of tech systems analysts back home trying to walk my mothers through a troubleshooting process. "You're telling us to reboot? Do the ceremony again? See if the power resets to Nimh?"

"THE THEORY IS SOUND," it replies. "THOUGH IT HAS NEVER

BEEN ATTEMPTED BEFORE, AND I CANNOT PREDICT WITH ANY PRE-
CISION WHAT WILL HAPPEN."

"We don't know where the heart is," I point out.

"No," says Nimh slowly. "But I believe the Sentinels may."

We find Matias in the archives with Anasta—seeing him standing there in his Fisher King's robes is almost as much of a jolt
as seeing Nimh in Miri's jacket, and the sight of him standing
with my heartmother brings back the flood of questions I still
desperately need answered.

Anasta is a Sentinel. What has she known all this time?
What has she kept from me? Can she possibly help us now?

Matias and Anasta are deep in conversation, and they turn
toward us as Nimh and I hurry across the archives to Matias's
desk.

"Matias," she greets him. "Is there anything in your lore
about the heart of this world or that of Alciel's? One heart that
created my divinity and bound me to the faith of our people or
one that kept Alciel in the sky?"

Matias's brow furrows as he looks between us and then
glances at Anasta, "Hearts," he echoes slowly. "As in the story
of the Oracle and the Lightbringer's broken heart?"

I nod. "We need to find the hearts' location. Do you know?
Do you have any clue where they are?" Anasta shakes her head.
Matias looks bewildered. My spirits begin to sink—all of this is
clearly new to both of them. If the Sentinels once knew how our
worlds were linked, the knowledge must have been lost.

Nimh turns away, pacing a few steps, agitation in her

movements. "There must be something—if only I had not been so young when I was chosen, maybe I would remember where the ritual took place."

Matias's eyebrows shoot up. "You mean the ceremony to initiate you into the divine line?"

Hope kindles inside my chest. "Yes! Do you know where they took her for that?"

"Of course," he says, in mild surprise. "The ritual takes place in the divine's ritual bathing chamber."

With a start, I remember that moment I witnessed Nimh in the bathing pool the night of the Feast of the Dying—where we came so close to touching, where I first realized just how much I wished I *could* touch her.

She stares at him for a moment, and I see something click into place. "I thought that was a dream," she murmurs. "Come—follow me."

Matias and Anasta ask no questions, but simply fall into step behind Nimh as she turns to stride from the archives, spearstaff in one hand, every inch the goddess once more. I grab for my heartmother's hand, though, and she tucks her arm through mine, as she always has when we walk together.

"You think you can stop her—Inshara?" she asks quietly.

"It's a long and complicated story involving an ancient supercomputer," I reply. "But yes. I think so. You want to tell me how you became a Sentinel while we walk?"

That draws a tired laugh from her, and when I glance across, I can see lines on her face that are usually hidden by the softness of her smile. It's one thing for me to force the image of

Beatrin's glazed-over eyes from my mind. Anasta had to watch it happen for weeks.

"It's . . . hereditary, after a fashion," she says.

"And you, a member of the Sentinel line, just happened to marry Beatrin?" I ask. I know how truly my mothers love each other. Could the marriage have been arranged?

"No. It is in connection to the royal line," she replies. "The monarch's spouse becomes a Sentinel. Your grandmother was, before me. Your spouse would have been, after me. Deep in my personal files there's a recorded explanation of everything they'd have needed to know, in case I died before you married."

"Was I ever going to find this out?" I ask. "Did grandfather know? Does Beatrin?"

Anasta shakes her head. "Only the line of Sentinels have ever known," she replies. "But now the map we were following has run out—we've reached its edges, and we have no choice but to seize the moment. What happens next is up to us."

Nimh has claimed an oil lantern and led us into her private passageways. She opens the carved wooden door ahead of us and leads us into the private bathing chamber I saw once before, the night Daoman was murdered and we fled the temple together.

The room itself is hewn from rock, an intricately carved wooden screen looking down on the great hall below. From here, Nimh and I watched the party. The hole that Inshara blew through the wall when she arrived is still there—the rubble has been cleared and stacked against the wall, but nobody's had time to try and fit it back into the ragged gap it left behind.

I wonder if the bloodstain from Daoman's murder is still there on the stone floor—but it's impossible to see from here.

In the bathing chamber itself, plants tumble down from high ledges, alive in their own misty ecosystem. I remember that the night I came here, Nimh thought I was a servant. Which was why she let me in. When she was naked.

There may as well have been an electrical current running between us that night. She glances back over her shoulder, and I wonder if her brain's also spinning with that memory—then she turns toward the pool in the center of the room.

Without hesitation, Nimh walks down the carved steps into the water, her spearstaff still in her hand, her robes floating and flowing around her. She stops when she reaches the bottom, turning and feeling with the bottom of the staff for something under the surface.

It slots in somewhere below, and Nimh turns onto her back, her arms spread out to either side, her robes billowing around her.

An instant later, there's a soft humming that I can't quite place—and then I realize it sounds like home—an almost unnoticeable electronic buzz coming from somewhere just out of sight.

And the pool beneath Nimh begins to glow green. Softly at first, and then more and more brightly, until we're forced to step back and shield our eyes. Until she's simply a silhouette, outlined against the glowing light . . . of her temple's heart.

THE GROUNDSKEEPER

The palace groundskeeper keeps their head down, trying not to pay any attention to the small army gathering on the eastern edge of the grounds. The guards are arrayed before a strange rent in the air, a blistering purple-and-green wall of energy that appeared when the city fell.

The groundskeeper should probably be somewhere else— with their family, maybe, except that they all live on Hosri, one of the smaller islands, and they've been unable to get home since the train service was suspended. But the truth is that the groundskeeper is most at home in their garden, anyway. They can now say with confidence that if the sky was falling, literally, they'd prefer to just keep working.

So they keep focused on their task, applying a sod patch to a bit of grass dug up by one of the network technicians yesterday.

People rarely ask for their permission before digging holes in the grass—just two weeks ago, a man came and buried something in that exact spot. The groundskeeper said nothing about it. None of their business, really, what a councilor does. Except that it'd be nice to have just a few weeks for the sod to take root before getting torn up again.

A scream echoes out across the lawn, making the groundskeeper's head jerk up. Someone's dragging a prone body away from the energy barrier; the prone figure is thrashing and keening in an inhuman voice.

Then comes a woman's voice, raised in anger—with a jolt, the groundskeeper realizes the voice is the queen's. They never would have recognized her, shouting that way.

"Keep trying! Fetch more people from outside the gates if you must—Nimhara says we *will* find a weak spot in this barrier, and I do not mean to let her down!"

The groundskeeper glances from the milling crowd of guards to the energy barrier. Sliding their hand rake into their tool belt, they ease back into the shrub-lined path leading west. Perhaps, they decide, it would be a good time to leave their work alone for a little while after all.

NINETEEN

NIMH

I am only five years old. Daoman is holding me in his arms, speaking softly in my ear.

"I know you're frightened, Nimh, but it won't hurt, I promise you. I was there when the goddess before you stepped into her divinity, and she said it was like meeting an old friend—wouldn't you like to meet her friend too?"

We are standing in the ritual bathing chamber, and an acolyte is holding a staff just my height in his outstretched arms.

"Pardon, High Priest," says a man by the entrance to the chamber with a shaved head and ornate robes, fearsomely stylish and put together. "This ritual was never meant for a child—she won't even be able to stand in the pool, she'll drown."

I lift my face away from Daoman's shoulder. "I can swim," I tell the colorfully robed man, with a flicker of hurt feelings.

Daoman's chest quakes with a silent laugh. "There, Techeki, you see? And you were concerned about a riverstrider being chosen—destiny knows what it's doing. Where is Kachoro? The Master of Spectacle ought to be here."

"He is feeling delicate after last night's celebrations," says Techeki, his face very still and careful. "He sent me in his stead."

"It seems your master has begun handing over his responsibilities at an auspicious time," Daoman says dryly. Techeki says nothing in reply, though his eyes twinkle. *He is not so bad,* I think, a little more of the knot of fear in my chest slipping away.

Daoman stoops to set me down on the stone, and then crouches in front of me so he can gently take my chin in his hands. "Nimh, are you ready? Once you step into the waters, your name will be Nimhara, and you will be a goddess. All those people who came to see you at the party last night, and everyone in the city and all the villages beyond, they will all love you—but they will also need your help. This is a very big thing for someone your age to do, and—"

His voice cuts out. I have only known him a few days, but we've spent almost all that time together, and I've never seen his face look like it does now. Everything he's saying is nice, but his eyes . . . his eyes are sad, so sad.

"It's okay," I tell him, reaching up to pat his cheek, where a tear glistens in the light of the spellfire lanterns. "I can do it. I want to do it. Helping people is good."

"I still wish I didn't have to ask it of you." Daoman exhales, reaching up to gently take my hand and pull it away from his face. "That is another thing, Nimh. After you go into the water, you cannot touch me again, or anyone else. It's the most important rule of all, and you must never, *ever* break it. Do you understand?"

I blink at him, not quite understanding, but not quite willing to tell him so. "Yes, Daoman. I won't, I promise."

Daoman's face twists, and he leans forward to press a quick, startling kiss on my forehead. "Thank you, Nimh."

The air seems to ripple, a whisper of breath sweeping across the room, a greenish light rising all around me. When it clears, the pool is still there, but Daoman and Techeki and the acolytes are gone. Instead, standing by the pool is a girl in red robes, with a boy in black finery just behind her, helping her with the ties at the nape of her neck.

I try to open my mouth to speak, but I can't—I can only watch as his fingers trail down the red lacing, and the girl shivers, her eyes closing because she can almost feel him there, almost imagine his touch. Her breath catches, then quakes as it releases again.

"How is it," says the boy, his voice soft and aching, "that you can live your life without touching anyone? Never being touched?"

The girl hesitates a long moment, and then, abruptly, she whirls and wraps her arms around the boy's neck, pulling him down to kiss her.

I try to cry out, for this is wrong, this is not what I remember— and then the light rises once more, and when I can see again, the faces of the two people by the pool have changed. They're standing on the first step of the pool together, their ankles submerged in the water. With a jolt, I recognize the woman, though her hair has no white in it anymore and her face is unlined: *Jezara.*

The man kisses her in return, passion in the clasp of their arms—and when they break apart, there is a gleam of light between their lips, like the sun cresting a mountain peak, blinding and bright. Then he pulls back, the light moving with him before sinking into his skin and vanishing. It's as though something of her has settled within him.

"I thought we couldn't—" The man is saying, though his arms are tight around her, his forehead pressed to hers. His back is to me, only his dark hair visible over the black clothes he wears, but his voice is strangely familiar. "I never meant to ask for this."

"You didn't," whispers Jezara, her eyes filled with tears. "I just—I can't believe that I will serve my people better by being so far away from them. I am not just a goddess, I am *human* too. And I love you."

The man lifts his hand to cup her cheek, exhaling a long breath. "Skyfall," he mutters. "I love you too."

A sound comes from outside the chamber and they fly apart, both turning toward me, toward the entrance.

I stare at the man, whose features are a haunting mix of familiarity and strangeness; the features of someone I know well, but changed somehow, different.

Then the light flares once more, and I can see nothing but brightness. A warmth deep in my chest rises like an embrace, and I lean into it, letting that warmth surround me.

I know you.

Clarity comes like a lightning strike, and I remember everything—why I'm here, that I was here once before as a child, at the beginning of all this, that the others are waiting just beyond the light to see if renewing my bond with the temple's heart will remove its bond with Inshara.

But there is no renewal—just a gentle wash of warmth that never left me.

And I can still feel her. There's a dark well in the fabric of belief that stretches across the land, and she crouches there, clinging to the threads connecting her to the heart like a spider in its web. I can almost *see* her, a shadowy form in that dark pit, her back to me—

And then she turns, her eyes two burning pools of mist, fixing on mine.

With a gasp, I lurch backward. Water splashes all around me, and for a moment I can't see anything, my eyes blinded and flashing with afterimages.

"Nimh!" North's voice, a tether, calls me back—I open my eyes to find him kneeling at the edge of the pool, leaning close, looking half a second away from throwing himself into the water after me. "Are you okay?"

"It didn't work," I gasp, shivering, turning to find the others watching me, wide-eyed with concern. My robes cling to me, winding around my legs in the water, and I remind myself that I am safe here, that the Inshara I saw was just a vision.

"What do you mean?" North asks, eyebrows drawn in. "How can you be sure?"

I wrap my arms around myself, shaking my head. "I can still feel her, somehow, through the heart."

"So we're back at square one." The disappointment in his face is like a knife in my gut. "No closer to stopping her."

"Perhaps not." I can't help but stare at him, the features I know so well after just these few weeks—and the features I just saw changed, less familiarly formed. My heart's still thudding as though I'm in full flight; I reach out to grab the spearstaff for support. "I know who Inshara's father is. Who's been talking to her all this time through that chrono she wears, convincing her she's chosen by the Lightbringer."

North's eyebrows fly up, lips parting in surprise. "What? How?"

"I had a vision." My voice is shaking, and I can't take my eyes off of North. "The heart remembers—they first touched here, by the water."

"Jezara and her lover? Techeki said he was a cloudlander who he helped get back to the sky." North braces his palms against the stone, leaning forward. "If it's someone in Alciel, then maybe we can get to him, use him to talk Inshara down from her delusion. You think you know who it is?"

I swallow, my eyes scanning the faces of Matias and Anasta behind North, watching and listening—but my gaze finds its way back to North as if tied there. For a long moment, I can't speak. North has lost so much today, learning of his grand-father's death and his mother's madness; I wish I did not have to give him this, as well.

But I must speak.

"North . . . where did you leave Talamar? Where is your father?"

TWENTY
NORTH

Nimh's hair is still damp, curled into a knot at the back of her neck, instead of loose, like she usually wears it. As we follow her toward my quarters, where I left Talamar, Miri, and Saelis, I find myself focusing on the way the damp tendrils cling to her neck, caressing the slope of her shoulder.

She's clad in dry robes, but her hair tells me that what we witnessed in her bathing chamber was real. The gut punch of discovering we can't separate Inshara from the temple's heart, that we're back to square one, was real.

Anasta's at my side, Matias behind us, and my heartmother wears a resolute expression that might surprise others. They always think she's Beatrin's sweeter counterpart—being under-estimated has always served her well.

We meet Techeki in the hallway—he rarely looks like he's hurrying anywhere, but Nimh sent an acolyte scurrying to fetch him as we left the library, and both the boy and the Master of Spectacle must have made record time. Techeki takes in our expressions and holds his questions, simply falling into train behind us.

The door to my room's ajar, and Nimh pushes it open, walking through without hesitation, though she automatically steps to one side to ensure none of us run into her when she stops. It's only a moment until I see why she has: Talamar isn't here.

Miri and Saelis are rising from the couch where they were sitting together, wearing twin expressions of concern.

"North?" asks Miri. "What's happening? Is everything okay?"

"Where is Talamar?" asks Anasta, crisp, her hand coming up to rest between my shoulder blades, a steadying touch.

Saelis lifts one hand to point through to the study, and I'm over to the door in an instant, pushing it open with too much force. Talamar stands by the window, already turning toward us with a quizzical expression.

"Talamar," I manage, aware of the others at my back.

"North?" He turns toward me, takes a step forward.

"Have you . . . ?" I don't want to ask. Because then he's going to answer. And everything's going to come undone. "Have you been here before, Talamar?"

He simply stares at me for a long moment, and then his gaze shifts past me. It takes me a moment to realize it's settled on Techeki. The hawk-nosed Master of Spectacle is staring back at him, his mouth slightly open, the shock of recognitition transforming his face.

"What are you doing here?" Techeki manages, pushing past me to take a step toward Talamar.

My father doesn't take his eyes off me, though, and simply inclines his head. "Yes," he says. "I've been here before. When I was young."

Techeki swings around to look between us, gaze locking onto me. I can see every wheel in his mind turning furiously, trying to put the pieces together. Belatedly, I remember that Techeki was the one who helped Jezara's lover return to Alciel after she was banished. Techeki and Talamar—old friends. My mind refuses to get past it.

"The boy who fell Below," breathes Saelis from behind me, gazing at my father. "I thought that was just a story. How could you possibly . . . ?"

They're all in the room now, and I walk toward Talamar, past Techeki. My father takes a step backward as I approach.

"An accident with an aircraft," he says. "I doubt I was the first, but perhaps I was the first to survive. I did survive, though, and the ones that found me brought me to the temple. And I met Jeza—Jezara, I mean—and she knew I wasn't a god." His mouth quirks to a weak smile. "It doesn't take much figuring out, once you meet me."

"I sent him home," Techeki says quietly, looking like he's conducting furious mental calculations.

Talamar nods at him, a weary smile on his face. "I never had the chance to thank you, my friend."

"I knew it was what Jezara would have told me to do, if she were still at the temple," Techeki says slowly. Then he turns, addressing Nimh and me. "I used the only relic capable of transporting him and destroyed it in the sending. I always wondered if he arrived home safely."

Anasta speaks quietly, her hand still steady at my back. "The next part of the story is mine, North."

I turn toward her, my mind reeling. "Yours?"

She nods slowly. "Talamar arrived in a chamber known only to me—known only to the Sentinels. I had no idea who he was, this bruised, filthy stranger who was suddenly inside a room that had been locked for centuries. I'd kept to my duties since they became mine, but I didn't know if any of it was really true. Until suddenly Talamar was there, saying he'd been Below."

"And I was panicking, because the princess's wife had just opened the door," Talamar puts in, scrubbing at his face with one hand.

I want to push him on with the story—I want to ask, to say the words out loud.

Are you Inshara's father?

But there's something inevitable about the way this is unfolding, and instead I simply stare at Talamar, trying to imagine him younger, trying to imagine him walking the temple as I have been. Trying to imagine him falling in love with its goddess . . . as I have a generation later.

"That was how you met?" I ask him and Anasta, instead of all the things I want to know.

"Yes," my heartmother says simply. "Over time, he earned my trust. He kept the secret of Below, and of the Sentinels. And when Beatrin and I needed a donor, I suggested Talamar as your father."

Techeki's bronze skin looks sallow, and his gaze is flickering back and forth between us now—he manages a small, tight shake of his head. "*Your* father," he murmurs, and my heart sinks a little deeper.

"You were such a gift, North," Talamar says, stepping forward as if he wants to come to me and he's holding himself back. "I couldn't tell anyone you were my son—that was part of the agreement—but I was proud of you from afar. When the newsfeeds outed me, it was a relief. It meant we could talk. But . . ."

"But," I echo, barely a whisper.

"But," he says, just as soft, "I had left my chrono behind with Jeza, and I always hoped—I tried a dozen different ways over the years to broadcast, to bridge the gap between here and home. And eventually it worked. I was too late for my love, but I discovered that my daughter was still alive."

"Inshara," I whisper, my throat dry. "Inshara is my sister."

There's a gasp from the doorway behind me that I know must be Miri, but I can't look away from my father.

"Tal," Anasta whispers, stricken. "Why did you not come to me . . . ?"

"What would you have done?" he asks, spreading his hands wide. "What *could* you have done?"

"Maybe nothing," she concedes. "Maybe only mourned with you."

Nimh steps forward to my side now, and I glance across to her, every part of me crying out to take her hand. But I can't—not here, not now.

"I do not understand," she says, trying for calm, and perhaps sounding that way to other people. "Why were you too late for Jezara, Talamar?"

"She was gone," he murmurs. "It took me nearly five years. She had died by the time I managed to make contact."

Nimh blinks in confusion, but I'm immediately drawn back to that last conversation between Jezara and Inshara, before Jezara's death. To the confession her daughter made, before she killed her mother. I'm quiet, searching for the right words to break the news, but Techeki beats me to it.

"My friend," he says slowly. "My friend, that's not so. Jezara lived more than twenty years after you left. She died only weeks ago."

Talamar backs up until his legs hit the couch, and there he stands, his mouth moving like he's working for air. "What?" he manages eventually. "I don't understand. She died when Insha was young. Insha told me so."

His expression is shifting, brows crowding together in confusion, mouth slackening, and I can see the tug-of-war between bewilderment and heartbreak right there on his face. Which makes what I have to say next so, so much worse.

"Talamar, it was Inshara who killed her mother. I was there. I tried—I tried to stop it."

My father's face collapses, and his legs give out—he thumps down onto the couch, drawing in a deep, shuddering breath as he stares up at me. "North, I don't—that can't be true. Why would she do such a thing? Why would she tell me her mother was dead, all those years? All those years we could have spoken?"

"Because she wanted you to herself. She wanted something all of her own," I say, my own legs barely steadier than his, caught between the knowledge that I have a sister, and that she's holding my mother—my *world*—hostage, and that Talamar has known about her all these years and never said a word. "What did you tell her?" I ask, forcing myself onward. "What made her think she was going to become divine?"

"I—" Talamar's breaking, his face buried in his hands, his voice muffled. "I only wanted to help her feel special. She told me tales of a world that hated her, that spat on her."

"Those tales were true," Techeki says, his face drawn. "I got supplies out to Jezara when I could, once I found out where she had gone. But she was an outcast."

"I loved her," Talamar whispers.

At my side, Nimh lets out a breath, and I glance across at her. There's an intensity in the way she stares at my father, like she's trying to drink in every last detail about him. His and Jezara's choices—their love—are the reason Nimh was taken from her own life and thrust into this one.

Is that true, though? Or was the prophecy already at play? Is Nimh the Lightbringer, the Destroyer of Worlds, because she was always going to be? Or did she become so because the devoted started to believe the world was ending after Jezara cracked their faith so completely?

"Tal," says Anasta softly, from somewhere behind me. "Tal, what did you tell Inshara?"

"That her father was a cloudlander," he whispers. "A god. I told her bedtime stories about what I could remember from the prophecies. And then . . ."

"Go on," I choke out.

"This world," he says, lifting a tear-streaked face to me. "You're the only other person who can understand, North—full of magic and monsters, impossible that it even exists. Danger at every turn, and yes, there's beauty here, but these people— North, I watched them drag her away, her own guards. She screamed for me, and they held me back, and—" His voice breaks, and he drops his head, gulping for breath, fumbling inside his jacket for his breather, then hesitates, for it isn't there.

And skyfall, I *can* understand. If I had to watch them drag away Nimh . . .

He pauses, waiting to catch his breath without the help of his medication. Finally, he manages, "There is nothing safe about this place. I learned that when I came here. I was caught in a mist-storm—it's how my lungs were injured. The animals here, the trees, everything was twisted. People like Jeza were punished, and innocent children like Insha."

Nimh makes a soft noise beside me, and when I look across I see my own turmoil mirrored on her face. We met Jezara. What was done to her was beyond terrible. And he's not wrong about the dangers of this world, either, for all its beauty.

"I couldn't get back to my daughter," Talamar says, lifting his head, "but I wanted her to feel powerful. To feel special. So I used some of what I'd learned about their prophecies, about the Lightbringer . . ."

"You told her she could claim her mother's divinity as . . . a bedtime story?" Anasta murmurs, dismayed.

"I never, *ever* meant for her to become what she has. Please—" And now his gaze shifts from me to Nimh, to Anasta, to Techeki. "I beg of you, believe that much."

And looking down at him . . . I do.

I fought with everything I had to get back to Nimh. If I'd been stranded above, thinking her murdered by the people here, thinking a child of ours was alone in a world that hated her very existence?

I've had the chance to find the good in people here, for all I've found their dangers. But I understand why Talamar couldn't. In his place, I would only ever have seen my grief as well.

Nimh's the one who breaks the silence. "You must speak to your daughter," she says. "Help her to understand that what you told her was a lie. That she can still turn back from this path she's walking."

Talamar recoils, his eyes widening. "Have you seen nothing she's done? I spent every moment she was in Alciel trying to hide from her. I knew as soon as she heard my voice, she'd recognize me—and of course I had no power to pass on to her. I didn't know what would happen, but I could see it wouldn't be good."

"As opposed to what's happening now?" I ask, my voice rising. "Talamar, the time for hiding, the time for protecting yourself—that bird has flown. You have to do something. Perhaps she would have killed you up there, seen what you were. But here she might believe you. She might be prepared to leave Alciel and come to you."

"To what end?" Saelis's gaze swings between me and my father, his expression drawn. "We don't have any way of stopping her. She could just take us all over."

Anasta's still watching Talamar with sad eyes, but she gives herself a little shake and looks around at the rest of us. "Inshara only took over those closest to her in the palace. Beatrin—and then, just before I escaped, a few of the guards. If she can't control people at a distance, maybe we could get Beatrin away from her. Even if Talamar can't talk her out of her quest for power, we might be able to rescue my wife." She swallows, but that's the only outward sign of the panic and grief she must be feeling. "She is also Alciel's queen," she continues, her voice even. "Having her free of Inshara's influence, able to rally her people and give orders, would be worth a great deal."

"We could go in," Miri says slowly. "While you're talking to Inshara, someplace away from the temple, Saelis and I—and Anasta—could go in and try to get the queen out of Alciel."

I glance at Nimh, who looks back at me, her eyes sparking at last with the faintest glimmer of hope. When her gaze swings over to rest on my father, I look at him as well—sitting there on the couch, glancing between us, his lips pressed together. My temper is still running hot—the secrets he kept from me, the lies he told Inshara, the betrayal of my mothers' trust . . . it all makes me wish I'd never learned who my father was in the first place.

Seeing me look at him, he shakes his head. "North, I don't think she's going to listen to me. What if I can't talk her down?"

"You *are* still her father," I snap, taking a step forward. "You can still be that for her—it might not be too late. Tell her what you did—that you lied to her, that you've *been* lying to her—and maybe she'll realize she isn't supposed to be a god. That she never was."

His gaze locks with mine, and for a long moment, neither of us seems to breathe. Then he closes his eyes. "I will send her whatever message you think best," he says simply.

Anasta sinks down on the couch beside him—I can't tell if she wants to comfort him, or shake him, or both—and I turn toward Nimh, Techeki and Matias stepping forward to join us. There's no sniping between them now, their expressions equally grave. I force myself to take a slow breath, to smooth out my thousand whirling thoughts about my father, my sister, my mothers, Nimh—about the endless numbers of my people, whose lives I want to protect.

"We have to draw her out of Alciel," Techeki says, buying me a moment to calm myself. "To somewhere outside the city, where there'll be enough mist for Nimh to use against her."

"And fewer innocents," Matias agrees, rubbing his chin thoughtfully.

"The plains," Nimh says softly. "North, you know them—we sheltered under the mounds in the ruins there."

"The old shopping arcade," I remember. "You played there as a child."

"I know it well," she agrees. "Every corner. I am sure Inshara does not. It would give us avenues of escape, if . . ." She doesn't finish the sentence, but her eyes go to Talamar's face, finishing it for her.

If we fail.

TWENTY-ONE
NIMH

I stand by the window in North's room, looking out over the view far below, the bindle cat sitting on the sill with his warm fur pressing against my ribs. From this angle, the ruined city is not visible—there's only the curve of the river, gleaming like onyx in the starlight, speckled here and there by the barges of the riverstriders. Beyond the river, less than a day's journey from the temple, is the ruined city of the ancients that will serve as our neutral ground to meet with Inshara.

Talamar is in the study, speaking to her through his chrono to try to convince her to meet with him.

North and his mother sit near the door, their heads together. She's doing most of the talking, North merely listening and occasionally nodding a fraction, his face grim. As if sensing my eyes on him, he lifts his head, eyes swinging over to meet mine.

I have no desire to interrupt his time with his mother, so I only smile a little, raising my eyebrows. *Are you all right?*

The corner of his mouth rises a little in a sad, answering smile. *Yeah. I'm okay.*

I stifle a sigh and force myself to move my gaze away from

him again. Miri is curled up on the bed with her head in Saelis's lap, fast asleep—Saelis himself is asleep too, his head tipped back against the wall, mouth open, snoring softly. Matias sits at North's breakfast table, head bowed—either asleep himself or meditating.

I know I ought to try for some sleep. I tell myself I will, just as soon as we know from Talamar what his daughter's response is.

His daughter.

My heart is still reeling from that revelation, and I have to fight not to look back over at North again. First his beloved grandfather's death, and then his mother's madness, and then his father's secrets. And now he has gained a mad person for a sister, one who wishes him dead. I wish I could hold him the way Saelis holds Miri. I wish I could offer him a safe place to lay his head until his heart has had time to settle.

"Divine One," comes a voice at my elbow. I lift my head to find Techeki there, inclining his head as I turn toward him. The bindle cat gives a low chirp of greeting. "I have ordered food and tea to be brought here. If you will not sleep, perhaps you will at least eat something."

"Thank you, Techeki." Despite my best efforts, the smile I offer him in thanks is weak at best.

"May I join you?" he asks, nodding toward the window, and waiting for my answering nod before easing close enough to gaze out at the river himself. He's quiet for a while, his well-trained features giving away nothing of his thoughts. Then he gives a long, slow sigh. "Memory is a strange thing."

You have no idea. I can't help but think of the person I was just a few days ago, lost and confused, wandering the streets of Alciel searching for answers to who I was. "How so?" I reply.

Techeki shakes his head a little, his eyes on the night outside. "When that cloudlander prince first appeared, arriving with you at the temple after we feared you were——" His lips twist in a grimace, and he doesn't look at me. "It was like the world was repeating itself. It was Talamar and Jezara all over again."

"Is that why you found it hard to trust him?" I ask gently. "Because you could tell he was a cloudlander?"

"I didn't trust him because of how he looked at you," Techeki replies with uncharacteristic bluntness and a sidelong glance at me. "As I said. Talamar and Jezara all over again."

He's watching me with a quizzical expression on his face, and for a moment I'm not certain why—and then I feel the blood start to rise to my face, and I break eye contact, hoping the night is enough to conceal any telltale darkening of my cheeks. "We never touched, North and I," I tell him, watching the river as the bindle cat shifts his weight uneasily. "Not before Inshara took hold of me."

Techeki huffs a soft breath, though whether it's a laugh or an expression of relief, I can't quite tell. "Daoman would have been proud of you." He pauses, and then adds quietly, "For that and for so many other things."

My throat tightens a little. "I still failed him in the end," I whisper, keeping my burning eyes fixed on the river below, the river I vaporized in my fury, turned to a dead thing like the city nearby.

"In the end?" Techeki's voice is sad, but there's something else in it too, a warmth I can't define. "How can you say so, when nothing is over yet? You are still here; so is North. So are your allies."

I just shake my head, emotion gripping me too tightly to allow me to speak until I've taken a few breaths. I wait until my vision stops blurring before turning to look at him again. "I saw him, Techeki. In the same vision that showed me Talamar and Jezara together. You, as well. I saw my initiation ritual. You were arguing with Daoman about whether I would drown in the bathing pool."

Techeki's eyebrows go up, and he runs a hand over his shaved head, fingers curling against his scalp. "Well, it may have taken me a few years, but I learned to stop underestimating you, Divine One." He flashes me a rueful smile. "The old know-it-all never could resist proving me wrong."

The fondness in his voice surprises me, and my face must show it, for he glances at me again.

"Yes, we were rivals, certainly," he says gently. "You cannot offer up that kind of power to men like Daoman and I and not expect a lifelong game of strategy between us. But he was also my friend."

My heart gives a little twist, and my gaze falls from his. "I know you have been running the temple while I was away, holding everything together. It is unfair that you have worked so hard, and now you must return all that power to me."

When I glance back up, I'm surprised to see something strange on Techeki's face—a fleeting pain, something stricken.

He's quick to smooth it all away, but I have known him almost all my life, and I can see the hurt in his eyes.

"Divine One," he says slowly, "I have never been more glad than when the guards brought you back up from the city today." He swallows. "Nimh, I was only ever holding it all together for *you*. You are my goddess, and I will serve you as long as I am able."

I exhale shakily, moved by the look in his eyes that, for once, he doesn't try to conceal: Faith. Relief. And something else, something like that warmth I heard in his voice earlier.

Techeki's eyes scan my face, and he tilts his head a little to one side in that habitual gesture of his. "I know you thought of Daoman as something like a father," he says, voice still quiet. Very carefully, he raises one hand so he can pluck at a lock of hair dangling just by my cheek, so that he can lift it back into place among the rest twisted back into a knot. "But you ought to know that he wasn't the only one who thought of you as something like a daughter."

Speechless, I can only gaze back at him, tears burning my eyes and choking my throat. The bindle cat rises, then stretches out his front legs in a bow before strolling across the windowsill to bump his head against Techeki's arm, purring.

Before either of us can say anything else, the door to the study opens, the noise startling Miri awake so abruptly that Saelis jerks upright and bangs his head against the wall with a stifled cry of alarm.

Talamar stands in the doorway, head bowed, one hand braced against the frame as though it's all that's keeping him on his feet.

North's jaw is tight as he regards the father he'd only just begun to know. "Well?" he prompts in a low voice.

Talamar bobs his head once. "She will come," he says simply. "We are to meet her at sunset tomorrow in the ruins of the ancient city. I say 'we'—but she believes I am coming alone. It was the only way."

But North's eyes narrow, not moving from his father's face. "What did you tell her?"

The man looks over at him, guilt and dignity mixed together in his expression. "That it was finally time for her to receive the Lightbringer's power. She still believes she was chosen, that the voice she hears through the chrono is that of a god who will grant her even more power than she already has. What else would bring her out of the palace, away from all her guards?"

"So you lied to her," North replies through gritted teeth. "Again."

I can hear the pain in his voice—he may not have known his father well, but to learn he is a liar and a coward so soon after reuniting with him must be a devastating blow. I move away from the window, taking a few steps toward North. "He's done as we asked," I tell him gently. "The lie will get her there, so we can talk."

"And you think she'll be *easier* to talk to when she finds out the truth?" But North's turning away, shoulders hunching— he's conceding the point.

"Either way," Techeki breaks in, "we ought to get some rest. We'll have to leave at dawn if we're to get to the city of the ancients by sunset. And," he adds, glancing between me and North, "I want us all at our best. Just in case."

Techeki wakes us just before dawn, and together we creep down one of the servants' corridors, through the kitchens, and out the exit that opens up onto the river below. We have no desire to explain to Elorin and her Graycloaks where we're going or why—and the Deathless still patrol sections of the city, too numerous for the temple guard or the Graycloaks to round up. Our party is small, just me, North, Techeki, and Talamar, and in our drab cloaks and jackets, we draw little attention.

The chill of the morning air makes me shiver, and I see North's gaze flick toward me, sensitive to any shift in my manner. I shake my head when he raises his eyebrows, wanting to savor the way the cold chills my skin. We've all slept far too little after such a world-shaking day, and I have to cling to alertness like a lifeline.

Matias is waiting for us at the river's edge on the riverstrider's barge he promised us. He pushes out the gangplank, and Techeki takes the other end, securing it wordlessly on the bank. I see the way their eyes meet as they work together, for just a moment longer than necessary. Something unspoken passes between them—a truce, I think, in service of my cause—and together they lock the gangplank into place.

We file across to the barge one by one, to join the Fisher King and his crew. North comes last of all, pausing to push the plank back across from the shore, and making a light-footed leap to join us. Matias steadies him by the arm and greets him with a nod that's deeper than I expected, almost like a bow of respect.

I can't help but wonder what transpired between them while I was gone. The news that not only was my quiet, humble Master of Archives secretly the riverstriders' fabled Fisher King but that he was also a Sentinel out of ancient legend was one of the hardest to digest bits of information Techeki briefed me on when I returned to the temple.

The barge is manned by a trio of riverstriders, plus the captain. They push off from the riverbank, and for a time, the only sound is the gentle swish of the water as they use poles to usher us into the current of the river, not able to use the engines until we're past the ring of sky-steel anchors still inhibiting the use of magic in the city.

The bindle cat is busy inspecting the barge for mice, poking his nose into the coils of rope here and there. Matias and the captain take Talamar down into the engine room to satisfy his curiosity about the integration of magic and machinery.

North and Techeki are standing by the railing, talking quietly. When I pass by, I overhear North trying to explain what he learned from ORACLE to my Master of Spectacle—how he will navigate the concept of an ancient computer, the truth about the two halves of the broken heart in their ancient story of how the world began, and the channeling of mist and faith into divinity, I do not know.

Then again, Techeki is already naturally inclined toward the importance of belief. He has spent his life on the ceremonies and spectacles that have bolstered my people's faith. Perhaps his keen mind will grasp it well enough. It would make sense to him, that faith should matter so much. I wish I had the words to tell him how much I value his.

I gaze out at the sky to the east, where the sun waits just below the horizon, a little of its light touching the undersides of the clouds with mauve.

After a time, North joins me at the railing, setting his hands down next to mine. When I turn my head, I realize Techeki is gone, and we are alone on the deck but for the riverstriders some distance back, wielding their poles through the dark.

We stand in silence together, watching the water ripple past, and eventually I speak. "Are you thinking about the others?" I ask quietly. "They will be all right. It is a good plan."

Miri, Saelis, and Anasta are most likely in Alciel now, even as we speed down the river away from them. Anasta was to use the rings that are her Sentinel's artifact to open a door in the mist for Inshara—once she is gone, it should be a simple matter to retrieve Beatrin, and invaluable in the long term. If we break Inshara's hold over the queen, we break her hold over Alciel's people.

Ours is by far the more dangerous task: facing Inshara with no way of defending against her powers, except for the slim hope that the truth might shatter her belief that she was chosen to rule this world.

North's face is grim in the low light, and he shakes his head. "I know the plan is sound," he replies. "I just wish I was with them." I can't help but remember that he saw them, *his* people, more and more of them succumbing to Inshara's control as he was forced to flee. And it's into this world that he's sent three people that he loves so dearly.

For the first time since he told me he was a prince, I can see the weight of that crown bearing down on him. For the first time, he looks like a king.

My heart gives a weary twinge, and I look into the murky water, so still and dark. "You will be with them," I tell him firmly. If it is what North wants, I will not try to stand between him and Miri and Saelis, no matter how much it hurts. "As soon as we return from dealing with Inshara."

"I still can't help but feel we're doing exactly as Inshara wants," he admits. "Until now she's been held inside Alciel by the mist. By opening a door for her, we let her out, back into this world."

"From what your heartmother told us, her power is only growing. If we leave her there and wait, who is to say that she will not have all of Alciel under her control by the time we feel ready to face her? Whether she intends to rule both worlds, or believes she is the true Lightbringer and tries to end them, we will not be able to stop her."

North's fingers tighten around the railing, and he doesn't answer, staring at the lightening sky.

I glance over my shoulder. The riverstriders are still fixed on their tasks, little more than dim outlines farther along the deck of the barge. North and I are alone.

I can imagine myself sliding my hand toward him on the railing of the barge, and letting my fingers brush his. I can imagine myself turning in to him, letting him enfold me in his arms. I can almost feel the brush of his shirt against my cheek, hear the steady thump of his heart as I lay my head against his chest.

But I remember as well the way my self-control threatened to crumble in the garden, when our fingers touched. What happened the last time I let go. I cannot take such a risk.

My hands tighten around the railing instead, an echo of North's grip.

I still remember the words Talamar and Jezara spoke to each other in the baths in my vision. *How is it,* he said, *that you can live your life without touching anyone? Never being touched?*

When I look up, I find North watching me, now, instead of the sky.

I am not just a goddess, Jezara replied. *I am* human *too. And I love you.*

There's another piece of that memory tugging at me too, though, insistent and nagging.

I can feel North turn his head to look at me, and after a moment, he murmurs, "Where'd you just go?"

I look up at him, briefly distracted by the way the dim light blurs and softens his features. "You are beginning to read me too easily, cloudlander," I mutter, though I cannot quite stop my lips from quirking a little, feeling oddly pleased that he knows me so well. "I was thinking of the vision I had, when I was connected to the temple's heart through the pool in my bathing chamber."

"The one of Jezara and Talamar?"

"It was the moment they first touched each other—first

kissed each other. They were standing in the pool. And I thought I saw something . . . *pass* from her to him. A shard of light."

When I glance up, North's eyes are wider, his expression thoughtful. "Like a piece of divinity?"

"Maybe. They were in the water, both close to the heart when it happened."

"You think my *father* is somehow connected to the heart now?"

"Or was." I search North's features, more and more easily seen as the light to the east grows stronger. "If he carried that within him when he returned to Alciel, and then he sired *you* . . ." I trail off, not sure how to articulate the tangle of confusion in my mind and heart.

North's eyebrows drawn in a little. "You think somehow that I'm carrying in me whatever it was she gave to him?"

I lift my shoulders in a small, helpless shrug. "You and I keep arguing about science and magic, technology and faith—but if the truth is something far more complex, if it is somehow both and neither . . . then destiny and fate must have a vehicle, some tangible way of working in the world. What if that connection to the hearts, that fragment of divinity, is what brought you here to fulfill your part in prophecy? Brought you to me?"

North has gone very still. "Go on," he urges. "Say it."

"What if—" I have to stop and swallow in an effort to clear the lump in my throat. "What if that connection is what we feel when we are together?"

He's motionless for a few breaths. Then, carefully, gently, he's wrapping his arms around himself, visibly withdrawing, his eyes going back to the horizon.

I don't bother to hide the hurt in my voice. "You cannot tell me that you have not wondered—I know you have. We've only known each other a few weeks, and most of that time, we were apart. You must have wondered if all of this between us is just prophecy. Just . . . magic."

North swallows, eyes falling a fraction, and I see it on his face—I'm not wrong. "I know what I feel," he says stubbornly, voice a little muffled.

I wrap my arms around myself. The cold is no longer bracing—now it just feels miserable and aching. "When you came to this world you were in love. And now that Miri and Saelis are here with you . . . I know it must be tearing your heart in two."

North's jaw clenches, but then he lets out a breath and shifts his gaze to me out of the corners of his eyes. "And what about you?" he asks tightly. "If there were no prophecy, no destiny, no heart connecting us—what would *you* feel?"

It would make no difference, my heart begs me to say. *I would love you if we were not a prince and a goddess; if we were farmers on the smallest of the sky-islands; if we were riverstriders fishing for our suppers. I would love you if I was nothing.*

But I cannot stop seeing his face when Miri and Saelis first threw their arms around him in the street yesterday.

"I cannot say," I mumble. "That is exactly my point. How can I know how I would feel if things were different?"

It takes me some time to be able to look at him, but when I do, he's watching me intently. I had expected to see hurt there

312

in his eyes, or anger—but instead he's searching my face, scanning my features, and for an instant I wonder if I spoke my true thoughts aloud. Or if he somehow reads them anyway.

He opens his mouth, but before he can speak the barge's engines kick into life with a sputter that shatters the dawn, and the vessel gives a lurch that makes us both jump.

The riverstriders along the deck stow their poles, and one of them vanishes up the ladder and into the cabin where the captain is. A few moments later, the captain himself emerges, having passed the steering of the barge over to his second, and comes sliding down the ladder and striding toward us.

With a start, I recognize Orrun, whose barge North and I stole the night of the Feast of the Dying when we fled the city.

"Divine One, Last Star of prophecy." Orrun shoves his hands into his pockets with a nod to each of us. "We're past the sky-steel now. It'll take us about six hours to get to the point in the river closest to the city of the ancients. Matias tells me that none of you have slept much—I recommend you all rest while there's nothing to do but wait."

North nods, clapping Orrun on the shoulder and then moving past me toward the ladder leading below deck. I start to follow, but Orrun clears his throat deferentially, making me pause and look back at him.

"This time," he says, face solemn but eyes gleaming, "may I ask that you not let anyone set fire to my new boat?"

THE QUEEN

The queen watches as her goddess paces back and forth, those beautiful, multicolored eyes alight. Her joy seems to grow with each passing moment—and with each passing moment, the queen's heart breaks a little bit more.

"Can you not stay?" the queen begs, her hands clutched together, fingers twisting. "Alciel needs you—her people *need* you."

Inshara does not stop her pacing, nor does she take her eyes from the archway filled with that crackling, purple-green barrier. "Be still," she snaps, though even angry her voice is lovely, compelling, irresistible. "I have no more need of queens, or the people of Alciel. When I return, I shall be a god unlike any either world has ever seen, and the people of *both* will worship me alone."

"You are *already* unlike anything I have ever seen," the queen chokes, her voice breaking in a sob. "And I already worship you—if you will not stay, can't you take me with you?"

Inshara snorts, a strangely musical sound for all its brusqueness. "He tells me they will open the barrier for me if I, and *only* I, pass through it."

"But how can you trust this man?" The queen can feel tears streaming down her face, but doesn't bother to wipe them away. "What can he offer you that could possibly make you any greater than you are?"

"My destiny," Inshara replies, her footsteps halting, so she can gaze at the barrier—*past* the barrier, her eyes distant. "They tried to convince me he was nothing, Beatrin. That all the promises he made me were nothing. But I knew—I had *faith*. All of this was a test, don't you see? A test of my power and my conviction. I brought down the home of the *gods*."

"But—"

"His power is what will give all of this meaning!" Inshara whirls around, fixing the queen with a stare that makes her fall to her knees. "Everything I've done—my mother—" Her voice cracks.

"You told me you lost her when you were very young," the queen whispers. "And I have lost my son. It would be the honor of my lifetime to love you and support you as you deserve—will you not stay, and be my daughter?"

Inshara's stare falters, those enchanting eyes softening a moment with confusion. Before she can speak, however, the barrier behind her gives a grating crackle, and then parts like a curtain being drawn back.

Inshara draws herself up, casting one last glance at the queen on her knees before her. "I have no need of queens," she mutters again, and vanishes through the portal.

TWENTY-TWO

NORTH

The riverstriders wanted to come with us, but I'm glad they stayed back at the boat as we hiked from the river to our meeting place.

There are a hundred places to hide here, where the grassy plains seem to ripple and wrinkle, as if someone had tugged at a huge blanket and created a messy spot in its middle. There are far fewer places that are also within earshot of Talamar and Inshara's meeting place, though—and within running distance to a tunnel down into the maze of ancient shopping avenues below.

"How do you think all these boulders got here?" I ask, patting one with my hand.

"A mist-storm, perhaps," Nimh says.

As if I didn't have a hundred other reasons to be highly stressed right now—my mind obediently conjures an image of the wild mist-storm that chased us here shortly after my arrival, sending us down into the caverns below.

Techeki pulls off his coat, setting it on the ground for Nimh to kneel on, despite her quiet protests—in the end she accepts it and crouches to be sure she can press her eye to the gap in the stones through which she'll watch.

Should I have offered mine? I know she doesn't need it, and after our conversation on the boat, I think maybe she'd rather I didn't. What I really want is to offer her my hand.

I settle beside her instead, finding my own gap between the stones. When I lift my head, she's watching me, her dark eyes thoughtful.

"You should keep this with you," she says quietly, reaching into her pocket and pulling out the protection stone.

"I gave it to you," I say, a little too quickly, and I'm not sure if the faint edge to my voice is my nerves, or an echo of the conversation we had on the boat, or both.

"It makes more sense for you to have it," she replies. When I hold out my palm she drops the stone into it, still holding the warmth of her skin. It feels like she's giving back more than just the charm she made me.

I don't know how to answer her questions about whether I'd have loved her if we had simply met and there was no prophecy guiding either of us.

I could tell her that I love her generosity, and the mischief in her smile, and her quick wits, and that none of those things would change if we were in another time, another place.

But a part of me knows I have no right to protest her words, no right to the hurt I'm feeling. Because I've wondered too—is the prophecy coming true because we're falling in love, or are we falling in love so that the prophecy can come true?

And if we truly are entwined as tightly as it feels to me,

what can I say to Miri and Saelis? Seeing the two of them, feeling their arms around me—it felt like coming home. It felt like sunshine after a storm. And I *do* love them. I just wish I knew whether I was still *in* love with them.

"The sun has nearly set," Techeki says quietly. "She cannot be far away, if she has come straight from the city, as we must hope."

"As we must hope indeed," Nimh agrees. We took a boat and traveled faster, but we left only enough time for Inshara to walk here after Anasta opened the way for her. We didn't want to give her an opportunity to try anything else.

"Talamar is ready," Techeki says, nodding to my father, who I can see between my own gap in the stones.

He stands alone, hands folded behind his back, apparently calm. Then, as if to belie that appearance, he reaches inside his jacket, feeling for his inhaler and failing to find it. He folds his hands together once more, keeping his eyes fixed on the middle distance. Perhaps he's watching something, or someone, approach—I can't tell.

"We will be ready too, if we must," Nimh murmurs, nodding to our right. We're all aware of the dark space where the boulders meet the hillside. It's an opening that leads down to the labyrinth of tunnels beneath the hills, the ruins of an ancient arcade and who knows what else, probably there since before the Exodus.

I'd love to ask ORACLE about it—it's been incredibly easy to get back into the habit of looking everything up as soon as I wonder it, the way I've done all my life, up to the last few weeks.

That will have to wait, though—the bracelet is safe with Miri. I wasn't willing to bring it near Inshara, not when my blood is the key to accessing everything it knows. If what we're trying here goes wrong, then at least she won't have that.

Talamar straightens, folding his hands behind his back, and now I know he must see her approaching. Beside me, Techeki clicks his tongue and nods at my father to make sure Nimh and I have both seen the change in his posture.

I don't know if he can pull this off.

On one hand, I watched him for years as a councilor in Alciel—he represented the smallest of the islands, but things so often seemed to fall his way in the final vote. I know that he knows how to put his case persuasively.

But I also know that when it comes to Inshara, he doesn't think straight.

I brace myself, unsure what I'll see when Inshara comes into view—all I can remember is her mad, twisted face as she grabbed for Nimh's ankle, the mist raging in her eyes.

Then she steps into my line of sight, and my breathing shallows as I press my eye to a gap between the rocks, as if she might hear my slightest exhalation. She matches Talamar's upright posture—she's clad in black, smart enough not to wear red out across the plains—and her hair is drawn back in a braid. Unbidden, my mind tries to slot her into a picture of me, my mothers, Talamar.

Her eyes are shining, her lips pressed together hard, but still quivering just a fraction. She's gazing at our father like she's a bride arriving at her wedding, and all her dreams stand before her. Her movements are slow, measured—she's drinking in everything about this moment.

As she comes closer to Talamar, though, her eyes widen a little, and her lips part. "I recognize you," she says, her surprise audible, her steps slowing. "I have seen you above."

Talamar clears his throat, then speaks, his voice even. "I'm glad you came, Insha."

Her mouth falls open in recognition as she hears his voice, and she takes an involuntary step forward, both hands lifting to clasp in front of her chest. "*You* are the Lightbringer?"

"We have much to discuss," he says calmly, inclining his head.

"You," she repeats, her eyes raking over him. Her expression has dimmed a fraction, as if she'd been expecting something else—something more godlike, perhaps. Something that would live up to her lifetime of imagination. "Why did you not say anything to me? Why did you bury the chrono you used to speak to me all those years?"

Talamar swallows—I can see his throat move from here—but he stands his ground, avoiding any telltale shifting or fidgeting to betray his nerves. "It wasn't time yet," he says finally.

Beside me, Nimh's breath catches faintly. My own heart is pounding—*tell her*, I urge him. *Who you are, why you did what you did.*

"Not time?" Inshara's voice thins, becoming sharp like a blade. "But you were there, I recognize you from the palace. You saw my power. How could you let me think you had abandoned me?" She reaches inside her tunic, pulling out the chrono she wears around her neck, clutching it in one hand. "I would hold it, you know, on the worst days. A merchant who had agreed to sell us food waited until the day before the cold came, then tripled his price. A section of the cliff fell down on our garden, and we had to dig out every piece of stone by hand until we bled. There was nobody to ask for help—it wasn't safe, they hated us so. You were all I had, a voice whispering to me from this relic. And you let me think you had no more use for me."

Her voice is dropping lower, until I can only just make out her words, and Talamar steps in closer. The setting sun blazes between their bowed heads, turning each of them to silhouettes.

"I would hold the chrono," she whispers, "and know that you would call again. And that when dawn came, we would be one day closer to this moment."

"I am sorry," Talamar manages, his own rich voice soft. "Insha, I barely know where to begin. You look so like your mother. I wish she had been here to see us meet."

She blinks at him once—then her eyes narrow in confusion. "My mother?" she echoes. "How can you know what she looked like?"

Now, Talamar. Tell her the truth, for once in your miserable life.

Talamar hesitates for one long moment—I don't think any of us in concealment so much as breathe.

"I am the Lightbringer," he says finally, his voice thick. "I know all."

What did he just say?

Inshara takes a long, shaking breath, her eyes shining.

"Then do as you said you would. Grant me your power—make me your instrument in this world. I am ready."

"I—" Talamar swallows again, his fear becoming more obvious. Too obvious. "It's still not time. We must continue to prepare."

"What?" she spits. "Tell me you jest."

I feel like standing up and shouting the same thing: *Tell me you jest, Talamar! Tell me you didn't just keep on with the lie you've been telling her all these years!*

"I did not tell you to take hold of the queen of the cloud-landers," he says, his tone growing more formal. "You should have shown more restraint. That is why I stopped speaking to you—I wasn't sure you were ready after all. You should have treated their world with more respect."

With a sudden burst of clarity, realization dawns on me. He spent fifteen years building up her madness, and now he stands before her, a powerful magician, and he's not willing to risk his life. Simple as that.

My father is a coward.

"Their world? The world of the gods, you mean? But the queen is not a god." Inshara snaps the words. "None of them are! So I took charge of them all—what else should I have done?"

"You should have waited," he replies, his own voice rising.

Techeki whispers something under his breath, and though I can't make it out, I share his incredulity. What's Talamar's play here? What's he going to do if she agrees to stay with him and keep learning? How long can he possibly string her along?

She's staring at him now, as if she's trying to decode something about him. She stands perfectly still, her brow creased. And then that furrow disappears.

"My mother said you were not a god," she says slowly. "She said you were only a man, but I knew better. She said this artifact you used to send me your messages was neither magical nor divine. But I *thought* I knew better."

She looks down at the chrono in her hand, then slowly lifts the leather band on which it hangs from around her neck, so she can swing the device back and forth.

Everything is quiet. Everything is still.

"But it's just a chrono," she says slowly. "Everyone in Alciel has one."

"Insha," says Talamar, slow and careful, lifting a hand.

Her fury is sudden, her voice rising to a shout, her hands lifting, the chrono catching the last of the sunset. "It is *nothing*," she spits, throwing it to the ground. She shifts her weight, lifts her foot, and drives her heel down onto the chrono with a *crunch*. When she moves again, sparks fizz in the ruins, and the light fades from it. "It is nothing," she repeats, softer now. "It is a lie, and you are no more a god than the rest of them. All my life, your voice in my ear, your false words in my heart. All my life, everything I have done—and it was for *you*?"

"Insha, you were alone," he protests. "I wanted to——"

"I do not care!" The mist-storm raging in her eyes whips up, her face twisting, her fists clenching. Then, slowly, her head turns, until she's looking directly in our direction. We're hidden behind the stones, but it can't be a coincidence.

I glance across to Nimh, who's waiting wide-eyed to meet my gaze. She's shifting her grip on her staff, preparing to rise to her feet, resolute. We came here because it was isolated, so innocents won't be harmed if Nimh and Inshara clash. But that doesn't mean Nimh will be safe.

I glance back at Talamar and Inshara—he has his hands lifted, trying to pacify her, but she's beyond listening.

"The gods of the cloudlands are no more than men," she shouts, voice rising, "but *I* will show you real power! You think you have known divinity?" She gives a bark of a laugh, a crackling sense of power rising all around her, as if she holds an entire mist-storm within her. "I am already more powerful than any god you have ever known. Worship me, and I shall let you live."

For in an instant there's a strange twist in my mind, like a fish flickering past on its way somewhere else—and then I'm sprawling to the ground as Techeki springs to his feet, pushing past me. His face is twisted into an impossible grimace, and with one shaking hand he reaches out toward me.

I grab for him, but he wrenches himself away, striding out of cover, pulling his knife from his belt as he walks unhesitatingly toward Talamar and Inshara. He must be trying to end Inshara before she can exert her power over the rest of us, but he'll never get there in time—she can see him already as they both swing around to face him—he lifts the knife, the blade flashing in the dying sun.

I come to my feet, reaching out with one hand, and I sense Nimh beside me. Techeki's too close—there's nothing I can do to save him, and a part of me shies away from hoping for him—still, after all of this, shies away from the thought of that knife plunging into Inshara.

Talamar simply stares, his breath shuddering, one hand raised as if to ward off the Master of Spectacle. And it's that hand that Techeki grabs in order to yank Talamar back against him, the blade of his knife held to my father's throat.

Talamar swallows, the blade so close it brushes skin, and slowly, the pair of them turn under Inshara's triumphant gaze, until they're facing Nimh and me.

And that's when I see the tears in Techeki's eyes, spilling slowly down his cheeks. My mother's face flashes before me, bringing with it the memory of seeing her heart twisted to serve Inshara—and those same tears on her face.

"No," Nimh whispers, horror creeping into her voice as she realizes the truth a moment after I do.

"I can feel the rest of you," Inshara says, calm now, her words slow. "Your hearts beating away there, behind the ruins. Come out and join your friend, and we will return to the cities together. *Then* you will know I am worthy."

TWENTY-THREE
NIMH

"Techeki!" His name bursts out of me, and I leap to my feet to go after him. Something drags me back, though, and for a moment I'm so confused by why I'm not moving that I can barely think.

"You can't go out there," North is saying in my ear—he's got hold of my spearstaff, keeping me at his side.

"What—let *go!*" I could let go of the spearstaff myself, but the anguish in North's face stops me, keeps both of us holding on. "I can't lose him too!"

"And I can't lose you!" North doesn't budge, doesn't release his grip.

For the span of a few heartbeats, we're no longer in the ruins—we're standing on that winding path from Jezara's house, with a sheer cliff face on one side and a long, deadly fall on the other. And his grip on the staff is all that's keeping me from falling.

I could let go—I could run. North wouldn't be able to stop me, not without grabbing hold of me, and I know he won't. But to let go would be to use that faith and respect against him. To tell him the trust between us means more to him than it does to me.

Inshara's watching, her face grim; Techeki stands beside her, tears rolling down his cheeks, tension in every line of his body as he holds the blade to Talamar's throat.

"Use the Lightbringer's power." North pulls the spearstaff, and me along with it, back behind the rocks so he can look into my face. "There's mist all around us, right? Use it to hold her, and Techeki, and we can get my father out of there."

My body, so intent on running after Techeki, goes still. My mind floods with the consequences of releasing my iron grip on my control, even to this small degree. I'm aware of North's presence just beside me, can feel his warmth like the coals of a fire. I can feel his desperation.

Gasping for a breath, I blurt, "I—I can't."

His face ripples with frustration, and he risks a peek over the rocks. "There's no time. Nimh, I *know* you can do it—you used it to stop the train car from falling."

"And I used it to destroy my city." I'm still frozen, unable to look away from his face. From the way he looks over the rocks again, I can tell Inshara is closer, coming for us. "I can't go to that place again."

North's eyes find their way back to my face, and he hesitates for a long moment, his internal struggle written clearly in his expression. "Then we have to go. Now. *Now!*" He shifts his grip on the staff and leaps up to pull me along with him.

The movement jars me from my paralysis, and I manage to get my legs working so that North isn't forced to drag me like a bundle of laundry. We chose our position well—the entrance to the buried ruin is just behind us—but I'm so certain that

Inshara is on our heels, that my dear Techeki will be there with his knife, slashing at us, that my skin crawls.

But when we reach the shadow of the ruin, I look over my shoulder and see that Inshara is standing just where she was, watching us go, her face unreadable. Talamar, still held at her side by Techeki's unyielding grip, has gone white.

We keep running, half sliding down an ancient marble floor that's now tilted at an angle. Fragments of daylight filter down from gaps in the earth and stone ceiling, but they do little to light the way—then my foot catches on a bit of detritus and sends me sprawling, my spearstaff clattering to the ground. North halts a few paces away, doubling over for a few breaths and then backtracking to kneel at my side.

"Are you all right?" he manages, panting.

I'm too winded to reply with anything other than a wordless sob, picking myself up onto my hands and knees, which are bleeding sluggishly from being scraped against the stone.

North sinks back onto his heels and scrubs at his face. "I'm sorry I—" But there he stops, unable to articulate what passed between us in that moment when he held me just by a touch on my spearstaff.

I shake my head, trying to catch my breath and swallow my feelings at the same time. "No. You were right to stop me. I just—" My voice halts again, and I shake my head again.

"I know." North's face is uncharacteristically grim. "I just hope the others were able to get my mother out of Alciel." He runs his hand through his hair, disheveling his curls, and looks back at me. "We'll get Techeki back. I was hoping there'd be *some* sign that reconnecting you with the temple's heart affected Inshara's power."

I wrap my arms around myself miserably. "So what do we do? Ask ORACLE if there's any other way?"

"We'll have to get the bracelet back from Miri," North replies, grimacing. "Or get back to ORACLE itself, but that means heading across the city."

I reach for the spearstaff and use it to help myself to my feet, my body aching from its collision with the ground. *We have to go after Techeki,* I want to say—but I know there's no point until we find a way to interrupt Inshara's power over those she holds in her grip. I dare not say it to North, at least not until we've seen his mothers, but we don't even know for sure that those whose minds she's taken can ever recover their own will. "We ought to get back to Matias," I say instead, the words slow and quiet. "Before Inshara stumbles across the barge and we lose our way back into the city."

North's eyes are on the ground as he rises to his feet, gaze distant—remembering, perhaps, that last glimpse of his father standing at Inshara's side. "I don't think she'll be sticking around," he says quietly. "She got what she wanted."

The night is thick and heavy by the time we get back to Orrun's barge, the starless sky threatening rain. The bindle cat, having chosen for once to remain with the riverstriders rather than accompany me, greets us from the railing of the ship. His calling brings the others, all clamoring to know what happened. Only Matias is quiet, eyes raking across our group—just two returning, when there were four who left his boat a few hours before.

"You had to make the attempt," he says quietly, once the riverstriders have gone back to their tasks and gotten the boat underway back up the river. "If there was any chance of piercing the veil of her delusions, it was a chance worth taking."

"If Talamar had just told her the truth . . ." North bursts out, bent over with his forehead on his folded arms against the railing.

Matias waits, but when North shows no sign of finishing the sentence, says pointedly, "She might have reacted even more poorly if he had. The truth is that your father has been whispering in her ear since she was a child. In a strange way, he knows her better than anyone—perhaps he sensed that the truth would only make things worse."

"Worse than having lost both him and Techeki?" North straightens and turns to put his back to the railing. "Skyfall, I hope Miri and Saelis and my mothers are at the temple waiting for us. That's the only thing that might salvage this."

"It'll be a few hours before we reach the city again—we must go carefully, to avoid attracting the attention of any Deathless who might be patrolling downriver from the riverstrider encampment. If I were you two, I'd get some rest. You have a habit of going without."

He vanishes back below the deck, leaving North and I—and the bindle cat—alone.

I hesitate, part of me wanting to simply follow Matias below deck and let the sounds of the river and the engines drown out my thoughts. I can feel North's eyes on me, though when I glance his way, he's gazing fixedly at the wooden deck.

The bindle cat gives a little chirp and sashays over toward North, arching his back and bumping up against his legs. Without seeming to think, North moves his arm, making room for the cat to jump up onto the railing at his side and then bump his head against North's jaw.

I can't help but smile a little, crossing my arms and taking a few steps toward them. "And to think that a little over a fortnight ago you had never seen a cat before."

North curls his hand and tickles the cat under his chin, triggering a purr loud enough to be heard over the sound of the barge's engines. "I still maintain they're terrifying creatures."

As if to prove his point, the cat opens his mouth and snaps at North's hand—though he pauses there, teeth resting lightly against the skin, and eyes the prince thoughtfully. *Your move.* North flinches, but manages not to jerk his hand away, and after a moment the cat lets him go and jumps down off the railing huffily.

The quiet threatens to settle in again, my heart aching at this new divide between us. North won't meet my eyes. He speaks, but he's . . . conversational.

I thought it would help him to know what I saw in my vision, that his father may have passed some form of connection to the temple's heart to him. I thought it would let him see his own feelings more clearly—know where he would be happiest.

Instead, he feels as far away from me as he did when we were worlds apart.

"I—I'm sorry," I mumble into the heavy darkness. When he looks up at me, eyebrows lifting a fraction, I add, "About Talamar."

"He made his choice when he decided to keep lying to her." North shakes his head, eyes falling again. "I'd only just begun to know him, you know, before I fell. I know who my real parents are. And if we saved my mother today . . . it's worth it."

"Maybe I could have stopped them," I say quietly.

North huffs a breath and glances at me, his gaze uncharacteristically opaque. "I shouldn't have asked you to try. I can't imagine what it's like to have a power like that in you and not be able to control it."

"After what happened the last time Inshara and I did battle . . . I think it may be why I could not remember anything, when I first arrived in Alciel. I think perhaps my mind was trying to protect me, knowing that if I remembered what I had done to my own people, I might . . . I might become the Destroyer again."

"You used to think it was your destiny to destroy the world. What changed?" North asks—and though the words are a challenge, his tone is gentle.

The question hurts anyway, tugging at that deep place of uncertainty in my heart. I let my breath out and cross to the railing, an arm's length away from North, so I can look into the water. Even this far away from the city, the river is changed—I didn't vaporize this part of it, but all the dead plants and animals and loose sediment I stirred up flowed downstream, and I can smell that underlying odor of decay.

"The story of the original Lightbringer," I say finally, "is that he was destined to be the world's end, to wipe the land clean of life so that it might start anew. But when the time came for him to fulfill his destiny, he balked, and fled along with the rest of the gods into the sky." Again I feel North's eyes on me; this time, when I glance his way, he meets my gaze. "Maybe that's part of the cycle too. And I am just one more in a long line of gods too frightened of fate to do what must be done."

"I don't think that's it." North's voice is slow and thoughtful. "The story isn't done yet, and nothing is quite as it seems in this prophecy of yours. We know now what ORACLE really is—we know the two halves of the broken heart are real. We know there's more to the tale than we've been told. There's still time for us to figure out what it really means."

"But my power—"

"Is yours," he says. "You're supposed to use it. You may have forgotten that in Alciel—but you remember everything now, don't you?"

"Almost everything." I hesitate, scanning his features. There's a question I have been too frightened to ask, even as more and more of my memory returns. If my mind is truly protecting me from truths too horrible for me to bear, then perhaps there's a reason I haven't regained this last piece of the puzzle. "North . . . where is Elkisa?"

He stiffens, lips tightening. His expression tells me everything—the fragments of memory begin to fit together. Elkisa, finding Jezara and I by the burned remains of Orrun's boat. The revelation that she'd been working for Inshara all that time—my dearest friend and oldest companion, a traitor. The remnants of North's red sash tossed down onto the riverbank. Her lips forming the silent words: *North is dead.*

And then . . . nothing.

Perhaps the destruction of my city wasn't the memory my mind was protecting me from. Perhaps it was trying to shield me from a horror far worse.

He sees the truth dawning on my face and says nothing, but simply watches me, his eyes softening with the compassion that's only ever a heartbeat away, for him.

The real question, the core of the missing memory, I haven't the heart to ask—instead, I turn my gaze out toward the water, leaning on the railing once more, dropping my head. A shiver runs through me, echoing the ripples of the water below.

Then something touches my shoulder, and I startle, turning my head—but though North's close, it's not him. Slowly, carefully, he's draping his jacket around my shoulders. It carries with it the warmth of his body—the reminder that I am only ever a word away from his touch. That he would fold me up in his arms if I asked him to.

My tongue feels thick in my mouth, my throat too tight, and to my surprise, I find tears rolling down my cheeks. These are no gift from Inshara, though—the question that drives them is all my own.

Did I kill her? The words bounce around in my thoughts, but I stay silent, turning my head to touch my cheek to the warmth of North's coat. He stands silently beside me, as if to keep guard, while I cry over my lost friend—for she *is* lost to me, one way or the other, forever.

The riverstriders tie up the barge in the same place where we left this morning, outside the entrance to the temple kitchens. North and I leave Matias to pass orders for the riverclans along to Orrun, unwilling to wait even that long to get back and find out if North's family has made it safely out of Alciel.

The kitchens are dark and empty, the strangeness of that sight making my skin crawl as we make our way toward the staircases leading up to the rest of the temple. We pause at the bottom so that North can light a lantern. When I look behind us, the bindle cat is sitting in the far doorway, feet planted, tail twitching anxiously, ears flicking around as if listening to sounds I can't hear. I drift toward one of the hearths, not sure what I'm looking for until I reach it. I stretch a hand over the ashes there: *cold*.

"North . . ." My voice sounds strange. "Something's wrong."

The lantern flares to life, illuminating North's features as he adjusts the flame down a little. "What do you mean?"

"Where is everyone?"

"It's the middle of the night—they're sleeping, I assume."

I shake my head, stubborn. "There should be a few people working even at night. I've never seen this place empty all my life."

North's brow furrows, and he opens his mouth—but then his eyes fall upon the lantern, or rather, his hand upon it. With a sharp intake of breath, he lets go of it, the whole thing falling to the floor with a crash of glass, the oil spreading into a flaming pool.

I hurry to North's side, where he's crouching, wiping at the floor.

"Blood," he manages, gesturing at the crimson streaks his fingers leave behind on the stone. "I felt something sticky on the lantern—I just thought, it's the kitchens—"

The sight of blood on the floor of the kitchens; the sight of the bodies of my guards hanging from that clearing the night North fell to this world; the sight of the dust settling after Inshara blew a hole in the wall of my temple.

This is all wrong.

Before I can say anything else, North is stiffening, rising to his feet—and then breaking into a run, up the stairs.

"Wait!" I gasp, reaching out to try to grab him, but missing. "North—stop!"

"My family is in there," he shoots back over his shoulder, taking the stairs two at a time.

I'm forced to pause long enough to stifle the lamp oil fire with an empty sack before I can run after him, encumbered by robe and spearstaff. By the time I reach the top of the stairs, I can no longer see him—but there's only one way to go, down the long corridor that eventually opens out into the passages for servants and acolytes.

I turn the corner and skid to a halt, for North is there, shoulders hunched, one hand braced against the wall. For a moment, I can't tell why he's stopped—and then I see the shadowy forms scattered here and there along the length of the hallway. They look like bundles of rags, the careless leavings of a servant bringing linens to the laundry.

Then one of them moves.

North and I break into a run together, hurrying down the hall; he drops to his knees, his shock registering on his face before I follow his gaze to see—

"Elorin?" I gasp.

The leader of the Graycloaks groans, her eyes vague as they move past my face and North's without much sign of recognition. Her cloak is gone, and her clothes stained with blood—a sticky crimson pool surrounds her, and there's an ugly tangle of flesh, cloth, and blood in her side. North takes her hand, even as mine go to my chatelaine of herbs and spell reagents—but we're inside the ring of sky-steel again. There's nothing I can do.

"What happened?" North's voice is taut, his whole body showing his urgency.

"Deathless," Elorin manages, her breathing wet and labored. "Came at . . . dawn. Took the temple. They're still here, you must be careful. Dressed like temple guard. *Was . . .* temple guard."

I look at North, on the other side of the Graycloak, holding her hand. He looks back at me, expression grim and fearful.

Elkisa.

"Said . . ." Elorin pauses, her whole body wracked with a sudden cough. Blood sprays against my robe, a darker crimson soaking into the fabric against my thigh. "Said . . . orders of the true divine."

North lets out a sound, half strangled in his throat. The hint of despair in it tears at my heart, even as it sinks into a deep pit of anguish.

This was where he was meant to meet his family. And instead, the temple is lost.

Inshara played us. We'd thought to distract her by summoning her to the ruins to speak to Talamar, and sneak in to retrieve the queen. Instead, she took advantage of our absence from the temple, got word to Elkisa somehow, and had her take the temple from us in a single day.

"Tried to run," Elorin continues, her breathing quickening, each rise and fall of her chest growing shallower and shallower. "The others—did they make it?"

I look past her, at the other bodies scattering the hallway. North meets my gaze, and in that moment we have no need to speak to each other.

"Yes," he says, squeezing her hand. "Yes, you bought them enough time. They made it out."

Elorin's urgency eases a fraction, relief lending more life to her dull eyes as she eases back again. She blinks once, twice— then her eyes focus on my face. "Divine One," she croaks, as if just realizing I was there. "Will you . . . ?" Her mouth works for a moment, possessing not enough breath to finish the sentence—but I recognize the shape of the words.

For a moment I can't move, my mind flooding with the pain of the last few years, the rise of the Graycloak movement that hated me so and preached against my divinity. I remember that boy in the floating market the morning I left the city in search of the Last Star—his voice still echoes in my ears. *The last of the gods has gone, and all that is left is nothingness in the form of an empty girl called Nimh.*

"Yes." I take a breath and whisper, "Yes, I will bless you. Blessings be upon you, Elorin. May you walk lightly through the void until you live again when the world is new . . ."

North keeps hold of her hand until the blessing is complete, and the final words—*until we meet again*—finish echoing in the still, dead corridor. When I've finished, he carefully folds the woman's hand over her body, concealing the wound, a tiny gesture to make her look a little more at peace. The shallow, rattling breathing has stopped—she lies still now.

North rises to his feet, and I clumsily follow suit. "We have to move quickly," he says in a low voice, his eyes fixed on the far end of the corridor.

I'm about to agree when I realize he didn't mean what I'd thought. "North—no. You cannot go look for them."

"You should stay here." North doesn't look at me. "Or better yet, go and wait with Matias and Orrun. I'll meet you once I've found them."

"You don't know that they're here!" I burst out, though I know my arguments mean nothing—North thought he lost his family once. If I were in his place, there's no power in this world that would stop me searching the temple for them now. "You heard what Elorin said—Inshara's people have taken the temple. If Miri and Saelis and Anasta *are* here, they're prisoners." *Or worse,* my mind tells me. "We have to hope they never made it out of Alciel, that they're still there with the queen."

"If there's a chance," North says through gritted teeth, "then I'm going to find them."

Without looking back at me, he begins striding down the corridor, his long legs eating up the space. For a moment, I can't move—then I break my paralysis and lurch after him.

I catch hold of his sleeve, torn by the need to grab hold of him and stop him—but knowing that now, of all times, I cannot afford to lose my control. "North, *stop!*"

His sleeve drags at his arm for a moment, and he jerks it away without difficulty. But then he halts, breathing hard, his whole body vibrating with the need to keep moving. For a moment, I can't breathe—despite his urgency, he knows I cannot take hold of him and stop him bodily as I wish to do. Just as I let him stop me with a touch on my spearstaff—he is *letting* me stop him now.

"We need to retreat and make a plan," I tell him, trying to catch his eye, though he keeps his gaze fixed on the floor. "There are only two of us, there is nothing we can do alone. We must find some way to get past the Deathless, get the river-striders to fight—"

North makes an inarticulate sound, hands curling into fists as his weight shifts. Everything in him is telling him to run in search of his people. "Let me go, Nimh, I have to—"

"North—I can't lose you too!"

My voice echoes down the corridor, emerging in a wail, urgency overcoming the need for quiet. North freezes, only the harshness of his breathing to suggest he hasn't turned to stone. My heart is pounding with fear, knowing I should not test him this way, ask him to trust me over his need to find the people he loves. Moving carefully to avoid jostling him from this moment, I step close until I can duck my head and force him to meet my eyes.

"*We will come back*," I tell him fiercely, ruthlessly ignoring my rising desire to put my arms around him. He relaxes a fraction in response to my voice, head bowing so that our foreheads are so close I can feel his curls against my brow. "I swear it, North. This is my home—my family—too. We will come back, and we will fight. But we can only do that if we live through the night and figure out what to do next."

North's hand lifts, pausing a fraction of an inch from my cheek, and his shoulders quake as he surrenders. "They were supposed to be here," he manages, his voice thin and tight. He raises his head once more, and a tear drops from his long lashes onto his cheek.

"We'll find them," I whisper, my eyes on his, my own heart swelling. He didn't have to stop for me—I could not force him to, and he knew it. But he chose to listen. He chose to stay. "I promise."

TWENTY-FOUR
NORTH

The riverstriders are up at dawn, the sounds of mixed voices rising in a work song rousing me from my stupor. I remember very little of our retreat from the temple—I let Nimh lead me back out to Orrun's boat at the river, stopping only briefly to bandage up a few bleeding puncture marks on my ankle where the bindle cat bit me. He hadn't moved from the place he stopped on our way in, and I can't help but feel like his bite was a punishment for not heeding the warning he gave us with his twitching tail and flicking ears.

Now, he sits ensconced in a nest of blankets on Nimh's berth, his golden eyes watching me steadily. Upon meeting my gaze, he gives me a slow, lazy blink.

All is forgiven, I guess.

I don't think I properly slept, my mind drifting in and out of true wakefulness. My whole being is itching to do something to help Miri and Saelis, not to mention my mothers, but I have to acknowledge the truth in what Nimh said: we don't *know* that they're in there with Elkisa and the Deathless. They're smart, and though this is unfamiliar territory, there's at least a chance they've found a way to hide or escape back into Alciel.

And I have to believe that if they *are* in Elkisa's grip, they're too valuable to kill outright.

I roll over as quietly as I can, not wanting to disturb the still, quiet mound of blankets that's all I can see of Nimh. But the moment I move, her head appears from the pile, her eyes finding me in the meager morning light filtering in from the portholes. She looks weary, but her gaze is alert.

She must not have slept either.

I hunt for a smile and find to my surprise that I don't have to work that hard at it. Despite how much I ache for action, I also want to linger in this moment. In waking up with her there, looking utterly human with her mussed hair and rumpled robes, and yet undeniably something more. She smiles back at me.

We join Matias and Orrun up on deck, along with Hiret, and a few other riverstriders I don't recognize. The others have feathers and stones woven into their hair of different colors than Orrun's—Hiret has none, her widow's hair shorn too short for it.

I think the difference in color means they belong to other clans, but they all look at Matias with the same kind of respect my bloodmother's advisors show her. When Nimh appears, all of them turn toward her and offer up variations on that salute I've seen—and occasionally received myself, as the Last Star, while Nimh was gone—where they cover their eyes with their hands. Hiret lingers a moment before she lifts her hands, as if she wants to take in the sight of Nimh—her husband died to protect her, after all, the night I fell from Alciel.

"We've been discussing what to do next," says Orrun when the formal greetings are done with. "We've got a number of our 'striders fortifying and patrolling our perimeter so that we can try to dig in against the Deathless."

"We only have perhaps a fortnight of food," points out one of the riverstriders from another clan. "Ordinarily we could fish for more and last indefinitely, but . . ." She manages not to look at Nimh, but I know everyone is thinking the end of that sentence anyway: the river has no fish, because Nimh's fury vaporized it when she came for Inshara before they both Ascended.

"We cannot wait that long." Nimh's voice is quiet, but cuts through the others effortlessly.

"Wait before what?" asks Hiret, watching her goddess with a neutral expression. I can't imagine what it costs her—in her place I'm not sure I could have forgiven Nimh. Perhaps she understands that her husband's death was Inshara's fault.

Nimh meets Hiret's gaze, then looks around at the others. "Before we launch an assault on my temple."

Even I catch my breath, eyes snapping back to Nimh's face as the others begin spluttering their own surprised responses. "You want to attack the temple head-on?" I ask, not bothering to raise my voice over the rest, because Nimh is watching me, waiting for my reaction.

"We cannot stop Inshara if she holds the temple, for that means she also holds all of Alciel and both hearts," she says. "We cannot get across the city to consult ORACLE on how to break her control—the Deathless are too well-established. Elkisa will know we may try to reach that place, and she will have cultists watching the streets by now."

"And Miri has the ORACLE bracelet," I add miserably. "So we have no way of speaking to the computer." This is to the confusion of most of the riverstriders, but Nimh nods at me, her face grim.

"I have thought all night on what to do," she continues, raising her voice over the murmurs of her people and demanding their attention. "We cannot wait here, because Elkisa knows of the riverstriders' loyalty and piety; she knows North and I will have come to the river clans for help. Sooner or later, she and her Deathless will come for us here, and no amount of fortification and patrol will be able to withstand them. Our half of the heart lies within the temple—if Inshara learns of its existence, there's no telling what she might do. We also cannot wait for her to find North's family, either in the temple or in Alciel, and realize how valuable they are as hostages—it may be that she has them already, but if we can prevent it by acting now, we must."

I'm watching her carefully, and I don't miss the tightening of her features as she takes a breath, halts, and then closes her mouth again.

"Those aren't the only reasons, are they?" I ask.

Nimh's troubled gaze doesn't leave my face, even though the riverstriders have calmed enough to listen to us. "The temple is a symbol," she says finally, her voice a little halting. "The longer it stands as a testament to Inshara's strength, the more my people may turn to her with their faith. I have already lost so many of them." Her gaze flicks over toward the riverbank and the swath of ruined city beyond it.

"And if they start believing in her instead of you, you'll have less of the heart's power." I finish the thought for her, my own heart sinking a fraction. "Without a way to consult ORACLE, we have no way of stopping her."

"How can belief in her give her any greater power than she already has?" Orrun asks, glancing between us.

Nimh shakes her head. "I cannot say—except that our half of the heart is designed to channel belief into power. Perhaps it will mean she is able to control even greater numbers of innocent people."

"But attack the temple?" Orrun breaks in, his brow furrowed and eyes worried. "We have no idea how many Deathless might be in there, plus half the temple guard by now, following Elkisa out of misplaced loyalty or through deception."

I glance involuntarily at Hiret for his words, and her expression is grim. Her sister Didyet was one of the Graycloaks inside the temple. I can't help but think that if she survived the massacre, we'd have seen her back here by now. Does that add to Hiret's appetite for the blood of the Deathless? Or does she nurture some secret hope that Didyet has become one of them and is somehow still alive?

"My people are fishermen and foragers," adds one of the other clansmen, his colors red and dark blue. "Not fighters."

Nimh swallows, not looking at me now, as if seeing my face might in some way weaken her resolve. "We must try," she insists, and I can hear the hint of despair under her voice. "I wish I did not have to ask this of any of you, but I cannot think what else to do. We cannot afford to wait for a better solution to come to us."

Matias clears his throat, and the other riverstriders turn toward him, as if on instinct. Even Nimh turns to look at him, waiting; to her, he is still her Master of Archives, the crotchety librarian responsible for her lessons as a child.

"We must have the use of magic back," Matias says slowly. "As it stands, we would be badly outnumbered and outfought. But if our people could use magic, then one riverstrider magician could handle half a dozen of their Deathless."

"We're still working on the sky-steel anchors," says Orrun, "but even if we put all the riverstriders working on the fortifications in shifts to keep cutting away the sky-steel, it would take weeks to fish enough of it out of the river for magic to work at the temple."

"Weeks we don't have," Matias agrees. But he's not watching Orrun—his eyes are on Nimh. He waits, and I see the moment Nimh realizes what he's saying through his silence.

"No," she says tightly, her eyes wide and lips pressed together. "No, Matias, not under any circumstances."

"You negated the anchors once before," Matias argues, his tone still calm, but relentless. "If you vaporized the river again, we could have 'striders standing by ready to carry out the anchors before the water rushed back."

"Look what else I did when I destroyed the river!" Nimh cries, her calm flying over the edge as she waves a hand in the direction of the city. "I destroyed my people's homes, their faith, their *lives*. No," she adds, as Matias draws breath to speak. "I will not draw on the Lightbringer's power for this, or for anything else. I won't become the Destroyer again." Energy flickers and crackles about her as she speaks, reminding me that we're within the riverstrider's meager territory where magic works again.

I resist the urge to reach out for her hand, and instead take half a step forward to put myself in her peripheral vision. But when I take my own breath, Nimh's eyes snap over toward me, her expression half ferocity, half terror, and I find I can't bring myself to pile on to those all asking her to risk becoming a monster again.

A flicker of relief touches her features when she realizes I'm staying quiet, the barely visible lines of power around her fading, and then her eyes sweep across the semicircle of riverstrider leaders as if challenging any of them to try again.

No one does.

"We will attack the temple in the hours after midnight," Nimh tells them, in a tone I recognize from her ceremonies and rituals as the goddess of this world. "Let us all make sure we are ready."

She turns, walking away with the cat stalking her heels, his steps as quick and light as hers.

Orrun turns to Hiret, who runs a hand over her short-cropped hair, and the two begin discussing preparations, as do the others. Their voices are grim and low, but no one mentions vaporizing the river again—Nimh's word, to the faithful river-clans, is law.

Matias alone is quiet—Matias and I, that is. When I look over at him, I find him watching me. He says nothing across the circle of riverstriders, but I can feel the expectation in his look as if he were speaking it directly into my thoughts.

I find my hand dipping into my pocket, where the protection stone rests in its cocoon of red thread. My fingers tighten around it, remembering the story he told me about becoming the Fisher King, the night before Alciel fell.

I turn away, but then pause, looking over my shoulder. Matias is talking to the others now, discussing strategies and preparations—but I could have sworn that for a moment there, watching me slip my hand into my pocket for the stone, he smiled.

I lose track of Nimh for much of the day—she's everywhere, overseeing preparations for the attack on the temple, but never any one place long enough for me to catch up to her. I catch glimpses now and then of her crimson robe fluttering on a nearby barge or vanishing below deck, but I get no chance to speak to her.

So instead I fall in with Orrun's clan of riverstriders running through combat drills, a few of them pulling out ancient-looking weapons from their storage cabins, the rest using what tools they have that could be weapons: clubs and fishing knives and stout staves. My own experience with combat is next to nothing— the only lessons I had at the Academy covered just enough so that I could hold a ceremonial sword without cutting myself or looking like an idiot during royal events. There was a fencing team at school, but I opted to spend my after-school hours in the aeronautics club.

Fat lot of good that does me now, I think sourly, letting the tip of my borrowed, rusted blade fall, giving my aching arm a rest.

All the magic in this world, all the tech in mine, and tonight I'm supposed to face trained killers with a secondhand sword. This feels like a nightmare, but I can't wake up.

It's nearly night when I find Nimh sitting in the bow of a nearby barge, her head bent over her work. I give the bindle cat—who's been watching our efforts all day with aloof bemusement—a pet on his head, earning myself a cranky mutter in return, and head for Nimh.

I find her working a stone along the edges of a blade, each stroke removing a little of the rust and making it gleam in the red-orange light of sunset. Her spearstaff rests next to her, a weapon she's far more used to wielding than any sword, so I conclude she must be working on someone else's weapon.

I start to murmur a greeting, but then what I'm seeing sinks in—her fingers are red and cracked and bleeding from a few places. So instead I give a rather inarticulate sound of protest, dropping to my knees and reaching out to stop her work.

She jumps, having been too absorbed in what she was doing to notice my approach; her arms jerk away, habitually avoiding my touch, but then she sees my face and stops, blinking at me.

"You won't be any good to anyone tonight if your hands are so bloody you can't hold your staff," I tell her, reaching out to gently remove the sword and the whetstone from her hands, our fingertips coming within a whisper of each other.

She resists for a moment, but then gives in and joins me in inspecting her hands. "I only cut myself at first," she protests. "I know the way of it now."

"Still. Take a break, Nimh. Come walk with me. We have a long night ahead."

Or, if things go poorly, a very short night. Our last night.

I keep that thought to myself.

Nimh mumbles a protest, but she rises to her feet and retrieves her staff with one more glance for the sword she was sharpening. "You think I am being foolish in trying to take the temple back. Yet you were the one who wanted to single-handedly tear through every hall and corridor until you found your family."

I let out a slow breath as we head down the barge's gangplank and onto the spongy soil at the river's edge. "Maybe I've thought better of that plan. Thankfully, I had someone to talk me out of it."

"I see no other option," Nimh says quietly, her eyes fixed on the ground a little way ahead of us. "Wait, and we lose whatever hope we have of making a dent in Elkisa's forces. And that's not including Inshara, wherever she is—Orrun says nobody has seen her come back into the city, but if she returns, then what people we do have on our side, we'll lose."

Her voice is thinner—I know she's thinking of Techeki and that mindlessness that sat so strangely over his keen, intelligent features.

"No, I agree with you. We have to do something, and we have to do it now." I turn my steps, and she falls in beside me.

For a little while, we walk in silence, but I can feel her eyes on me, and a gathering tension that tells me she's got something to say. Eventually, she blurts, "You think I should become the Lightbringer again—destroy the river a second time."

I come to a halt, hands in my pockets, and meet her eyes. "I don't know what I think," I tell her truthfully. "I don't know what it's like to have that kind of power inside me."

"If we wait," Nimh whispers, her gaze sliding away from mine and drifting out across the river, "and we hold off our attack, the Deathless will come. The riverstriders will try to defend me, and they will all be cut down, one by one, until Elkisa has what she wants." She says the name of her old friend without a quaver this time, her jaw squared. "If I run, she'll kill them all anyway looking for me. If we attack now, there's a chance some of them might live."

I have no answer to that. Of all the things I was trained for as the eventual heir to the throne, war was never one of them. Who would we fight, in our city in the clouds? It's just one more thing I never thought about before falling into this world.

As much as I hate that Nimh is facing this impossible choice, a tiny, shameful part of me is glad it isn't mine to make.

The setting sun to the west has cleared the bulk of Alciel that sits atop the temple, so that the stone and metal underside of the city is lit with fiery red. Reflected in the river, it seems to wrap the whole landscape in that orange glow. The sight is beautiful—but I can't dismiss the way it just reminds me of the fire that spread from the lantern I smashed in the temple kitchens. As if the whole world is a breath away from being wreathed in flames.

"Our stories say the riverstriders were the first to come to this land," Nimh says quietly, leaning against her staff a little, and then setting it to one side with a sigh. "They were sailors then, generation after generation upon an endless sea, searching for a home. When they found this place they feared they would not be welcome, for whoever lived here would surely fight to keep ownership of such a beautiful and bountiful land. So they made their homes upon the river, ready to sail away should the need to fight arise. Even though no one else ever appeared to claim ownership of the land, they never left the river, for they found it was an even more perfect home for them than any place the land had to offer." She swallows. "My people have never been warriors."

"They were explorers," I murmur. I can't help but think of that tug in my own heart, that calling I've had since I was a child, to know what was beyond the cloudbank below Alciel— to see for myself what lay Below. If Nimh's stories have any truth in them, then I, too, am descended from voyagers.

From one of the barges, little more than an ember-like silhouette on the river, a voice floats back to us across the water. Rising in an undulating song unlike anything I've heard in Alciel, the words are lost across the distance. Other voices join in from other boats, other clans, until the sound rises to surround us—until the river is singing.

Beside me, Nimh draws a long and shaking breath. When I glance her way, there are tears clinging to her lashes. The fire is there, too, reflected in her eyes.

"It is a song of farewell," she murmurs, eyes moving from

boat to boat. "They sing it when they leave these lands at the end of the rains and travel with the river toward the Mirror of Divinity and the delta beyond. That is as close as they ever get to returning to the sea that brought them here."

I ache to reach out to her, but she has her arms wrapped tightly around herself in that way that tells me she has no desire to be comforted, that she wants to be this miserable and grapple with this choice. The sun, barely more than a sliver against the horizon now, touches every ripple of the water, every blade of grass, every bit of floating debris, casting them in golden fire and throwing long shadows behind them. Even the stones at our feet are gold.

This is the place where Matias brought me to tell me the story of his calling to be the Fisher King. This is where he showed me that power comes from belief, making me gasp as he threw an unremarkable stone into the water.

The realization hits me like a blow, and I find myself gasping again for a moment, too moved by the tableau of the fiery river and the voices rising and falling in farewell to do anything other than reel at the fact that Matias had it right all along, without ever consulting ORACLE, or knowing about the twin hearts of our two worlds, or where the source of divinity came from.

Power comes from belief.

With a choked sound, I turn toward Nimh, willing her to look back at me. "Nimh—you *can* save them. The riverstriders. Your people. All of them."

Her eyes are wide as she looks across and takes half a step

toward me. For a moment, I wonder if maybe I read her body language wrong—perhaps that way she has of wrapping her arms around herself just means she wishes someone would hold her that way. "What do you mean?"

"Power—yours, Inshara's—it comes from belief. Faith. Trust. That's what ORACLE told us—that your people believe in you, and that's what makes you divine. That my people believed Alciel's engines would keep us aloft, and that's what kept us in the sky for all those centuries. That our faith channels through the hearts, and our belief becomes reality. Who's to say what you will be when you step into the role of Lightbringer? Who's to say *that* doesn't come down to belief?"

"The city," Nimh manages, turning her head to gaze through the gathering darkness at the silhouettes of the few buildings still standing tall enough to be seen over the trees. "What I did to it, to them—I *can't* go back to that place, North, that dark place—" Her voice is thin and frightened.

I keep my gaze steady on her, and after a moment she looks back, though I can see how much she wants to retreat from what I'm saying. "You're afraid what happened then will happen again, because this power feeds off your emotions. But you were grieving then, Nimh. Elkisa had betrayed you, you thought I was dead, and you thought destiny had turned its back on you. Where is it written that *that* is the place you have to go when you channel the heart? Who is to say *you* can't choose what you become?"

"What if you're wrong? How can I take that chance?" she whispers.

She's letting me hold her here, the way she did in the ruins of the ancient city. The way I let her hold me in place, back in the temple. I have to make her understand, to see my certainty, my *belief.* She may be afraid of the power inside her, but I've never been more certain that she was meant to wield it.

"It isn't chance," I tell her.

"How can you know that?" Nimh's voice holds a tiny note of accusation.

I keep my eyes on hers. "Because Alciel was falling, and *you* brought it down safely. You didn't hurt anybody. You *saved* my people and the lives of my two best friends. It wasn't an act of destruction—it was an act of love."

I can see the tiniest of shifts in her eyes, though she tries to hide it. Some part of her wants to believe me. "Maybe in saving Miri and Saelis I was just saving my own skin."

A tiny laugh escapes me before I can stop it. "That is the most ridiculous thing I've ever heard you say," I tell her, leaning a little closer. "And I've heard a lot of pretty insane things since I fell out of the sky."

"So what?" Nimh asks, her eyes searching my face. "I let myself become the Lightbringer again, destroy the river all over again, in order to save my people? How do I even begin to do that, when every instinct tells me to run from the emotions that bring me close to that power?"

The last of the dying sun still warms her face, lighting her dark hair with hints of fire-red and glimmering in the tracks her tears have made on her cheeks. I long to lean closer, to touch my lips to those places—as if sensing my thoughts, she shivers

356

where she stands, a breath away. She closes her eyes, her face upturned toward me, an unshielded look of longing transforming the sadness that had been there.

The urge to lean down again and kiss her is so strong I almost can't think, my whole body tense with it, but I bite down on the inside of my cheek. By the time I can see clearly again, her eyes are open and watching my face.

"Do you trust me?" I ask hoarsely.

"You must know by now that I do, cloudlander." Her lips curve a little, distractingly close to mine. "Gods help me."

I'd laugh if I weren't buzzing at her closeness—instead I huff a soft breath. "Good. That's all you have to do. You've had to believe in yourself, and in your divinity, and your importance to this world, all your life—and over the past few weeks, I think it's been an impossible thing to ask. But *I* believe in you, Nimh."

My voice gives out for a moment, the weight of the words proving too much for me.

She doesn't speak. Instead, she lifts a hand, running the tips of her fingers along the collar of my shirt. That tiniest of pressures is as warm as the glow from a flame—it lets me find my voice again.

"I was afraid of you, that morning on the clifftop, when you first manifested your power as the Lightbringer. You talked about destroying the world, and I couldn't understand how this person I'd come to know as kind and thoughtful and brave could think that destruction was her destiny. I was wrong when I left you there." My own eyes burn, facing up to that moment we've never talked about—when we parted ways, when I thought I could run away from having to choose between Nimh and the world. "I was *wrong*, understand? That's why I'm here, I think—why the prophecy brought me to you. You don't have to keep believing in all of this, in yourself, because it's too much for any one person. But I believe in you. All you have to do is trust *me.*"

My breath catches, because I've run out of words, even though there's more I want to say: that I didn't know then what I know now, that I love her, and there's nothing she could do that could make me leave her again. But her eyes are scanning my face, her lips lightly parted in surprise, or wonder, and I can't help but think perhaps she's read my thoughts anyway.

Then, slowly, so slowly I don't dare breathe for fear of changing her mind, she leans closer. Those fingertips against my shirt shift, until I can feel the pressure of her hand against my chest. She smooths her hand across the fabric, and with a faint intake of breath—hers? mine?—her palm is on my skin.

Her touch moves up over my collarbone, her eyes following the path of her hand. She doesn't rush, watching her fingers' path across the tendon along my throat, into the hair at the nape of my neck; and yet, somehow, it's a shock when I feel her pull me down to her. I go, unresisting, unthinking—and then she touches her lips to mine.

For a moment, I can't move, my mind flooding with a thousand different things—protests that anyone could see us here on the riverbank and the others don't know that touch doesn't change her divinity; that we should go slowly, because for someone who'd never touched another person until a few weeks ago, a kiss is a monumental thing.

That I didn't mean to ask this of her, as badly as I wished to do it myself.

Then she pulls back a little, and I feel her exhale, the warmth of it quaking across my lips, and my mind goes utterly, blissfully blank. I tighten my arms, lean down, and lose myself in her.

It's a long time before a flicker of rational thought trickles back into my mind—and it's to realize with some distant confusion that instead of the light of the setting sun continuing to dim beyond my closed eyelids, it's growing brighter.

I open my eyes as Nimh eases down away from me, her skin glowing with a kind of white fire; when she opens her eyes, they're white too, as if her body is just a shell to contain the power inside her. Before I can be afraid of her, though, she smiles a little, and it's Nimh's smile—the private one, just for me. She doesn't speak, but there's mist gathering around her already, and a tendril of it reaches out to caress my cheek.

And then she's tilting her head back, the mist swirling around her and lifting her up into the sky.

TWENTY-FIVE
NIMH

The world is wrapped in white, blinding, deafening. There is no end to it, no shape—and I am nothing more than a vessel, a part of an endless void, swept up like a speck of dust in a storm.

Then something shimmers, a flicker of substance in this vast, white sea: the faintest of lilac wisps. I focus on it, desperate for anything to anchor myself within this sea of white. And, as if my eyes are adjusting to the light, the whisper of color grows. Thread by thread, it forms a shape in the negative space inside, the tendrils surrounding it trembling and flowing like sand blowing around a stone in a desert.

The form of a man stands there below me, his head tilted upward. I cannot see his features, but the threads of mist surrounding him grow stronger as I focus on them, flowing and scattering off his body, and drawn to some point at his hip. Like a knot in the fabric of mist, the threads swirl toward it, making it gleam.

North.

The word, the name, rings through my consciousness, and I cling to it like it's a piece of driftwood, the only thing I have to hold on to in this sea, in this storm. And then I remember: I am Nimh. I am my people's goddess. I am channeling the power of the heart of my temple. And I have a purpose.

I linger one more moment in watching North, as he looks up at me. I'm seeing the protection stone in his pocket, the lines of mist drawn in toward it; I'm seeing his belief in it, in *me*, affecting the mist around him. I'm seeing his faith.

Slowly, painfully slowly, I let my awareness broaden, keeping North at its center, grounding me.

The mist lies across the land like a palely colored fog, outlining the shape of the places I know so well. It curls in across the river, through the avenue that the riverstriders cleared for it by chipping away at the sky-steel anchor, and pools just where the barges are clumped most tightly together. Following the line of the river, I can see where the other anchors lie beneath the water, like darkened beacons against the sea of mist beyond them. Though I try to reach for them, I cannot budge them— even divine power cannot touch sky-steel.

The mist reveals to me every bit of life in the river: the few fish that have returned, gleaming green in their flickering webs, the reeds and roots at the river's edge a steady deep violet.

The river is only just beginning to recover from what I did to it two weeks ago. It will take months, maybe years, for it to go back to what it was before. It would delay it only a little while to empty the riverbed of water again, as I did in my rage and grief. The mist lies across the water, moving slowly, shifting in time with my thoughts—it lies ready to enact my will, to vaporize the water and accomplish my purpose. All my lessons, all the stories upon which my faith was founded, tell me that this—the cycle of destruction and rebirth—is meant to be.

And yet I find I cannot bring myself to destroy the river a second time, just as it is beginning to live again.

The mist quickens, leaping to do as I ask—and then I see a way. Carefully, gathering all my will, I part the water of the river, making it scatter back from that point like dust blowing before a breeze. As if sensing my goal, the mist tries to race ahead toward the sky-steel, to destroy the river I'm trying to preserve—but I hold fast, bringing all my focus to bear.

All along the twin rivers surrounding the temple, the river begins to part, making pathways for the waiting riverstriders to scurry through, like ants on a hirta tree. I can no longer make them out as anything more, drowning in the torrent of raw power that is the Lightbringer's gift.

As if frustrated in its desire to destroy the river, the mist begins to gather again in the city—and flow toward the temple. Squatting somewhere inside my home, cleaning the blood from her blade, is Elkisa, the traitor who betrayed me not once, but over and over again, to my face, every time she let me believe she was my friend.

Now, without the river turning the disparate pieces of sky-steel into an unbroken ring, the mist is rushing back into the rest of the city. Magic is returning—and Elkisa's advantage is vanishing.

I could take the temple now. I could snuff out the lives of everyone inside as easily as I would blow out a candle. I could leave the corridors empty for my riverstriders to reclaim and make this place mine again. My whole being tingles with the need to act, to do as legend tells me I must. I could destroy them all with a single thought.

And beyond them, beneath them and around them, the temple's heart. I can feel its fragility. How easy it would be to focus my will and shatter that ancient mechanism forever . . .

Who's to say what you will be, when you step into the role of Lightbringer?

North's voice is as close and intimate as if he were here with me, his hand in mine, his lips by my ear. With a wrench that takes all my effort, I yank my attention away from the temple and my enemies inside it.

The white light drowning me vanishes, leaving me in fragmented darkness. Groping for something, anything to ground myself with, I turn again—

And meet a pair of wide, mist-touched eyes.

Inshara.

Recognition and horror jolt through me, but I cannot look away, held fast. I can no longer sense the city around me—nor the temple, the riverstriders, or the sky-steel they're removing.

Inshara's eyes meet mine, unflinching, though there's something like fear in their depths, the longer I look. As if she is caught, as well, the two of us bound by our twin connections to the ancient mechanical hearts that grant us our powers. She may have stolen her bond the night she grabbed me on the temple terrace, but it is real and burns just as strongly now as mine.

My thoughts flicker, as if recalling a memory—but the image that comes to me is unfamiliar. A tall woman in purple robes, her veil held close about her face, moving quickly through a street lined by staring people. *Jezara?* She holds a little girl by the hand, her grip too tight. The people watching them are jeering, glaring—the little girl can feel their hatred like the electricity building in a storm against her skin. In another moment, the storm will break, and she and her mother will have to run.

Inshara's face twists—she's trying to pull away, no more able to control what passes between us in this moment than I am. A memory of my own flashes before me: Daoman and Techeki, instructing me as a child in the ways to perform the rituals and duties of my calling. Then, an earlier memory: standing with my high priest by the ritual pool in the temple.

With a wrench, I jerk my thoughts away. Nearly too late, I remember that we cannot afford to let Inshara know what I do about the hearts—not with both Alciel and the temple under her control. We cannot let her know about the importance of belief and the way faith gives us both our power.

We stare at each other across the thin, unbreakable line of connection between us, still held, still unable to break apart. The mist surrounds us, as it did when she touched me on the terrace of the temple, when she forged her own path to divinity.

Her eyes, holding the same swirling storm as the mist around us, narrow.

And then I see it.

She already knows.

Understanding courses through me like icy water through my veins. She knows about the hearts, somehow. She knows they control our divinity. She knows they're the key to her power as well as mine, and she . . .

She has a plan.

Inshara lashes out then, a soundless scream twisting her features, as her mind shoves mine away with all her might. Reeling, I try to cling to the scraps of my focus, but I can feel it falling away—the Lightbringer's power receding, fading, exhaustion swimming up to drag me downward.

Having fought so hard to keep my mind and my will my own despite the power's eagerness to destroy, I have nothing left. And as the last white-hot fragments of light fade away, I finally, gratefully, give in and let the darkness claim me.

TWENTY-SIX

NORTH

The moment Nimh's feet hit the ground, it's over. The light fades, and like a puppet with its strings cut, she crumples.

I throw myself to my knees to catch her before her head hits stone and gather her in against me as a gasp goes up from the riverstriders around us.

"He is the Last Star." It's Orrun's voice, unhurried, confident. He stands beside me, his hands still covered in muck from hauling the sky-steel from the river, and his voice immediately quiets the whispers. "The gods may touch one another."

A murmur of understanding goes through them, and Nimh stirs in my arms. It's only then I realize I'm as muddy as Orrun, and now so is she. I think I'll be dreaming for the rest of my life about standing inside that churning corridor of water as Nimh parted the river. "Stay still," I murmur as she tries to shift. "You just—"

I get no further.

A shout goes up from the riverstriders who are farther from the riverbank, wordless at first, though the alarm in their tone has me carefully easing Nimh down to the ground so I can push to my feet, every nerve in my body on edge. Then I make out the words.

"The Deathless! The Deathless are coming from the temple!"

Elkisa.

"Ready yourselves," shouts Orrun, and I glance back to check Nimh—the cat has taken up position over her slumped form—then rub my muddy hands against my trousers, wishing I'd known to bring one of the riverstrider's swords with me. And then I see it: Nimh's spearstaff, in the mud at her side.

In my mind, I see it resting where Matias hid it, deep below the heart of the temple, waiting for someone to claim it in Nimh's absence.

Someone to fight for her while she couldn't.

"They will come here," Orrun's saying as I take up the spearstaff, his voice firm and calm. "They saw what she did— the whole city saw. They'll know we have our magic again, and they have no choice but to move before our magicians can act against them."

All around us, riverstriders are readying their weapons or adjusting their stances as flames spring to life in their hands or the air shimmers around them. When I shift my gaze to the temple, I can see black-clad figures pouring down the steps, weapons in hand.

"They will come here," says Orrun again, and suddenly I realize he means *here.* This spot, a small grassy rise by the river's edge. "They'll have seen where she landed."

There's nothing left in him now of the man who smiled,

who bowed to the cat when they met, who teased me about not burning a second of his boats. He's all focus and grim determination, gripping a knife in each hand.

I adjust my hold on the spearstaff, my breath coming so fast now I can't seem to catch it, my heart hammering, my mouth dry. *I'm about to stick this in a real person,* I tell myself, looking down at the weapon, trying to make myself believe it.

Then they're on top of us, the sudden din of clashing weapons and shouting voices making me stagger back. I lose track of Orrun, raising the staff instinctively when a gleaming weapon comes jabbing out of the chaos toward me—the spearstaff's edge sends it harmlessly off to the side, and its wielder staggers back, whirling to face some other opponent. The riverstriders may not be warriors, like Nimh said, but all around me they're fighting with such ferocity it's hard to think of them as anything else.

They're fighting to protect their goddess.

I shift my grip on the spearstaff again, my mouth dry, my heart pounding, trying to force myself to enter the fray again—to go against everything I was ever taught about avoiding violence and join Nimh's defenders. The cultists begin to spread out, flanking us on all sides. Soon we won't have any avenue of retreat left.

And then I see her.

Elkisa's face is marred by sweat and grime, the tips of both her knives dipped in red. She moves with ease, ducking a bolt of pure, crackling magic from a nearby riverstrider, her jaw set as she fights her way toward us. Every move is economical—she's fluid as she ducks again, then seamlessly swings around to kick at the magician's knee, sending her to the ground with a crunch and a scream.

"Traitor!" It's a moment before I realize that raw shout came from me, but her head snaps up, and our eyes lock across the battlefield. I see that one word land as none of the blows around her have—I see her relive our trip together, the words we spoke, all in the space of a heartbeat.

Promise me you're going to try and keep Nimh alive, I said.

You know that is what I want, she replied.

But *want* and *promise* are two different things.

And the next moment there's a cultist coming at me with a knife, and I'm swinging the spearstaff in a wide arc to keep him at bay, planting my feet where I stand. Nimh's behind me and then the edge of the river—I can't give ground.

"North!"

"Hiret!"

She's fighting like a madwoman, a knife in each hand, her eyes wild, and she's everything in her fury and grief that Elkisa is not. There's no calculation to Hiret's strikes, just rage, but that alone seems to drive back the cultist before me as she reaches my side—he turns to Orrun instead, who's waiting for him with bared teeth.

"We can't hold forever," I say as Hiret swings into place beside me, and I shift to make room for her in front of Nimh. "They must want Nimh alive, it's the only reason we haven't been overrun yet." I can't bring myself to ask her if she's seen her sister Didyet anywhere in the battle—it would at least mean

369

she survived the massacre of the Graycloaks, but at the cost of turning toward Inshara.

"Last Star of Prophecy, there is something I wish to confess," Hiret says as Elkisa downs a riverstrider, teeth gritted as she works her way toward us.

"Now?" I clutch at the spearstaff, glancing across at her. "Hiret, we're kind of busy."

"Now," she replies. "In case there is no later. I want you to know that my faith wavered, after Maita died. It was difficult to believe in a goddess who had led him to his death."

"Nimh would understand that, Hiret."

"When the Fisher King sent you to retrieve the spearstaff, I told Elkisa where to find you." She pauses just long enough to lash out as a cultist runs toward us, her knives bloodied. Catching her breath, she adds, "I am ashamed that I doubted. Maita believed, enough to give her his life. I should have been as strong."

"You're looking pretty strong from where I'm standing," I reply. "So you wavered. You're here now."

"Will you tell Nimhara I am sorry?" she asks.

"You can tell her yourself," I reply. "Watch out!"

She turns, just as two cultists launch themselves at us. Hiret throws herself at the nearest, tackling her to the ground, and they lock together, knives drawn.

I lunge for the other, but he dives past me.

And everything slows down.

The man rolls and comes to one knee beside Nimh.

His knife flashes in the light of someone's spell as he draws it back.

My mind automatically draws its trajectory, as if it was a glider launching from the pads at home.

The cat yowls, throwing himself at Nimh's attacker.

The blade begins to descend toward her.

I'm moving, both hands gripping the spearstaff, swinging it around, and I'm watching as it slides into the man's side, I feel the impact as the blade's point glances off his ribs before shuddering deep into his body, and he goes sprawling to the ground, and there's so much blood.

So much blood.

Blood on the spearstaff, on the charms that dangle from its blade, blood on his side, blood at his lips. Blood on Nimh's unmoving form, but it's all her attacker's, because I stabbed him.

I *stabbed* him.

He rolls onto his back, looking up at me, and though our gazes lock together, I see nothing there that helps me understand—no madness, no magic. Just anger.

And then that furious light behind his eyes fades, and a moment later, he's gone.

TWENTY-SEVEN

NIMH

I have no time to process what I'm seeing as I swim out of darkness: North, holding my spearstaff stained crimson to the shaft, standing over a man's body, standing between him and me. The bindle cat is at his side, fur bristling, making him appear twice his size. Just past them is Hiret, a knife in each hand, climbing off the still body of one of the Deathless.

But another cultist is running at North from his other side, movements disjointed—or else my vision is fragmented, my mind struggling to come back from the sensory overload of connection to the heart. I try to sit up, to reach for him, but my body won't move. I gasp for a breath, willing him to raise his head, but he cannot stop staring at the man he's killed, his body frozen, his eyes wild.

"North!" His name bursts out of me in a cracked scream, and it's enough to jar him from his stupor.

He raises his head, and then the speastaff a half second later, and the cultist's blow deflects off to one side. North staggers back, but then Orrun is there, grimly taking over the fight, slashing with his fish-cleaning knife until the cultist drops and rolls back with a cry of agony.

The tip of the spearstaff hits the earth with a thud and a jangle of its udjet charms, and he drops to one knee. "I—I didn't mean to—" he manages, his face ashen. "Is he—"

With a wrenching effort, I manage to move my hand—not enough to reach for him, but he sees the movement, and in an instant his fingers are wrapped around mine. As if his touch restores something within me, I'm able to sit up, the world spinning dizzily and turning my stomach.

I try to reach for the mist, thinking to create some sort of barrier around us, some way to push the cultists back. Something snaps deep in my mind, and I cry out, starting to fall into darkness once more—only North is there, dropping the spearstaff and grabbing me before I can hit the ground, wrapping an arm around my ribs.

"I can't use magic," I gasp, holding onto his arm like it's my only lifeline. "Inshara threw me out of the connection to the heart—"

"Inshara?" North echoes, flashing me a fearful glance— the name is enough to stir him from his horror.

I shake my head, unable to explain, not here and now. I squeeze his arm instead, leaning back into him, exhaustion sending tremors through my body. The cultists are pressing closer—in the distance I can hear a cry of effort and triumph from Elkisa, and I know she must have cut someone down. I know that voice— that cry—from the many years she's spent defending me.

Shuddering, I scan the riverstriders around us, realizing with sinking horror that there are fewer and fewer of them with every passing moment. One of the cultists, flanking Orrun as he tangles with another, swings a blade at him, and I try to lurch forward, only to lean helplessly against North—but then a stone flies out of nowhere, slamming into the cultist's chest and sending him rolling back down the slope.

I crane my neck to find Matias standing some distance away, his walking stick in hand—each time he slams it into the ground, a handful of stones fly up from the soil, hovering ammunition that he then lets fly at the enemies with a weaving gesture of his hands.

North, following my gaze, lets out an explosive breath. "It worked," he manages. "Getting rid of the sky-steel—the riverstriders can use magic."

A flicker of hope springs to life inside me, and I tug on North's sleeve—he helps me to my feet, keeping hold of me when my wobbling legs threaten to send me sprawling. All around us, riverstrider magicians are throwing down their weapons and channeling the mist instead as it returns. I reach for it myself, but my vision clouds, exhausted tremors worsening, until North gives me a squeeze, his face rigid with alarm. "You need to rest," he shouts over the sounds of battle. "We've got to get you out of here."

I want to protest, to declare that I won't let my people fight for me while I flee—but before I can so much as open my mouth, North is muttering an oath, his head craned to look behind us. When I twist to follow his gaze, I see what he did: cultists behind us, now, cutting off our retreat.

We're surrounded.

A voice I know cries out in pain, and Hiret crumples, a gash on her thigh deep enough to expose the bone. Orrun is able to knock her attacker away before he can finish her off, but beyond her I can see others falling.

Even with magic . . . we're *losing*.

"We have to find a way to retreat," I cry in North's ear. "Help me stay standing—maybe I can—"

His protests fade into a dim buzzing as I try to concentrate, reaching for any scraps of remaining strength. The mist is there, still ready for my command, but my will is in tatters. My head throbs with pain. I try to ignore it, try to retreat back into that blazing white storm, even as the effort threatens to split my skull—

"Nimh, *stop!*"

I come back to myself to find North shaking me, his eyes wide with fear. I open my mouth to speak, but an inarticulate moan escapes instead. The cat is there in an instant, shoving his furry head against my legs, as if helping me stay on my feet. North pulls me in against him and then stoops, retrieving the spearstaff, turning to try to keep the other riverstriders at his back. Orrun is there somewhere, and Matias still; so many others have fallen, *too* many others. The cultists have sensed the same thing I did; they press the attack all the harder, sensing their victory.

Then the sky splits open with a roar.

I fall back against North, who grunts with the effort of staying upright himself, a sudden gale of wind threatening to drive us from the spot where we're making our stand. All across the battlefield the fighting has stalled, faces turning upward to stare. I shift my weight, throwing my head back and peering through my streaming eyes at the thing that now hovers above us.

Silver metal gleams in the light of the riverstrider's spell-fire torches, white accents defining a long, sleek outline. Two elegantly curved arches spread on either side of the thing, unmistakable imitations of wings. Spots of blue-white fire underneath its belly emit the thick, heavy whine of engines, flaring and dimming as the thing adjusts to keep hovering where it is, tipping minutely this way and that. Instinctively, I glance at North, but he's staring too, openmouthed, at the flying machine.

My belly tightens, dread returning after the momentary reprieve of shock. *What new horror has Inshara uncovered?*

With a hiss, a seam appears in the sleek side of the thing; an instant later, it widens into the shape of a door. A figure stands there, silhouetted against the gleam of monitors and control panels behind it—before I can make out any features, an orange burst of fire sprays out from the figure, cutting across the battlefield with a roar.

"Back off!" shouts a voice, high and intense, as the cultists and riverstriders scatter apart, all faces turned upward. "You all back up *right* now or I'll set your faces on fire!"

My mind is reeling, shock and confusion making it even harder to keep my feet, but I recognize that voice, distorted with agitation though it is.

I recognize it—but North is the one who bursts out in utter bewilderment, "Miri?!"

A pair of cultists, trying to recover from their shock, begin to move up on us again—but the flames shoot out once more from something in Miri's hands. One of the cultists dances away, but the other, less quick, ends up with the edge of his coat on fire.

"Oops." Miri's voice is jittery with nerves, as the cultist throws himself to the ground to roll and tamp out the flames. She staggers a little against the side of the door as the flying machine tips a little more violently. "Saelis, keep her steady, you're gonna throw me out! Hey, North!"

The appearance of a flying machine spitting fire proves too much—before anyone on our side can react, I hear Elkisa's voice lifted in a bellow. "*Retreat!* Back to the temple!"

A few more skirmishes break out as the cultists attempt to follow her orders, a few of the riverstriders trying to press their new advantage.

The flying machine dips again, as Miri calls out commands to Saelis, unseen somewhere and evidently controlling—or sort of controlling—their flight. The edge of the door, acting almost like a gangplank on a riverstrider's barge, brushes the ground.

"Come on, quickly!" Miri tosses aside the thing in her hand, which seems to be just a small cylinder of some kind. "We don't actually have weapons, better get on board before they figure that out."

North's arm tightens around me, trying to move with me toward his friend. We make little progress, my legs still refusing to work properly, until I feel another arm encircle me from the other side—I lift my head to find a familiar, worn face there, grim and exhausted, but resolute.

Matias helps North get me onto the gangplank, until Miri can grab my hand and pull me aboard. Behind Matias, Orrun is shouting orders, organizing the riverstriders' retreat. Some are diving directly into the river, covering the distance between the banks and the barges out in its center with long strokes; others are helping to carry the wounded to fishing boats and dinghies, to haul them to safety.

Orrun turns, sweeping across us, and then closes the ground between him and Matias with a few strides of his long legs. "Go," he shouts over the noise of the engine. "I'll handle the wounded here—the Divine One will need you."

Matias leans forward to wrap his arms around the younger man, speaking in his ear in a voice I can't hear over the din. I watch as he reaches toward his own neck, pulling something off over his head, and then draping it over Orrun's—it's a necklace, one of his many strings of beads. Orrun meets his gaze, nods, and squeezes the older man's arm. Then he's gone, turning away, helping the last of the riverstriders carrying Hiret toward the boats.

Miri half supports, half drags me away from the door, making room for North to toss the spearstaff onto the metallic floor with a clatter and then leap aboard. He turns to offer Matias his hand as soon as he gets his feet under him, helping the old man up onto the ship. Then Miri slams her hand into a dimly lit panel, and the door hisses closed, sealing out the noise from the engines and leaving us in ear-ringing silence.

Panting, pushing her disheveled, lavender curls back from her face, she manages, "Well, that was exciting. Everybody okay?"

North, who'd been standing motionless, hands on his knees, half-stooped, lets out a sound that's half sob, half shout of relief, and throws himself at her, to wrap his arms around her.

My legs begin to fold, as a familiar warmth winds around my ankles, purring furiously. As if this momentary safety, however impossible and unexpected it might be, was all my mind was waiting for, the glowing monitors and blinking lights of the controls dim in my vision. I let them and don't bother to fight the exhaustion as it claims me a second time.

TWENTY-EIGHT

NORTH

I squeeze Miri until she squeaks, burying my face in her hair, inhaling her familiar scent.

"North!" It's Matias, and in a second I'm away from Miri—I think she shoves me to get me moving faster—swinging around toward him.

He's got one arm under Nimh, and I take her other side, sinking to my knees and lowering her to the ground. The cat, who must have leaped aboard in the chaos, paces anxiously beside us. A soft breath escapes her, and my heart starts beating again.

"What's wrong with her?" Miri asks, dropping to one knee on my other side, giving the cat a wide berth and a fearful look.

"She needs rest," Matias replies. "I think she has only over-extended herself—she will recover."

Saelis's voice sounds from the door through to the cockpit. "North, are you—oh, what is *that*?" His eyes are on the cat, who returns his stare with a steady, unblinking one of his own.

Keeping my eyes on Nimh, hungry for the sight of the slow, gentle rise and fall of her breathing, I huff a weary laugh. "It's called a cat. He's . . . uh . . . a friend. But maybe don't try to touch him."

Saelis mutters something under his breath, giving me the distinct impression that of all his reactions to seeing an animal for the first time, scooping it up in his arms was not among them. He takes a few steps forward, his eyes on Nimh. "Is she okay?"

"She just needs to rest, apparently," Miri supplies, pushing to her feet. Then she freezes, her eyes widening. "Sae, is someone still flying this thing?"

"I found the button for some sort of auto-hovering pattern," he replies, with a faint smile, and just seeing it, the ground seems to steady beneath my feet a little. "Let's take Nimh out back, she'll be more comfortable. There's a kind of medibay, maybe, even if we can only use the beds."

As I scoop Nimh up in my arms, and she stirs, murmuring something into my chest, Saelis and Miri exchange a look I can't interpret, a faint, fleeting smile, though it reminds me of . . . anticipation, maybe? Then Miri's pushing past me impatiently, hurrying down toward the stern.

"Through here," she says, practically snapping her fingers, and as I always have, I obediently make my way after her, the cat weaving so tightly through my legs that he nearly trips me up.

I turn sideways to carefully carry Nimh in through the door, and stop dead in my tracks. It's a small room, dominated by equipment I don't recognize and two high-tech beds with blue gel mattresses.

And seated on those two beds are my mothers.

Both my mothers.

And they're both looking at me, both smiling—both with clear gazes, their hearts in their eyes. Anasta's crying. Beatrin looks terrible—her eyes shadowed, her face gaunt, seeming decades older than before—but she's herself.

We're all frozen in place, until Anasta suddenly snaps to her feet. "Put her here," she says, gesturing to the bed she's just vacated. "Matias, she's all right?" It's her Sentinel's voice, all business, but she reaches out to squeeze my arm as I gently set Nimh down on the mattress. She lets out a soft breath as I smooth her hair back from her forehead, and despite everything here in the room, every*one* here in the room, a part of me just wants to keep watching her breathe, keep reassuring myself she's okay.

"She must rest," Matias says, patient.

I tear my gaze away from our sleeping goddess as the cat marches around in a circle and then plunks himself down on her legs. Looking back at my mothers, I'm held in place by something almost like shyness, as if I can't quite work out how to make the first move.

Then Beatrin speaks, more tentative than I've ever heard her. "North?"

An instant later I'm in her arms, and she's squeezing me as hard as I'm squeezing her, and she's cradling my face in both her hands, kissing my cheeks—kissing my tears—and she's weeping too. Up close, I can see the new lines around her eyes, the exhaustion in her face. I can feel her tremors. I can see the toll Inshara's taken on her.

"North, I'm so sorry," she whispers, her eyes wet with

unshed tears. "Please tell me you understand. I love you—no one could ever replace you."

"Of course," I whisper. "None of it was you."

And I know that. I *do* know that. But still, the tiniest part of me twists inside—I've spent all my life listening to my blood-mother tell me to step up, to act like an heir, to set aside dreams of study and discovery. I have *never* doubted she loved me, but the way Inshara took those small seeds of my mother's frustration and turned them into the words she spoke. *It is no stretch to see that she makes a better heir than he ever did . . .*

"It wasn't you," I repeat. "It was *her.*"

Because that's the terror and the horror of it. The idea of losing myself—of the seeds within me being twisted into gnarled, ugly, thorny weapons. The idea of hunting the ones I love, of *hurting* them . . .

"I'm so glad you're safe," Beatrin murmurs, one hand pushing back my curls—longer than she's seen them in years—drinking me in like I'm cool tea on a hot day. "When I thought I'd lost both of you . . ."

I have to close my eyes against that. For her to lose me, and then lose her father just a day or two later, stepping up to the throne in the depths of her grief . . . I can picture her in her mourning clothes, picture the firm line of her mouth, her refusal to waver. I can picture her crying at night in Anasta's arms.

"No guilt," she chides, reading my mind, and when I open my eyes, she's smiling through her tears. "Though I *did* tell you that glider wasn't safe."

Miri's voice cuts in from the doorway. "In fairness, Your

Majesty, I serviced the *Skysinger* with him, it was as safe as—"
She cuts herself off, because she was probably about to say "the royal palace," and we all saw how safe my home ended up being. "It was sabotaged," she says, lifting her chin, as if daring us to contradict her.

"By who?" Beatrin and I demand in unison. *I knew it.* I was so sure of it, after I fell—but I haven't thought of the *Skysinger* in weeks, haven't had a moment to consider something that couldn't take or save my life.

"We're not sure," Saelis admits from his place beside her. "But she's right."

The statement hangs in the air. There will be time to figure out who wanted me dead.

"Well, forget how I got here," I say, perching on the edge of Nimh's cot and glancing down to check on her. She's quiet—she looks more peaceful already, with the cat curled up in a ball against her, eyes just slits even as his ears twitch and swivel, tracking us all. "How did *you* get here? And in this thing?"

"The short version," says Saelis, cutting off Miri as she readies herself to speak, "is that we did get into the palace and found the queen already breaking free of Inshara's hold. Things are bad in the city, though, and the palace. Everyone's panicking—and if Inshara's gone back to the city, she can probably control many more minds now than she could before."

Anasta picks up the story, adding, "The guards were beginning to shake off Inshara's influence as she moved farther away—they were willing to take my orders again. We came back to the temple and found a pitched battle underway."

"So we ran for it," Miri supplies. "Plenty of acolytes and Graycloaks were heading for the exits, so we joined in."

I glance down at Nimh again—the only other person here who saw Elorin and the others who didn't make it to the exits. Were my friends and family among the ones she tried to buy time for, to save? I'll never know.

"We got out of the temple," Miri continues, "and we remembered ORACLE"—and she brandishes her wrist, on which she wears my bracelet—"and it helped us navigate a way up to its mountain lair. We thought it'd be the best place to hide until we could figure out what to do. So, you know, thanks for making us authorized users."

"We were watching from there when Nimh . . ." Saelis trails off, not sure how to describe what all of us witnessed.

"Performed her act of magical badassery," Miri supplies. "And then this wild mist came rolling in, all green and purple, thicker than storm clouds. The whole of ORACLE's HQ lit up like an Ascension Day parade, and this thing"—she knocks twice on the surface she's leaning on—"activated."

"ORACLE needed fuel," I murmur. "The sky-steel ring had cut off the mist, but when we broke the ring, the mist came back."

Miri grins. "Seriously though, it was *wild*. I wish we'd had a camera on us to record the whole thing. We'd make a fortune."

"Anyway," Saelis gently interjects. "When the place lit up, the bracelet overloaded—too much battery charge at once, perhaps. We haven't been able to get a sound out of it ever since, but it died in noble service of the cause. Thankfully the main computers started working again when the mist arrived, and ORACLE suggested the shuttle could be of use, so . . ."

"That's how I came to be hanging out of the doorway with an aerosol can of engine lubricant and a welding torch cobbled together to make a flamethrower," Miri concludes.

"And how I came to fly an ancient shuttle," Saelis agrees.

"How does she fly?" I murmur, a part of me twitching to go inspect the cockpit, however serious our situation.

"She's pretty basic," Saelis replies. "Joystick controls, a lot of pictograms." He studies me in that quiet way of his, tilting his head. He's had a lifetime's practice—I know he sees how close I am to the edge, to letting the tangle of fear and relief within me spill out. He knows I'm asking about the shuttle's controls because one small thing is all I can handle, in this sea of big things. Nobody's ever been better at reading me, until Nimh. "You're the pilot," he says. "Why don't you come up front, I'll show you."

Matias speaks from his place next to Anasta. "Go, North. Nimh will be all right. If this contraption can remain aloft, then let us do so. We must wait until she awakens to decide our next course."

"I'll sit with Nimh," Anasta says softly, taking up a perch beside me on the edge of her cot. She seems far less concerned about the cat than Miri and Saelis were, and I can't help but wonder just how much my mother, in her secret role as Sentinel, knew about the world Below.

But I let Miri take my hand and lead me out of the medibay— she gives my fingers a quick squeeze as she looks back over her shoulder. "We'd really better not crash this thing," she says, voice lowered. "With Nimh *and* the queen on board?"

Saelis is leading us, but he stops before we reach the cockpit, turning to face us. And Miri mirrors his action, turning toward me, studying me for a moment, and then stepping in to wrap her arms around my neck. A moment later, Saelis's arms wrap around both of us.

That's all it takes to bring me undone, and I'm crying again, half choking on the words. "I thought you were both dead."

"We're safe," Saelis murmurs. "So are your mothers. Are you? Is any of the blood on your clothes your own?"

I shake my head without releasing my hold on them. "No, I had to——" But my throat closes against the rest of the words.

"You had to defend yourself?" Miri says, soft.

"In a fight you didn't start?" Saelis adds.

"But we did," I whisper. "We're the ones who decided to storm the temple."

"And Inshara's the one who took the temple, who took Alciel, who tried to take everything," Saelis replies, quiet, firm.

"*None of this* is your fault," Miri whispers, fierce. Then, easing back just enough to look up at me, her own cheeks streaked with tears too: "But we'll definitely get you the best therapist ever when we get home, because you'll have a *lot* to tell them."

"Is Nimh really all right?" Saelis asks after Miri manages to draw a faint smile from me.

I nod. "She overstretched her powers, I think. And she said something about Inshara—they're both connected through the hearts. It's a long story," I add, noting their blank faces. "If

Matias says she'll recover soon, she will. He's a powerful magician, he'd know."

"Good," says Miri. "And also, did you just hear yourself?"

"Magicians," Saelis murmurs, shaking his head.

"I know," I murmur, shaking mine.

The three of us are quiet a moment, and without speaking, we lower our heads to press our foreheads together, all of us, just as we've always done. But though it feels familiar—though it feels like home, like safety, like everything I should need—a part of me's already being tugged back toward the shuttle's stern.

Back toward Nimh.

Before the battle, when I spoke to her about faith and about how much I believed in her, my mind never hesitated. My *heart* knew what I hadn't been able to admit aloud.

I love her.

And then, a flicker of panic welling up in me, I think: *How can I ever tell Miri and Saelis, after all that's happened?*

Then Miri growls and tightens her hold on me, squeezing hard. "One really good hug," she says, her voice still rough with tears. "And then back to your goddess you go, lover boy."

My protest is automatic. "But you two—"

She silences me with a finger to my lips and waits until our eyes meet. "North," she says, as solemn as I've ever seen her. "We love you."

"We do," Saelis says quietly.

"And you love us," she continues.

I nod, still silent. It's always been this way with Miri. There's no stopping her.

"But," she says, "you can call it prophecy, you can call it destiny, you can call it a very complex set of personality factors, socio-historical forces, and traumatic experiences that you should also discuss with your therapist. You can call it whatever you like. She's your person."

"You're my . . ." I try to speak, but my throat's closed, and my words won't come.

"And we always will be," Saelis says softly. "We were best friends before we could walk. Or before we could run after Miri to stop her breaking something. But you shared something with Nimh, down here." His voice grows softer, more serious, as gentle as he always is. "And North, we shared something too, those weeks we thought you were dead. . . . We've all changed, and that's okay."

He reaches for my hand and brings my fingers to his lips, pressing a soft kiss to my fingertips. As he does, Miri goes up on her toes to press a kiss to my cheek.

"We know you love us," she says softly. "Go be *in love* with her, and do it with your whole, huge heart. Got it?"

I still have no words, gazing at the two of them, my whole heart full of the knowledge that they're friends nobody could ever deserve.

And then Matias's voice cuts through the cabin, quick and urgent. "North, she's awake! Come quickly!"

TWENTY-NINE

NIMH

Despite Matias's soothing voice in my ear and the comforting weight of the cat leaning against my legs beneath the blanket, I cannot quite convince myself that I have woken up safe—the room is shifting, lights blinking in the walls, which vibrate to the touch, a muffled roar from without threatening to drive me mad—and then North is there, in the doorway, breathing hard.

For a moment, my heart slows, meeting his eyes—and then I see the blood all over his riverstrider's tunic. A wordless cry bursts out of me, horror seizing me before memory has a chance to assert itself. North abandons the doorway and comes to my bedside, his mother moving aside to make room without being asked.

"I'm fine," he croaks. "The blood isn't mine." He pauses then, his eyes a bit wild—I remember, now, a little. I remember him standing over me, bloody spearstaff in his hand. Not just over me—*between* me and danger. I reach out, my trembling fingertips brushing the back of his hand. It turns, and curls around mine, his touch warm and strong. "Are you okay?" he murmurs.

I nod, ignoring the way it makes my head spin all the harder.

"It was the hardest thing I've ever done," I admit, wishing I could lean into him—but the room is full of people, including Miri and Saelis, who watch us both intently. My skin tingles against his, the sensation still so new that it's difficult to concentrate on what I'm saying. "I wanted to destroy it all—I was myself, this time, but I almost could not control myself as the Lightbringer."

"You were perfect," North is quick to reassure me. "We're all still here."

"I could see the temple's heart," I tell him, my own heart beating faster. "It would have been so easy to destroy it, like ORACLE said in the garden—it is so fragile, this thing that makes us all who we are."

"But you didn't," North replies, squeezing my hand. "That's what matters—you saw its vulnerability, but you didn't destroy it. And you didn't hurt anyone."

A little of the pressure of anxiety in my heart eases. But only a little.

"I could sense Inshara," I murmur, lifting my eyes to scan the room—those from Alciel look as grave as Matias does, that name striking equal dread among both populations now. "I could feel her, through our connection to the hearts. I could feel what she wanted to do."

"You could read her mind?" Miri leans forward, her eyes bright with curiosity. "That's so cool."

"And horrifying," Saelis reminds her, raising an eyebrow.

Miri flushes. "Well, yes, that too."

North glances their way with a faint smile on his face. I

can only imagine the happiness of their reunion, and that of North with his parents, while I slept; my heart aches, a little, that I missed seeing him that way. A small, exhausted part of my heart sings too, to see Beatrin alive, her mind her own once more. If she can return to herself, perhaps Techeki can too.

But when North looks back at me, his face is grave again, that smile he offered Miri and Saelis gone, and my heart hurts anew.

"What is she planning?" he asks. "If we know, maybe we can stop her."

I put aside that ache and sit up a little more in my bed, trying to focus. "Somehow, she's found out about the hearts, like we have. She knows that belief is what grants divine power, and she believes she has a way to . . . twist that, somehow. Use the hearts to make *everyone* believe in her."

"What, like mind-control everybody?" Miri asks, her eyes widening.

Beatrin starts, like a sleeper half waking from a nightmare. When she blinks and finds us all watching her, and North half risen in concern, she swallows and raises a hand to forestall him. "When she had me," she whispered, her voice tired and wispy, like that of an old woman, "it wasn't like she controlled my mind. I was still me. But what I *cared* about . . . she twisted it. I felt as though everything I did, I did for what I believed in, what I loved. Alciel, the throne, my duties as monarch."

She's shivering as she speaks, and her son's hand beneath mine is rigid with concern. Carefully, I slide my hand away from his, and he rises so he can go to his mother's bedside instead. North's face is drawn, his eyes fearful—I can see his heart recoiling from what's been done to his mother. Seeing her now, she's nothing like the way he described her to me: powerful, strong, unwavering. She must seem like a shell of herself to him—and he's afraid.

Beatrin flashes him a weak little smile, a tear spilling out onto her cheek. "I'm all right," she assures him. "But what Nimhara said about belief . . . that's what it was. She took my deepest beliefs, all that I had faith in, and perverted them for her own use."

Matias draws a long breath and lets it out slowly, grimly. "So she believes she's found a way to use the hearts to twist *everyone's* beliefs all at once. To bend them to her own purpose; to make everyone who has ever believed in *anything* believe instead in *her.*"

I shiver too, tightening my hands around the blanket to try and prevent North from seeing, so that he stays with his mother. "She'll become more powerful than any deity that has ever lived since the hearts were forged."

For a long moment, no one speaks, everyone imagining their own version of the nightmare Inshara is envisioning for us all.

Then Saelis's breath catches, uncharacteristic frustration flashing across his face. "How does she know about any of this?" he asks, glancing from me to North and back again. "She can't have learned about these hearts you're talking about in Alciel, no one knows about them there."

"Techeki knows." Matias bows his head, lifting one hand

393

to rub at his brow. "We spoke of the hearts, he and I, when the cloudlands first came to rest atop the temple. I felt he deserved to know. Techeki knows about the power of belief."

"And she has Techeki," North murmurs.

"Her mother might have spoken of the importance of faith too," I point out grimly. "Jezara told us that she didn't stop being the people's goddess when her lover first touched her— she only stopped being divine when people found out. When they stopped believing in her."

"But there's no way she'd know how to corrupt the hearts," North points out. "She'd have to ask ORACLE for that kind of information, wouldn't she?"

"And she can't get to ORACLE," Miri says. "She doesn't know it exists. And she couldn't get into the chamber anyway, she's not an authorized user."

"I told Techeki about ORACLE," North breathes, closing his eyes. "On the boat, on our way to meet her. She has his mind—we have to assume she knows everything Matias and I told him about both ORACLE and the hearts."

"She'd still need access to the system," Saelis says, uneasy.

"And she doesn't have Beatrin anymore," says Anasta, watching her wife as her son slips an arm around his blood-mother's shoulders. "So no royal blood."

The others exchange glances, confusion and dread mingling together to thicken the air, make it tense. I feel it, though I alone keep my eyes on the floor—for a truly horrible thought has just seized me, its icy fingers trailing down the nape of my neck.

"North," I manage, my voice hoarse. "Does the . . . What is the word for it, the power that governs your locks? The magic in your royal blood?"

"A DNA lock you mean?"

"Yes. DNA. Does it go away when you . . ." I almost can't finish the words, for his eyes are just puzzled, thoughtful, and I find I cannot bear to give him the same thought that's just frozen my heart. "Does it go away when you die?"

North's face drains of its color. He says nothing, but I see my answer in his face, the eyes that are suddenly so grief-stricken and so sad.

Beatrin's breath catches in a sob. "She doesn't need me or North—because she has Alciel. She has my father's body in stasis."

The end of Matias's walking stick clangs against the metal floor, and he gets to his feet. "We must get to this ORACLE relic of yours. We must find out what it told her and hope we can stop her before it's too late."

The shuttle's flight across the city is swift, the occasional dots of spellfire in the night below passing by like shooting stars. Saelis insisted that North try his hand at flying the thing, and he and Miri stand behind the chair at the controls—her shouting advice in North's ear, too excited to moderate the volume of her voice; and him nudging her, pointing at various controls.

I can't help but watch the three of them, so familiar with each other, so easy in each other's company. Ahead of us, out the window at the front of the craft, the grassy hillside beneath the Congress of Elders building splits and opens into a wide doorway. The good-natured bickering intensifies as North maneuvers the craft into its hangar.

I look away to find Matias watching me, his expression thoughtful. My spearstaff rests in his lap, as he works a rag over the bloody udjet charms; my heart aches a little, that he would think of such a kindness in all of this. His eyes never missed much, even when I thought he was just my Master of Archives—when I knew nothing of his involvement with the Sentinels, or that he was the same Fisher King in my hazy memories of being a riverstrider child.

There is the faintest hint of a question in those thoughtful eyes now, as they watch me watching the trio together.

"They were his long before I knew I wanted him to be mine," I murmur softly. "I do not begrudge them their time together. I could never ask him to give them up, not for me."

"Have you asked him what it is *he* wants?" Matias replies, his eyebrows rising a fraction as he folds the bloody side of the cloth away, using a cleaner part of it to wipe down the blade. "Truly *asked* him, not just assuming you know?"

I shake my head, fighting the urge to let my eyes stray back to where they long to go: watching North as he pilots the shuttle, going back to what he loves—flying, engineering, exploring.

"Perhaps," I whisper, "when this is over, there will be time."

But the truth is that I can't see past what lies ahead of us, even in my own imagination. There's only stopping Inshara—I can't let myself think what might lie beyond that end.

Matias must sense that sadness, that anxiousness, for he

shifts, the beads around his neck clinking together and the fabric of his robe rustling as he sets the cleaned spearstaff carefully aside. When I lift my eyes, I see his hand half stretched toward me, his face a study in contrasts—he wants to comfort me, but even knowing that others have touched me, the taboo is still strong, and he hesitates.

So I slip my hand into his, watching as he swallows, his old eyes closing a moment. He wraps my hand in both of his for a moment, head bowing again, reminding me that in all his guises—archivist, Sentinel, riverstrider—he has still always been serving his goddess, his faith.

Before I can stop myself, I lean forward and wrap my arms around the old man. His breath catches, and then I feel him embrace me in return, hesitant at first, and then more tightly. "I am proud of you, Nimh," he murmurs, withdrawing enough to kiss my forehead, as Daoman once did. The memory, and the comfort of being hugged by this man who's been so much like a father to me, makes my own tears spill over. "As are your people."

On his lips, those words evoke a very specific image: the riverstriders, arrayed around me on that hilltop as the cultists closed in, ready to defend me to the last.

Just then the shuttle gives a little sideways lurch, eliciting a faint cry from Miri—and then a jolt as it settles onto the floor of the hangar.

"Skyfall," mutters Miri into the silence that follows. "We need to work on your landings, Your Highness."

North stifles a laugh, hauling himself up out of his chair

with a groan that reminds me how weary he must be, and sore from swinging a weapon he's not used to carrying. I remember that ache all too well from my own days of training, years ago, to use the spearstaff in self-defense.

I get to my feet, keeping hold of Matias's hand—though who's helping whom to rise, I'm not sure. He lets me go then, and together North and I make our way to the gangplank, the others following behind us.

The room is vast and invisible in the darkness beyond the pool of illumination cast by the shuttle's lights. From somewhere in the gloom, a mournful meow from the cat echoes back to us. Despite the darkness, North seems to know where to go and leads us to a door in the side wall that opens at his touch.

We spill into the darkness beyond it, and then North freezes, so abruptly that I run into him. He reaches out to take my arm as I stagger back, steadying me. His hand is rigid, though, his body tense.

"What's wrong?" I whisper, glancing around fearfully— but the blackness is absolute here, without the lights from the shuttle.

"The lights should be coming on automatically," North replies. "Can you—"

But I'm already moving, reaching into one of my pockets, where I stuffed a few basic spell reagents while preparing for battle with the riverstriders. The light spell comes back to me automatically, though it feels strange on my lips. It's the first time I've cast a true spell since returning from Alciel, since regaining my memory—the raw use of mist is different, like trying to ride a lightning bolt, whereas this is easy and comfortable, like slipping into a familiar bed. As I whisper the incantation against the pinch of fireseed in my palm, I can feel North's eyes on me. The grains begin to glow, that gentle greenish light rising in a pool around us and illuminating our faces.

I can't help but remember the first time I cast this spell in front of him, making him jump back, scrambling away as if I'd just sprouted wings. And I can't help but remember our arguments about it later. *Science,* he'd insist, outlining the ways in which different chemicals could luminesce. *Magic,* I would tell him, making him bristle with frustration.

He's remembering too, his eyes meeting mine, a spark of amusement there.

For a moment, he and I stand that way, watching each other—and then someone behind us shifts their weight, reminding me that we're not alone.

I draw a breath and then blow it at the fireseed, sending it out across the room before us, to settle like distant stars against the floor.

And then the air goes out of my lungs when I see what the light spell has revealed.

"No . . ." North turns in a slow circle, his face haggard in the pale green glow. I recognize the wreckage around us only because of the machinery I saw here and there in Alciel—what must have been banks of screens and control panels are reduced to mere shards of metal and glass. Everything is gone, from the panels in the ceiling that must have been used to illuminate this space, down to the chairs that once stood before the controls.

Muddy footprints all across the floor tell a story of a frenzied group, rushing here and there, destroying anything they could find.

Inshara and her Deathless. They found whatever information she needed—and then they destroyed the ancient computer, ensuring that no one would know what she did, and that no one could follow her from here.

We're too late.

"She must have come after we took the shuttle," says Saelis, his voice grim and weary. "Damn it!" A muted crash and scrape tells me he kicked some part of the rubble—but I can't take my eyes from North's.

He gazes back at me, my own despair echoed in his eyes. If Inshara has found a way to corrupt the hearts, to use their channeling power to pervert the beliefs and faith of everyone, then it's only a matter of time before we too are overtaken. We stand motionless, frozen—too tired, too full of dread, to think of what to do next. I can see that fear in his eyes, the same fear he had as he looked at his bloodmother, and I know he's imagining having his own heart corrupted and used to Inshara's purpose. The thought of him, his faith in me, in us, his love, all stripped away from him . . . it makes me want to weep. All I want is to take the two steps needed to go to him and let his arms go around me and stay there until we lose ourselves.

Ping.

The sound, tiny and artificial, echoes in the empty, shattered space. Nobody speaks, though the air seems to electrify—for a moment we're all thinking the same thing, that we imagined that little beep, conjured it out of our desperation to find some sign of life in the wreckage of the ancient computer.

Ping.

Everyone starts moving at once, searching through the wreckage, turning this way and that, searching for the source of the noise. Voices rise and tangle, quickened with hope.

"I think I heard it over here——"

"Is that it? Wait, no, that's just more of that light magic. . . ."

"Miiaaow?"

"Can you still hear it?"

North's voice rises over the rest of them. "Stop!" And, like magic, the commotion ceases. "Listen," he adds, in a quieter voice.

Ping . . .

"Ah! It's coming from this!" Miri steps up, struggling with something at her wrist—a moment later, she holds up the bracelet that North gave to her, the one we used to communicate with ORACLE in the garden.

North takes it from her, holding it up higher after the cat makes an attempt to bat it from his hand—and after a few moments, it makes the sound again, and a tiny little light glimmers weakly deep beneath its metallic surface.

"I thought it was broken," Miri breathes, gazing at it in North's hand.

"It is, I think," North replies, drawing it close to inspect it. "You said it overloaded or something?"

"Yes," Saelis chimes in. "When the mist came flooding in, when Nimh was . . . you know, doing her thing."

"May I?" I reach out, and North gives the bracelet to me. I blink in the gloom, focusing my eyes until I can see the threads of mist that wind around the object. Carefully, using my free hand, I brush aside a few that seem tangled up around the little blinking light; and then, coaxing a mist tendril of my own to form, I use it to brush at the place, urging it back to life. Into my mind flashes a memory of watching Elkisa light a fire this way—of using her breath the way I'm using the mist, to blow upon the embers until a flame sprang up.

Before I have a chance to let the memory distract me, the light gives a series of flashes in a distinct pattern. The bracelet makes another sound, a different sort of chime from the first— and then goes silent.

For a moment, nobody speaks—nobody even breathes, the silence of the room absolute.

Then North manages breathlessly, "ORACLE?"

A ring of light springs up from the bracelet, and then shifts into patterns as a voice emerges: "HELLO, NORTH."

A shout of surprise and relief bursts out of North, and behind him I can see Miri and Saelis clutching at each other in relief. Matias passes a hand over his face, leaning heavily on his walking stick—even Anasta, carefully supporting her wife on her arm, heaves a gasp of relief.

"ORACLE, how are you—how is this possible?" North asks, too agitated to form a more coherent question.

But the computer seems to understand. Its voice comes again, though the sound is fragmented and thin. "WEAK SIGNAL," it reports. "TOO FAR FROM MAINFRAME."

"Mainframe," North echoes, his brow furrowed as he bends over the artifact. "This place, you mean? We're right here—but it's destroyed. How are you still connected?"

"Too far from mainframe," the bracelet repeats. "Networked terminal down."

North's eyes snap up to meet mine, his mouth falling open. "Mainframe, of *course*. It kept asking us to sync with the mainframe the first time we were here, and I *thought* there was no room for the size of the computer needed to do all of what it did—the holographic projections, the storage of all that data and interactive programs. It would need banks and banks of servers—"

"North!" I blurt, forced to interrupt him and the spate of unfamiliar words.

He blinks, refocusing on my face. He lets out a slow breath. "I don't think this place is ORACLE at all," he says. "I think ORACLE is still safe, somewhere else."

"What do you mean?"

"I think this is an outpost. The main computer—the mainframe it kept talking about—is somewhere else. This place . . . it just accessed the information stored there. Like the bracelet does—the bracelet itself isn't the computer, it just *talks* to the computer."

I reach for his wrist, to hold it steady. North's giddy with relief at his deduction, but my mind is already skipping ahead. "ORACLE," I say, focusing on the bracelet. "Do you know where Inshara is going? The woman who was here before us, who destroyed this . . . this . . ." I glance at North.

"This terminal," he supplies.

"Right. The woman who destroyed this terminal?"

The bracelet gives a distorted beep, and then the ring of light shifts to a projected image, not unlike the way I'd seen North's chrono do. The image shifts, playing like a memory, hovering over the bracelet.

In it, Inshara crouches by a door—not the hangar door, but one I don't recognize. North does, though, by the swift intake of breath. It shows her pressing something to a panel by the door, her body language tense and furtive—and the door swings open.

Beatrin, gathered with the others forming a loose semicircle around North and I, gives a muffled cry and then turns away, hiding her face against Anasta's shoulder.

The thing Inshara is holding is a severed finger.

"Yes," I say, forcing myself to shove that image from my mind, even as the bracelet starts to shake in North's hand. "Her. Where is she going? How do we stop her?"

"A-A-AUTO-FUNCTION OMEGA." The voice is getting weaker, stuttering in an unsettlingly mechanic way.

"What does that mean?" I cry, giving the thing a shake, forgetting for that moment that I'm actually shaking North's hand—he reaches out to touch my shoulder with his free hand, steadying me.

"A-AUTO-FUNCTION O-O-O-MEEE-G-G-UHHH . . ." The voice drops in pitch, slowing horribly, becoming a parody of itself. And then, before anyone can so much as move, the tiny little light dies, and the computer falls silent.

"No!" I shout. "Come back!" North's arm around me supports me, his breathing quick and tense in my ear.

I reach for the mist, fumbling in my desperation, and thread it through the bracelet's mechanisms again, trying to revive it once more—but nothing happens. The bracelet is dead.

Tears of frustration spring to my eyes, even while North squeezes me. I hear him swallow hard and reach up to fold my hand over his, not sure whether I'm seeking his comfort or trying to offer him some of my own.

Then, the sound of someone clearing his throat breaks the silence. "Um . . ." Saelis says haltingly. "I think I might know what 'auto-function omega' is."

Every face turns toward him in the darkness, even the cat's, the gloom starting to gather around us as the light spell begins to fade.

He glances around at us, nervous, as if half-afraid to offer another splinter of hope after so many repeated blows. Miri reaches out, brushing his arm, then threading her fingers through his when he shifts automatically to let her take his hand.

Saelis takes a deep breath. "On the shuttle, when we were first trying to figure out how to fly it, we were looking for some kind of autopilot program. We found something that had a bunch of preprogrammed locations, and they were all labeled with code words, which didn't help us at the time." His eyes scan the faces gathered around him. "There was one called 'Omega.'"

We race back toward the shuttle. For a moment, the chaos of too many bodies trying to crowd around the control panel stops any of us from seeing what we're looking for. The bindle cat gives an outraged shriek as someone steps on his tail—Miri lets out a wail of a curseword, and an apology—then North leans forward, one hand jerking out to hover over a button.

Below it, written in the text of the ancients, is the word *Omega*.

He hesitates, and when he lifts his face, his eyes find mine among all those watching him so intently. "What if it was a glitch?" he whispers, a question in his gaze. "The last jumbled bit of code from a dying machine?"

My heart is pounding from the rush back to the shuttle, from the weight of the decision North has just handed me. For all we know, the shuttle could take us to some far distant land, away from Inshara, in the opposite direction of where we need to go to stop her. For all we know, there's no way to stop this automatic pilot once we've started it.

"We have to stop her," I tell him, my voice pitched for his ears, not caring just now about our friends. "I believe we are *meant* to stop her. The prophecy brought us together for a reason—that machine hung on for a *reason*. I have to believe it. I *choose* to believe it."

North's lips curve a little. It's not quite a smile, the tension too thick for that, but his eyes move across my face a moment, warming, some of his fear and uncertainty easing away. He nods, just a little—and then hits the button.

The shuttle gives a little shudder, and the engines make their distinctive whine, and the hangar bay doors open so that the aircraft can slip out into the starlit night beyond.

THIRTY

NORTH

The two moons hang before us in the sky, close together in their dance. Nimh told me once they're lovers in the stories her people tell. I like the idea that they're side by side, just now.

Below us stretches the forest-sea, the river winding its way through, cutting a curving line amid the dark treetops and offering glints of moonlit silver now and then.

Beside me, Miri sits with her feet up on the dashboard, carefully avoiding any navigational instruments, joining me in admiring the view. The two of us aren't doing anything to pilot the ship—we're just keeping watch and waiting to find out whether our destination will be near or far.

"Is it *a* cat?" she says suddenly, nibbling on a lavender curl. "Or *the* cat? How many of them are there?"

"Both," I say, with a twitch of a smile. "He's one of many, but he's most assuredly *the* cat." I'm about to continue—to admit to her how wary I was of him at first, to laugh at the way I asked Nimh if he could speak, what his name was—when the motion of the shuttle changes subtly.

We're slowing down.

"Nimh!" I call, sitting up straighter. There's a break in the trees up ahead—and I think I know where we are.

She's there in a moment, crowding into the cockpit along with the others—she pushes along to stand directly behind me, one hand on my shoulder, and leans in to study the view.

We're approaching the edge of the forest-sea, definitely slowing now, and perfectly smooth salt flats stretch out ahead of us, as far as the night will let us see. They're bigger than all the islands of Alciel put together, covered in perfectly calm, perfectly still water. It's not deep enough to cover the toes of my boots, but from here, it could be bottomless.

"The Mirror of Divinity," Nimh breathes softly.

And so it is, the stars above us in the night sky reflected perfectly below us in the still stretch of water. It feels for a dizzying moment as if the shuttle could turn upward and accelerate toward the two moons, or could dive, passing straight through the water and into the reflection there, to chase them below instead.

This is the place my glider crashed, and I can see a scar at the edge of the water where Techeki's people dragged it from the Mirror, toward their barges and the long journey back to the temple. We thought perhaps we could salvage something from it, use some part of it to find a way home for me. We didn't, and in truth, I knew we wouldn't before I began.

This is the place I crawled out of its wreckage, discovered to my shock that I was alive, and then found myself surrounded by mist-bent boars, fearsome creatures furious at my invasion of their territory, intent on ripping me to pieces.

This is the place Nimh came to find the Last Star of

prophecy, fallen from the sky, and found me waiting for her.

We're back here, in the end, where our story began.

"Did it stop on its own?" Saelis asks, leaning in to take a look at the water below. "Did either of you touch anything?"

"No, I didn't," Miri retorts, huffing softly.

"The reason will reveal itself," Matias says, and I turn my head to take in his serene expression. For a guy who'd never set foot in an aircraft an hour ago, he's doing pretty well.

Then Nimh gasps, and leans past me, and I twist back toward the water. My breath catches in my throat as I see what she saw. A line's appearing along the surface of the salt flats, splitting the stars in two. At first I can't make out what it is, but then it thickens and grows wider.

Nobody breathes.

The ground is opening, divided by a line so even it must be manmade, and the reflected stars are shimmering as water begins to pour in through the newly created gap. The stars waver and dance, and for a moment it seems as if the two moons themselves will be drawn in, tipping over the edge and vanishing into the black below.

The two edges widen, a perfect waterfall appearing in the moonlight, and Danna and Miella hold their places, showing us what's been hiding beneath the Mirror of Divinity all this time.

At first, I only know it's something huge. I see a matte silver surface. Then a communications arrays, and hatches, and—there's some sort of massive building down there, the architecture strange, reminding me of something I can't remember, its surfaces gently curving away into the distance.

"How big is it?" Miri whispers, my own awe echoed in her voice.

"And how long has it been waiting for us to arrive?" I murmur back.

The water pours down between the open hangar doors, the lake of stars tumbling endlessly down. And as we all gaze at the sight in wonder, the shuttle slowly begins to descend. A hatch appears in the curved surface of the massive place, the doors dividing in an echo of the way the salt flats themselves split a few minutes before.

As we all strain our gazes to see into the darkness, we descend into a gloomy chamber—and then with a soft glow that grows to a light as bright as day, it illuminates. We're in a long, sleek hangar, half a dozen other shuttles just like this one parked in rows to either side. This is where our shuttle must have come from—and I can't help but feel as if the shuttle is glad to be home. There are still more places that are empty, and I wonder if the shuttles that belong in them are sleeping under the mountains somewhere, just as ours did.

With the softest of kisses, the shuttle touches down, and everything dies away to silence. I glance across at Miri, expecting a crack—*now that's how you land a shuttle, next time you're wondering*—but her eyes are wide, her face still lit with wonder.

Beatrin, who's behind the others, in the doorway into the cockpit, looks back over her shoulder as the shuttle door hisses open, sending a hint of a breeze through to my face.

"I suppose we should see why ORACLE sent us here," says

Anasta, but it takes a long moment for any of us to move. One by one, though, we leave the cockpit. Nimh and I are the last out, and I wait for her to retrieve her spearstaff—someone must have cleaned it, for which I'm immensely grateful—before I reach for her hand. A part of me still hesitates to curl my fingers through hers, but she slips her hand into mine without pause, as if she'd been doing it all her life.

The shuttle has opened its hatch and extended a small set of stairs that lead down to the hangar floor, and we follow the others down, our footsteps not echoing, but swallowed up by the size of the place. The ceiling is still open above us, the stars gazing down on this place they haven't seen in centuries.

Beatrin and Anasta stand with Matias to one side of the stairs—the past hours have begun to catch up with him, and he looks older than I've ever seen him, leaning on Anasta's arm. Miri and Saelis stand to the other side of the stairs, close together. The cat runs down them ahead of Nimh and me, and we keep our hands joined as we descend.

"Hello, North," says an electronic voice, and I nearly fall down the last two steps in my fright, grabbing at the handrail to save myself from sending Nimh flying.

"Oracle?" I ask, glancing up and around, as the two of us regain our balance.

"Affirmative, North. We interacted at an outpost terminal, where my functions had degraded. Fortunately, it seems you were able to find this place once power was restored to the shuttle. My mainframe remains at full functionality."

"How?" asks Saelis, turning in a half circle, searching for

411

something to address, though there isn't anywhere a light shines, or anything to give us a focus.

"MY NETWORK TRANSMITS VIA THE M.I.S.T.," ORACLE replies. "DIVINE ONE, I APPRECIATED YOUR ASSISTANCE IN RETURNING IT TO THE CITY."

"Of course," Nimh murmurs weakly.

"ORACLE," I say, leaning right back. "What is this place? Is this all to house your computer machinery? It's massive—how did they ever build it?"

"THIS PLACE WAS NOT BUILT FOR ME," ORACLE replies. "IF ANYTHING, *I* WAS BUILT FOR *IT*. I AM THE OPERATIONAL REVIEW, ADVICE, AND COMPUTATIONAL LOGISTICS ENGINE FOR THIS VESSEL."

For a moment, I can only stand there, rooted to the metal floor, my mind spinning. The words, their meaning, hit me all over again. "*Engine,*" I echo, hearing the word properly for the first time, staggering back a pace, and tilting my head back as if I might be able to see the massive size of the thing through the metal hangar around me. "I thought you meant you powered some sort of computer. . . ."

"For this *vessel?*" whispers Miri, catching up with my realization.

"You're an engine for . . . this is a *skyship?*"

I hear Nimh's breath escape her in a gasp, her shoulders gone rigid.

"YES," says ORACLE, oblivious to the foundation-shaking awareness shuddering through us all. "THIS WAS ONCE A COLONY SHIP, AND I AM THE COMPUTER AND PROPULSION SYSTEM DESIGNED

TO GUIDE IT. WE BROUGHT YOUR ANCESTORS TO THIS PLACE."

"From where?" I ask, my heart thudding in my chest.

The computer pauses for the tiniest second. "FROM EARTH," it says finally.

For a moment, nobody speaks. Then Nimh leans forward and asks, "What's Earth?"

THIRTY-ONE

NIMH

"EARTH," ORACLE repeats. "THE THIRD PLANET IN THE SOL SYSTEM, LOCATED APPROXIMATELY TWO THOUSAND EIGHT HUNDRED AND ELEVEN LIGHT-YEARS AWAY. ONE OF SEVERAL PLANETS KNOWN TO HAVE DEVELOPED LIFE. ORIGIN POINT OF HUMAN SPECIES. ATMOSPHERE CONSISTS OF APPROXIMATELY SEVENTY-EIGHT PERCENT—"

North is staring vaguely upward, as if that might be where to find ORACLE itself, his mouth open. There's a strange, compelling light in his eyes as we stand together in this ancient skyship, his wonder and awe written so clearly in his features that my heart gives a lurching, almost painful squeeze as I watch his face.

I swallow as the computer continues on, and lean in as I try to get a grip on myself. "North . . . what is a planet?"

North blinks, looks down at me, and then just shakes his head, confused. "Another world, I guess," he says, looking nearly as puzzled as I am.

"Like Alciel?"

North lifts his shoulders in a shrug. "I don't know, maybe.

Our legends say there are other sky-cities out there somewhere, lost to us—maybe this Earth is one of them."

ORACLE cuts in, having apparently been listening to us while it lectured. "SHALL I INITIATE EDUCATIONAL PROGRAM?"

I open my mouth, but before I can speak, North jumps in. "No!" he replies swiftly, voice quick. "No, thank you." Catching my eye, and my unspoken question, he shifts his weight from one foot to the other. "I, uh . . . I spoke with that program before. He thinks I'm an idiot."

I find my lips quirking, amusement sparking despite my weariness and the urgency of our mission. "Perhaps you could just explain it to us, ORACLE?" I murmur.

There's a slight pause before ORACLE answers, but when it does, there's no sign that it finds the request unorthodox. When it does speak, its language is modified—it no longer sounds as though it is reciting a text. "THE HUMAN RACE ORIGINATED ON A PLANET CALLED EARTH. A LONG HISTORY FILLED WITH STRIFE ULTIMATELY LED A PART OF THE POPULATION TO SEEK ANOTHER WORLD IN WHICH THEY COULD LIVE FREE OF CONFLICT. THEY BUILT A SHIP DESIGNED TO BRING THEM HERE, A NEW PARADISE."

"Free of conflict?" I echo, uneasily. "Earth must have been a truly terrible place, to think that *this* is a more peaceful world by comparison."

"It's just like our ancestors, and the Ascension, and Alciel," North murmurs, glancing over his shoulder at his mothers. "We keep trying to run away. Apparently we've been trying to run away for a lot longer than a thousand years."

Matias makes a disparaging noise in his throat. "This is

why stories are important," he says quietly. "As soon as we forget where we came from, we start losing track of where we should be trying to go."

The computer's words have left a strange tightness in my stomach. "If Daoman were here," I say slowly, "he would remind me that all life is a cycle—all this has happened before and will happen again."

North raises one eyebrow a fraction, in that way he has when he's about to make an important argument. "To that, I think I say that we write our own stories. That Nimh will choose what it means to be the Destroyer. Just as Matias says, learning from where we've been, so she can decide where we go next."

I swallow, that tension in my body intensifying. "No pressure."

North gives an almost startled huff of laughter, joined a moment later—to my surprise—by Matias, whose chuckle echoes down the corridor. The cat, sitting just close enough to me for his fur to brush my calf, flashes the old man a haughty look and then stretches up onto his feet to weave between my legs.

"Of course," I tell him softly. "We may not have much time. ORACLE, why did you bring us here? Is this where Inshara came?"

"I DO NOT RECOGNIZE USER 'INSHARA.' CANNOT ANSWER QUERY."

North and I exchange a glance. "She's the one who destroyed your other terminal," he explains. "She wants to use the hearts for her own purposes, terrible ones. Is there something here that could help her do that, ORACLE?"

"Yes. Me."

Everyone is silent for a long moment, trying to process the many roads that information could lead Inshara down, each of them worse than the last. I stoop to retrieve the cat, who is winding around my ankles in agitation.

"How?" North asks. "Are you connected to the hearts?"

"Your ancestors required my help to utilize the M.I.S.T. and create the hearts," ORACLE replies.

North's breath comes out in a long rush. "So you're like the brain that controls the hearts. And now *she* could use you."

"You mean ORACLE is what Inshara is here for?" I say slowly. "She wishes to use it to change the purpose of the hearts?"

"She plans on corrupting ORACLE the way she corrupted me," says Beatrin, her voice startling me in the sudden silence. I'd nearly forgotten she and the others were there, in my horrified fascination.

"Can she do that?" Anasta murmurs, her eyes wide. "Take a computer the way she takes people?"

"She clearly thinks she can," North answers her. "And if ORACLE is connected to the mist, as it says, then she might be right. ORACLE, did anyone else show up here before we did? Through some other entrance, maybe?"

"Negative. There is only one entrance, and it has been closed for centuries."

North starts to ask another question, but Saelis takes a step forward, raising a hand, his brow furrowed in thought. North falls silent, waiting for his friend, who takes another moment before speaking.

"You said no one showed up before we did. Has anyone showed up *since?*"

The computer pauses for a long moment, and my stomach hollows out more with every moment I wait for its reply. "I APPEAR TO BE EXPERIENCING A MALFUNCTION. MY SENSORS ARE RETURNING FRAGMENTED DATA."

Miri looks around, as if half expecting to see Inshara and a horde of her Deathless coming for us. "She's here."

"And we opened the door for her," Saelis adds, expression twisting.

North gives a quick, sharp shake of his head. "Now we know where she is. Now we can stop her."

He glances at me, and I nod at him, though dread has settled in my bones, making me struggle not to shiver visibly. It's easier to proclaim faith than it is to feel it—easier to tell North I believe that we are destined to stop Inshara than to trust myself. Because when North says "we," the truth is that *I* am the one meant to confront her.

The last time I tried, she bent me to her will without once using her powers, manipulating my pain and my emotions to bring Alciel crashing down into the world Below.

And now, we must face her with the hearts of both worlds at stake.

THIRTY-TWO

NORTH

"Go!" says Matias, lifting one hand in a sweeping gesture.

"Run!" echoes Anasta, looking first to the Fisher King, then to my bloodmother, both worn and weakened. "I have them, go!"

I hesitate for one long, agonizing moment, and then Beatrin looks up at me, and our eyes lock. "You can do this," she says quietly.

And we *run*.

We race along a dimly lit hallway, following an illuminated green spot that ORACLE projects on the wall to guide our way. Nimh and I are out in front, Miri and Saelis close on our heels, and the cat streaks ahead of us all, chasing ORACLE's guide with single-minded determination.

Nimh's face is grim, her jaw squared as she takes the corner beside me, her spearstaff held close. We're headed for the center of the ship, still near its top—my lungs are aching, my tired legs screaming at me as we burst together into a huge, circular room with a domed ceiling, and abruptly we stop.

There are banks of computers all around the edge of the

room—it reminds me of a flight tower, and perhaps that's what it once was. The ceiling is transparent, but I can only faintly make out the stars above us—the light in here is too bright.

A huge, crackling ball of red-and-gold light is suspended in the very center of the room, beneath the dome, with metal walkways crisscrossing from the room's perimeter to its heart, several stories above the floor far below. It's wider across than I am tall, and it's as if it's made of living light, strands of Nimh's red robe twisting and turning and roiling around strands of the same gold as both our crowns. Green and purple tinge it here and there, touches of mist woven through.

And there, dwarfed by the massive sphere—and yet impossible to miss—stands Inshara. The sheer power humming from the computer's core makes her robes and hair shift as if in a breeze, as if the core is generating its own weather. Her face is riveted to its surface, eyes wide, hands raised.

Techeki is to one side of her, Talamar the other, both standing perfectly still. Tears roll slowly down Techeki's cheeks. Talamar bows his head, as if in silent grief.

Elkisa is a few steps closer to us, as if she'd started forward when she heard my approach. She meets my eyes, but her gaze is inscrutable, and after a moment, it shifts across to Nimh.

"Isn't it beautiful?" Inshara doesn't take her eyes off the great ball of light, her tone admiring, but . . . not quite right. There's an edge to it. "The mind of this place, I think. I can sense the power it has over the hearts." Her lips twitch, and finally she looks across at us. "My mind controls hearts too. This place was meant for me."

Techeki gazes at her in sheer adoration, scarcely sparing a glance for the sight of the computer core. "I wish our people could witness this moment, Divine One. I will create a new festival of light to commemorate it—there will be reenactments, celebration, and splendor." His eyes are alight in a way I've never seen before.

I snort, my words coming out before I have a chance to choose them, my instinct to provoke her, to keep her off balance. "Are you so desperate to be Nimh that you couldn't find your own Master of Spectacle? Do you want everything she has?"

Inshara lets out a breath and then turns, her lips tightening as she looks at me. She didn't miss our entrance after all—she's just pretending not to care.

Or she doesn't think we're any kind of threat to her.

I only get a moment to dwell on her attitude, though—because something's moving behind her and Elkisa. Techeki stands as still as ever, ignoring the glorious light display right beside him, the tears trickling down his cheeks illuminated red and gold.

But Talamar . . . slowly, carefully, he's shifting his weight. And when he glances across at us, he's alert. His cheeks are dry. His eyes meet mine, urgent with some concealed purpose. Inshara's grip on him has slipped, or else she never had him.

Moving slowly, carefully, he drops to one knee, and slips a hand inside Elkisa's bag. On instinct, I draw Inshara's attention away, every nerve in my body alive. Perhaps my father was just waiting for this moment: something to distract Inshara and give him an opportunity to stop her.

"You aren't going to try and fight us?" I ask, pulling up a mildly insulting tone.

"I have no more need for violence," she replies, voice tight. "All of it was a means to an end. *This* end."

"We found a temple full of dead, after Elkisa went through it for you," I counter. At Inshara's side, Elkisa closes her eyes. "We watched you kill Daoman—the world watched you kill your mother. Claiming mercy now seems out of character, Insha."

With a sharp intake of breath, Inshara takes a furious step toward me—and Talamar *strikes*.

As he lunges for Inshara, my gaze flicks to him involuntarily. Someone cries out behind me, and then Techeki is moving in a flash with reflexes far beyond his natural ability, seeming to turn almost in the same heartbeat that my father moves.

He throws himself past Inshara to tackle Talamar to the ground, pinning him with both knees against his chest and knocking the blade from his hands. The face of the Master of Spectacle is twisted with passion in defense of the goddess he now serves, giving him unnatural strength as he holds my father down.

Inshara has stopped in her tracks, staring at Talamar, and for a long, silent moment, the only thing moving in the chamber is the slowly writhing ball of red and gold—ORACLE's mind, the key to the hearts. The key to Inshara's rule.

"You," she whispers, her eyes wide and full of hurt fury. "You were . . . *pretending* to be under my power? How?" The silence that follows only seems to enrage her, for she shouts the question again, voice echoing: *"How?"*

Talamar groans, gasping for air, his already-labored

422

breathing worsening beneath Techeki's weight. He gurgles, attempting to answer—but only manages to speak once Techeki eases back a fraction.

"You take what people believe in," gasps my father, "and you twist it. Your power is the corruption of love and faith—but what have I left to believe in? What have I left to love?"

"You only ever *pretended* to love me," she says in a shaking voice, which then rises to a shout. "What do I care? You are no god—you are *nothing*!" In a quick, vicious movement, she kicks at his knee.

He screams, and Techeki clamps one hand over his mouth. His chest rises and falls urgently, and his free hand shoves into his jacket pocket, but his breather isn't there.

"Inshara—" I try, and she spins to face me.

"Yes, *brother*?" The word is like poison. "You think I owe our father mercy? Come, then. Decide his fate for yourself." She stoops, claiming Talamar's dagger from where he dropped it and taking two steps toward me to hold it out.

I glance from her to Nimh, tense at my side, and back. *Keep her talking. Find a way past her madness.* "Why would I hurt my own father?"

Inshara's expression ripples. "I will tell you what he told me, when all his secrets came spilling out in an attempt to save his own skin. Then you can choose what to do with the knife."

More than fury, more than madness, I see *pain* in her eyes—the betrayal of our father has stripped her of what little sanity she had left. She's nothing more than a raw nerve, screaming out in the darkness.

"I don't need the knife, Insha," I say, approaching her slowly. "I know he's hurt you—I know I'll never forgive him for his secrets, and what he did to you. But I'm not going to kill him for it."

"I never expected you to kill him for what he did to *me*," she says softly, her eyes fixed on mine. "Take the knife, young prince, for *he* is the reason your glider fell."

For a moment, I can't move, my stomach dropping, my breath freezing in my lungs. Then my body staggers, one hand going out to clutch at the railing. "What are you talking about?"

"He hates this place," she replies, stepping forward to keep pace with me. "Hates us—fears us. He wanted to burn the bridge between our worlds—he wanted to destroy the key."

"The royal bloodline," murmurs Nimh from behind me. I can hear her shock and pain, but it barely penetrates the roaring in my ears.

"That doesn't make sense," I shoot back, pushing away the growing dread inside my chest. "Ever since he joined the council he's been arguing that we should send an expedition Below."

Inshara scoffs. "And you think he would have let such an expedition fare any better than you did, princeling? What better way to ensure its failure, than to steer its course?" Another step forward, and then she's grabbing for my wrist, wrenching my arm around, and shoving the hilt of the knife into my hand.

My fingers close around it.

Ice is creeping through my gut, twisting and swirling as if that living ball of light has a smaller twin inside of me.

This is the man who told me I was right to dream of flight.

So that I could fall?

For a moment, that pain and anger surging through me snaps, and I tighten my hand around the knife's hilt. This man—my father—*our father*—is the reason for all this death and pain. If I had never fallen Below, Inshara never could have used me to reach Alciel, never hurt my mother; Alciel would still be in the sky; I would have been there with my grandfather at his end; I would know nothing of war or grief or despair.

The tiniest of sounds, little more than a metallic tinkle, draws my hyperalert senses. I know the sound: one of Nimh's charms, on her spearstaff, clinking as she shifts her weight.

I would never have known Nimh.

I squeeze my eyes closed and take a breath, wishing I could just unknow what I've learned.

I open my eyes again and take a step back from Inshara, adjusting my grip on the knife's hilt. "It doesn't matter," I say slowly. "There is no crime for which I would take someone's life."

"He tried to take yours," she snaps.

"*I am not him,*" I shoot back.

My eyes are fixed on my father, who gazes back at me, expressionless. The churning in my gut is rising up my throat now, making it hard to breathe. I can't feel my fingers, but I know I'm gripping the knife.

"He does not deserve your protection," Inshara murmurs at my elbow. "Kill him, and I'll let you walk away."

I wrench my gaze from Talamar to stare at her. "What?"

Inshara is intent, those mist-colored eyes unsettling as they

425

fix on mine. "Take the ship you came in and go far from here. I will leave you undisturbed." Those eyes slide from my face to Nimh's behind me. "You never wanted this life that was thrust upon you, sister. I do. Let me unite these broken worlds under my banner, and our paths need never cross again. Kill him, and go."

And as she speaks the words, I can see it. For the longest moment, I live in the picture in my mind—in a humble place, far away, where we've escaped all the death and pain that will soon overtake both our worlds. Where we're protected.

But where could we go, that the memory of what we left behind couldn't follow us?

I can still feel Nimh there behind me, and I let her tether me, let her hold me in place. "I'm sorry, Insha," I say softly. "But I'm not like you. I could never kill my father."

Her response is a roar, like a sound of pain—she swings around, lunging for Talamar, her knife lifted.

I throw myself after her without time to think about what I'm doing, and everything happens at once. I hear voices cry out behind me. Elkisa dives for me, and Inshara for my father—

Their eyes lock, and she lashes out with her knife.

THIRTY-THREE

NIMH

My feet are already sprinting toward them as Inshara and Talamar collide and tumble together, scrambling for the knife; a cry tears its way from my lips as I watch North throw himself between Inshara and his father. *Their* father. I get there in time to see Inshara raise the knife, its blade glimmering in the light from the computer's mind—

Then Inshara goes staggering back, her feet skidding on the metal. She stands there, panting, staring at the person who's put herself between her and North.

Elkisa.

"Stop this!" my former guard cries, her arms outstretched—one pressed against North's shoulder, the other stretching, palm outward, toward Inshara. "You have what you sought, Insha—just take what you need from this ancient relic and leave them be."

Inshara, gasping for breath, her face distraught, clutches at the guardrail. "H-how *dare* you," she manages finally, her eyes flashing with pain. "You claim to be on my side—"

"I *am* on your side!" Elkisa replies, drawing herself up onto her knees, not even looking away from Inshara long enough to glance back at North. "But this cannot be what you wished for—this death, this bloodshed, when it serves no purpose. Attacking Nimh's camp and trying to capture her before she could find her Star, I understood that. Retaking the temple to stand as a beacon for your new divinity, I knew that to be right. You even convinced me that Daoman had to die—that my hands would be washed clean of his blood if I just *believed* enough—"

Her voice breaks, and she pulls herself up the rest of the way, her gaze intent on Inshara's face, pleading.

"But your mother?" Elkisa whispers. "And now you would kill your father too? How can all this death be right?"

"She never loved me," Inshara spits, her eyes wide, as if Elkisa's whisper were a terrifying roar. "Neither did he. They both used me, manipulated me—"

"I cannot speak for him," Elkisa says, jerking her chin toward Talamar, who crouches behind North, his eyes wide with fear. "But Jezara loved you, Insha. You told me enough stories of her to prove that to me." She takes a cautious step toward her beloved, her hand still raised, as if to calm a skittish creature.

"Stop!" Inshara's voice is high and thin. "You're trying to distract me—you're still loyal to *her*." Those blazing eyes focus past Elkisa on me, the hatred and agony there hitting me like a visceral blow.

"No." Elkisa shifts her weight, stepping so that I am half concealed from Inshara's gaze. "I am loyal to *you*. Have I not proven that? Let me prove it to you now—let us just leave this place together. You have already shown your power over this world. Do not do this monstrous thing."

Inshara's eyes dart between Elkisa and what little of me she can see beyond her, and then to North, who crouches before his father, poised to match any move she makes. "I am no monster," she hisses. "Everything that I have done, I have done because I was *destined* to do it. Fate has made these choices—not I! You used to believe in that. In me. If I leave now, then I am just— just a—a . . ."

"A murderer?" North murmurs hoarsely.

Inshara's throat moves as she swallows hard, her mist-touched eyes wet with tears—of grief or fury, though, I cannot tell. "Shut up!" She emphasizes her words with a jab of her knife, causing Elkisa to twitch, adjusting where she stands, putting herself between Inshara and North now.

"Look at me, my heart," Elkisa says as she takes another careful step closer, her voice that familiar combination of gentle and firm that I remember from our years growing up together, quieter now as she takes another careful step closer. "I will not let you kill your brother too. I will not let you become this."

A part of me recoils, wants to scream that the woman she loves already *is* this, that her hands are already stained with her mother's blood. But the flickering light from the center of the room glints off the tears standing on Inshara's cheeks— Elkisa's approach is *working*. She's reaching Inshara, where I could not—where North failed—where her own father could not touch her.

And so I press my lips together, taking what solace I can in the warmth of the bindle cat as he leans against my legs, his fur bristling and body tense.

"Just take my hand," Elkisa continues, still gentle, still not taking her eyes from Inshara's face. "We can go together. Just . . . just put down the knife . . ."

I see it, a moment before it happens—my eyes, sensitive to the shifting mist in the room, can see the bloated, sickening tendrils of power that snake out from Inshara toward Elkisa. Like black snakes, shimmering as if coated with faintly iridescent oil, they reach for her the way they sit around Techeki, coiled around him like bindings.

Elkisa steps forward, her arm still outstretched, unaffected. She wraps her fingers around Inshara's arm, making her flinch.

"No!" Inshara's voice is a wail, confusion and fear mingling together. "How are you resisting?"

Elkisa doesn't answer, wrapping her arms around Inshara, the gesture half embrace, half restraint. "Just leave with me," she pleads.

Those serpentine coils reach for Elkisa again, only to slide away, Inshara trying in vain to gain a toehold in her mind. "Why can't I make you worship me like the others do?" Inshara cries, her voice echoing throughout the chamber. "Why can't I make you *love* me?"

The final words are punctuated with a thick, sickening sound: a wet, sucking squelch. Elkisa jerks, but doesn't let go.

I feel my own voice crack in a scream, and I try to run for them, forgetting in that moment all of Elkisa's betrayals, needing only to reach my friend—but North is there, catching me around the waist, holding me back. His face is haggard in the light of the ancient computer, his body immovable as I fight to be released.

Inshara gasps, letting go of the knife, whose handle protrudes just below Elkisa's ribs. Horror transforms Inshara's face as she looks down at the blood beginning to stain her clothes.

Elkisa draws a shuddering breath, voice cracking with pain as she loosens her arms enough to pull back and look into Inshara's face. "You don't need that power," she manages hoarsely. "Not with me."

"El—" Inshara's arms are around her now, half supporting her. "Oh gods, I didn't—"

But Elkisa just smiles, her voice weakening. "I . . . always loved you . . . my heart." Her knees buckle, her weight dragging both of them up against the railing. "You never needed . . . magic."

"No—no—!" Inshara's grip fails as Elkisa's body goes limp, draping across the railing and then, after one last desperate grab, topples over the edge to fall down, down, tumbling slowly, down into the darkness below.

I gasp a sob, staggering, North's arms holding me up. He's speaking in my ear, but I can't hear him, my eyes glued to the spot where Elkisa had stood—where she sacrificed herself for us.

No, not for us. For Inshara herself.

El, my mind wails. *Come back.*

Inshara falls against the railing, a guttural sound emerging from deep within her, a wrenching moan of grief and horror.

She holds her hands before her, shaking, the stains on them so thick she might be wearing crimson gloves. Her eyes are focused on them, then dart to the railing, to the drops of blood where Elkisa was standing, to where her father still sits on the floor, cringing away from her gaze.

Then they swing toward us—and her eyes meet mine.

For a moment, her pain is all I can see. There's no mist-touched monster there, only a girl who was told as young as I was that she was destined to change the world—a world that hated her, spat upon her mother, told her that her very existence was a cosmic mistake. A girl who had to watch while some other child was raised into the light, worshipped, praised—and, ultimately, given the exact power she'd been promised by the gods.

She gazes at me, that girl twisted by false destiny, her heart in her eyes.

Help me, she seems to say, some last shred of humanity dangling over a pit of despair and misery so thick that my heart shifts, all of her crimes seeming to fade away.

I open my mouth to speak—and in that moment, the shutters come down in Inshara's eyes. That gulf of despair encloses her, and the mist transforming her eyes grows into brilliance.

With a scream of pain and rage, Inshara whirls to face the massive, gleaming ball illuminating the vast cavern of a room. Silhouetted against its light, those corrupted tendrils of mist gathering all around her, she raises her bloodied hands . . .

. . . and plunges them deep into the ancient computer's mind.

THIRTY-FOUR

NORTH

Light blazes like the sun—red and dazzling gold so bright that even when I close my eyes and turn my face away, the colors still dance behind my eyelids. Even with the protection stone in my pocket, I can feel Inshara pressing up against my mind—her madness and her fury writhe like the light she's consuming, tugging at my edges, whispering to me to hear her.

My eyes sweep across the walkway, and I realize there's no sign of my father—I have barely a moment's thought to spare for his cowardice, though. Let him run; he isn't the one I'm searching for in the sudden glare.

"Nimh," I gasp, swaying on my feet. My gaze snaps over to her with a sudden shiver of fear, but she's still herself. Her grip on her spearstaff is white-knuckled, her lips pressed together, and when she turns her head to look at me, there are tears in her dark eyes. She doesn't have the protection stone that's shielding me, but she's holding on, fighting back against Inshara's rising power.

But for how long?

The power radiating from the computer is growing. Soon it will have engulfed the whole room, and beyond that, the forest-sea, and Nimh's temple, and Alciel, both hearts falling to her corruption . . . and then everyone within their reach will turn to worship Inshara.

With a gasp, understanding flashes into my mind with all the clarity of a lightning bolt. Turning, I reach for Nimh, holding her, willing her to look at me.

"You are the Lightbringer," I say, raising my voice above the crackle of power. "The Destroyer. Nimh—she can't corrupt the hearts if there are no hearts to corrupt."

Nimh's wide, fearful eyes fix on mine. For a moment, she doesn't understand—and then I see the same realization settle in her features, along with a flash of the horror she showed when ORACLE first presented the idea to us. She recoils, pulling away from me. "No! If we destroy the hearts, we could bring destruction to everything. No more divinity—Alciel could never rise again—we would be killing destiny itself—"

"None of that matters," I insist, stepping close again. "Yes, you'll be ending the world as we know it—but Nimh, if Inshara succeeds here, it'll be the end anyway."

The light around us flares again, making it impossible to see anything—for a desperate moment I think maybe it's too much for Inshara, that she won't be able to control the hearts—and then it dies, and I can see Nimh's face again. And, beyond her . . . I see my best friends.

Saelis stares at us like he's trying to solve a problem, seeming not to notice the tears slowly spilling down his cheeks. Miri's lips curve to a slow, calculating smile as she takes a threatening step toward us, her eyes bright.

I can barely look away from them—they're still themselves, and that's the worst of it. Saelis, still thoughtful. Miri, still scheming without missing a beat. Inshara has taken those beautiful parts of them and twisted them into her service. The thought that she could take my devotion to Nimh, my determination to do what's right, and make those things rotten . . .

I swallow my terror, turning back to Nimh. This time she doesn't pull away when I reach for her, shaking in my arms.

"I understand it now," I murmur, now that I'm close enough that I don't have to shout. "Prophecy. Fate. Everything that has led me to you—to a girl who believes she's meant to destroy the world." A lock of her hair, whipping about in the press of mist and power emanating from the computer, falls across her eyes, and I raise a hand to brush it aside. "Nimh—this is it. *This* is your destiny."

She shakes her head, leaning forward, holding onto me with the strength of desperation. "Don't ask this of me," she whispers, her eyes searching mine. "I can't—we can just run, think of a way to undo what she's done once we're safe—" She breaks off, gasping in pain as Inshara assaults our minds once again—she's there at the edges of my thoughts now, pushing relentlessly at my defenses.

I draw a long breath, slipping one hand into my pocket so that I can curl my fist around the protection stone, the only thing preventing Inshara from taking my mind the way she's taken everyone that I love, everyone but . . .

I keep my eyes on Nimh's. She's so strong, but she can't hold out against this power of Inshara's, not forever. She needs every bit of strength and protection I can give her, even if the thought of surrendering—of letting Inshara twist my mind, turn my love into a weapon—makes me want to turn and run as fast and as far as I can, until my lungs burn, until my mind goes blank.

But this is why I'm here. To believe in her when there's no one else left to do it. Not even her.

"I love you," I say quietly, holding her gaze. I pull the protection stone from my pocket, as Inshara's power ripples against my mind with an oily, hungry darkness. "It isn't prophecy, it isn't magic. This is just me, loving you. Believing in you, Nimh."

She lifts one hand to cup my cheek, her fingers warm against my skin. I've ached for her touch, dreamed of her touch. Slowly, carefully, I lift my hand to press the protection stone into her palm.

Nimh gasps a sob as she sees the stone, her hands fumbling now to press it back into my hands—she knows what I'm about to do. "North, no—please. I can't do this without you."

I can hear Miri and Saelis close by, but I can't look away from Nimh, can't break this moment. Inshara pushes at me, relentless, stronger than ever, and Nimh groans as she holds the line.

"You won't be alone." If these are going to be my last words to her, I want them to count. I press the stone into Nimh's palm and lean in to whisper my words to her. "You have my faith. Always."

Our lips meet, and I can taste her tears.

I close her fingers around the protection stone, and I let go.

THIRTY-FIVE

NIMH

North's body stiffens in my arms, his muscles going rigid, his breathing slowing. My own body is frozen, the air crystalizing in my lungs. The fingers he curled around the protection stone won't respond to me, ready to let it go, to push it back on him. If not for his hand over mine, I would have dropped it.

All at once, the pressure against my mind, the encroaching darkness choking my thoughts and my heart, eases away, the power of the stone—of the layers of belief woven into it, my own spells to protect North, and his faith in return—settling over me.

Power comes from belief.

And he believes, with all his heart, that the stone will protect me.

Then North's fist tightens around mine, an excruciating grip that makes me cry out in pain, my knees buckling. When I look up, he's watching me with a fierceness that robs me of breath, tears spilling from his eyes and tracking down his cheeks. I've never seen him look at me like that—like I'm nothing more than a thing, some object to be mastered.

He opens his mouth, and in that moment I realize I can't bear to know what he sounds like, with the depth of his love and faith twisted to Inshara's purposes. I shove at him, breaking free of his grip and eliciting a grunt of surprise.

I scramble away, but he recovers quickly, regaining his balance and lunging after me. Before he can grab at me, though, the bindle cat gives a howl of rage and launches himself at North's face, claws extended, fur sticking straight out, teeth bared and ears back. I get my feet under me and run, trying to shut my ears to the sound of North's shout of pain and surprise and the cat's howls of distress.

I lift my head and skid to a halt, my feet sliding against the metallic walkway. Miri and Saelis stand there, their bodies blocking the way, their gazes as intent as North's.

When I turn, Inshara is there, standing before the massive sphere of light—only it isn't made of light anymore. Shadows crawl across its surface like oil on the river, individual tendrils of darkness writhing free and then settling back again. The air is thick with darkness.

I reach for the mist, trying to exert my will and buy myself time—a bolt of fiery pain lances through my head. With a cry, I stumble, hitting the railing hard enough to jar my bones.

"Stop fighting," comes a familiar, beloved voice. "You'll hurt yourself."

North walks forward, his face a study in concern, seeming not to notice the rows of bleeding scratches covering his face and throat. There's no sign of the bindle cat, and my battered heart gives a weary lurch of fear for him.

"The mist is hers now," he continues, dropping to a crouch before me. His eyes glisten with the strength of his emotion. "You must see that."

"Stop it," I manage, my voice barely a whisper—but Inshara hears me, I know, for in the distance beyond North, I hear a noise of triumph. "Stop this—you're not him."

His eyebrows rise a little, the gesture so familiar, so *North*, that my heart aches. "Of course I'm still me. I just . . . *understand* now what I didn't—what I *wouldn't*—before." His eyes are almost gentle now, so much so that I wonder for the briefest of moments if I'd imagined that change in him. "You never wanted to be the Lightbringer," he murmurs. "And now you don't have to be. Let go, stop fighting, and you and I can be together again."

"Stop!" I cry again, though this time I turn my face away from North, focusing on Inshara behind him. "Stop using him—if you want to gloat, talk to me yourself!"

"You think I am speaking through him?" she says, with an exaggerated air of innocence. Her bloody hands are black now, as if burned by the computer, but she seems not to feel any pain. "You misunderstand what I am offering these people, Nimh. I am not forcing them to do anything. I am simply giving them something greater than themselves to believe in. Something greater, even, than *you*."

"North believes in me," I whisper, tightening my hand around the protection stone nestled in my palm. "Nothing you do, nothing you make him say, will change that."

"I bear you no ill will," says Inshara, taking another step, her eyes full of swirling, raging mist—a storm, there, violent enough to tear a person apart, were it not contained behind her gaze. "Give me the stone, Nimh. Give it to me, and I will let you and him be together in the new world I will forge."

I draw myself back up to my feet, holding on to the railing for support. "No."

"He can take it from you," Inshara says, voice sharpening a fraction. "I have but to ask."

As if to prove her point, North lets out a breath, straightening to his full height and looking down at me. I had not quite realized that he was so strong, not until I felt his touch myself—he is no burly riverstrider lad, but he's no temple acolyte either. I only escaped his grip the first time because of the bindle cat and the element of surprise.

This time, if he grabs me—I won't be able to get free.

I gather my intention, letting my will pool in my mind. I can feel that grief and fury that fueled my manifestation into the Lightbringer, feel it filling my heart in an eager rush. But I also remember North's lips on mine as the sun set behind our two worlds, and his faith that there was more than grief and fury in my heart.

Shifting my gaze from North's face to Inshara's, I say, "Let him try."

The words take a moment to sink in—then Inshara's giving a shout of frustration, and North is lunging for me.

I dodge to the side just enough to duck under his arm, and then I throw myself at him, wrapping my arms around him and ducking my head against his shoulder.

Hold on, love. Stay with me.

Pure white light explodes against my eyes, blinding me, drowning me, carrying me into some other kind of existence— the Lightbringer's power fills me, threatening to rob me of my will and everything I am.

And then I open my eyes.

Inshara is there, surrounded by her darkness and shadow— she meets my gaze with a cry of alarm and fear, staggering back. The black tendrils around her recoil like insects in a sudden beam of sunlight.

North is still as stone in my arms, but I hold on, unwilling to let him go—he is my anchor. My tether to myself, my own heart, my own choices.

You have my faith in you. Always.

Beyond Inshara is the computer, the ancient engine that brought our ancestors to this place. Some of its light is still there, glimmers of red and gold beneath the blackness—but the roots of Inshara's corruption have run deep, my eyes able to see it there now. The corruption is nearly complete, its threads impossible to untangle.

I let my awareness shift, sending the light that fills me outward, into the ship, beyond it, above the Mirror of Divinity. I can see the wave of Inshara's power rushing outward from this place, its crest approaching the river and racing along it.

She is only moments from taking the hearts of North's world and mine.

I throw myself forward, urging the light to overtake the shadow—for my will to reach the hearts before hers.

The light responds as if it were an extension of my body, and despite the desperation of this moment, a wild exhilaration courses through me. Now that I'm not fighting the Lightbringer's power, it fills me, inhabits me, in a way that sets every nerve and particle of my being on fire. I can no longer separate myself from this power—I *am* the light itself.

I catch up to the leading edge of Inshara's control, and before I can go farther, the shadow turns and crashes into me, the world flashing infinitely bright and then casting us both into darkness.

For a moment, I can see nothing—not the shadow-encrusted computer or Inshara before it, not the larger world without. I can't even feel North in my arms—I cannot tell if I even *have* arms anymore.

And then a tiny pool of light illuminates a figure in the vast emptiness.

Inshara.

She sits, her legs drawn up, her arms wrapped around them, her face pressed down into her knees. When she lifts her head, she looks at me, her eyes full of anguish. Her hatred is gone, her expression offering none of that rage and ferocity. Instead, she gazes at me in appeal.

"Please don't," she whispers. "Let me have this. I won't hurt anyone else. Everyone will be at peace."

There's a faint, glimmering thread leading from Inshara off into the emptiness—when I look, I see that I have one too. That same connection that bound us at sunset, when I felt her plan to corrupt the hearts, binds us now. Our spirits are still tethered, both of us, to the two halves of our world's broken heart. I can feel them, their delicate structures within my reach. I could destroy them now, the urge to do so rising in my heart—but I turn toward Inshara, instead.

I move toward her, coming into my body again as I do. "I cannot let you coerce their devotion," I tell her gently. "You know that."

"Why not?" Inshara's voice is a wail, her gaze beseeching. "How is it that you *know* your way is better? I can offer peace. A united people under *one* god. Isn't that the whole point? All this death and bloodshed comes when we keep running away from each other, and I can unite everyone, once and for all. How can you be sure you can unite them if you can't control them?"

I reach her and drop down to my knees so I can look into her face. It shimmers and blurs, her concentration wavering—but then, I must seem as ghostly and strange to her, as well.

"I suppose I can't," I whisper. "But I don't think it's about that. If this endless cycle of exodus and strife tells me anything, it's that it is the most human thing in the world to disagree. But I think it's in the *trying* to come together that we find our purpose."

"How can you be so sure?" Inshara whispers back.

"My people, the riverstriders, tell stories of the first explorers to come to this land. They say they navigated the dark, endless ocean by the light of the stars." I find myself wishing I could reach out to Inshara and take her hand, but I hesitate. "I had such a Star to guide me."

Somewhere, in the real world, the other world, my arms are

still around North, holding him on that walkway suspended in space, refusing to let him go.

The last star on that long journey, to guide me in the end to this place.

Inshara's face twists, and she squeezes herself down all the more tightly—she seems smaller, now, as if the power giving her form in this void is draining away. "Destiny never gave me a star," she mumbles.

My breath catches—and when she looks up at me again, the words come spilling out. "Oh, Insha—it did. You just didn't see her for what she was."

Inshara's eyes fill with tears, and I abandon hesitation, abandon the strangeness of this encounter, this world apart from the world where she isn't hiding her agony with rage, and put my arms around her. She collapses against me, her darkness no longer recoiling from my light; she sobs, there, heartbroken.

I wrap my arms tightly around her—around North, in the real world—and call upon the Lightbringer again, gathering my focus, reaching out toward the hearts of our worlds. I linger for one more moment, feeling the delicate shimmer of power there, the beauty of the system my ancestors put in place, the strength of the faith being channeled into me.

There is a certainty to it now, here at the last—North was right. This is my destiny, my reason for being. I *am* my people's goddess, and I am finally what they have always needed me to be. For the first time in my life I am content—I am enough.

And I must give it all up.

Closing my power around the hearts like a fist, I squeeze until they're ready to shatter.

North, I think, holding the image of him in my mind, clinging to the shape of his soul. *My heart. My guiding star.*

And then—surrendering myself at last to my purpose—I destroy the world.

EPILOGUE

NORTH

Music echoes up from the city below, a strange mix of the drums and flutes of Nimh's people, and the electronic instruments of mine. The pace of it quickens, laughter drifting up through the night, as the musicians challenge each other to follow more and more complex rhythms and harmonies.

Spellfire lanterns line the terrace below, illuminating the crowds milling there enjoying the festivities. I see mostly the colors and fashions of Below, but here and there I spot one of my people. Miri's hair is sky blue this week, and I can pick her out of the crowd as she dances with Saelis and the small but steadily growing pack of friends she's bullied and cajoled into coming along. I promised I'd join them later.

Most of those from above have kept to Alciel in the weeks since it fell from the sky, hesitant about emerging into a world full of unknown animals, strange customs, and magic—but it seems like every day, a few more of them end up braving this new world. Like it or not, it is their world now too—Alciel will never return to the sky, with its engines permanently dark now that the hearts are gone. My people are going to have to get used to the idea of magic, one way or another—but there's no rush. We have time.

Up here, on a higher terrace without the spellfire decorations, only the light of the moons illuminates the stonework. The Lovers, Miella and Danna, hang low over the river, casting their dual rose-silver glows across the water. The stars are bright in the sky; the city below full of song; and I find myself letting out a groan, dropping my head to rest it on my hands folded against the stone.

A light touch against my leg makes me lift my head. The cat, his wide, furry face turned up at me, voices a query.

"I wanted to see Nimh tonight," I tell him, by way of explanation. "We might as well be worlds apart again, for all we've seen each other the last two weeks. I don't suppose you could remind her I'm up here?"

The cat gives himself a shake, then bunches up his muscles to leap lightly onto the stone railing beside me. He spends a moment looking down at the celebration unfolding below, then deliberately turns away and begins grooming a paw in meticulous fashion.

Techeki started planning the festivities while still in bed, recovering from the injuries he gave himself under Inshara's control. Rejoining Day, they're calling it—a name that made me smile. It sounds like *Rejoicing Day*. I rather like the idea of our descendants, centuries from now, celebrating on this night.

In theory, the day marks the signing of the treaty uniting Nimh's people and mine. In truth, it's little more than a symbolic gesture. There are too many details to work out, with one city resting atop another and two whole peoples trying to coexist for the first time in a thousand years. Nimh and my bloodmother have spent nearly every day since the destruction of the hearts holed up in a council chamber, along with an endless parade of representatives: riverstriders, councilors from the other islands, former Graycloaks, royal advisors . . .

One advisor who wasn't there was my father, and the gap where he should have been among Alciel's councilors is still raw.

I saw the moment he disappeared to hide, during the confrontation at the great colony ship. One last time, as he always had, he tried to save himself.

With a look that told me what she thought of him, Miri nevertheless went running after him, Saelis on her heels. They followed his trail all the way to the ship's edge, stopping where he'd climbed out onto the rippling surface of the Mirror of Divinity.

"I don't understand how he thinks he can walk all the way back to the city," Miri said when they came back to us. "Or what will happen when he gets there?"

Nimh opened her mouth to reply, and then stopped.

The howling of the mist-bent boars cut her off.

The sound of the hunt.

So his place sits empty at the table, and other voices fill the gaps where his once was. I've been at that table too—not in his chair, thankfully. Sometimes I speak, often I listen. Occasionally I just gaze at Nimh, I'll admit it.

But seeing her across a strategy table is . . . not the same as her being here, in the quiet moonlight, within arm's reach.

The cat, satisfied with the cleanliness of his paw, rises up onto all fours again and approaches, burbling another curious meow.

Before I can answer, a voice behind me makes me jump and look over my shoulder.

"I believe he wants you to pet him," says Matias, amused, his walking stick rapping gently on the stone as he steps out onto the high terrace.

"You think?" I reply, stifling an irrational surge of disappointment that he's not the person I wanted to come find me. Cautiously, I hold out my hand, halting a few inches from the cat's face. "Better to be sure. I've been burned before."

The cat sniffs delicately at my fingertips for a moment, then curls his lip and thrusts his cheek at my hand, purring like an engine.

Matias, chuckling, moves out farther into the moonlight. "I think he misses her too."

I focus on the cat, trying to hide the flicker of annoyance that I'm so easily read—and the guilt that I could resent how hard Nimh is working to forge this alliance with my mother. "It's just for a few weeks. It'll get easier soon."

"You think so?" Matias's voice is mild. "Hmm."

I glance at him, resplendent in his Fisher King's attire—though I notice he wears fewer beads around his neck than he once did. I haven't seen Orrun much lately, but I imagine he must have his hands full as he begins taking over the duties of the Fisher King's heir.

"Out with it, Matias," I tell him, a little more wearily

than I'd meant. "Do we really need to do the mysterious thing tonight?"

Matias makes a sound suspiciously like a snort and shakes his head. "Still so impatient. Still thinking you can rush a good story."

"What story?" I ask, exasperated. "It's over now, isn't it? The hearts are destroyed. There's no more prophecy. No more Song of the Destroyer—no more *Destroyer*, even. Nimh's not divine anymore—she's just a normal magician. Inshara's mind is gone—she's only a mist-touched shell now, no threat to anyone."

Matias reaches out to stroke the cat, his gnarled fingers curling through the orange fur, and sighs. "And you think all that is happening out there," he says, gesturing at the celebration below, the river teeming with barges beyond, and the edge of Alciel perched overhead and against the cliff, "is what . . . epilogue?"

I shake my head, my frustration with Matias's way of conversing fading a little. "No. I know it's important work. People coming together. Ancient secrets being learned. Worlds colliding."

"Indeed." Matias rests his walking stick against the railing and presses his palms against the stone. "I imagine that, if anything, all this will be prologue when the Fisher King of some future age tells this story. The real work, the true test of faith, begins now. Here, tonight."

I make a noise of agreement, shifting my weight. That Matias has something else to say, I don't doubt—the old man never just lingers, unless it's for a reason. But I'll be mist-touched before I give him the satisfaction of asking him.

Finally, he lifts his head, turning half toward me, half toward the door he came through, and exhales. "There's been some discussion about what to do with the temple now. I think Nimh, in her eagerness to prove to everyone that she's no longer divine, wants the matter settled. I expect it will be some time before the temple stops being a temple, though—her people have worshiped the divine for a lot longer than she's been their focus."

"It's the same with the throne of Alciel," I point out. "The royal bloodline existed to protect the DNA key to traveling between the worlds. You can't really be monarch of half a people—I expect my mother will end up abdicating her throne some day, and rule will fall to the councilors and the Congress of Elders."

"So you will never be king?" Matias asks, raising his eyebrows as if in surprise. "After all that effort your parents went to to teach you to reign over Alciel?"

I eye him sidelong. "What're you getting at?"

Matias lifts one shoulder. "Nothing. Except that I imagine it's unsettling, not knowing what your future holds, when you were so certain, for so long. To be one thing for all your life, and then . . . what?" He shakes his head a little.

"You're talking about Nimh." It isn't a question, and Matias doesn't answer; he waits, and this time, I find I can't let the silence drag. I lean over onto the railing again, propping my elbows on the stone. "It's just that . . . if prophecy was what brought me here—if fate brought my father to Jezara, and led him to sabotage my glider, and created Inshara, and had me fall in the exact spot where Nimh would find me . . . if *destiny* was what brought us together, and there is no destiny anymore . . ."

I trail off, finding myself unable—unwilling—to say the rest aloud, my heart starting to pound, almost like saying it might make it true.

Matias tilts his head, thoughtful, adjusting a few of his bead necklaces. "You find yourself wondering if there is anything left to keep you together."

I can feel blood rushing to my cheeks—I only hope the moonlight isn't strong enough to show the darkening of my face. "I know there is," I tell him quickly. "I miss her. I . . . I *love* her." I glance at Matias, half expecting to see some flash of surprise or disapproval—but he just gazes back at me, unperturbed. Of course he knew that, curse the old man. "I just—I just want a chance to *tell* her that, away from all this ceremony, and peace treaties, and politics."

"I know." Matias's lined features shift to a little smile. "You are certain. But only of your own feelings, not hers."

I shoot him another glance, a little more pointed this time, and then fix my eyes on the cat instead, saying nothing.

The old man gives a groan, shifting his shoulders in a way that makes his spine pop audibly. "I suppose I ought to leave you in peace. You may not know what path lies ahead of you, but I certainly have work to do. I mentioned that they're talking about what to do with the temple now? One idea—the one I rather think will win out in the end—is to expand the archives and turn the entire temple into a grand library, containing all the stories and wisdom of both our worlds, open to anyone wishing to learn." He's watching the temple now, his back to the night sky, eyes distant as though he's already seeing that other place.

I find myself smiling in spite of myself. "That does sound like a project worthy of an ex-Sentinel." But then a little pang of disappointment needles at me. "I just wish ORACLE hadn't been destroyed when the hearts were. There's so much we could've learned from it."

Matias is still for a moment—then his head shifts so he can look at me out of the corner of his eye, his lips twitching just a fraction. "No story is ever truly lost," he says quietly, over a burst of laughter from the terrace below. "Perhaps all it lacks is someone with the vision to uncover it again."

He slips his hand into his pocket, pulling something out, and then leaning across me to set the object down on the stone. He catches my gaze for a moment, and then—he *winks* at me. Before I can summon an appropriate reaction, he's leaving again, the tapping of his walking stick on the stone fading away as he returns the way he came.

I roll my eyes, and then look down—and freeze.

On the stone before me, gleaming darkly in the moonlight, is the bracelet ORACLE gave to me.

I swallow, my fingers hovering over its surface. It's dark now, no light or life to indicate it'll ever work again. But Nimh used the mist to revive it once.

Maybe . . .

"North?"

The sound of her voice has me whirling around, my heart leaping in my chest.

Nimh is there, her eyes meeting mine and catching there, as she tucks a strand of hair behind one ear in a nervous gesture. Her eyes are still lined with kohl, and her lips are dusted with gold, but she's wearing—*green*?

I blink at her, utterly unused to seeing her in any color but crimson. She takes a few more steps forward, her smile a little wry. "Techeki's idea," she says, as if reading my mind. "He says it'll be a long time before people *really* stop thinking of me as divine, but that in the meantime . . ." She lifts one shoulder, left bare by the cut of her dress, drawing my gaze as if by magic.

"In the meantime, you can wear what you want," I finish for her, trying to speak evenly despite the thudding of my heart.

Her smile flashes again, gaze falling for a moment—when she looks up, she's oddly shy, her manner hesitant in a way that's uncharacteristic. "What do you think?"

I don't have to hunt for an answer—the words are there, fighting to get free. I have only to try not to blurt them out in a rush. "You look beautiful."

Nimh bites her lip, a dimple appearing briefly in the shimmer of gold there, and I have to drag my eyes away from her mouth with a monumental effort.

Get a grip, North, come on.

She crosses the rest of the terrace, coming up beside me so she can stroke the cat, whose purr emerges once more in

454

response. "I . . . brought you something." She turns, lifting her other arm, and I see that there's a small parcel in her hand, wrapped in red fabric.

Trying not to let myself be distracted by her closeness, after so much time apart, I focus on the red parcel with some effort. "A present? What for?"

"Your mother tells me it is the anniversary of your birth in a few weeks. In your world, you celebrate this with gifts." She hesitates, her eyebrows rising a hair, a flicker of anxiety passing through her features. "Do you not?"

Not bothering to hide my smile, I reach out to accept the gift, my fingers brushing hers. She jumps at my touch, and my eyes fly up to her face automatically, my unspoken question there: *Are you all right?*

Nimh breathes out shakily, a rueful smile already reassuring me. "Most everyone still avoids . . ." She bites her lip again. "I don't think anyone has touched me in days."

I gaze back at her, momentarily frozen by warring desires. To kiss her, to take her hand, to touch her cheek, to pull her into my arms—instead I do nothing but stare at her, like an idiot.

"Well?" she says after a moment. "Will you open it?"

I clear my throat, shifting my weight and turning my attention back to the parcel. I pull the fabric away—red silk, as it turns out, like one might wear as a sash—to reveal an odd-looking book.

Her eyes are waiting for mine, when I look up again, puzzled. "They found it when they were exploring the rest of the skyship beneath the Mirror of Divinity. There will be whole archives full of artifacts, I think, recovered from our ancestors' living quarters—but whoever brought this along had a particular fondness for the stars."

She reaches out, gently turning the book and my hand with it until I can see, written along the spine in faded letters, *Ancient Astronomy and Celestial Navigation.*

My throat tight, I look back up to find her watching me, her gaze searching. "Nimh," I manage, my voice hoarse. "This . . . I don't know what to say."

"I read some of it," she whispers, as though admitting some great secret. "Much of it, I did not understand. But it is full of stories about the skies above Earth. Their ancients navigated across their own oceans by starlight just as ours did."

I run my fingers along the book's cover, feeling the dips where the letters were once emblazoned there, that paint too faded now to see. "I suppose some things are the same across all worlds."

Nimh's still watching me intently, as if searching my face for an answer to a question she's gathering the courage to ask. "They had one particular star," she murmurs. "It had many names—as many names as there were different cultures in that world. Cynosura . . . Arcady . . . Polaris. It was special to them because of all the stars in the sky, it alone never wavered—never changed position, even as everything else in the sky whirled around it in a never-ending dance."

I'm scarcely listening to her words, too captured by the way she's looking at me—but I hear her, and after a moment, greatly daring, I take a step closer, so I can rest my empty hand alongside hers on the balustrade.

Nimh's eyes are wet, and she blinks furiously as my fingers brush her hand. "Do you want to know what else they called it?" she whispers, her heart in her eyes, no longer able to fight the smile transforming her features. She steps close, lifting her free hand to touch my cheek, gulping a breath. "The North Star."

I exhale sharply, torn between a laugh and a gasp, my every nerve ending alive and reaching out for her touch. "That," I whisper, giving in and setting the book carefully on the balustrade so that I can slip a hand around her waist, "is the strangest coincidence I've ever heard."

Nimh sniffs and shakes her head, leaning into me as I pull her close. Her smile is radiant, brighter than the moonlight, her eyes shining with laughter, pleasure—relief.

She was afraid too.

"No," she says, summoning the briefest and least convincing of frowns. "Not coincidence. It's fate. I was right."

"Don't be foolish." I lean close, touching my lips to her temple, breathing in the scent of her hair, reveling in the way she softens under my touch. "There's no such thing," I add as her hand slides along my shoulder, leaving fire in its wake before her fingers creep into my hair, cradling the nape of my neck.

She draws back enough to look at me, laughter fled, her eyes soft and grave. "Magic, then," she whispers.

I swallow, my hands tightening around her. The sounds and lights of the revelry below us seem to fade away, leaving only the night sky, its stars, and the Lovers rising in the east. I dip my head, unable to resist a moment longer, and find her mouth with mine in the darkness. She stretches up to meet me, a shiver running through her that makes me ache.

I break away only long enough to breathe a reply: "Magic, then."

ACKNOWLEDGMENTS

Many years ago, we began daydreaming about this series set in two worlds. We never dreamed we'd finish it from two different continents, without being able to see each other, as utterly separated as those in Alciel and Below. We're looking forward to our own worlds meeting again one day soon, but in the meantime, writing this duology has been a comfort in tough times. We'd like to finish it up by thanking some of the people who have helped bring it to life.

Firstly, we'd like to thank all the readers, reviewers, booksellers and librarians who urge others to read our books—we're so grateful for all that you do.

We must also thank, as always, the wonderful team at Adams Literary—Josh, Tracey, Anna, and Stephen, without whom we'd be lost. We value both your advice and your friendship.

Our team at Harper has worked so hard to bring you this book—our editor Kristen was there for every word, pass, and rewrite, and this story simply wouldn't have worked without her. Many, many thanks as well to Clare, Erin, Mark, Jenna,

Alison, Kristen E., Michael, Lauren, and the teams in sales, marketing, publicity, and managing ed.

To our Aussie team at Allen & Unwin—Anna, Nicola, Simon, Yvette, Sheralyn, Eva, Matt, Lou, Megan, Alison, and Kylie—a thousand thanks for all the wonderful stuff you do for us.

To Artem Chebokha, a thousand more thanks for the truly beautiful covers you gave us for this series. They're better than anything we'd ever imagined.

To our friends—you have kept us afloat through the toughest of times, and we will never stop being grateful for you: Michelle, Steph, Marie, Leigh, Jay, Kiersten, Alex, Sooz, Nic, Kacey, Soraya, Ryan, Kate, Maz, Cat, the Roti Boti crew, the Council, and the Asheville crew. Jack, Sebastian, and Viola kept us company for every moment of writing, and Icarus is all over these pages, a part of him always living on in the bindle cat.

And to our families, who always merit the deepest thanks—all these books, and we still don't have the words to say everything we wish we could. To the Spooners, the Kaufmans, Cousinses, and Mr. Wolf, a world (or two!) of thanks. From Amie, an *I love you*, as always, for Brendan. And for Pip, enough love from both of us to fill two worlds.